KNIGHTSWRATH

The Dragonkin Trilogy: Two

MICHAEL MEYERHOFER

Unlocking New Worlds

Knightswrath
The Dragonkin Trilogy™ Book Two
A Red Adept Publishing Book

ISBN-13: 978-1-940215-51-8
ISBN-10: 194021551X

Red Adept Publishing, LLC
104 Bugenfield Court
Garner, NC 27529
http://RedAdeptPublishing.com/

Winnersea

Sorocco

Dhargoth
Peninsula

Ivairia

Phaogos

Syros

Lotus Isles

Dead Shores

Quorim

Cassica

Lyos

Simurgh Plains

Cadavash

Godsfall

Hosod

The Red Steppes

Stillhammer Mtns.

Armahg's Tears

Ash'bana Plains

Atholon

Wytchforest

Quesh

Dendain

Runn

PROLOGUE

T
HE KING STOOD NAKED ON his terrace, surrounded by darkness. From his vantage point high in the city of Shaffrilon, built into the soaring boughs of the World Tree, Loslandril could look out over half of his father's kingdom. Of course, the kingdom was not his father's anymore. King Rhil'thys had been dead for three years. In his absence, Loslandril had commanded the Sylvan armies in their endless skirmishes against the Olgrym, traded with the Humans inhabiting the Dead Shores, negotiated with the Wyldkin north of the forests, and presided over the fierce and ongoing debate over what to do about the Shel'ai. Still, Loslandril chafed at his title.

I am not my father. I will never be like him...

Loslandril glanced up at the night sky awash with stars. As it extended even higher overhead, the expansive World Tree blotted out a portion of the sky before vanishing into the blue-black clouds. He traced his fingertips along his terrace railing. He remembered how, as a boy, he'd touched the smooth, white bark of the World Tree and felt as if he were touching his father's silk robe—so different from the dark, gnarled texture of wytchwood trees. He smiled thinly.

I won't become him... but isn't that what all sons say, in time? Isn't that what my son will say about me one day?

Loslandril touched the faint scar beneath his left eye and shook his head. No, Quivalen would never have so much cause to hate his father as Loslandril hated his own. Loslandril had sworn that to the Light, to the gods. He had sworn it days ago, kneeling beside Jalthessa's grave.

My sweet wife... how much easier it would be to keep that vow if you were here! More than anyone else had, Jalthessa had taught him compassion. She had saved him from whatever poison ran in his veins, giving him through her demonstrable love the precious antidote to his father's malice.

And now she's gone.

Loslandril fought back the tears that still came every time he thought of her. Sylvan women did not give birth easily, and Jalthessa had been no exception. Despite all the wealth and ancient medicines at his disposal, Loslandril had been forced to watch her die. Yet she had smiled weakly, held her newborn son, and nursed the infant one time before her spirit went to the Light. That, Loslandril knew, should have given him comfort. Strangely, it only made him angrier.

Quivalen had not opened his eyes before his mother died. That was not uncommon for Sylvan babies—especially sickly ones, like Quivalen—but it also meant that the boy had never even seen his own mother. Now she was gone, and her son would grow to manhood without even the vaguest, ghostly memory of her inhabiting some dim recess of his mind.

Loslandril clenched his fist and struck the ornate stone railing of his terrace. It hurt. He struck it again, even harder. This time, his knuckles left a smear of blood on the smooth white marble. His hand throbbed, but the pain was a welcome distraction.

Like most Sylvs, Loslandril had not come from a large family. He had no siblings or close relatives, and his own mother had died when he was young—drowned after too much wine, his father had insisted. Loslandril had never believed that explanation, and the scar under his left eye was the result of questioning the circumstances of his mother's death one too many times.

While Sylvs usually mated for life, exceptions were made for royalty in order to preserve the lineage. Loslandril had no doubt that before long, potential mates would be not-so-subtly introduced to him at court. But for the time being, he had no intention of humoring them. Loneliness was all that he had left of Jalthessa—he kept it to honor her.

No, he amended, *that's not all I have of her. I have Quivalen. I have my son.*

The pain eased a bit, like a knot going slack. He considered summoning the midwife and having her bring the babe to his arms. But Quivalen was still only a few days old and uncommonly weak. Loslandril still feared injuring him somehow—though he still savored those bittersweet moments when he watched the child sleep, frail but alive.

Loslandril took a deep breath and let it go. Trying to clear his thoughts, he stared out at his night-wrapped city with its twisting towers, arcing walls, sloped rooftops, countless temples, and statues. There would be time to dote over his son—years and years. For now, he had other concerns.

He glanced again at the heavy parchment unrolled on the table behind him. Though he had already read the missive enough times to commit the words to memory, he picked it up and read it again. Once again, the words, written in flowing Sylvan script, made him shudder.

A king should not be afraid, he reminded himself, echoing one of his father's favorite sentiments. But it was not every day that one received a message from a Shel'ai. *A message... or a threat?*

Loslandril cursed, allowing a little of his lingering bitterness to turn into anger. Like most Sylvan kings dating almost all the way back to the Shattering War, King Rhil'thys had waged a tireless war of persecution against the Shel'ai. Rhil'thys had taken a special liking to the persecution.

Under most previous kings, Sylvan children born with the violet eyes and white pupils—an unmistakable sign that they had been cursed with the gift of Shel'ai magic—had simply been raised in neglect then banished as soon as they were of age, left to wander the outer lands alone, to seek shelter in Human realms that wanted them no more than the Sylvs did. But under King Rhil'thys, as a formal tenet of the king's law, such children were torn from their mothers and murdered.

Magic is a stain, Loslandril had heard his father say again and again, his eyes made frightfully wide with rage. *Better the poor souls afflicted with its curse be given a quick death! Better for them and essential for us, if we trueborn Sylvs are to survive.*

Still, sometimes, Shel'ai survived. If their parents did not have the heart to kill them and concealed them instead, they might live long enough to escape the mobs, inquisitions, and long knives. Loslandril did not know whether to call that salvation luck; such children almost certainly faced a lifetime of misery, evading Sylvan mobs and fleeing the forests only to face the even harsher outer world—alone. But if they survived, in time, their abilities would grow. They would wield the last vestiges of the old magic. They would be powerful. And no Shel'ai was as powerful as the two men who had signed their names to this parchment.

El'rash'lin and Fadarah... Loslandril cursed again. He tossed aside the parchment, noting the smear of his own blood on the message.

He did not know how the Shel'ai had delivered the message, and his palace guards had been unable to find out. Loslandril had returned from his wife's funeral to find the parchment lying neatly in his bedchamber. At first, he had assumed a connection between the two events. Certain the Shel'ai had somehow contributed to his wife's demise, he had momentarily burned with a wrath for the magic-born that would have rivaled even his father's. But his wrath slackened. He knew it had to have been a coincidence. After all, Jalthessa had possessed strength of spirit but never much strength of body. It had come as a surprise to no one—least of all her—when childbirth proved her undoing.

"Yet you still insisted on having a child," Loslandril spoke to the darkness. "For me. And gods forgive me, I let you do it." Loslandril pushed such thoughts from his mind and considered the sorcerers' proposal instead.

A bargain between Sylv and Shel'ai, a returning to the alliance of old... Loslandril laughed bitterly. The sorcerers' demands—that the Sylvs halt the murder of the Shel'ai children, no longer hunt them, and welcome them back into Sylvos—were impossible. What they offered in return—help in fighting the Olgrym, plus the threat of revenge if Loslandril refused—was no small matter, but it would never be enough to convince his people. If Loslandril agreed to the sorcerers'

8

demands, as part of him wanted to do, he would almost certainly be the first Sylvan king in centuries to feel an arrow in his back.

Still, he had no other choice. The letter made it clear that if Loslandril continued the genocide perpetuated by his father, all of Sylvos would pay the price. The threat was not an idle one. He had been receiving startling reports of late: Fadarah, El'rash'lin, and their ilk had been interceding to save Shel'ai children from the mobs. Each child saved was, in turn, added to their ranks.

According to the wisdom of midwives, one in a thousand Sylvan children was born with dragonmist eyes. The children seemed chosen simply by chance, though some said that children with even one Shel'ai parent were guaranteed to have magical abilities. That meant that one or two Shel'ai were born each year.

Of course, most Shel'ai infants are strangled by their fathers the moment they open their eyes. He clenched his fist, flexing his sore fingers. He glanced down at his knuckles. The bleeding had stopped.

But Fadarah might still have fifty Shel'ai with him. That might as well be an army. Given the perpetual violence and endless border skirmishes between the Sylvs and the Olgrym, not to mention the tension between the forest-dwelling Sylvs and their Wyldkin cousins, Loslandril could not afford the soldiers it would take to defend his kingdom against fifty righteously vengeful sorcerers wielding wytchfire even more deadly than Sylvan longbows.

I must bargain with them. I cannot give them everything they want, of course, but I must give them enough.

He could not permit the Shel'ai to live once more in Sylvos... but perhaps he could spare their lives. An edict declaring it unlawful to kill Shel'ai children—a simple law that threatened banishment into the care of their fellow sorcerers instead of death—might be enough. Of course, that would mean letting the Shel'ai grow stronger, but at least it would stave off a war that Loslandril had neither the strength nor the will to fight. Besides, El'rash'lin and Fadarah were saving many of those children anyway. Better that Loslandril gain a measure of credit in their eyes.

It will be hard to convince my people, though... He flexed his fingers again, winced as jagged pain radiated from his knuckles, and wondered if he'd broken his hand. Then someone knocked on his bedchamber door. Far from the usual gentle rapping of his servants, the knock was fast and frantic. Loslandril's heart froze.

My son! They've come to tell me my son has died. He bolted for the door, touching a luminstone along the way. As soft blue light flooded his bedchamber, he remembered that he was naked. He grabbed a robe and tied it tight then unbarred the door and flung it open.

Old Hanwen, the midwife who had served his family all her life, stood in the hallway, flanked by guards. In place of her usual smile, her lips were tight, and her eyes were wide with panic. She was holding a small bundle wrapped in a blanket of the finest silk patterned with the broad weeping limbs of wytchwood trees.

No...

Old Hanwen spoke, but Loslandril did not hear. Grasping her arm, he yanked her into his bedchamber then wrested the bundle from her arms. The guards started to follow, but Loslandril kicked the door shut with a heavy, oaken boom.

No...

Forcing himself to be gentle, he peeled back the blankets until he saw pale, naked flesh. He reeled at the sight of Quivalen's tiny face. The infant's eyes were closed.

No...

Loslandril pressed his fingertips to the infant's throat, feeling for a pulse, but his hands shook too much to tell. He raised the infant until his face was nearly touching his own. He prayed that he would feel his son's breath on his lips. Nothing.

Loslandril reeled and might have fallen, dropping his son's corpse in the process, but Old Hanwen, in a moment of unheard-of familiarity, steadied him then gently but forcefully pried the infant from his arms. Loslandril wept, falling to his knees.

Gone... he's gone. I'm sorry, Jalthessa. I should have kept him closer. I should have kept him with me.

Then he heard the infant cry. Loslandril stiffened as though struck. He stood. Quivalen was alive. He took the infant from her again, as gently as he could, and held him close. He laughed and wept at the same time. "My son..."

Old Hanwen's face was still taut with horror. He examined his son's tiny, soft body for injuries. Nothing. Quivalen's face was pinched and crying, his small limbs weak and flailing, but his skin was cool. His breath still came in tiny, quiet gasps that were easy to miss. Still, the infant bore no obvious wounds or indications of fever. The midwife was still talking, her voice rushed and frantic.

Then Loslandril caught the word. *Impossible...*

Quaking in disbelief, he held his son closer. Quivalen's face was mere inches from his own when the infant opened his eyes. For a moment, Quivalen's squalling stopped. The only son of the Sylvan king stared up at his father with wide, unblinking eyes. Violet eyes with white pupils.

Loslandril stumbled, nearly dropped the infant, and choked back a sob. Once more, the midwife took the baby from his grasp. Quivalen began crying again, his small body quaking with angry sobs, but Loslandril hardly heard the sound. He sank to his knees.

Old Hanwen was shaking him, repeating something over and over, but Loslandril did not understand. Her figure blurred as he began to weep. Then she shifted the sobbing infant to one arm, reached into her robe, and withdrew a knife.

Loslandril thought for a moment that she meant to stab her own king. He tensed. He was no fighter, though he had received a measure of training from the Shal'tiar. He was certain he could get the knife away from her, though she would surely cut him in the process. But she offered him the knife, hilt first.

Loslandril stared at the knife for a moment, not comprehending. Then he stood, wrenched the dagger from the midwife's grasp, and threw it away. The steel clattered on stone. He took his son from her and slapped her across the face.

As Old Hanwen recoiled, Loslandril shouted for his guards. They burst into the room so quickly, shortswords drawn, that he knew they had been waiting for the slightest reason to rush in. Loslandril pointed at the cowering midwife. He told them that she had gone mad, mistaken her son for a Shel'ai, and tried to kill him.

"Take her," he ordered, seething. "Gag her. Take her down to the garden. Cut her throat."

The guards blinked. One said, "My king?"

"You heard me. And tell no one. The kingdom is still mourning my beloved queen. The last thing they need is a vicious rumor souring them against their innocent prince."

The guards glanced at each other. Old Hanwen had been a fixture in the palace longer than anyone living, but these particular guards had been chosen from the ranks of the Shal'tiar, for their loyalty as much as for their skill at arms. They could not refuse an order from their king.

Old Hanwen's blue eyes widened. Her mouth opened as though to protest, but the guards were on her in an instant. One removed his glove and stuffed it in her mouth. The other pinned both her arms behind her. The midwife did not struggle. Instead, she looked at Loslandril with confused, pleading eyes. Loslandril did not waver as the guards hauled her away.

Loslandril closed and barred the door. He held the crying infant close to his heart, those small limbs flailing angrily against his chest. *He's hungry*, Loslandril realized. *Hungry and scared. But I have no milk for you, little Quivalen. I have nothing for you but my love. And my pity.*

Quivalen's eyes were still wide open—twin pools of white and purple fire.

The midwife could be silenced… but what about the guards? Surely, half the palace had already been startled awake by the commotion. How long would it be before they insisted on inspecting Quivalen to ensure that the midwife had done the infant no harm? How long could Quivalen be hidden? How long before mobs ascended the winding streets of Shaffrilon to lay siege to the palace itself, for the first time since the Shattering War?

I must save the kingdom… I must save my son…

Loslandril glanced about his bedchamber, from the big, empty bed to his wife's ornate dressers and mirrors. He went to the knife and picked it up. He inspected the tip of the knife's glint, so sinister and unforgiving.

No, I won't kill you, my son—but I must protect you, as Jalthessa would. Forgive me. He moved the knifepoint closer to his son's wide, violet eyes.

12

His hands quaked. He needed to wait a moment and calm his nerves. Once he'd regained his composure, he would have the steadiness to do this ghastly thing. He would do what needed to be done, then claim Old Hanwen had done the deed before bringing the child to his arms. Quivalen would become the object of pity instead of revulsion.

Loslandril looked from blade to infant then back to the blade. He asked himself if he could really carve out his own son's eyes to save his life. He realized he could. A dreadful calmness filled him.

Quivalen was still sobbing, but Loslandril hardly heard him. All he saw were his son's eyes—and the knife in his hands. *I can do this. For Quivalen, for Jalthessa, I must do this.*

He flexed his fingers around the knife's brass handle, carved with an undulating pattern of wytchwood leaves. He took a deep breath, held it, and let the knife descend. With a certain detachment, he watched the knife's tip moving closer to his son's eyes, as though he were in a dream.

A moment's courage, and it's done. I'm sorry, my son. I have no choice.

A shadow passed over him. Loslandril jumped. He feared the guards had reentered his bedchamber somehow, despite the barred door. He turned. A cloaked and hooded figure stood before him. His hands were folded in his sleeves, making it impossible for Loslandril to tell if he was armed. He glanced past the dark man and saw that his door was still closed.

Loslandril thought of the parchment. Perhaps this man was one of the Shel'ai who had written to him, and he had come to obtain Loslandril's answer in person. He raised his knife. "Keep back, sorcerer. Another step, and I will call my guards."

But the hooded figure stepped forward. Shadows hid the man's eyes. Loslandril fell back, holding his crying child close. He repeated his threat, but he heard the fear in his own voice.

The hooded figure raised his open hands in a sign of surrender. "No need for threats, my king. I intend no malice toward you, your kingdom, or your child."

Loslandril frowned. Though the stranger spoke flawless Sylvan, there was an oddly saccharine accent to his voice. The stranger slowly

13

brushed back his hood. Coldly handsome features came into view: a strong, thin jaw; tapered Sylvan ears; sloping eyebrows; and eyes so blue they looked as though they had been painted. His clean-shaven head made telling the man's age even harder, though Loslandril doubted he could be much older than the guards who had just hauled away the midwife.

Loslandril scrutinized the man's eyes: blue—not purple. Whatever else this man was, he was no sorcerer. However, he'd breached the palace and gotten into Loslandril's bedchamber. He would be a remarkable assassin indeed if he could kill an armed man with his bare hands while a whole host of fiercely loyal bodyguards stood within earshot.

"Who are you?"

The stranger bowed slightly. "Not a Shel'ai—as you can plainly see. My name is Chorlga. I have come to help you... and your son."

Loslandril winced, puzzled as much by the man's strange name as his words. Though the stranger had barely whispered, his voice was overpowering as though he'd shouted loud enough to burst Loslandril's eardrums. "I don't believe you."

Chorlga smiled. Despite his handsome features, his teeth were black and rotten. "I did not expect you to. Not yet. But I am not here to earn your trust." He pointed. "I am here for your son."

Loslandril's heart leapt into his throat. He considered summoning the guards, even knowing that they would have to break down the door to reach him. "You will not take my son. I swear this on the graves of my wife, my mother, and all the kings who came before me since the days of Shigella."

Chorlga's sickening smile broadened. He regarded the king in such unnerving silence that Loslandril required all his willpower not to look away. Only then did Loslandril realize Chorlga had not blinked even once since appearing in Loslandril's bedchamber. Finally, Chorlga said, "Apologies, great king. I have not come to steal your son. I have come to help him. And you." Despite the deference in the man's voice, his tone held not the slightest fleck of humility.

Quivalen had stopped crying. The infant's eyes were wide with terror, and his small mouth opened and closed without sound, as if

14

he were a fish drawn out of the water. This frightened him more than anything.

Loslandril fixed his gaze on Chorlga again, tightened his grip on the knife, and once again considered calling for the guards. *He may not be a Shel'ai... but he's no Sylv, either!*

"You can't help me. I don't know whether you're an assassin or a fool, but I'll give you one last chance to explain yourself before I call my guards and have you torn limb from limb."

Chorlga tucked his hands back into his sleeves, seemingly unafraid. "It could be that I know your people better than you do. I know, for instance, that they will not suffer a king whose seed bears Shel'ai fruit. They will depose you, or they will kill your son—or both."

Loslandril shook his head. "No one will harm my son. I swear it."

"I have been watching you for some time. You have a soft heart... much too soft for a king. I know that you received a message from the Shel'ai. A threat, couched in a plea... Sylv and Shel'ai fighting side by side, like in the days of old." Chorlga's voice exuded derision. "You will reject their offer. You will renounce the Shel'ai, just as your father did."

Loslandril shifted Quivalen, jostling him a bit, half wishing the infant would cry again. "And why should I do that?"

"Because in return," Chorlga said, "I will rinse the magic from your son's blood and wash the purple from his eyes. I will make him every bit as frail as you are. I will save his life... and yours." The cloaked man bowed, though Loslandril sensed no warmth in the gesture.

"How could you do that? You said yourself, you are not a Shel'ai—"

"I spoke the truth." Chorlga took a step closer. "But there is more magic in this world than that of the Shel'ai. Much more. I wield a little of it. And I will use it to help you... if I have your word."

Loslandril fought to keep his composure. Each time Chorlga drew closer, the king felt icy dread snake through him. He glanced down at Quivalen, saw the infant's violet eyes still wide with terror. *Quivalen feels it, too...*

Loslandril imagined what Jalthessa would have said if she were there, and he found his courage. "I don't know what your goal is here, but I know better than to trust an offer so tempting and timely. I didn't trust you a moment ago, and I trust you even less now. Obviously, this is a trick. You must be allies with the Shel'ai."

Chorlga looked as if he were about to laugh but stopped himself. "Oh, I am many things, great king—things you cannot possibly fathom. But I am no friend to the Shel'ai." Chorlga paused. "Do I have your word?"

Loslandril wondered what would happen if he said no. Even with his guards right outside, he had the terrible feeling that neither he nor Quivalen would survive if he refused. He nodded. "You have my word."

Chorlga answered with a wolfish grin. "Good. Then place the child in the bassinet and step back. Once I have begun, do not speak. Do not move. Do not even breathe until I have finished."

Loslandril meant to question him but found he could not speak. He looked down at Quivalen again. The feeling of dread intensified, but through supreme effort, he placed the infant in a bassinet, made sure he was securely wrapped in his blanket, and stepped back. He gripped the knife tighter than ever, prepared to fling it into Chorlga's smirking face the moment he sensed the stranger was hurting his son.

Chorlga approached the infant and leaned over him. Quivalen had begun crying again, his little arms and legs flailing madly. Chorlga flipped aside the blanket. He held his open palm over the naked, crying body then pressed his hand to the infant's face.

Quivalen instantly went still. Loslandril tensed. Instinct begged him to attack, but he held his ground. The very air seemed to change, thickening and turning cold. Loslandril had the feeling that not just warmth but life itself was being drained from the world. He wept.

But a moment later, Chorlga straightened. His unnaturally blue eyes flashed, turned a bright and blazing purple, then became blue again. He exhaled, an almost lustful smile tugging at his lips. He stepped back and gestured. As though on cue, Quivalen began sobbing again.

"It is done. You can move, great king. Retrieve your son and look at his eyes."

Loslandril sheathed the knife in the belt of his robe and did as he was commanded. The moment he was picked up, Quivalen stopped crying. The infant stared up with wide, trusting eyes. Loslandril breathed in awe. The pupils of Quivalen's eyes had turned black, and the irises were as blue as his own. It seemed too easy, too quick, to be real. "An illusion…"

"No illusion, great king. All the magic your son might have wielded has been drained away. I have swallowed it like wine. In me, it will live forever." Chorlga's smirk disappeared, replaced by a frightful seriousness. "I will be watching you, Sylv. Henceforth and forever more, the Shel'ai are your enemies. Break your vow, and all the swords and arrows in Sylvos will not keep me from killing your son. And that death will not be quick. It will take days—months, if I wish it—and you will watch. Do you understand?"

Loslandril knew at once that this man had spoken the truth. Then he remembered the knife. He returned his son to the bassinet. Pretending he only wanted to lean over him, he touched the knife, fingering the handle. He rehearsed the simple motion it would take to turn around, draw the knife from the belt of his robe, and throw it.

He tensed and spun. The knife flew from his hand—but Chorlga was gone. The blade struck the far wall and sank deep, quivering slightly.

Loslandril lowered his arm. He looked around, both for Chorlga and for another weapon. Then he heard Chorlga's voice, so close that he felt the man's breath on his ear. "Before I leave, great king, permit me one more simple demonstration."

Loslandril could neither move nor cry out. Chorlga stood in front of him. With frightful gentleness, he opened Loslandril's robe and pressed his fingertips to the king's chest.

Wytchfire sprang from Chorlga's fingers, lancing deep into his flesh. Loslandril's mouth opened wide—the only motion he was allowed—but he could not scream. Raw pain flooded his senses, freezing them, scalding them.

"I trust you will appreciate this reminder." Chorlga slowly drew his fingertips like fiery claws down Loslandril's chest, past his navel, to his groin.

Loslandril wept. Chorlga laughed. Then his body shimmered, faded, and disappeared altogether.

Released from whatever spell had immobilized him, Loslandril toppled to the floor. In time, he woke to the splintering sound of the guards breaking down the door. Loslandril sat up. Pain screamed through him. He heard his son crying in the distance, but for a moment, all he could do was stare in horror at what had been done to him.

From collarbone to crotch, his flesh was blistered and seeping. Shaking with agony, he forced himself to rise. He grasped his robe and tied it shut, wincing as the soft fabric pressed into his wounds. Then he went to retrieve his son—just as the door shattered and his guards rushed in.

With strength Loslandril did not know he had, he composed himself and stilled them with a ferocious look. He held his son before him, hoping Quivalen's small body would conceal the blood and pus already seeping through his dark robe. He ordered the guards to leave and said he had only been sitting on the terrace and had nodded off after too much nightwine. As an afterthought, he turned Quivalen toward them, letting them see his blue, wet eyes.

The guards exchanged looks then left him alone. Closing the broken door behind them, they promised he would not be disturbed until morning. Loslandril waited, fighting to keep his composure. When they were gone, he crumpled. Reeling with pain, he returned Quivalen to his bassinet and stumbled to his bed. He lay down in agony, biting the sheets to keep from screaming. He wished he'd had nightwine, after all, though he doubted all the wine in Sylvos could have eased his pain.

In time, he slept. When he woke, he approached Quivalen and found his son staring up with clear, blue eyes. Loslandril touched his chest through his robe. The pain had slackened. Loslandril wept, though he could not say for certain why. He gathered his courage and opened his robe. The wounds had closed and healed, as though it had been months since Chorlga touched him. Still, ghastly scars raked his torso, leaving a reminder, accompanied by a dull ache, of whatever bargain he had struck and a warning of what would happen if he disobeyed.

Fifty years later, he still felt it.

CHAPTER ONE

THUNDERHEADS

ROWEN REINED IN HIS HORSE, scowling at the approaching thunderheads. Though it was only midday, the grassy horizon to the west had taken on a blue-black stain reminiscent of twilight. Rowen glanced back at the two figures riding with him. "So much for luck."

Jalist laughed, though his faintly gray, Dwarrish skin made it look as though the storm had already hidden the sun. "Locke, when in all the hells have we experienced anything akin to luck?"

A distant rumble unsettled Rowen's horse, a piebald palfrey he had taken from the stables of Lyos. He patted the horse's neck. "Easy, Snowdark. It's just thunder."

Jalist urged his own horse up alongside Rowen's. "You know, that's a silly name for a horse. Besides, aren't Knights of the Crane supposed to ride big solid-colored destriers?"

Rowen shrugged, resisting the impulse to smooth the azure tabard hanging over his new kingsteel cuirass. Though his armor was light and well fitting, it still chafed him. "I've been an Isle Knight for barely a week, and already, that's probably the least of my transgressions."

The Dwarr glanced down at the sword Rowen was carrying. "True enough."

A week, Rowen thought, surprised that it had been that long. Lyos had fallen far behind them. Unbelievably, it seemed they had not been followed. Then again, if the Shel'ai wanted him dead, he doubted he would see them coming. The Shel'ai were not even his most pressing concern at the moment. He glanced down at his azure tabard, eyeing the emblem of a balancing crane. Then he touched the exquisite dragonbone hilt of his sword. It seemed faintly warm to the touch, as though alive.

By now, most of the Knighthood surely knew that he'd fled Lyos with Knightswrath, the long-lost sword of Fâyu Jinn. They would hunt him. They would catch him. They would rescind his Knighthood. They would call him a traitor, possibly even behead him. After all, he'd not only set out on his own without permission, but he'd also taken a sacred relic with him—one that he would surely have had to relinquish to his superiors had he remained in Lyos.

But I'm not a traitor... am I? Rowen realized he could not definitively answer his own question. He told himself that he'd come by the sword honestly, as a gift from Hráthbam for his service as a bodyguard, and that he'd left to keep Knightswrath from falling into the wrong hands. He told himself that what mattered was taking the blade to the distant Wytchforest. He had to invoke the Oath of Kin and enlist the help of the Sylvs before the Dhargots rampaging across the continent ground all the kingdoms and all the Free Cities under their heels.

Maybe I just didn't want to give it up. The sword... the notion that I was chosen by the Light to bear it... the wild idea that some low-born, grave-digging sellsword could follow in the footsteps of Fâyu Jinn!

Before he could stop himself, Rowen laughed. Luckily, a clap of thunder muffled the sound. "No caves nearby. No trees, either. We could backtrack, maybe reach Cadavash before the storm hits, but—"

"And trust the hospitality of fanatics who mutilate themselves and pray to the bones of dead dragons? No, thank you. I'll take a storm over a dragon worshipper any day."

Rowen scowled. "Then we're about out of options. We can either ride through it or hide under our cloaks and spend all of tomorrow trying to dry off."

"Perhaps I can be of service." Silwren, the final member of their motley trio, spoke up. She had come on them so quietly, like a shadow, that they had not heard her. In her blue-black robe, she was almost invisible, save for her face.

20

Rowen's breath caught in his throat. Even after several months, Silwren's appearance still startled him. She was more than pretty—fine features, a lithe frame, and platinum curls—but her eyes were those of a Shel'ai. As often as he'd seen her eyes, the pupils especially still both unnerved and fascinated him. Rowen was beginning to find them beautiful, but their beauty was haunting, given what they represented.

Realizing he was staring, Rowen forced a smile. "I've seen Shel'ai cast fire and heal wounds. Can they wave away storms, too?"

Silwren answered with the faintest of smiles. "Not exactly." Slender hands came up, emerging from her blue-black cloak. Tendrils of violet wytchfire ignited from thin air, coursing through her wrists, fluttering without smoke or sound.

Rowen had seen wytchfire before, but the sight still made him jump. He heard Jalist swear. Rowen was glad he had a firm grip on the reins, or else Snowdark might have bolted.

Silwren raised her hands over her head, fingers moving. Her hood spilled back to reveal more platinum curls. Her mount seemed unperturbed. More and more wytchfire, bright and hot, exuded from Silwren's palms, though it left her skin untouched. Jalist swore again. The growing mass of wytchfire broadened and became more concave until it swirled over their heads like one of those ridiculous umbrellas used by the rich noblewomen of Ivairia.

Silwren lowered her wrists. The wytchfire continued to float over them. "It will keep us dry, at least," she said easily.

Rowen had to clear his throat before he could speak. "Thank you." He wondered if his own expression bore the same unease that he saw on Jalist's face. The Dwarr had not known Silwren as long as Rowen had, but everyone knew that Silwren should not make frequent use of her magic. By her own admission, she was no longer a mere Shel'ai. The machinations of her old allies had effectively turned her into a Dragonkin, enhancing her magic so that its mere presence crackling through her bloodstream threatened to drive her mad. Yet there she was, casually employing abilities she'd spent months avoiding.

Maybe she's just getting better at controlling them. Rowen eyed the wytchfire hovering over them and hoped that was the case.

21

"Don't be afraid, Human," she said. "This small expenditure is not enough to turn me into another Nightmare."

Small expenditure? Rowen remembered the Nightmare—another Shel'ai impossibly twisted and ruined, left raving mad by the magic forced into his body. He wondered if Silwren had read his thoughts. She must have. He shook himself, forcing his mind to clear. He felt both Jalist's and Silwren's eyes on him, but he focused only on the distant thunderheads. "We ride on."

True to Silwren's word, her hovering umbrella of wytchfire kept them relatively protected from the storm, causing all raindrops that struck it to hiss ominously. Yet the thunder rumbled terribly all around them, making controlling the horses increasingly difficult. Rowen eventually ordered them to stop and wait out the storm. Silwren's horse seemed to be faring far better than the others.

Can't be a coincidence. She's using magic to calm the beast—that means she's using magic continuously. He'd never seen her do that before. He checked her expression, but she seemed calm. The hovering dome of wytchfire stopped when they did.

"My magic can soothe your horses, too, if you wish to press on," she offered.

Rowen forced a smile. "No need. We could use the rest." He might have said more, but the thunderclaps drowned him out.

The group made camp, working in the surreal glow of wytchfire. Rowen worried that the glare might attract other travelers or even bandits, though he suspected they would run for their lives when they got close enough to see what was causing it. When Jalist complained of cold, lamenting their lack of firewood, Silwren gestured, and a campfire wrought of sorcery appeared in their midst, burning without any visible source of fuel.

Jalist jumped. "Gods, woman, you should warn us before you do that!"

Silwren made no answer, and Rowen could not tell in the flickering light if she was smiling or frowning. Rowen stretched his hands toward the wytchfire, which was warm enough. Its violet tendrils matched the color of the dome hovering over them. Still, he fought the impulse to shrink away from the ghostly campfire. He reminded himself that, like other Shel'ai, Silwren seemed able to control whether or not her wytchfire harmed those it touched. Rowen was not about to thrust his hand into the fire, though.

"You seem more willing to use your magic lately," he began carefully. He made a show of warming his hands. "In Lyos, you barely used it at all." He risked a glance at her.

Silwren seemed neither perturbed nor surprised by his comment. "I am gaining more control over it. You need not be concerned."

He caught a hint of rebuke in her melodic Sylvan accent. He knew he should let the matter drop. "Sorry, can't help it. El'rash'lin said that use of the magic could drive you mad—or cripple you, like it did him. And the Nightmare. I'd... like to avoid that, if we could."

She flinched at the mention of her dead friends. "I know what he said. But each of the Shel'ai exposed to the power of Namundvar's Well responded differently. My mere appearance proves that." She paused. "I am getting stronger."

Rowen could not argue. El'rash'lin had been badly disfigured by the magic leached from the Light and was covered head to toe in ghastly sores and scars. By comparison, Silwren had remained beautiful. Just a few wrinkles around her eyes made her seem to have aged years overnight. But her personality seemed mostly the same.

But how would I know that? I barely even know her! Still, he knew that wasn't exactly true. In the jails of Lyos, in an effort to help him understand their plight, El'rash'lin had used magic to share minds with Rowen. Many of El'rash'lin's memories still echoed in Rowen's brain as though they were his own. If he concentrated, he could remember Silwren as a child—wide eyed, staring at clouds—as though he had known her then himself.

Not for the first time that afternoon, Rowen shook off his thoughts. The last thing he needed was *another* life when he could barely manage his own. "Maybe I'm the one being driven mad," he muttered. Jalist's scowl told him he'd been thinking out loud. He blushed and turned to Silwren. "Forgive—"

She waved him off. "Ten thousand apologies are already called for in this war. Be assured, yours are far down on the list." Nevertheless, she stood and walked away. Her dome of wytchfire did not follow, though the campfire she'd conjured began to dwindle. The downpour soaked her cloak, making it cling to her. Before he lost sight of her, Rowen thought she looked small, almost childlike, and afraid.

Jalist grunted with disapproval. "Locke, I'd appreciate you not antagonizing a woman who could turn our cocks into candlewicks with a wave of her hand."

Rowen faced the Dwarr, biting back rage. "She won't hurt us. You know that. She's saved my life. I trust her."

Jalist raised one eyebrow. "Is that why you almost pulled steel on her a moment ago?"

Rowen blinked, realized he was holding his sword hilt. "I wasn't angry. She just... startles me sometimes. Her eyes—"

"That, I understand. But why is she even with us?"

"She's keeping me alive, helping me get to the Wytchforest in one piece. And no offense, Jalist Hewn, but she's a prettier traveling companion than you are."

"Fair enough. But has it occurred to you that your chief bodyguard is a wytch the other Sylvs will likely fetter with arrows the moment they see her? She's *using* you, Locke! No way a Shel'ai banished from the Wytchforest would go back unless it was in her own interest to do so."

Rowen was quiet for a moment. "I forget how much you hate them."

"The Sylvs?" Jalist shrugged. "Never met any from the Wytchforest. Met a few of those Wyldkin, though. No sense of humor, but they seemed like a decent lot."

"I don't mean the Sylvs, and you know it. I meant the Shel'ai."

"Same thing."

"Not really." Rowen changed tactics, eager to reduce conflict as much as he was to soothe his old friend. "You fought with them. You fought *for* the Shel'ai and the Throng... or have you forgotten? And as I recall, you tried to get me to do the same."

"I was *paid* to fight for the Throng. When was the last time you really cared two coppers for the man renting your sword arm?"

Rowen thought of Hráthbam, the dark-skinned Soroccan merchant who had not only befriended him but also given him Knightswrath in the first place. "Don't worry about Silwren. She's nothing like Fadarah. We can trust her."

Jalist scoffed. "Trusting a Shel'ai is like trusting a tiger just because it purrs. If you had half a brain, you'd have learned that by now."

Rowen smiled faintly. "Well, I never was very bright."

"Or willing to back down from a fight. That's your weakness. You're as hotheaded as your idiot brother."

Rowen winced, and his hand moved of its own accord, touching his sword. His fingertips traced Knightswrath's dragonbone hilt. He remembered his sword quivering when he drove it through his brother's neck. He remembered his own name bubbling from his brother's lips before he fell as a single exhalation of blood and gratitude.

"Kayden was your friend. He died on my sword. You know that. Don't talk about him like—"

"Not all killing is murder. Some deaths are a kindness. From what I hear, Kayden's was one of them. Or would you rather he live on like he was?"

Cursed, crazed, forced to murder on behalf of the Shel'ai like some kind of trained hound... "The Shel'ai *made* him that way. It wasn't his fault. They tortured him—"

"Yes, they did."

Rowen sighed. "*Some* of them, I mean. Silwren and El'rash'lin didn't have any part of that. And I think some of the others objected, too."

"But they still went through with it." Jalist waved him off before he could reply. "Point is, Locke, they did what they did. No sense denying it. I'm not one to defend those bastards, but if you want to assign blame for Kayden, save half for your brother. He *let* them make him their thrall. So he gets half the blame, and the Shel'ai get the other half. You get what's left." Jalist uncorked his wineskin and took a drink. "Who knows? Maybe there's even something to what she said about the Light."

"About it guiding our actions?" Rowen snorted derisively. "If the Light fated me to be reunited with my own brother only so that I could set him free by killing him"—he turned away, stung by his own words—"then maybe I'm on the wrong side."

Jalist stretched out on the ground. "Stop your gods-damned brooding! You're finally an Isle Knight. Aren't you supposed to be a pillar of moral certainty now?"

Rowen scoffed. "I used to think that's how the Knights were. Then I spent some time with them."

"Yet you wear their tabard."

Rowen glanced down at his armor again. He shrugged.

Jalist laughed quietly. "Exactly how far is this Wytchforest, anyway?"

"A week. That's what Silwren says, anyway." The Wytchforest was one of the few realms of Ruun that he'd never visited, though he'd had little choice. Some people, like the Dwarrs or the nomadic horsemen of Quesh, could be unfriendly to foreigners. Others, like the Dhargots, tried to convince them to join their empire and partake in one of their bloodthirsty campaigns. Then there were the Sylvs. In the Wytchforest, foreigners were simply peppered with arrows and left to rot in the sun.

Rowen hoped his group would fare better than that. True, he had Knightswrath, but he would have little chance to invoke the Oath of Kin if the Sylvs killed him on sight. "We'll have to stop somewhere along the way and resupply. Hesod isn't far. Wasn't there a blond boy you fancied there a few years back?"

Jalist laughed. "Cornflower hair, skin as soft as a woman's. If I remember right, you had your eye on some pretty, big-rumped lass you tried to talk out of joining the Iron Sisters." He glanced around at the storm. "Maybe they're even still alive."

"You don't sound so sure."

Jalist shrugged. "Fadarah never went that far south. But the Dhargots might have. If so, what those bastards will do to the Iron Sisters..."

"It's a long ways from Dhargoth to Hesod. The Dhargots might just be focusing on the northern cities for now."

"How about Atheion?"

Jalist opened his mouth, but another massive clap of thunder rolled over them, punctuated by a vehement splash of lightning. Rowen jumped, reaching out to catch Snowdark's reins and soothe the animal before it could run off. Jalist did the same with his mount, cursing all the while. Both men gazed up at Silwren's umbrella of wytchfire. Rowen figured they were wondering the same thing: would a bolt of lightning pierce it and kill them? "If we *do* run into the Dhargots, it'll be good to have Silwren with us."

"Maybe. Troubles follow that woman like they follow you. Gods, Kayden used to say that you drew disasters like shit draws flies!"

Kayden again. "Then maybe you should be rid of us. You might live longer."

Jalist snorted. "Between bandits and my bad luck, I'd never make it all the way back to Tarator—even if they'd have me, which they won't. So I may as well see where this goes."

The storm was worsening, almost completely veiling the midday sun behind bruise-colored clouds. He glanced westward, in the direction Silwren had walked. He thought he saw her statue-still form: a faint shadow cloaked in rain. He could not tell if she was facing them. He shuddered, realizing that no matter how far away she was, she might very well be able to hear their every word.

They set out again as soon as the storm cleared. The smell of rain filled the air, along with a faint mist that made the plains appear to be steaming in the afternoon sun. Rowen's spirits rose. But they did not ride far before he was forced to call a halt. Already, something else had replaced the fresh smell of rain. He scowled at the western sky, noting a dark smear on the horizon. He turned to Jalist. "Is that what I think it is?"

"If you mean the dark chariots of Fohl, come to carry off our enemies, probably not." Jalist touched the shaft of his long axe. "If you mean smoke, yes."

Rowen turned to Silwren, remembering stories about the famed sight and hearing of Sylvs. "I don't have a spyglass, and your eyes are better than ours. What do you see?"

Silwren was quiet for a moment. Instead of leaning forward in the saddle as Rowen and Jalist had done, she closed her eyes. When she opened them a moment later, she stared straight ahead. "A city, burning."

Jalist swore. "Hesod?"

"If that's what you call it."

"Is it under siege?" Rowen touched his sword hilt, resisting the urge to ask if and how she would be able to answer his question.

"The siege is finished. I see smoke pouring over the walls. In front of the city, I see... hundreds of people stripped naked, mostly women, impaled on spears." Despite her dispassionate tone, Silwren trembled.

Rowen and Jalist exchanged worried looks.

Jalist said, "Sounds like our old friends from the north, all right."

Rowen stared at the horizon for a moment. "We'll have to go southwest," he said finally. "We'll avoid the Dhargots then reach the Wytchforest by skirting the Noshan Valley. Won't delay us more than a few days."

Jalist's dark eyes narrowed. "Unless we get our skulls axed in! Nosh isn't the friendliest place on Ruun, you know."

Rowen scratched his beard. Even though he'd never been to Nosh—including Atheion, its famous City-on-the-Sea—he'd heard a little about it during his travels. "Noshans are sailors and goatherds. They won't trouble us."

"I'm not talking about the Noshans who live around Atheion. I'm talking about those damn wildmen who live in the mountains. Supposed to be as mad as dragonpriests and as cruel as Dhargots."

Rowen scratched at his beard. "A few thousand Dhargots or a few hundred barbarians..." *And behind us, Shel'ai and Isle Knights! Gods, how did I get so many enemies?*

"Welcome to Ruun," Jalist snorted.

"I can get us past the Dhargots," Silwren offered.

Jalist tapped the shaft of his long axe. "How's that?"

Silwren faced Rowen. "I can blind them to our passage. We can ride right past the city, and they'll never see us." She trembled faintly as she spoke.

Silwren's new unsettling eagerness to use her magic sent a chill down Rowen's spine. "I don't think that's a good idea. If something goes wrong—"

"El'rash'lin gave his life, Knight. He died for you, as much as anyone. It's time I did my part. If I say I can get you past the city unharmed, then I can." Silwren's violet eyes flared as she spoke.

Rowen resisted the urge to reach for Knightswrath. "Something will go wrong. Something *always* goes wrong." He relaxed his voice. "I trust you. I do. But you dying right now to keep me alive just means I'll die a little later. I need your help, not your sacrifice."

Silwren smiled faintly but said nothing.

"We go south." Rowen turned his horse.

The others fell in behind him. As he rode, Rowen thought of the hundreds of Hesodi dragged in front of the city, stripped naked, then impaled and left to endure a slow, agonizing death in the baking sun. He'd seen such things before. For a moment, he imagined himself riding to the victims' rescue, Knightswrath gleaming in the sunlight, an army of Knights at his back. He pushed the thought from his mind.

CHAPTER TWO
CAPTAIN OF THE SHAL'TIAR

EVEN FROM HALFWAY ACROSS BRAI'YL Run, the stark grassy swath that separated the Ash'bana Plains from the looming Wytchforest beyond, Essidel could smell the reek. At least, he thought he could. He reminded himself that the distance was too far even for Sylvan senses, but he had been fighting Olgrym three fourths of his life, long enough to be all too familiar with their grisly ritual of painting themselves with blood and dung before battles.

He felt his pulse quicken and that familiar knot of fear. Even from such a distance, they looked like giants...

Giant as trees before the axe, he told himself, reciting the ancient phrase often intoned by the Shal'tiar before battle. He steadied himself and counted.

Counting Olgrym was not easy—they moved in a broad, heaving tide of malice and muscle—but he estimated at least a hundred of them. The main host was still farther east, clashing with General Seravin and trying to muscle past the stronghold of Que'ahl. The horde before him was just an upstart party sent to test Sylvan mettle.

They should know better. Then again, he doubted the Olgrym were acting under Doomsayer's orders. The chieftain who had somehow united all the Olgish clans had a rare and wholly uncharacteristic appreciation for cunning and strategy. That made him dangerous. But the group probably consisted of renegades from one of the other clans—the Ash-Hands or the Skullshards—out to distinguish themselves.

That was fine by him. He would have preferred sneaking up on the Olgrym that night to cut their throats or doing battle behind the strong walls of Que'ahl, but every Olg they killed right away was one they would not have to fight later. He signaled.

A squad of Sylvan footmen in black leather brigandines and blackened mail took up positions on either side of him. They formed a long row of grizzled fighters armed with longbows and curved shortswords. None flinched. Most had been fighting Olgrym nearly as long as he had. But he caught other small indications of fear: fingers tightening around weapons, a restless step, and a deepening frown.

Essidel cast a critical eye over their defenses again. His men had taken up position in a shallow trench. One side was piled with earth and bristling with sharpened stakes angled to face the charging Olgrym. The Olgrym could simply have wheeled east or west and tried to flank them, but for a suicidal war-band such as the Olgrym's, the only honorable attack was one delivered straight at the enemy's throat.

All the better for us. Essidel issued no orders. None were needed. Each Shal'tiar warrior took a firm stance behind the heaped earth and sharpened stakes. They loosened their blades and nocked arrows to their longbows. The tips were poisoned with burgundy smears of quickdeath, a deadly mixture of crushed felberries and wytchwood sap—the strongest poison the Sylvs had. But against Olgrym, a killing shot to the throat, the eyes, or the liver was better than relying on poison. They were just too big.

Essidel loosened both his curved shortswords, withdrawing them a finger span from their well-oiled scabbards of tooled leather. Then he picked up his longbow. Like his clothing, it was black. He reached for the quiver at his belt. It contained a variety of footed arrows: broadheads, bodkins, and even flint-tipped arrows designed to break apart once they entered the body. He chose a broadhead because it would make a larger wound. He fit the slender arrow to the string, sighted down the shaft, and waited.

Sunlight glinted off the arrow's tip, shimmering off the thin sheen of quickdeath. The taunts and bloodcurdling shouts of the enemy grew more intense, as did the reek wafting off their bodies. The Olgrym were almost within longbow range, provided the Sylvs aimed high. Another force might have decided against firing right away. Despite their great size, Olgrym could sprint nearly twice as fast as any man. Some would think the best tactic was to wait, aim, and make the shot count.

But as fast as Olgrym could run, Sylvs were even faster at nocking arrows. Essidel raised his bow to a forty-five degree angle and let the bowstring slip from his fingers. The other Shal'tiar warriors followed suit. A dark cloud of poisoned arrows rose into the air with an ominous *snap*. After rising higher and higher, they fell, their steel tips glinting in the sun. Metal sought flesh, sank through gray muscle, and bit bone. A dozen Olgrym were struck—some in the neck or face, others in the chest and shoulders—but even the mortally wounded pressed on, taking a few more steps before they stumbled and crashed to the plains.

Essidel reached for another arrow, nocked it, and aimed, all in one smooth motion. The other Sylv followed his lead. They fired a second volley, reduced their arc, and fired a third. The Olgrym were less than fifty yards away. Their feet pounded the earth, shaking the ground.

Essidel swallowed his fear and counted. A third of the Olgrym were dead already, but he knew that was not enough to stop them. He drew out three arrows at once and nocked them all. He pulled the string back, steadying the bow despite the unusual weight. The other Shal'tiar did likewise. The tide of Olgrym rolled closer. Essidel waited, waited, then fired.

A thick mass of arrows leapt from the Sylvan line, nearly parallel to the ground, and shredded the foremost Olgrym. Some still pressed on, blood crazed, half a dozen arrows in their bodies. Essidel cursed. He tossed his bow over his shoulder, drew both his shortswords, and braced himself.

The Olgrym must have seen the sharpened stakes, but they did not slow. Instead, they hurled their bodies at the Sylvs' position, impaling themselves, howling and thrashing like rabid greatwolves in their efforts to move forward. Essidel kept from flinching as Olg blood splattered his face.

Each wooden stake, as wide as a man's arm, sank three feet in the earth, but the wood buckled and snapped under the weight of Olgrym bodies. Howling, those in the rear shoved their mortally wounded comrades on, inadvertently using them as shields. Essidel stepped back. The other Sylv did the same. The bodies of Olgrym fell like a leaden rain where they had just been standing. Fresh Olgrym clawed and shoved past.

Then the real fighting started.

Minutes later, after what felt like a lifetime, the battle was over. Essidel wiped the sweat from his forehead then wiped the blood from his shortswords using the corpse of the Olg at his feet. He counted again. All the Olgrym were dead... as were half his men. He maintained a stoic expression.

No tears in victory, he thought, echoing another Shal'tiar motto, though he had never really cared for that one. He studied his surviving fighters and chose one who appeared unhurt and the least winded. "Briel, take word to the general. Tell him the Olgrym—"

The crisp blare of a trumpet shattered what he had been about to say. Essidel tensed. He thought for a moment that a fresh host of Olgrym was bearing down on them. Olgrym wrought their booming war horns from the bones of dead dragons, but that horn blast had been crisp and metallic.

He turned in time to see a thick mass of armored figures gathering on a distant rise. They spread out, forming a long line of men and horses. Essidel stared. The men wore flashing mail, gleaming half helms, and brilliant-azure tabards. He wondered for a moment if he had lost his mind.

Briel cleared his throat. "Captain, should we—"

Essidel sheathed his blades. "No, go report to Seravin. The rest of you, at ease. Humans or no, these are Knights... *allies* from the days of the Shattering War. Wait here. Tend the wounded. I'll go and see what—"

The Knights' trumpet sounded again. Essidel turned in time to see the glinting formation explode into action, rolling down the hill like a ribbon of azure and steel. Essidel thought for one wild moment that the Knights had spotted a second force of Olgrym bearing down on them and were spurring to intercept them. He looked around. Aside from the Sylvs, the corpses of the Olgrym, and the wave of Knights thundering toward them, Brai'yl Run was empty.

Even then, Essidel could not believe it. *Humans... Isle Knights... attacking Sylvs?* He grabbed Briel, who was just finished cleaning his blades and was turning to go. "Forget the Olgrym. Tell the general we're being attacked by Isle Knights!"

Briel's eyes widened. Stunned, he stood for a moment then ran. Essidel glanced back at Sylvos. Sylvs were quick runners, nearly as fleet-footed as Olgrym. He and the rest of his fighters could make it to shelter, even on foot, but they had to cover Briel. Essidel started to draw his swords but changed his mind and retrieved a longbow. "Aim for their horses. The Knights will be thrown from their saddles. Don't bother trying to cut through their armor. Nothing can cut through kingsteel. Just stab their necks below the helmet or right through their visors."

He glanced at his men's faces again, noting both their weariness and their confusion. Still, they sprang to action. They retrieved their longbows and formed up in staggered lines, using the corpses of slain Olgrym as a barrier between them and the onrushing Knights. Those Shal'tiar who were too wounded to stand nocked arrows, willing to fight as long as they had breath in their bodies. Luckily, Shal'tiar trained to fire their bows even when kneeling or lying down, to fight even when in agony.

Essidel nocked an arrow. If they could get the poison around the Knights' famously impenetrable armor, the men would die almost instantly. *If...* He drew back the arrow until the feathers touched his cheek. He held his breath, cursing whatever new trick the Known Gods seemed to be playing. Then he let the bowstring slip from his fingers.

CHAPTER THREE

A CHANGE IN DIRECTION

A s her group rode south, Silwren glanced to the right.
Sylvos, what her new companions called the Wytchforest,
was still just a blur on the western horizon, a wall of green
gowned in clouds. She doubted the others' eyes were sharp enough to
see it, but the sight of her homeland filled her with dread.

*They drove me out. The other Sylvs... my own people... they tried to
kill me! They killed my birth parents. Why am I going back?*

Fadarah had been fond of saying that the next time an exiled
Shel'ai set foot in Sylvos, it would be at the head of an army. She no
longer wished to see all her people suffer and her homeland burn, but
that did not change one basic fact: Sylvs born with Shel'ai abilities
were routinely murdered or, at best, exiled. Her people—if they could
be called that—had the direst of crimes to answer for.

*But I am only one woman. One Shel'ai can neither change their minds
nor punish them for their sins.* Then again, she was not quite a Shel'ai
anymore. A sense of loneliness flooded her, accompanied by memories
of Namundvar's Well. She fought back a sudden swell of tears, though
she could not quite say what had caused them. She had seen, even
been submerged, in the Light. She should still carry some remnant of
that joy, that bittersweet serenity. But the raw power drawn from the
Light also threatened to drive her mad—if it didn't kill her first. *Me...
and those around me.*

Besides, Rowen had gazed into Namundvar's Well, too. He had
seen the Light, just as she had, but he seemed to be devoting all the

energy he could spare to not thinking about it. She could not blame him. After viewing paradise and having it torn from his grasp, how could he think about it with anything but despair?

Rowen touched her arm. She jumped then looked where he was pointing. A band of travelers had made camp in the distance.

Her companions tensed. Rowen had one hand on his sword, and Jalist was trying to look casual as he palmed his long axe. There appeared to be about fifty of them: some women and children but mostly old men, all dressed in rags.

Rowen asked, "Refugees from Hesod?"

Jalist shook his head. "Not bloody enough. Clerics and pilgrims, I'd guess. Doesn't look like many of them are armed."

"Looks like they follow Tier'Gothma and Armahg," Rowen said, scrutinizing the emblems on their colored robes. Some had a cluster of grain stalks under a quarter moon, and others a swirl of stars.

"Should we ride around them?" Jalist asked.

"Let's see if they need help first." Rowen dismounted and led his horse on foot. He held the reins in one hand, resting the other casually on his sword hilt.

Jalist did the same, pretending to use his long axe as a walking staff. "I'll save you the trouble of asking, Locke. They do." He gave her a sidelong glance. "Are you coming, sorceress?"

Silwren caught the wariness and disdain in the Dwarr's gravelly voice. She wondered if these pilgrims would hate her for what she was, just as so many other Humans had. She wondered if they would threaten her. *If they do, I'll kill them.*

She dismounted and followed after the others. As Rowen's group drew nearer, the travelers shrank back. A few produced staffs or small knives, but only one—an old man—wore a sword. That man left his sword sheathed and came ahead of the others to greet them. The old man's robes might once have been blue, but they had long since faded to almost white. He wore the starry, swirling emblem of Armahg, but his gray beard was patchy and uneven. He looked less like a cleric than a beggar, but he smiled warmly. Sunlight glinted off his coppery skin and earrings—he wore several in each ear—and she heard a faint

Queshi accent in his voice when he said, "Welcome, friends. Will you share our fire?"

Rowen spoke for them. "If it pleases you. Are you from Hesod?"

The cleric's smile faded. "No... but we heard the screams while we were traveling. We're pilgrims from half a dozen towns to the north. We're bound for Atheion, to visit the Scrollhouse and the temples. If all goes well, we're hoping to stay there." He lowered his voice. "We *did* find one refugee from the city, but she's asleep now."

Rowen nodded, unkempt red hair hanging in his eyes. "We aren't clerics, but we might be able to help, if you have wounded who need tending."

Silwren wondered if he meant for her to heal them. She'd kept her hood drawn so far. Despite her trepidation, she smiled. She could tell how hard Rowen was trying to sound courteous, ever mindful of the balancing crane he wore on his tabard. *If all the Isle Knights were like him, the Lotus Isles might actually become what it claims to be.*

The cleric smiled. He looked Rowen up and down. "A Knight of the Crane! Why, I haven't met anyone from the Isles in years. You don't have the appearance of an Isleman, though."

"I'm Ivairian by birth. I trained on the Isles. Knighted less than a month ago." Rowen introduced himself, then Jalist. "And this"—he gestured, a faint worry in his eyes—"is Silwren, our friend."

Silwren braced herself and lowered her hood. The cleric's smile vanished, and he reached for the rusty sickle-sword hanging from his belt. Whatever courtesy had been poised on his lips was replaced by a vulgar oath.

Rowen stepped in front of Silwren, sword half drawn. Jalist followed with a sigh, readying his long axe.

But the cleric held up his hands. "Peace, Knight! You only caught me off guard. My eyes may have been soured from countless hours reading books by firelight, but they still know white-and-purple eyes when they see them."

An uneasy murmur swept through the company of pilgrims. Some reached for makeshift weapons. Others pulled children close or backed away, muttering curses and oaths.

Rowen said, "We're travelers. Nothing more. We mean no harm to anyone."

"Good news for us." The Queshi priest turned and waved and his companions. "Lower your weapons, brothers. An invitation is an invitation." He offered Silwren a wary smile. "Whatever blood's in your veins, you're free to join us, if you like. But first, you'll have to forgive me. My addled brain didn't catch your name as it flew by."

"Silwren," Rowen repeated.

The old cleric's eyes widened. "The Wytch of Lyos?" He grinned and turned to Rowen. "And you're the Knight who protected her."

I need no protection now.

Meanwhile, the Queshi priest laughed. "The Heroes of Lyos, right here in our camp. I should have guessed! We've heard your story... a version of it, at least. I'll wager such tales take on a life of their own, after a time. Perhaps you could tell us the version you like best."

Rowen smiled slightly. "Perhaps."

The pilgrims relaxed a little at the sound of their leader's laughter, though they still gave the trio a wide berth as they followed the cleric to one of many campfires erected in the center of camp. Several priests offered to care for their horses. One offered them a wineskin, though Rowen offered it to the Queshi priest first.

With a forced smile, Rowen said, "Honor does not permit me to drink before our host."

Silwren concealed a smile. She did not need magic to know that Rowen was lying.

The cleric raised one gray eyebrow. "Don't worry, Knight. We had no time to poison it before you arrived." He winked, drank, and passed the wineskin back. Then he turned, issuing orders to bring food for their guests.

Jalist leaned toward Rowen's ear as the Dwarr accepted the wineskin next. Silwren's acute Sylvan hearing caught him saying with sarcasm, "The Heroes of Lyos?"

Rowen whispered, "If you could avoid telling them you fought for the other side, I'd appreciate it." The Knight faced the cleric again. "Forgive me, Father. You've shared your wine with us, but not your name."

The old cleric blushed. "Apologies. I am Matua. I'm originally from Quesh—as you might have guessed by the color of my skin, if your eyes are any better than mine."

"I've been to your lands once, years ago. I remember the red horses your archers ride. 'Lightning on four legs,' they say. I've never seen anything move so fast!"

Matua laughed. "Bloodmares? Fast, sure, but ill tempered." He indicated a scar just beneath his jawline. "One gave me a toss when I was a child. If you're a Queshi, falling off your horse is like being caught stealing from the temple coffers. My prospects as a fighter seemed bleak, so I went north instead. I think my father was glad to see me go. Been moving about the Simurgh Plains ever since, one village to another." The cleric's expression sobered. "And *your* story, Lady Silwren?"

Silwren felt all eyes on her. She'd taken the wineskin from Jalist and handed it back to Matua without drinking. "Not one I delight in sharing, if you'll forgive me."

Matua nodded, unfazed. "Some stories, especially the painful sort, are better shared. Others, not. As it's your story, we'll trust that judgment to you."

Clerics appeared with bowls of stew. Silwren took hers and smiled at the scowling man who delivered it, but she did not eat.

Rowen said, "I'm surprised you stopped for the night. If anybody got away from Hesod, the Dhargots will be hunting them. They can't be more than two days away from you."

"It's not the Dhargots we're afraid of. I don't think they'll come this far south. But I've passed through Nosh before, and I remember the Lochurites have a fondness for attacking camps at night. Better we sleep here, do most of the rest of our traveling tomorrow. Don't have to worry about being so quiet in daylight."

As though on cue, a baby began crying somewhere in the camp.

"I heard about the Lochurites while I was in Quesh. They're midland raiders, right?"

Matua grimaced. "You're too kind. I'd call them wolves, but that would be cruel to wolves. If you know anything about my order, you know that Armahg cautions us against passing judgments over entire people"—he glanced at Silwren—"but in the Lochurites' case, I make an exception." He spat in the fire for emphasis, muttering a Queshi oath over the faint hiss.

Jalist nodded in agreement. Silwren knew of the Stillhammer Mountains, where most Dwarrs made their home on the eastern shore of the midlands, but she had never heard of the Lochurites.

Matua seemed to read her expression. "The Lochurites roam the hills south of the valley. Don't know where they got their name since they don't have any cities or towns, much less a king. They just rove about, raping and reaving. They tried invading Quesh not too long ago, but our riders put a quick and bloody stop to that. So they moved on to the Noshans."

"Sounds like they'd get along well with the Dhargots," Jalist muttered.

"Lochurites don't even use iron. They think bronze is some kind of sacred metal sent by gods, so that's all they'll use for weapons. They're fanatics, even worse than dragon worshippers. They don't mind dying. They swallow some kind of poison before battles. It yellows their eyes and drives them mad. *Berserkers,* some call them. Even their women and children fight."

Rowen said, "Atheion has a standing army. Why don't they hunt them down?"

Matua scoffed. "Most Noshans stay near Atheion, tending their herds or trading goods brought in on ships. Lochurites don't attack cities. They just prowl about, scouring camps and villages, looking for easy prey. So the Noshans don't have much reason to get worked up about it. But I bet they *are* worried about the Dhargots."

Silwren said, "They aren't the only ones." She looked at Rowen.

Matua leaned forward. "There's talk of them sweeping across the Simurgh Plains. Makes me wonder, if things don't work out in Atheion, if we'd even have villages to go back to. And that's if we even make it to Atheion in one piece!"

Rowen asked, "Doesn't your group have any fighters?"

Matua laughed. "Guards cost money. We can hardly afford bread. But we've got a few weapons, here and there." He tapped his rusty sickle-sword.

Silwren saw the concern in Rowen's eyes. She guessed what the Knight was thinking. She could not decide whether to feel irritated by the Human or be proud of him.

"Maybe we could help," Rowen said. Jalist groaned, but Rowen continued. "We could escort you to Atheion. In the meantime, we don't have extra weapons, but we can help you carve some spears from old tree limbs. Harden them with fire, and even if they don't push through a bronze breastplate, they'll drive the wind out of a man—drugged or no."

Matua blinked in surprise then grinned. Some of the others looked displeased, but most wore expressions of relief. "You have our thanks, Sir Locke! And you'll have coin for your troubles—no, don't refuse it. If you know the Queshi and hospitality, you know that's an insult. Just nod and give me whatever courteous reply they taught you on the Isles."

Rowen grinned, and Silwren knew his pleasure came as much from the use of his title as from anything. She did not listen for Rowen's reply. She looked away.

Rowen, you're no figure in a tale of hope and heroes. By the Light, you have no idea what you're risking. We were supposed to make haste through the valley, not act as bodyguards. If there's a fight, if I lose control...

She studied the faces around her: gnarled priests, fretful old women, a few wide-eyed children gazing upon her with fearful fascination. She wondered how many would die were she forced to unleash her full power to protect Rowen. She spooned some of the stew and raised it to her lips. It was hot but bland. She ate it anyway and tried to smile.

CHAPTER FOUR
FOHL'S DAUGHTER

B
Y MIDDAY, ROWEN BEGAN TO wonder if he'd made a mistake. He had risen early and, with Jalist and the priests' help, begun fashioning crude spears. But the task quickly proved to be daunting and mostly useless. Some priests refused the weapons, claiming that even holding them betrayed their vows. Others accepted them, only to use them as walking sticks. None save Matua seemed to have any idea how to use them. As they set out, Rowen even saw a few of his meticulously crafted, fire-hardened spears simply cast aside, abandoned in the grassy plains. Silwren watched, always from a distance, and said nothing. But her stern, unblinking gaze made her disapproval clear.

That was only the beginning. The ragtag group rose late, traveled slowly, and stopped often. Though they had a handful of horses, all were laden with supplies and required almost as much coaxing as their masters did. Children cried. The old took only two steps for his three. Many seemed to breathe in air only to exhale complaints.

Rowen seethed, trying to conceal his mounting frustration. He'd offered to escort these people without first consulting Jalist or Silwren, thinking that the loss of a couple days would not seriously hinder them. In fact, if they traveled south around the valley, they could reach the Wytchforest and avoid the Dhargots entirely. But with every delay, he imagined his enemies—Dhargots, Lochurites, Shel'ai, and Isle Knights—drawing closer.

Jalist appeared next to him. "Well, *Sir Locke*, what did you expect?

Remember that Ivairian merchant we helped escort a few years back? He insisted on bringing his wife, his servants, his concubines, his legitimate children, and, what, a half dozen bastards?"

"I'd nearly forgotten. This bunch isn't that bad, though."

"You're right. They're worse. If we get killed doing this, I'm blaming you." The Dwarr kept a wary eye on their surroundings—plains, a few rocky hills, and a distant crescent of mountains—his long axe always in hand.

"We won't. Even if we're attacked, we have Silwren."

"Then why did you waste all that time carving spears?"

"Just a precaution, and one we probably won't need. We're well into the valley now. The Noshans must be patrolling these lands."

"Ah, yes. The brave Noshan warriors. There's some of them now." Jalist pointed to a distant rise, where three shepherds were tending a flock. One of them waved. Jalist waved back. "We're doomed."

"Don't worry. We'll be in Atheion by nightfall."

"And will we find the streets turned to wine and the rooftops to strawberries when we get there? At this pace, we'll be lucky to get there before winter!" Jalist glanced over his shoulder, scouring the priests and pilgrims with a murderous stare.

Jalist had a point. Rowen sighed and went to talk to Matua. Trying to smile to soften what he was sure was an unmistakable edge in his voice, Rowen said, "Forgive me, Father, but we must quicken our pace."

The disheveled cleric nodded, unsurprised. "I agree. In fact, I have been praying for that at least five times a day for two weeks now. So far, Armahg has declined to answer."

Rowen had already had his fill of sarcasm from Jalist and did not need it from the cleric as well. He took in their surroundings. They had a good clear view for miles. Aside from the occasional drover, the land seemed sparsely inhabited. In fact, were it not for Matua's tale, he might have thought this realm as safe and uneventful as any.

"If we *are* attacked, lead the group onward. We'll deal with the Lochurites."

"And you'll be welcome to them. But I doubt you'll dampen your sword here, Sir Locke. These Lochurites aren't an army. They rove

43

in gangs of three or four. If they see you and your friend, armed and armored, I'm sure that'll keep them away."

"Just the same, make sure everyone stays together. Even if someone has to relieve themselves, they shouldn't go alone. Modesty's not worth dying for."

"Tell that to Haesha." Matua added, "She's the young priestess of Dyoni."

Rowen scowled. "So far as I can tell, Priest, everyone in your group is wearing clothes."

"Oh, I don't mean she's naked. I mean, she keeps wandering off, then coming back. She's been drunk since we found her. She's the refugee who made it out of Hesod... though she hasn't said two words about that, or anything else, since we found her."

"Is she wounded?"

"I don't think the Dhargots got to her, if that's what you mean. We just found her wandering south of the city. She had blood on her, but it wasn't hers. Beyond that, I know nothing." He paused. "Have you ever known a follower of Dyoni?"

Despite his irritation, Rowen smothered a grin. Those who followed the God of Earthly Pleasures were famous for their lively barroom and bedroom exploits, to say nothing of their provocative attire—if they wore clothes at all. He had even known a certain flaxen-haired brothel worker who spoke often and longingly of becoming a priestess of Dyoni.

"I'm doing the work anyway," she used to say. "Might as well earn divine favor while doing it!"

Matua frowned. "I thought Isle Knights were above such things. Meaning no offense, of course."

Rowen shrugged. "Ivairian Lancers are supposed to be chaste, though few are. For the Knights of the Lotus Isles, though, the laws are a bit... *lax* in that area. The Codex Lotius only calls for restraint. All things in moderation, that kind of thing. Besides, I wasn't *always* a Knight."

The cleric did not smile at his joke. Rowen sighed. Remembering another prejudice of the Quesh, he was glad he had said nothing about Jalist's preference for men. He decided it was time to cut his

44

losses. He bid his farewell to Matua—who was already distracted, trying to help a mother with a colicky infant—and went to Silwren.

The Shel'ai woman rode stone faced, obviously keeping her distance from the group. He rode next to her for awhile. When she did not speak or acknowledge him, he finally broke the silence. "You're angry with me."

"Perhaps I am not the only one who can read minds."

Rowen considered telling her that he regretted his decision as much as she did. "I was hoping you'd say I was wrong."

"I already told you, Human—"

"Rowen," he corrected. "Gods, are you back to forgetting my name again?"

Silwren raised one eyebrow, looking down at Knightswrath. "That's no tin blade you carry, Knight. You wear one of the few relics left in all of Ruun that proves the Oath of Kin is real. With that sword, you might compel the Sylvs and the Knights to fight together. You could save thousands of lives. Instead, we're safeguarding fifty."

She's right. "You're wrong. These people needed our help. A Knight of the Crane doesn't turn his back."

"Don't they? I've heard otherwise."

"Enough. So what if the Dhargots keep killing? What do you care if Humans kill other Humans?"

"I don't. But you do."

Rowen was about to argue with her, to remind her that she herself had betrayed the Shel'ai to save Lyos from the Throng, but he sensed that was going too far. Instead, he decided to check on the priestess of Dyoni. He rode back to the ragged column of clerics and crying children. Some bowed at the sight of him. Others shied away when they saw his anger. Rowen ignored them and scoured the ranks until he spotted her.

At the rear of the column walked a young woman about Rowen's age, perhaps a few years younger. She wore mismatched traveling clothes. Her trousers, much too big for her, were held in place by a belt of knotted rope. Her tunic, on the other hand, was much too small.

The breath caught in Rowen's throat. The woman was clearly

Human, though her exaggerated curves hinted at Dwarr blood somewhere in her lineage. She had brilliant red hair, even more scarlet than his. If not for the color of her hair, he might have mistaken her for the brothel worker he had just been thinking about. But this priestess was even more striking.

She was also very drunk. One hand white-knuckled a wine pitcher, the contents of which sloshed over the pewter rim with her every other step. The other hand held a drawn knife. He would not have taken her for a priestess at all were it not for the silver emblem pinned to her clothes: a nude, androgynous figure holding a chalice, back turned to the viewer.

While followers of Dyoni could be irritatingly heavy drinkers, given what the woman must have seen at Hesod, Rowen could hardly blame her. Still, the other refugees were giving her a wide berth. He dismounted and led Snowdark by the reins, walking slowly until Haesha caught up with him. When she did not acknowledge his presence, Rowen cleared his throat.

Haesha answered by twisting on one heel and slashing at his face with her knife.

Rowen recoiled, narrowly avoiding a fresh scar. At the same time, Snowdark reared, and he almost lost hold of the reins.

"I'm in mourning," she slurred. "These knees stay closed. Fuck your horse if you're lonely."

She tried to drink from her pitcher, spilled a mouthful of wine on her tunic, and stumbled. When Rowen drew closer, about to catch her, steel flashed at his face again. The tip of her knife slashed his tabard and sparked off his armor, leaving a bright scratch in his breastplate.

"Wait, I just want to—"

"Half the men in the midlands want the same thing. I don't need a description." She turned away, dropped her knife. She tried to pick it up, missed, spilled some wine on her trousers, cursed, then managed to retrieve her knife and leap to her feet in one oddly graceful motion. Seeing that he was still staring, she gave him a mocking curtsy and stumbled on.

"I'm not a midlander," Rowen said, furiously inspecting the tear in his tabard. "I just want to talk. Matua said you might—"

At the mention of the Queshi priest, Haesha spat a string of obscenities.

Rowen recoiled, trying to keep his eyes on the blade flitting about in her hand. He was tempted to try to wrest it away from her before she cut herself, but he was not sure if it was worth the risk. Instead, he mounted his horse and gave her the same wide berth the others did. Some were trying not to snicker.

As he rode away, he heard Jalist in the distance, chuckling softly.

Rowen's mood had not improved when Matua found him later.

The cleric, on the other hand, looked as though he were fighting back a grin as he said, "I heard you had a conversation with Haesha."

Rowen had let a mother and child ride Snowdark while he traveled on foot. He'd done this not just out of generosity but also because he was tired of the priests' and pilgrims' snickering. Unlike the others, though, the Queshi priest seemed unamused.

"You could call it that."

"Careful with that one, Knight. I should have warned you better. She's a fetching sight, but so is a campfire. Only a fool would try to lay his hands on either."

"Save your breath, Priest. The only way I plan on touching her is at the other end of a sword, if need be."

"I don't think it'll come to that. She sleeps like a stone once she's drunk enough. That's why you didn't hear her when you met us on the road. Good thing, too, or else you might have ridden on."

I still might, Rowen thought, eyeing the scratch in his breastplate. The first dent in his armor had come not from battle but from a drunken priestess he had only been trying to help.

Irritated, he tugged at the straps securing his breastplate. Though his armor was made of kingsteel, lighter and stronger than most other armor on the continent, it still weighed on a man who was used to wearing nothing heavier than a brigandine. He had finally begun to grow accustomed to the weight, and he liked the respect it got him. However, the heat and straps still bothered him.

Once I get to Atheion, I'm going to pile it in the corner of some tavern room and let it gather dust while I gorge on that famous food and wine.

He chided himself. *Do I really intend to stay in Atheion that long?* Both Silwren and Jalist had only reinforced his certainty that he'd made a mistake in not riding toward the Wytchforest as fast as possible. Still, for better or worse, he'd become the leader of the group, and as vainglorious as he admitted it was, he rather liked the idea. He had spent most of his life taking orders—from his brother, from the gangs in the Dark Quarter, from whatever merchant had hired him as a sellsword, even from the trainers on the Lotus Isles. If he intended to remain a Knight, though, he might one day lead men into battle. He had better get used to the idea soon.

The hours wore on. They were still far from Atheion, though the strange inland sea known as Armahg's Tears, upon which the city resided, was in view. It shone on the eastern horizon like a broad, blurry sheen. Rowen could hardly believe the size of it. He had not seen such a thing since he'd stood on the Lotus Isles and stared at the ocean—though in the case of the ocean, the mists of the Dragon's Veil kept him from really seeing it.

But I'll see Armahg's Tears. I'll stand on the shores and watch the fishing skiffs come in. I'll see the city with streets of water.

He glanced up at Armahg's Eye. The starry swirls gleamed faintly in daylight. He thought how fine it would be to have so many beautiful things named in his honor then flushed with embarrassment at the thought. He walked ahead of the others and found Matua again. Tired of discussing Haesha, he asked about the distant sea.

The Queshi priest smiled. If Rowen had lost any favor by failing to show adequate ill will toward prostitution, he regained that and more by asking the right question. "The sea was formed from the tears shed by Armahg when the other gods cast her lover, Zet, also called the Dragongod, from the heavens. Some say that the sea was even used by Zet's dragons to wash his bones. And when Armahg's tears moistened those bones, they blossomed and gave birth to all the races of the world."

Rowen nodded carefully. He wondered if the cleric actually believed the preposterous tale. He remembered discussing such matters with Hráthbam, the dark-skinned Soroccan merchant who gave him Knightswrath, who agreed that most priestly tales were childish nonsense.

Rowen was about to ask about Atheion's famous Scrollhouse when he heard a familiar voice shouting his name. He whirled, Knightswrath already half drawn, and saw Jalist thundering toward him. Unwilling to surrender his own horse, as Rowen had, the Dwarr had taken to patrolling the surrounding lands. He rode back to the column so quickly that his horse's hooves kicked up a flurry of dirt.

Matua blanched. "Trouble?"

Rowen sheathed Knightswrath but reclaimed Snowdark and rode to meet Jalist. "Dhargots?"

Jalist shook his head. "Berserkers. But hear me out before you draw that sword and go charging off!"

Priests and pilgrims crowded closer, some gripping their new spears.

Jalist lowered his voice. "There's only about six of them. Looks like they just got done fighting somebody else, maybe those goatherds we saw earlier, because two of them are bloody. But when they saw me, they howled like jackals and charged."

Rowen looked over Jalist's shoulder. "How far away?"

"A quarter mile. Now listen, I know we can take six madmen, especially if Silwren helps, but there might not be a need. I'm the only one they saw. They're on foot. You take this bunch on ahead, and I'll lead the wildmen south. Once they're out of breath, I'll ride back and find you. Agreed?"

Matua was busy trying to calm his companions. Rowen spotted Silwren riding toward them. Priests and pilgrims hurried to get out of her way. Those close enough to overhear what Jalist had said nodded their agreement.

"No," Rowen said finally. "We let these berserkers get away, and they'll just hurt someone else. You said it yourself—there are only six of them. Two already wounded. Better we just kill them."

Jalist scowled. He looked as though he wanted to argue then shrugged. "Fair enough, Sir Locke." He reached for his long axe.

Rowen turned to Silwren just as she joined them. "Jalist saw—"

"I know." She turned to Jalist. "Stay with these others. Both of you. I'll deal with these barbarians myself." Before Rowen had time to answer, she turned in the saddle and looked down at Matua. "Father, lead these people on. I promise, no harm shall befall them. But be quick." As she spoke, wytchfire flared from her hands, turning in bright purple bands around her fingers. The reins smoldered.

Matua paled again but raced to the front of the column, shouting for the others to follow him.

Rowen faced Silwren. "You're not going alone."

"It's better if I do."

"Why?"

"Let her go," Jalist snarled. "She doesn't need your help, and frankly, I can herd these people better with you on the other side."

"I don't need your help," Silwren echoed. She smiled faintly.

Finally, Rowen nodded. "Be careful." He guided Snowdark out of the way.

Without a word, Silwren rode off toward the berserkers. Rowen watched her go then turned back to the column. Everyone had moved on except Haesha. The priestess stood in the distance, frowning, knife in hand. Despite the wine pitcher in her other hand, she appeared as sober as the clerics racing away from her did.

Rowen called, "Get going!" When she did not move, he rode over to her and offered his hand.

Haesha sheathed her knife in her belt. Though she took his hand, she leapt in front of him almost entirely on her own. She pressed against him in the saddle. "Keep your hands to yourself, Knight, or I'll cut them off," she hissed over one shoulder. She took the reins from him and urged the horse after the column.

Silwren had no trouble finding them. As soon as she rode away from the column, she used her magic to momentarily heighten her senses until they trumped even those of the strongest Shel'ai. Her nostrils, suddenly more sensitive than a greatwolf's, caught the scent of blood. When she spotted the barbarians, she reined in. She sat high in the saddle for a moment, waiting until they'd seen her before she dismounted. A quick mental command ensured that her horse would not move without her.

Her pulse quickened, warmed by magic she ached to unleash. Turning her back on her horse, she started toward the berserkers. Though the spell she'd cast to heighten her senses had already begun to fade, she could still see them as if they were right in front of her when they were hundreds of feet away.

The intensity of their emotions washed over her before she could shield herself against it. The berserkers—three men, two women, and a young girl—had just finished launching a sneak attack on a small group of Noshan farmers. Out there, though, the farmers had been prepared. Bows had sung in the morning air. Those six were all that remained of a party twice its size. But that did not matter. The farmers lay slain. The berserkers had paid dutiful homage to Fohl, the Undergod. They'd dipped their bronze blades in blood. Survival was their reward—and Silwren was merely another chance to prey.

Unwilling to see more, Silwren closed off her mind, but not before she sensed a glint of madness, even worse than what she'd sensed from the fey priests and dragon worshippers infesting Cadavash. She shuddered. As they howled and drew closer, she studied their gaunt, dirty bodies and yellowed eyes. All six were naked, armed with knives and hatchets of hammered bronze. Even the little girl screeched like a feral animal.

Silwren's rage waned. Killing murderous Humans was one thing; killing children was another. The mobs who butchered Shel'ai infants did that. But if Silwren spared her, the girl would only find others of her kind and go on killing. Silwren had already glimpsed enough of the child's mind to know she had already been thoroughly corrupted by the same madness as the others. She was past saving.

Like the Nightmare... "No." Too many innocents had already died. She would save the child from these wretched people then use whatever magic it took to draw the poison out of her mind.

Silwren strode forward. Wytchfire blazed from her fingertips, coursing along her arms. Brighter and brighter it flared. The Lochurites stopped, wide eyed.

A man stepped ahead of the others then knelt on the grass. "Are you Fohl's daughter?"

Silwren went closer to him. She wondered if this man was the girl's father and what he'd done to her. She considered extending her mind into his, but the thought repulsed her so much that she nearly vomited. So she stretched out one hand and held it over the man's face. Wytchfire snaked past her reach, caressing the man's face.

He screamed. His body tipped sideways, blackened and dead before he struck the grass. Silwren stepped past him.

Another man, a woman, and the little girl knelt, arms wide in supplication, but the others charged. Silwren did not know whether they were seeking revenge for their slain comrade or the simple favor of their god by dying in battle. She decided it made no difference. She lifted both hands. Twin blasts of wytchfire flung a man and a woman off their feet, turning them to ash before they hit the ground.

Silwren reeled. Magic coursed through her blood, faster and faster, blurring her senses. Panic rose within her, melding with wild exhilaration. Before she realized what she was doing, she turned on the kneeling ones. She blasted the man and woman into cinders then turned to face the child. Darkness clawed at the edges of her sight. The ground roiled beneath her. She lost her footing then fell. On her knees, too, she found herself looking into wide yellow eyes. Then those eyes became her own.

Silwren screamed. She lifted her hands and burned away the sight. The force of the fiery exhalation drove her backward. She lay on her back for a moment, staring up at the passing clouds. The clouds blurred. A horrible smell flooded her nostrils.

She closed her eyes, turned onto her side, and forced herself to stand. She stumbled away from the charred reek. After a few steps, she opened her eyes.

A Human in blue silk and bright armor stood before her, eyes wide. Part of her recognized him, but before she could remember, the long curved sword gleaming in his hands drew her eyes. The sword's glint terrified her. She lifted her hands again. Wytchfire spilled from her fingertips before she could stop it. The armored man shouted and leapt backward. Somehow, his sword drew in all the flames. Cinders dripped off its blade like blood.

Silwren stared for a moment. Then, with a strangled sob, she pitched forward into darkness.

CHAPTER FIVE
NEEDED REST

ROWEN STOOD STILL FOR A moment, his sword drawn, staring at Silwren. He'd changed his mind, left Haesha with the column, and ridden back to help Silwren just in time to see her burn one of the Lochurites—a child—to cinders. Though she lay unconscious, her eyes were wide open. Around her lay scorched, ash-strewn plains. He trembled.

She tried to kill me. He did not think she'd even recognized him. *Gods, maybe Jalist was right! Maybe I can't trust her after all. Maybe I should just leave her.*

He stared at her a moment longer then sheathed Knightswrath. Searing waves of heat continued to radiate from the blade, warming him even through the sword's plain leather scabbard. He knelt to gather Silwren in his arms as he had done at Cadavash and at Lyos. She felt so warm that were it not for his armor, he might have dropped her. She seemed practically weightless, though, as he carried her to his horse.

Despite Snowdark's sudden reluctance to carry the unconscious sorceress, Rowen held Silwren in the saddle in front of him, where Haesha had been moments before. Silwren whimpered but did not wake. Her platinum curls smelled of smoke and charred flesh. Slowly, afraid to wake Silwren, Rowen rode back to find the others.

Jalist met him halfway. "Is she dead?"

Rowen felt a lump in his throat. "No."

"Then close her eyes before she gives me even more nightmares than she already has." Jalist rode closer. When Rowen did not move, the Dwarr switched his long axe to his other hand, reached out, and, with surprising gentleness, closed Silwren's eyes. "What happened?"

Rowen shook his head, unwilling to answer.

"The Lochurites?"

"Dead."

"Good. I don't see any blood. Did they hurt her?"

"I don't think so."

"Then why is she unconscious?"

Rowen tried to edge his horse around Jalist's, but the Dwarr grabbed his arm. "Locke, you're pale as a shade. What happened?"

"Nothing. The wildmen are dead. We're safe. Let's just stop for a while and let her sleep, then we'll move on."

Jalist's eyes narrowed. "It's almost sunset. You sure you want to stop? The way things are going, we might not get any farther today if we do."

Rowen remembered the barbarian child's face, wide with awe and terror, a moment before she died. Sweat beaded on his forehead, though he could no longer tell if the heat came from Knightswrath or Silwren. He resisted the urge to push her off his horse completely. "We have to stop."

Jalist nodded and moved out of the way. Rowen felt the stares of the priests and pilgrims as he rejoined the column. Haesha stood in the distance, frowning, knife in hand, but he rode toward Matua and dismounted. He stepped close to the old cleric and whispered, "Silwren needs to sleep. We need to keep her out of sight. Are there any tents?"

Matua blinked. "Yes. That is, no, but we can make one out of cloaks and spears, if needs be." He turned to Silwren, who had slumped against Snowdark's neck, prompting the horse's eyes to go wide. "Is she hurt?"

"She just needs to sleep." Rowen pulled Silwren down from his horse. While Matua took the reins, Rowen carried the prone sorceress toward a soft patch of grass. "She needs to be left alone," he said loudly.

Matua followed hesitantly. "Does that mean we're stopping for the night? Your friend spoke of Lochurites—"

"They're all dead. We're safe. We just need to stop." *And the next person to ask me why is going to get a split skull.* Luckily, Matua did not press the matter, and despite their fear of the Lochurites, the others seemed relieved for the rest. As Silwren lay on the grass, shaking in short, unsettling spasms, Rowen gathered cloaks and spears. The priests and pilgrims seemed reluctant to part with their cloaks, even if only for a while, but Rowen's expression, coupled with Matua's urgings, persuaded them otherwise.

Rowen carried everything back to where Silwren lay. Jalist helped, silent for once, though the others kept their distance. The two jammed spears in the ground, forming an outline around her body, then draped the spears with cloaks. Shadows covered her. Rowen stepped back.

Jalist whispered, "Locke, you're still as pale as the bone handle on that sword of yours. Would you mind—"

"We can't take her to the Wytchforest like this." Rowen glanced toward the setting sun. "I know we don't have time to waste, but we can't go west until she's... better. We need time. Atheion's as good a place to wait as any."

Jalist cleared his throat. "That's... a change from what you've been saying."

Rowen turned to face him.

Jalist held up his hands. "All right, Locke, don't bristle. Atheion it is. I've always wanted to see the City-on-the-Sea anyway. Maybe I'll even spend some time in the Scrollhouse, make myself smart, become a merchant. Who knows? Maybe—"

Rowen walked away, ignoring the rest.

As the sun set, darkness swallowed the camp, keeping pace with Rowen's mood. The others lit fires, but Rowen stuck to the edge of the camp, careful to avoid letting the fire spoil his night vision as he scanned the darkness for enemies. He'd left Jalist to keep an eye on Silwren, though Rowen was certain that the others were too afraid of her to risk getting close enough to harm her.

Maybe they're smarter than I am.

Rowen walked the perimeter of the camp over and over again. Though he still wore Knightswrath, he used a fire-hardened spear as a walking stick. From time to time, fresh pulses of heat radiated off the sheathed sword, sometimes so painful that he wanted to ungird it and leave it behind.

Something was happening to the sword. Whatever had begun in Lyos, where the sword had transformed seemingly of its own accord from tarnished and rusted to bright and flawless, had accelerated. He suspected it had to do with Silwren, though he could not decide if it was because of the wytchfire the sword had absorbed—which it had done before, when Shade attacked him—or Silwren's mere presence. He had the terrible thought that as Silwren's power and unpredictability grew, the sword was trying to warn him.

Maybe I should just give the damn thing to Crovis Ammerhel after all. I might not need it to kill Fadarah anyway. Even without it, I might be able to invoke the Oath of Kin with the Sylvs.

He moved his hand to the buckle of his sword belt. He started to remove it, changed his mind, and paced the perimeter again. In the distance, a baby cried. Two old men argued over which of the gods was the strongest. Haesha threatened to kill someone for something they'd just said to her. Then Silwren emerged quietly from the darkness right in front of him, her pale skin a stark contrast to her blue-black cloak. He thought for a moment that she was a ghost or a hallucination and that the real Silwren was still asleep in the camp.

"It's me," she whispered, holding up her empty hands.

Rowen realized he'd rested a hand on his sword hilt. He removed it. "Are you all right?"

Silwren nodded then drew closer. Before he could stop himself, Rowen took a step back.

Silwren winced. "Are you?"

Rowen nodded stiffly.

Silwren stared for a moment, unblinking. "I'm sorry. I hardly remember... what happened. Just jumbled images. But..."

Rowen thought of the Lochurite child again. He wondered if he should tell her, then he washed the child's face from his mind in case

Silwren was reading his thoughts. "You should sleep. We'll leave at first light and get to Atheion by sundown. We can start west the morning after."

Silwren turned to stare off into the night. "You're right. I can't go west yet. If you want my help, we should go more slowly. If not, you should go on your own."

Before Rowen could answer, Silwren vanished into darkness. He cursed, wondering if he should follow. Instead, he returned to the camp. Jalist rose from a fire, a flask in hand, and met him.

"Thanks for keeping an eye on her," Rowen said dourly.

Jalist shrugged. "She woke. She walked off. I wasn't about to argue." He offered Rowen the flask.

Rowen ignored the flask and made his way to the heart of the camp. Priests and pilgrims were talking, but he silenced them with a look. After ungirding Knightswrath, he laid it on the ground at his feet. He forced a smile. "We're close to Atheion, but we still have a long day's journey tomorrow. There's still danger. We gave you those spears, but we haven't had time yet to teach you how to use them. If you like, I'll teach you now."

Some stared at him. Others went back to talking in low whispers. No one stood up. Jalist smirked.

"Listen, if not tomorrow, maybe you'll face a Lochurite or a robber or some other cutthroat a week or a month or a year from now. When you do, you'll be glad for this practice."

Some of his listeners copied Jalist's smirk. He cursed inwardly, reminding himself that many of these clerics were old and probably meant to live out the rest of their lives in Atheion. The other refugees—women and children—would likely do the same. The only person who indicated any interest in learning to use a spear was a little boy who stood up and was promptly restrained and hushed by his mother.

Rowen hoped the darkness hid his embarrassment as he felt himself blush. He tried to think of some joke to save face, but his mind was blank. He jabbed his spear into the earth and was about to sit down when a voice called out.

"If you're giving lessons on how to kill, Knight, call me your student."

Haesha pushed past the others and stood before him. She plucked Rowen's spear from the earth and threw it hard. He barely caught it before it hit him in the nose. She grabbed one for herself from a nearby pile. She twirled it between her fingers, making a deft circle, then nodded to herself. She threw off her cloak. A few more travelers chuckled. Others, like Matua, made sounds of disapproval.

Haesha's new clothes, smaller and badly torn, left her midriff exposed. Her slender waist glistened in the firelight, and Rowen caught a flash of jewelry in her navel. He eyed her with a mixture of arousal and loathing. If her breasts did not jostle free the first time she made a quick move, it would be a miracle.

"Only a fool fights while drunk," Rowen told her.

"Haven't touched a drop for hours. Kiss me and taste for yourself." She took a few brazen steps toward him. Then she lunged with her spear.

Caught off guard, Rowen backpedaled. The fire-hardened point stabbed at his face again—not with a clumsy lunge but a quick, balanced strike. Rowen parried with the tip of his spear, considered stabbing her in the gut, and sidestepped. She pivoted, as agile as a shadow, and swung at him, but he was out of range. She recovered easily.

Rowen noted her graceful footwork and easy grip. Though a spear was not his weapon of choice, he'd trained with them. He could tell right away that Haesha was at least his equal. *A cleric who knows how to use a spear? What is this madwoman's story?*

Haesha regarded him with cold green eyes. Then she flashed a crooked smile and attacked. Rowen ducked, parried, sidestepped, and parried again. He was glad the onlookers had left him room to maneuver. He was glad he was still wearing his armor, too, when the tip of Haesha's spear jabbed hard against his kingsteel cuirass, further snagging his tabard.

Rowen risked a sidelong glance at Jalist and saw the Dwarr's unconcealed expression of amusement. He hefted his long axe a little, indicating his willingness to intervene. Rowen shook his head. He used the spear like a quarterstaff, striking Haesha just above the elbow. He put only enough force behind the blow to catch her attention.

"Settle down," he warned.

Haesha's green eyes sparkled with mischief. Unfazed by the strike to her arm, she attacked again. She, too, used her spear like a quarterstaff. Rowen blocked a strike at his knee, sidestepped to avoid a broken jaw, then grunted when Haesha spun and thrust the butt of her spear into his stomach, hard enough that he felt the impact through his armor.

Anger withered his restraint. He drove the butt of his spear toward her ankle. But she moved away nimbly and struck his shoulder far harder than he'd struck her arm.

"*You're* looking a bit *too* settled, good Sir Knight." Her voice dripped with sarcasm.

Rowen glowered at her. "This is getting out of hand, Priestess."

"Let it." Haesha came at him again.

He blocked each of her strikes, but her fury drove him back again. He bumped into an onlooker and narrowly parried a spear point from his throat. Rowen's anger turned to rage, seasoned with profound irritation. He could not imagine that the madwoman really meant to kill him for no reason.

When she attacked again, he sidestepped and delivered a hard blow to the outside of her thigh. He took another sidestep and struck her even harder across the buttocks.

Haesha cursed and nearly fell then turned, grinning. "Were I still a whore, I'd charge you two silvers for that."

"Enough." Rowen used the butt of his spear to push her back a step. "I offered instruction out of kindness. If you want to kill something, go wander the countryside and find a Lochurite to tussle with."

"Thanks, but I prefer to rattle the skulls of pompous Knights." Haesha sank in a low crouch and sprang up, twisting. The movement caused her ample bosom to sway. A pink nipple caught his eye.

Too late, Rowen recognized her tactic. Before he could wrest his eyes from the distraction, Haesha's spear slammed into his groin. His armor absorbed most of the force, but he still doubled over. "Fohl take you!" He looked up to see her spear point angling toward his throat again.

But Jalist stepped between them. The Dwarr blocked the strike with his long axe and countered, lopping off the sharpened tip of her spear. He gave the priestess a cold stare. "Like he said... enough."

Haesha took a step back. Then she smirked and twirled the remains of her spear before tossing it at Jalist's feet. She faced the onlookers. "Some protector you've hired."

Rowen felt his face burning with shame, but he could not formulate a biting retort.

Again, Jalist came to his aid. "He could have killed you a dozen times. It takes no great skill to strike a cheating blow against someone who's only fighting for sport."

But Haesha was already walking away, vanishing into the night. Scowling, Matua went after her. Jalist helped Rowen to his feet.

Rowen whispered, "A dozen?"

"I was feeling generous. So, will you live to father a brood of redheaded bastards, or do we need to flay the girl for revenge?"

Rowen felt all eyes on him. He noted the onlookers' expressions. Some were embarrassed on his behalf or ashamed that a fellow priestess had behaved in such a manner. Others still looked amused. He resisted the impulse to reach under his armor and massage his groin. "Seems like Dyoni's followers have found a new way to worship."

Jalist laughed. "Did she rattle your brains, Locke, or do you really not know an Iron Sister when you see one?"

Rowen blinked. "But she wore the chalice and the crescent moon—"

"So she changed her robes and pinned on a different symbol. Doesn't change what she is. Or *was*."

Rowen's rage slackened, though the embarrassment remained. "Well, at least we know why she's been drinking so damn much."

Jalist nodded. "Come sit by the fire before you fall over."

As the Dwarr helped him along, Rowen cast a murderous look in the direction the priestess had gone. He half hoped that Haesha would try the same bravado on Silwren and get herself burned to cinders.

CHAPTER SIX

THE CITY-ON-THE-SEA

THOUGH ROWEN AND JALIST TOOK turns keeping watch on the camp with some halfhearted assistance from the people they were trying to protect, no Lochurites appeared to assail the camp. At first light, Silwren returned. Rowen noted her bloodshot eyes, but she appeared otherwise stoic and tireless as she mounted her horse and joined the column.

They set out to the east again. Silwren rode some distance from the others, while Jalist continued at the rear. Rowen spotted Haesha, too, though she kept her distance as well and snarled at Matua when he offered her water. Matua proceeded to the head of the column. Surrendering Snowdark to a mother and child again, Rowen walked with the priest.

Matua said, "I'll be glad when we get to the city. I still can't believe those berserkers attacked us in those numbers. It wasn't like this the last time I passed through Nosh. Things are getting worse."

Rowen eyed the growing body of water on the horizon. Anxious to put the Lochurites out of his mind, he said, "What can you tell me about Atheion?"

Matua shrugged. "Only what you've probably already heard in legends. The city's older than the Shattering War, built by the Dragonkin—or, more aptly, their metal servants, the Jolym."

"I've heard of them. I thought they were just killers."

"Mindless slaves, more like it. Not alive, exactly. My order says the Dragonkin used them as troops, sure, but also to build their cities.

Anyway, as for Atheion, there's still some kind of strong magic there. The city floats on skiffs that don't tip or sink, no matter how heavy they get."

"And the Scrollhouse?"

Matua's grin told him that he'd asked the right question. "Followers of my order tend it. It's as much a temple to us as it is a library. It's said that it contains all the knowledge in the world, all the way back to the days of dragons."

Rowen wondered if the library might also contain lore on the Isle Knights, not to mention the Oath of Kin. His pulse quickened, overshadowing his embarrassment over his encounter with Haesha. Perhaps he could learn more about Fâyu Jinn. Also, he'd heard nothing about Knightswrath on the Lotus Isles, but maybe the famous Scrollhouse could help him understand what was happening to the sword.

But what would I do with that information? Who would I tell? If I go back to the Lotus Isles, they're more likely to arrest me than listen to me. And there's still no telling what the Sylvs will do to me when I reach the Wytchforest.

Rowen glanced north, where Silwren still rode, distancing herself from the others. He wondered if she knew anything about the Scrollhouse. He knew that El'rash'lin had visited the place in secret, probing its histories for information on Namundvar's Well, but he had communicated none of those memories with the rest he'd seared into Rowen's mind. And he did not feel inclined to approach Silwren at the moment.

They traveled on and on, making good time for once. Finally, near sunset, they arrived at the shore of Armahg's Tears. Ruddy, golden light bejeweled the face of the sea. The sight was as welcome as any Rowen could remember. He relaxed a little and took in the view.

True to the stories, Atheion was a city of water. While the banks of the sea were littered with homes, shops, and windmills, most of the city floated on the backs of enormous skiffs, each far larger than any sailing vessel he had ever seen. The skiffs were arranged like city blocks, linked by gangplanks and more often by ornate bridges that somehow avoided being sheared apart by the continuous rise and fall of the sea. Beyond them, scores of plainly dressed fishermen headed out on boats or simply tossed their lines off the edge of the city. He even saw stone—true towers and temples wrought of everything from sandstone to marble—floating on gigantic skiffs. The whole city creaked and swayed in the salty air.

Matua said, "Shall we be on our way?" For the first time, the clerics and refugees did not need prodding. They hustled along, almost running toward the city. Rowen followed more soberly, glancing around for the others.

Both Jalist and Silwren had rejoined the column. They dismounted and led their horses toward him. Rowen accepted Snowdark from the mother he'd loaned her to. She bowed her thanks before hurrying down the hill after the others.

Jalist said in a low voice, "All right, Locke, we got these people here in one piece. No sense risking any more. If you still want to get to the Wytchforest, I'm sure the World Tree is as impressive a sight as this."

Rowen cast a worried look at Silwren. Despite her hood, any fool with eyes would see the wisps of brilliant platinum hair peeking out. He doubted it would be long before someone noticed her purple eyes. But they dared not camp in the wilds of Nosh, either. Silwren needed time to regain her composure—perhaps he did, as well—and they could not do so while fighting off Lochurite berserkers.

But what if the Noshan king turns out to be as dangerous to us as they are? "No," he said finally, "we'll stop here... at least for a day or two. Matua can vouch for us." He glanced at the old Queshi cleric and wished he'd thought to ask him to speak to the city on their behalf.

Jalist said, "And what do we do if the Noshan king decides to clap us in irons?"

Rowen glanced at Silwren and forced a smile. "Melt them." He turned before Jalist could protest. "Best we stick with the clerics instead of straggling in like fools."

"You mean, like the damn fools we are? May as well be true to our nature."

Rowen cast Jalist a cold look and rode after Matua.

With the bulk of the city built on the water, Atheion obviously had no great need for stone walls. Still, a squat wall of sandstone formed a half circle on the banks of the sea. From its wide-open gate, a squad of Noshan soldiers rode out to greet them. All wore Atheion's sigil pinned to the blue-and-white-striped tabards: a white sailboat between mountains.

Their lean sun-bronzed captain greeted Matua with formal friendliness, but his eyes widened when Matua introduced Rowen. They widened further at the sight of Silwren. When the other Noshans saw her, some swore. Others signed themselves superstitiously. Rowen tensed.

The captain tapped the hilt of his sword. "The Wytch of Lyos. We've heard of you here, too. They say you're different from the rest of your kin. Is that true?"

Silwren answered in a quiet, even voice, "I will trust you to decide that for yourself. But if you're asking if I mean any harm to you or your city, the answer is no."

The captain turned to Rowen. "Helps that you're with an Isle Knight... and that you have clerics to vouch for you. I'll let you in, but I'll have to take you to see King Hidas. As for you"—he turned to Matua, and his smile returned—"you may proceed unhindered. You'll find the Temple of Armahg on the southernmost skiff. The temple dedicated to Tier'Gothma is there, on the shoreline." He pointed.

Matua hesitated. "Captain, I hope I've been clear. These people aren't enemies. They protected us—"

"I believe you, Father. It will be up to my king if these people stay in the city or not, but they won't be harmed by me or my men. I swear it."

Matua nodded his thanks and approached them. He offered Rowen a handful of coins. When Rowen refused, he offered them to Jalist, who accepted them without hesitation. Then Matua stepped back and thanked them all, though he seemed to avoid looking at Silwren, before rejoining the others.

The clerics and refugees were already beginning to scatter. Haesha lingered alone on the plains for a moment. She cast Rowen a quick, indecipherable look, adjusted her cloak, and started toward the city gates. She appeared so lonesome that Rowen almost pitied her. Almost.

"This way, if you please," the captain said sternly. With the clerics and pilgrims gone, the captain openly wore the same distrustful expression his men did. But something in his demeanor told Rowen that he'd spoken the truth: they would not be harmed—at least, not until after they'd spoken with the Noshan king. He nodded at Jalist and started forward, hoping he had not just made another serious mistake.

As soon as they passed through the gates and set foot on the first skiff, the noise of a bustling crowd washed over them. The experience reminded Rowen of the King's Market in Lyos, but the floating market was accompanied by the smell of the sea and the faint sway of the ground.

Their horses seemed none too pleased with their new setting, and the Noshans appeared to have anticipated such. While their own horses seemed accustomed to their surroundings, the guards dismounted anyway. As soon as they passed through the first gate, the captain summoned a flock of stable boys, who led the horses toward a separate skiff that hosted a huge, sprawling stable. Rowen handed over Snowdark's reins, despite his hesitance to trust his piebald palfrey, along with the others' horses and the few supplies left in their saddlebags, to strangers.

"Don't worry about your horses. They'll adjust to the sea in a few moments. We have oats seasoned with a drug to calm their stomachs," the captain said.

"Wish they'd thought to offer that to us," Jalist muttered to Rowen. The Dwarr blinked rapidly, rubbing his stomach. However, Silwren appeared unfazed, and Rowen found the swaying strangely comforting.

The captain led them onward, through thickening crowds, toward the heart of the city. Given the short distance the guards had ridden, Rowen wondered why the guards had not simply gone out to greet the travelers on foot in the first place. He wondered if they had wanted the advantage of horseback in case a fight started, which made him wonder what had made them so jumpy. He pushed the thought from his mind, figuring he would learn soon enough.

The palace was a surprisingly plain but ancient-looking structure, three stories high, with stucco walls. The Noshans had obviously tried to pretty it up by draping it with tapestries and surrounding it with nude statues. Jalist eyed one statue depicting a strong young man, reclining to read some undoubtedly brilliant scroll of poetry.

The interior of the palace was more extravagant. Statues lined the walls, and bright tapestries hung beside brassy candelabras that flickered with candlelight, through which a crowd of merchants, dignitaries, and citizens moved. A few women in spangles and veils danced about, though no one seemed to notice them. The captain led Rowen's group past an impressive garden and pool in the center of the chamber.

Even indoors, the garden overflowed with exotic flowers of every color and shape, most of which he had never seen before. Jalist's eyes widened. "These flowers must be planted in darksoil," he said, referencing his race's greatest export, which allowed plants to blossom even in the absence of sunlight.

The Noshan captain hurried them to a closed door. There, they waited. He disappeared inside the next chamber, closing the door behind him, but the guards remained. Rowen was glad Silwren had kept her head down and her hood drawn. So far, everyone seemed too distracted to notice her, but it was only a matter of time before that changed. He eyed the figures around them. Most were haughty old men wearing rich silk robes and speaking in heated whispers. Each looked as though he bore the weight of the world, despite the glinting, gaudy jewelry.

Finally, the captain returned. A small, scowling man came with him. The captain introduced the man as a prefect, though Rowen failed to catch the man's strange, nearly unpronounceable name. Rowen braced himself for questions.

But the prefect simply cleared his throat and said, "You must surrender your weapons. You'll get them back, with the king's permission."

Rowen hesitated then unbuckled his sword belt and handed it to the Noshan captain, who passed it to one of his men. He did the same with Rowen's dagger, along with Jalist's long axe and shortsword. Jalist made no move to surrender the dagger in his boot—the captain saw it anyway. He held out his hand. Jalist apologized, feigned surprise, and handed over the dagger.

The captain smiled slightly and took the weapon. "These will be cared for. Don't worry. My men have never stolen a blade, nor have I."

Silwren opened her cloak, revealing that she was unarmed—as far as steel was concerned. Rowen wondered if the captain was thinking the same thing. *But how could they handicap her sorcery?*

Finally, the captain led them through the archway. The next chamber was nearly as large as the first. Decorated sumptuously, it was far less crowded. Though the room was well lit, Rowen saw no candelabras or braziers. Then he spotted glowing, blue-white stones the size of his palm all lined up on pedestals so that they formed a hallway of light leading into the chamber. The rest of the chamber was dim and shadowed.

"Are those magic?" Jalist whispered, surprised.

Rowen thought he remembered them from El'rash'lin's memories, but he was not certain. He turned to Silwren.

She said, "Luminstones, from the days of the Dragonkin. They're very rare. I've never seen one outside the forest."

Rowen wondered how the Noshans had come by them. Dwarrish darksoil was one thing, since the Dwarrs were renowned as traders and craftsmen, but as far as he knew, the Sylvs did not trade with outsiders. Then again, given how old Matua had claimed Atheion was, the luminstones could have been there since the Shattering War.

The captain and the prefect hurried ahead and conferred with the old man seated at the rear of the chamber, surrounded by other men who looked nearly identical to the prefect. Aside from the richness of his blue-and-white robes, the king did not appear much different than his administrators. The king raised one eyebrow before he nodded. The prefect joined his fellows. The captain stepped back but remained at the king's side, one hand pointedly resting on his sword hilt.

King Hidas stood. He frowned as if he were having trouble seeing them and waved them closer. They obeyed, the guards keeping in step behind and on either side of them. The king studied them a moment. "Dwarrs have visited our fair city before, as have Isle Knights, on rare occasions. We even had a Shel'ai visit us, many years ago. But never all three at once."

Rowen wondered if the king was referring to El'rash'lin. He had always assumed that, as with Namundvar's Well in Cadavash, the Shel'ai had accessed the Scrollhouse without their keepers' knowledge. He decided that was a question for another day. "I'm sure our appearance is unexpected, Sire, but we intend no harm to you or your city. We met some clerics on the road and escorted them here out of kindness. Along the way, Lochurites—"

"So I hear. I am sure our temple fathers will thank you for your service. But I do not think the famed Heroes of Lyos have come to our fair city just to safeguard clerics and pilgrims."

Rowen fought back a chill at the king's icy tone. "In truth, Sire, we were also hoping to buy supplies before we continue our journey."

"And where will that journey end?"

"In our graves," Jalist whispered.

"The Wytchforest," Rowen said, speaking loudly to drown out his companion.

An uneasy murmur passed through the chamber. The king's eyes fixed on Silwren, narrowing dangerously. "Lower your hood, woman," the king ordered brusquely.

Silwren obeyed. The luminstone light shimmered off her platinum hair. Her violet eyes met the king's stare.

The king blanched and faced Rowen again. "Well, Knight, we've heard stories of what happened in Lyos. But we've also heard stories of sorcerers razing half the realms to the north, that every Shel'ai in the world is part dragon, stained by the sins of the Dragongod. Which are we to believe?"

Rowen recognized the trap. The king expected him to plead their own good nature, which would make them sound desperate, perhaps even arrogant and insincere. Swallowing his nervousness, he said, "With respect, Sire, I don't know how to convince you that we aren't dragons, except to point out our lack of wings."

His response provoked both scowls and scattered laughter.

Siding with the former, the king leaned forward in his chair. "This isn't about wings, Knight. It's about purple eyes. It's about people who can summon fire out of thin air and burn a city to ashes. It's about Knights famed for honor and goodness, who, strangely, never seem to leave their islands." He sat back in his chair. "But more than that, it's about three dangerous, uninvited strangers in my city."

Jalist groaned, and Rowen felt his own face go red. He considered asking forgiveness. "Sire, if you think we are in league with Fadarah and the Throng, you should kill us. If you think we are the ones who broke the Throng and saved Lyos… and perhaps even Atheion, once Fadarah turned this way… then I *ask* that you let us go about our business in peace and treat us as one would any ally."

King Hidas smiled faintly. "Allies. *Allies,* he says! What amusing visitors I'm getting these days!" He gestured toward one side of the chamber.

Rowen turned, and his blood went cold. Six men stood along the far wall, in the dimmest part of the chamber. All had shaved heads and long braided goatees banded with brass rings. Their scale armor was decorated here and there with tassels of black silk, plus black silk sashes displaying the ominous sigil of a dragon impaled on a bloody spear. The rims around their eyes had been painted black as well, so that in the shadows, only the whites of their eyes were visible. And those eyes overflowed with contempt and derision. One of the men, the leader by his posture, was practically a giant.

Rowen eyed the gruesome necklaces the men were wearing— necklaces made from the dried, threaded ears of slain opponents. He remembered the old saying that one could tell a Dhargot's skill in battle by the number of ears he wore around his neck. He decided the men were not people he wanted to know.

King Hidas cleared his throat, drawing Rowen's attention. He made no move to introduce the Dhargots. "I think you are hiding something, Knight. But I also enjoy my trade agreements with the Lotus Isles, so I'll not risk them by wringing the truth out of you. Besides, something tells me you are the least of my problems."

He waved toward the captain who had escorted them. "Captain

Reygo will take you to the Borrowed Crown. It's an inn reserved for our city's more... *unusual* guests. I'll grant you two days in Atheion, provided you cause no trouble. If you do—or if that wytch works any mischief—it'll be *your* neck on the chopping block, Sir Knight. Bow if you understand."

Rowen bowed. "Yes... yes, Sire."

The king turned his attention to other matters. Captain Reygo rejoined them and wordlessly led them from the palace. The Noshan captain set a brisk pace through the swaying streets and over the bridges. When they reached the inn, his men returned their weapons. "Two days," the captain said before he left.

"Well," Jalist muttered sourly, "that's actually a warmer welcome than I expected."

"He didn't ask why we were going to the Wytchforest. And why didn't he introduce the Dhargots?" Rowen buckled Knightswrath around his waist.

Jalist licked his thumb and tested the edge of his long axe, as though to check if the guards had blunted it. "Your point?"

"Maybe nothing. But if he knows about Fadarah, he might have also heard rumors that Fadarah and the Dhargots are allies. Despite how he sounded, maybe he was trying to keep me from getting myself into trouble."

"Or maybe he doesn't like you any more than he likes them."

Rowen shrugged. He glanced at Silwren, who stood quietly, and sized up their lodgings.

While most inns had only one or two stories, theirs had four. The building was freshly painted and surrounded by dogblossom trees. Such trees were native to the Lotus Isles. Rowen wondered if that, too, was a coincidence. The sign above the door, depicting a crown tipped on its side, looked carved out of white oak, recently painted. There was real glass in the windows.

Jalist said, "Looks expensive. Sounds crowded."

"And who's to say if the king is paying for our rooms?" Rowen felt his purse. Before they'd left Lyos, King Typherius had given them more than enough coin, but they might need all of it for fresh supplies. He glanced over one shoulder. Two of Captain Reygo's guards stood nearby, stern faced and staring, making absolutely no effort to conceal themselves.

Jalist said, "May as well go inside. It's here or the wilderness, and I, for one, could use a good rest and a cup of mead before I head back out there again."

As he went inside, Rowen glanced back and saw the guards change position, stationing themselves right outside the inn's front door. *Unusual guests, indeed,* he thought, then resolved to get good and drunk.

CHAPTER SEVEN

THE IRON SISTER

Haesha felt her purse. She'd left Hesod with a bag of coins taken off a slain Dhargothi officer, but after buying wine, she had only a few coins left—not enough for a room at an inn. Still, an inn was where she was going, as soon as possible. After several days in the company of the priests and pilgrims, she doubted she would be welcome at the temples of Tier'Gothma and Armahg, where they—and their loose tongues—had already taken refuge. She glanced down at the emblem of a goblet and a crescent moon pinned to her cloak. She had no intention of seeking out the temple dedicated to Dyoni, claiming to actually be an adherent, and begging for assistance. Besides, temples of Dyoni were practically brothels anyway, and she'd had quite enough of that life when she was younger.

Then someone caught her eye. A pudgy man in expensive silk was heading in her direction. His haughty demeanor confirmed his life of privilege every bit as much as his clothing and glinting rings did.

Haesha placed herself in the merchant's path, opened her cloak, and batted her eyelashes. "Which way to the temple, love?"

The merchant did not even try to meet her gaze. "Plenty of temples around here. Even one for Maelmohr down the street, if you feel like smelling sulfur and getting a lecture on hard work."

She pouted and adjusted her clothing, affording him an even better view. "Not quite what I had in mind." She sidled closer and touched his chin. It was cold with sweat, but she winked anyway.

"How much?"

She feigned insult. "I am no whore!" She gestured to the emblem on her cloak. "I merely seek to bring greater happiness to those around me."

The merchant grinned. His breath smelled of mead and fish. "Indeed." He put his hand on her waist.

Resisting the impulse to drive the heel of her palm into his nose, she moved closer and kissed his cheek. As she was doing so, her nimble fingers drew the coin purse from his belt. She slithered away when the merchant's hands began to explore her body even more freely.

She whispered, "Temple of Armahg in half an hour. Meet me by the steps. I'll be the one who looks like this." She winked playfully and walked away, wiggling her backside so the merchant would be sure not to notice the coin purse in her hand.

She took two more coin purses from the crowd, then bumped into a Noshan guard and stole his dagger while distracting him with a well-rehearsed apology. By sundown, she had stolen enough to afford to stay at Atheion's finest inn for a month. But first, she bought new clothes. It was only a matter of time before embarrassed merchants fed her description to the guards. Though the new clothes were too conservative for her tastes, her plan was to take on the identity of a wayward merchant's daughter, overly sheltered and lost in the world. The story would make securing a benefactor much easier.

She stopped at a temple dedicated to Maelmohr, wherein an old cleric was angrily pontificating on the dangers of lust and material excess. Haesha pretended to listen, sidled close to a white-haired worshipper who'd fallen asleep. She spotted Maelmohr's burning fist pinned to his tunic. She took the pin. As an afterthought, she left the emblem of Dyoni—a smirking hermaphrodite—in its place.

Back on the street again, she wondered what to do about her hair. She could do nothing for the striking color unless she bought a wig or those foul-smelling dyes used by Ivairian noblewomen. Then again, she might be able to turn her hair to her advantage. Rich men liked unusual things, and red hair did not appear to be common in the midlands. She just had to make sure none of the people she'd robbed recognized her. Her new clothes and the sigil of Maelmohr would help. Besides, she had perfected the art of seeming to be someone else just by changing her demeanor and replacing her coy swagger with hunched shoulders and downcast eyes. So long as she styled her hair differently—in a plain braid, perhaps—its color would seem like a mere coincidence.

She bought a bowl of spiced stew and two cups of strong wine from a street vendor. The stew was good and the wine even better. She might have bought a third cup, but willpower told her to wait. As much as she wanted to stay as drunk as she'd been on the road, she did not dare in her current disguise—at least, not until she'd hidden her coin.

Three days. She could risk staying in the city no longer. Atheion was a big place, and she could move to a different district each day. Eventually, though, she would swindle enough noblemen and pick enough pockets that she would have to move on. *But to where?*

Hesod was out of the question. That city was in the hands of the Dhargots, making it no place for a woman—or any man who wasn't a Dhargot or a sellsword, for that matter. Besides, everyone that she had known there—Queen Sharra, Captain Ailynn, and even Haesha, whose name she'd borrowed—was probably dead.

She buried her rage and considered her options. Lyos wasn't far, and the city was still free, as far as she'd heard. But with the Dhargots surging east, that might not last long. She watched a few Noshan children run through the streets, waving at their father as he set out on a fishing boat. She wondered if the Dhargots would try to claim Atheion, too. It was certainly a fine target, nestled in a fertile valley in a time when many of the northern realms were reeling from food shortages. But even the Dhargots might not be so ambitious as to attempt extending their empire all the way to the midlands.

She made her way down Atheion's streets then over a bridge that swayed like a ferry. She wished she hadn't been so hostile toward that pompous Knight of the Crane. She needed a fresh start, and his fancy Isle sword, with its exquisite dragonbone hilt, might have fetched enough coin to start a tavern or a brothel of her own. But seeing him had only reminded her of the stories she'd heard about the courage and honor of Isle Knights and how none of them had arrived to prevent Hesod from being put to the sword.

Not their fault, I suppose. They're on the other end of the damn continent! Besides, coin is coin.

She considered looking for the Knight, but she was not a cleric of Dyoni anymore. Meeting him again would require too much explanation and raise too much suspicion. Besides, she doubted even her talents could soothe his injured pride. But if she knew where the Knight was staying, she might slip in and steal the sword while he slept. Surely, Atheion did not have frequent visitors from the Lotus Isles. Finding him would be a simple matter of asking around.

Then again, even if she got into the Knight's room undetected and evaded the suspicious Dwarr, she would have to contend with the wytch.

That platinum-haired Shel'ai watched over her bumbling Knight with a fierceness that seemed somewhere between a jealous but aloof lover and a mother wolf safeguarding her cubs. Haesha did not fear men or swords, but magic was another matter. She pushed the thought from her mind—at least for the moment.

She stopped to ask a passing merchant what inn he would recommend, mostly to practice the halting, nervous voice of her new identity. The man answered, and she thanked him without even robbing him.

When she reached the inn, Noshan guards stood outside. She tensed but reminded herself that they could not have been there for her. Not yet. Nevertheless, she decided to move on. She found a less fancy but adequate inn just down the street. She paid for her room and went up to hide the bulk of her coins. Stashing them under the straw mattress would have been too obvious, so she used her stolen dagger to pry up a loose floorboard. She checked the area for rats then hid two of the three coin purses within. She doubted any thief in all the realms could rob from her, but she saw no point in taking chances. She kept only enough copper on her to pay for her drinks. After taking the Maelmohr pin off her tunic, she went down and ordered an entire pitcher of wine.

Unwilling to spend the evening fending off men's drunken

advances, she chose the company of a muscular, kind-faced merchant she suspected of being a man lover. She introduced herself as Igrid—a name she'd used in Hesod—and filled his cup. Soon, they were speaking like old friends. She used the opportunity to test her story, adding fabricated details to her fictional past: a rich father gone missing, an ailing mother, a merchant husband who would be meeting her in two or three days. She concealed her pleasure when the man not only believed every word, but also offered to help search for her father. She grew tired, though, so she excused herself and started for the stairs that led up to her room.

At that moment, crude laughter echoed through the barroom, and she turned to see Dhargots swaggering in. She counted three of them, strong and leering, their painted eyes clearly scouting the common room for a fight. She scrutinized their faces, wondering if she'd met any of them in battle before she'd fled Hesod, but one Dhargot looked like another. Resisting the urge to hurry to her room, she sat back down. The merchant spoke to her, his voice filled with concern, but she ignored him. Her hand touched the hilt of the dagger at her side, hidden beneath her cloak.

No, not here. Not yet.

It made no difference if those particular Dhargots had been at Hesod. All Dhargots were the same. Still, she forced herself to relax. She could not avenge her sworn sisters if, in the process, she wound up jailed and executed—or worse, hauled out and brutalized by the very Dhargots she intended to kill. Besides, she could tell already that she was too drunk for a pitched battle. She determined to pace herself, keep calm, and wait for an opportunity.

Igrid took a deep breath and released it. She filled her cup, then the cup of the man next to her. Then she waited.

CHAPTER EIGHT

MATUA'S PLEA

ROWEN WOKE EARLY, SHOOK OFF his hangover by forcing himself through the martial poses of the sha'tala, then went to buy supplies. Though he had rented one room for Jalist and himself and another for Silwren, he saw no sign of the Dwarr. Rowen figured his friend was still in the company of the inn's cook, a young man whose acquaintance Jalist had made the previous night. Silwren had joined her comrades in the common room only long enough to eat and raise a single cup of wine before she retired.

Rowen could not blame her. Word had already spread through the city that a Shel'ai was in Atheion, and though no one dared voice animosity, the stares conveyed everything from curiosity to contempt. But unlike the people of Lyos, who had welcomed her only after first trying to kill her, the people of Atheion kept their distance. He wondered if they had other threats on their minds, and thought once more about the Dhargots. He guessed they were dignitaries, sent to persuade Atheion to join the empire. After all, without the Throng to help, Atheion might be too distant for the Dhargots to take by force, for the time being. Once they solidified their hold on the Free Cities of the Simurgh Plains, what they would attempt next was anyone's guess.

Thinking of the now-decimated Throng, Rowen wondered again why Fadarah had not simply used that army to fortify one of the other conquered cities and live there in peace. Silwren had said that Fadarah's ultimate goal was the Wytchforest. Beyond that, all past attempts to settle down had only seen the Shel'ai attacked by one superstitious people after another, from the Ivairians to the Dwarrs.

Maybe the Shel'ai don't want peace. Maybe they just want revenge. If so, this war won't end until Fadarah presides over an empire of ash.

Rowen took a deep breath and let it go. All he had to do was reach the Wytchforest, show Knightswrath to the Sylvan ruler, and invoke the Oath of Kin. The Sylvs would be honor bound to help the Isle Knights battle the Sorcerer-General's allies, the Dhargots. Once the Dhargots were defeated, Fadarah's mad plan would inevitably unravel.

Rowen touched Knightswrath's hilt. As far as the Sorcerer-General went, the only truce Rowen had a mind to offer was a twist of a blade in the man's gut. Kayden deserved that much, at least. But just then, Rowen had other concerns.

He considered wearing plain clothes. Jalist had been correct the night before—a resplendent Knight in enameled kingsteel armor was apt to get a far worse price for supplies than a bedraggled sellsword would. But Rowen had sacrificed too much for that armor to leave it at the inn. So he donned his armor, cleaned his muddied boots, and slipped on his tabard. His room had a mirror, a rare extravagance, and he blushed with pride at his own reflection, appreciating the sigil of a crane balancing on one leg as he girded his sword.

Outside the inn, the cries of seagulls and the creaking of boats mingled with the sounds of a bustling city. It was a cool day, and the smell of sea air reminded Rowen of the Lotus Isles. Though he smiled as he made his way, he was still careful to keep one hand on his coin purse.

He went to the stables first to check on their horses. Snowdark nuzzled him, clearly anxious to be gone from the place, but the other horses seemed content with their blankets and oat feed flavored with apples. Reminiscent of their stables in Lyos, the horses' accommodations were certainly better than anything on the road.

Then he heard a commotion, including the unmistakable stamping of hooves, and went to investigate. At the far end of the stables stood six enormous horses with blood-red coats. Each was a full foot taller than the others in the stable—all of which were keeping their

79

distance. Despite being even more muscular than destriers, they had a sleek appearance that promised quickness as much as fury. *Bloodmares.*

Though Rowen had seen such horses a few times in the past, he could not help but stare. He heard the sound of footsteps and tensed, wondering if the Dhargots had returned for their mounts.

Instead, a tall, gray-haired stable master approached him, glancing spitefully at the unruly horses. "Would you believe I was excited to see them? Damn things won't stop trying to bite the other horses." He lowered his voice. "You can tell they belong to Dhargots, all right!"

"Unless they're trained not to, bloodmares naturally try to kill any other horse that isn't one of their own. If you have a whole different stable, one that's empty, you're better off keeping them there."

The stable master scratched his face. "I do, but it's not well guarded. Something tells me those Dhargots will have my ears if one of these brutes gets stolen."

Rowen imagined a would-be thief trying to steal a bloodmare, facing red, flailing hooves that could kill a man in armor. "Don't worry about that. Bloodmares will also kill any man who isn't their master if he gets too close."

The stable master obviously wasn't convinced. Rowen couldn't blame him. When it came to punishment, Dhargots were every bit as vicious as Olgrym, who, according to legend, smeared their own bodies in the entrails of still-living opponents.

Gods, why are there so many damn madmen in this world? He handed the stable master a few coins and asked where he could find Atheion's market district.

The stable master laughed. "Which one? This whole city's one big market district, Sir Knight."

Rowen forced a smile, trying to take pleasure in the use of his new title rather than feeling insulted by the laughter. "I just need supplies for a week's travel. Rations, feed for the horses, some sweetbitter leaves, maybe a few articles of clothing. Nothing extravagant."

The stable master nodded. "If price matters, head for the vendors by the temple of Armahg. Quality's not great, but they're less likely to rape your coin purse. Oh, they'll try and tell you that those cranáfi of yours aren't worth as much as Atheion's coins, but don't listen. Copper is copper." He added, "It's a bit of a trudge, but I'll send a couple of my stableboys to help haul the goods back here. We'll store them until you're ready to leave. We keep the stables guarded. Your goods will be plenty safe."

Rowen thanked the man, handed him another copper cranáf, then waited for the stable master to select two stableboys to send with him. Both seemed glad to be leaving the stables for a while, and Rowen wondered if they were as anxious about the Dhargots' return as he was. They proceeded through the streets. Rowen's armor drew stares, but no one stopped him. On the next barge, he saw a breathtaking structure that put the palace of King Hidas to shame. He stared, dumbstruck by the towering, ornate pillars and stained-glass windows depicting everything from dragons to naked clerics, both male and female, holding scrolls. "Is that the Scrollhouse?"

The stableboys nodded with a touch of boredom. Rowen wondered how anyone could ever get accustomed to such a sight. Even the path leading up to the Scrollhouse, lined with statues, gardens, and exotic blossoms, was unlike anything he'd' seen in the fairest districts of Lyos. He thought again of his desire to search the ancient scrolls for further evidence that Fâyu Jinn and the Oath of Kin had actually existed. Then, as though on cue, he turned his head and saw Matua rushing toward him.

Rowen blinked in surprise, thinking the sight must be a trick of his senses, but it was indeed the Queshi priest. The rusty sickle-sword was gone, though. Rowen tensed when he noticed the grave urgency in the cleric's expression.

Matua had hardly greeted him when the words tumbled out. "Thank Armahg I found you, Sir Knight! I heard you were at the Borrowed Crown, but the innkeeper said you'd left already. I spotted the Dwarr, but he was... in an offensive condition." His shudder would have made Rowen laugh under other circumstances.

Rowen explained what he was doing and asked what was wrong.

The cleric grimaced. "Haesha. Turns out she caused... quite a stir last night."

Rowen smiled. "And what new mischief has Fohl's bitch wrought now?"

Matua glanced uncertainly at the stableboys. "She knifed two Dhargots in an alley behind a tavern. Knifed them dead then slashed a third one ear to mouth."

Rowen's smile melted. He'd expected to hear that she'd been caught picking pockets.

"She might have killed the third one, too, or gotten herself killed, but it seems a few guards were assigned to keep watch on the Dhargots in case they caused trouble. They stepped in, but from what I hear, Haesha gave one of *them* a good scar, too."

Rowen had no idea what the specific penalties for such crimes were in Atheion, but in Lyos, an assault on the guards alone would have meant death. If the foolish woman really had done all that, she was as good as dead.

"I found out myself just this morning," Matua went on. "Some merchant recounted it all. He came to pray for her at the temple. I spoke with my order, but the high priests have declined to intervene on her behalf."

Rowen frowned. "Intervene? Father, why in the hells would they do that?"

Matua blinked in surprise. "She's a priestess of Dyoni, Sir Knight! No matter our particular dislike for her, surely she deserves—"

"She deserves whatever she gets. She knifed two men in the dark." *Even if they were Dhargots...*

"But you're a Knight of the Crane. In the king's eyes, you represent the Lotus Isles. If you were to speak on her behalf, the king might show leniency."

"Father, she's probably not even a cleric. You saw how she handled that spear. And you said yourself that she came from Hesod."

Matua nodded. "An Iron Sister, then. All the more reason for her actions! Besides, my order teaches that no matter one's sins, everyone deserves to have *someone* speak on their behalf. Doesn't your order teach the same?"

Rowen scowled. Unbidden, a passage from the Codex Lotius came to mind: *Give aid and mercy when asked—but mostly, when they are not asked.* He cursed so vehemently that the stableboys blinked in surprise. "Fine, Priest. Once I'm done at the market, I'll go. And by the Light, I'll bet she shows neither of us a shred of gratitude."

Matua shrugged. "I am a cleric, Sir Knight. I am quite accustomed to ingratitude." He bowed hurriedly then was gone.

Seething, Rowen continued to the vendors. All the joy seemed to have been drained from his surroundings. When he had bought all the necessities, including two shortbows in case they encountered Lochurites as they headed west, he paid a few coppers to rent a wheelbarrow from one of the vendors and sent it with the stableboys. Although Rowen had intended to return to the stables with them, he decided to get this business with Haesha over as quickly as possible.

So dark was his mood that he did not ask for directions and so spent far more time than he cared to wandering Atheion in search of the king's palace, stomping over bridge after bridge, from skiff to skiff. It was late afternoon by the time he finally spotted the palace.

The place looked as busy and crowded as it had before. Despite his armor, Rowen still felt like a slumdweller from Lyos as he milled in the shadow of the palace, trying to decide how best to address the matter. Finally, he pulled aside a Noshan guard and conveyed his wish to speak with the king about the woman who had attacked the Dhargots.

The guard regarded him as though he had gone insane. "Sir, the king likely won't grant you an audience, but I'll see if I can fetch one of the prefects for you."

Rowen nodded, swallowing his impatience. He waited outside the palace for what felt like hours before a bald, wiry man in silk robes came out to meet him. The man introduced himself as a junior prefect. Rowen had not seen the man the last time he was in the palace. Still, Rowen explained his purpose. His listener frowned and asked him twice to repeat it. Then he curtly told Rowen to wait while he fetched a superior.

Next, an acolyte ushered him into the palace, where Rowen waited even longer. He had been gone so long that he feared his companions had started to worry. Soon, a prefect appeared and urgently drew him aside. The young man walked with a limp; one leg was a full handspan shorter than the other. The man introduced himself, then said, "His

Grace has been made aware of your desires but cannot meet with you today."

Rowen balled his hands into fists.

The prefect quickly continued, "I should add, His Grace is most displeased by last evening's bloody events. In addition to an injury visited upon a city guard, the priestess slew two Dhargothi dignitaries and wounded a third. There are even accusations that she may have poisoned their wine to weaken them before she struck. Jaanti, the Dhargothi ambassador, swears that if she is not turned over to him for punishment, he will report the incident back to the empire."

"Do you know what the Dhargots do to women who offend them?"

The prefect blinked. "Such matters are not within my purview, Sir Knight. However, I can assure you that the king's commitment to justice—"

"They're even worse than Olgrym. Olgrym just rape you to death. But the Dhargots... if they're feeling merciful, the offending woman is taken as a slave and used to birth as many fellow slaves as she can. If she objects to her children being taken away, they'll kill the child right in front of her and make her dine on its flesh. Even Haesha doesn't deserve that."

The prefect paled.

"When her womb is of no more use, they'll impale her. Shall I describe the process? First, they take a wooden stake and they smear it in pig fat. Then—"

"Enough!" The prefect wobbled heavily on his cane. "You've made your point, Sir Knight."

"Good. I'm just saying that if she has to die, make it quick. Don't send her back with the Dhargots."

The prefect cleared his throat. "I will... convey your message, Sir Knight."

Rowen nodded, turned on his heel, and stomped out of the palace. He thought of heading back to the Borrowed Crown or to the stables to make sure his purchases had arrived intact. He started that way, then stopped and approached the closest guard. After muttering a stream of curses that made the guard reach for his sword, Rowen asked for directions to the prison.

Haesha blinked as a torch was thrust through the bars of her cell, blinding her. She recoiled as cinders fell upon her clothing. She patted them out then looked up to see her visitor. The bottom dropped out of her stomach.

Igrid. That was my name in Hesod. That's who I have to be now.

Her visitor was a Dhargot, huge and well muscled, with painted eyes and a thick necklace of human ears. The man's eyes were narrow, despite his smile. "So this is the woman who does not fear a slow death."

Igrid glanced past the Dhargot and saw a trio of Noshan guards watching uneasily. She wondered if they would intervene should the Dhargot try to kill her. She had, after all, attacked a fellow Noshan guard in her fury—an action she regretted. The man was alive, she knew, or else she would not have been.

She closed her eyes. "I can't understand your accent."

The Dhargot laughed. "I think you understand Jaanti quite well." She heard the sound of metal scraping on leather. She opened her eyes. The Dhargot brandished a thin, curved dagger. He held it in the hand opposite the torch, turning the blade so the metal caught the light. The guards behind him scowled, but the Dhargot ambassador did not seem to notice. "Do you know where this goes?"

Igrid masked her fear with a derisive smile. "Well, I know where *I'd* put it."

The Dhargot grinned. "Jaanti is a patient man. He likes spirited women. That is not in your favor."

Igrid yawned, feigning boredom. "You make good threats for a captain whose men couldn't beat one drunk woman with a knife."

The Dhargot's smile vanished. "You poisoned them."

"Is *that* what the third one said?" Igrid laughed. "I can see why he'd lie. But I don't need poison. If you don't believe me, toss me a blade, and I'll show you what I can do."

The Dhargot said, "You are from Hesod, yes?" When Igrid did not answer, the Dhargot laughed. "I thought so. Strong women in Hesod. A whole cult of sweet virgins. I wish I'd been there when they were on their hands and knees, screaming… or were they moaning? Depends who you ask."

Igrid looked around at the straw littering the floor of her cell. She imagined the straw transforming into long, thin daggers that she could thrust, one at a time, into Jaanti's eyes.

Jaanti leaned against the bars of the cell. "How did you escape? Did you strip off that pretty armor and crawl through the sewers, shit caking those big pretty tits while your sisters screamed and—"

Igrid leapt up, charged the cell bars, and reached through. She tried to claw Jaanti's eyes, but the Dhargot ambassador stepped out of range. He laughed, waved his torch, and burned her hand. Igrid bit her lip, refusing to cry out. The prison guards glanced at each other, frowning, though neither moved to restrain the Dhargot.

Jaanti stared at her a moment, perverse enjoyment lighting his painted eyes. "You should know, I bought a whole squad of your Iron Sisters as slaves. They're waiting for me back home. Maybe you will recognize them. Like them, you'll serve as amusement for my men, my hounds, and my stallions—in that order."

Igrid retreated and turned her back on him. She fought back tears as the Dhargot continued taunting her, describing in graphic detail the punishments administered to the condemned.

Then she heard a new voice: "Step back, Dhargot. Or by the Light, *you'll* be the bitch split crotch to throat."

Igrid was so surprised that she turned without wiping her eyes first. She saw the Dhargot squaring off against the Isle Knight. Both had their hands on their swords. The prison guards finally intervened. It took three of them to restrain the Dhargot. The knight did not flinch, though the Dhargot was nearly a foot taller.

Jaanti seethed. "Dhargots and Islemen will cross swords soon enough. The Dead God wills it!"

The Knight of the Crane nodded. His voice was low and lethal. "Good. We'll be waiting. Look for us in the east. That's where the sun rises, in case you forget."

The prison guards hustled the ambassador away.

The Knight turned and scowled at her. "You look different— Priestess. Haesha, was it?"

"Actually, it's Igrid now."

"Fair enough. You didn't quite strike me as a cleric, anyway. A noblewoman, is it?" He eyed her vestments, still finely tailored, though splattered with blood and dirt.

"Actually, a merchant's wayward daughter in search of adventure and companionship."

"Were you ever really an Iron Sister?"

Igrid tried in vain to remember the Knight's name. "Do you really have to ask that?"

The Knight was quiet for a moment. "That Dhargot wasn't lying. What they'll do to you—"

"He'll try."

"He'll *succeed*, unless Iron Sisters are adept at fighting off armed men with their hands tied." The Knight paused. "Ask for mercy—not from the Dhargots, but from the king. If you describe... what you saw at Hesod, he might listen."

Igrid offered him a crooked smile as she wiped her eyes. "The king won't turn me loose any more than I can talk you into unlocking this cell."

"Maybe not. But that's not what I'm talking about."

Igrid shuddered. "If you're talking about a cup of poison, my sisters offered me that when we realized the city was about to fall. I decided to take my chances with the Dhargots. I'll do that again."

The Knight shook his head. "I don't know how you got out of the city, but whatever you did, it won't work here. Listen to me, Haesha—"

"Igrid," she corrected. "As true a name for me as Haesha was. Besides, Igrid has a nicer ring to it. Igrid of the Iron Sisters." She glanced down at her bloody clothing. "Now all I need is some armor and a sword. And a cup of wine. And someone I can bribe." She glanced up, directing her words at the Knight and the prison guards alike. After all, the coin purses she'd stolen were still hidden away in the floorboards of her room at the inn. But their scowls dashed her hopes. "Then why are you even here, Knight?"

"A certain cleric of Armahg found me. He heard what happened and asked me to speak to the king on your behalf."

Igrid answered with another smirk. "Matua? Gods, he must be

savoring this! Well, if you're here, I'm guessing your talk with the king didn't go as well as it could have. And all because I knifed two bastards who probably killed and raped a dozen women and children each. But I wouldn't expect you or the king to understand."

The Knight's answer was quick and low, little more than a whisper. "You're not the only orphan with a sword, Igrid."

The remark caught her off guard, but she forced herself to answer quickly. "Well, I seem to have misplaced my sword. Let me know if you find it."

"I will." The Knight gave her a hard look, turned, and walked away. She swelled with a sudden need to call out to him, to ask him to come back so she could plead for his help. Instead, she screamed a vile string of curses that followed him into the street. Then she leaned back against the cold stone wall, closed her eyes, and pretended to sleep.

CHAPTER NINE

THE SCROLLHOUSE

J ALIST SHOOK HIS HEAD. "No. If your brother were here, he'd tell you the same thing. So I'm saying it for both of us. No." He scowled across the table at Rowen. Along with Silwren, they sat apart from the other patrons. Sunset spilled through the windows of the inn so that the floor and the table between them seemed foggy with blood.

"All I'm saying—"

"Is that we take on more trouble than we already have," Jalist finished for him. "Do you really want to make for the Wytchforest with a hundred angry Noshans hurling spears at our asses?"

"It won't come to that. We can take her quietly—"

"Like hells. What? You think the guards will just *let* you walk in and open her cell door? I'm surprised they let you see her at all." Jalist glanced about, lowered his voice, and pretended to smile as though they were only sharing a joke. He drained his goblet then filled it again with the wine pitcher in front of them. "You're not using your head, Locke. You know the king won't turn her loose. He won't grant her a quick death, either. Why anger the Dhargots just to save one wandering madwoman you don't even know? And if you say *for honor*, by the gods, I'll break this pitcher over your skull!"

Rowen smiled. "I'm not going to quote the Codex Lotius. I'm just saying you didn't hear what that Dhargot said to her. I did."

Jalist pushed the pitcher toward him. "Such is life. Drink and forget it."

Rowen pushed the pitcher away. "No. We can get her out of there."

"Even if we could, why should we?"

"Because no one else will."

"Not good enough." Jalist took another drink. "Maybe you just want to let her have another go at your cock... with or without the sharpened stick this time."

Rowen flushed, glancing sidelong at Silwren, who sat at the head of the table but still had not spoken. Instead, she looked down, tracing the wood grain with her fingertips. Rowen met Jalist's gaze and said, "Don't act like you were chipped off the Wintersea. You know damn well why we should do it. And you know we can."

"Not without killing. Is that bitch worth Noshan blood on your hands?" Jalist took a drink. "Her life versus some fool guard with a wife and brats waiting at home. Or maybe his blade will get lucky, and it'll be *you* lying there, bleeding your guts out. Think about it."

"I thought Dwarrs had better hearing. I never said we'd get her out with fists and steel."

Jalist followed Rowen's gaze to Silwren again. He rolled his eyes. "Perfect! Your solution is to risk burning down half the city, just to free one woman you detest. A woman who's *guilty*, I might add." He drained his cup, filled it again, and faced Silwren. "Well, speak up! Talk some sense to this bastard."

Silwren was quiet for a long time. Her own cup sat in front of her, untouched. Finally, she said, "I could get her out of Atheion. But I won't."

Rowen said, "Why not?"

Silwren answered with an icy look. "Have you already forgotten what happened on the road?"

Jalist wondered what she meant, but she continued before he could ask. "You would risk everything for this woman when we both know we shouldn't even be here."

Jalist chimed in, surprised that he and Silwren were in agreement for once. "She's not worth it. You think she'd risk a drop of blood to save you? Gods, she tried to crack your skull on the road, just to show you she could!"

90

"I sided with you in Lyos. When the people wanted you dead, I stepped in. I asked nothing in return. Now—"

"You want to be the next Fâyu Jinn." Silwren's white pupils caught Rowen in an unblinking stare that made Jalist pity him. "You want to stop a war, but you also want to start one. You want to kill the Shel'ai who tormented your brother, while pretending to forgive me for helping them. You want to lash together some kind of alliance with the Wytchforest... between the people who killed my parents for refusing to butcher me when I was born, as the Sylvs have been butchering Shel'ai for centuries."

Her voice trembled dangerously. "Your thoughts are as loud as screams to me, Human. You *want* to be a hero. You crave it. I don't. I just want to fix a little of what I've broken." She stood and started to walk away.

Rowen seized her wrist. She broke free with surprising strength. Wytchfire sprang from her fingertips. Violet tendrils spiraled around her hands.

Jalist swore as a telltale hush fell over the common room. Silwren looked confused then glanced down. The wytchfire vanished as quickly as it had appeared. Without a word, she hurried away.

Jalist said, "Want to tell me what happened on the road?"

Rowen said, "Not really," and took a drink from his cup. The two sat in silence for a moment. "You always said women would be the death of me."

Jalist snorted. Taking the pitcher, he refilled Rowen's cup. "Well, here's to hasty words and bad decisions." He raised his cup. Rowen did the same. They drank together, scowling.

Silwren had intended to stay in her room, but the tension roiling inside her persuaded her otherwise. Leaving through either the Borrowed Crown's front or back door necessitated that she pass through the common room, so she opened the window and jumped.

She felt the air on her skin and smiled despite herself. She stretched out her arms. She slowed, landing on the cobblestones like a wind-tossed feather. Only then did she realize what she had done.

She had never done that before, though it had seemed as natural as breathing.

No Shel'ai spell can do that!

Luckily, her window overlooked an alley between the Borrowed Crown and a mercantile. No one had seen her. She drew her hood and became one with the shadows. She wandered the Atheion night, unseen by any save those who passed so close that she felt their breath on her face. Even those people saw nothing more than a shadow, a trick of light they considered only a moment before dismissing it.

I should go... Rowen doesn't need me. Not really. Fel-Nâya's power is waking. Rowen's honor will restore it—but slowly. Too slowly.

She crossed a marble bridge over the darkened waters of Armahg's Tears. The next bridge was less magnificent, wrought only of wood and rope. This led her to a quiet district of plain adobe homes and fishing huts. The place reminded her of the streets of Lyos, where she had walked unseen. She deliberately closed her mind to the people's thoughts, fears, and passions—something she had not been able to do before—and walked down to stand alone by the sea.

She saw a few night fishermen, an old man drinking tea, and a young woman nursing her sleepless infant while she dangled her feet in the water. But no one saw her. Silwren stood, cloaked in cloth and magic, and watched the night-blue waves of Armahg's Tears. A fisherman with a flute invoked a simple, melancholic melody over the waters. She wondered if the song was some sort of superstition that the Noshans thought would charm the fish to the surface and grant them an easier catch. She preferred to think the faceless fisherman merely liked the tune.

I could help Rowen. I could restore Fel-Nâya. But he's not ready... and neither am I.

She considered the irony that the general dishonor of the Isle Knights, which had driven Fel-Nâya's full power into dormancy, might also have been the reason Rowen was still alive. He did not yet understand the sword's true nature and potential, and she had not yet found the courage to tell him.

Maybe he won't need the sword. If he succeeds in reforming the alliance between the Knights and the Sylvs, he might be able to beat Fadarah without the weapon.

Silwren almost laughed. In truth, the Oath of Kin was as good as dead. She was escorting Rowen to the Wytchforest only because she did not know what else to do. She was not ready to reignite Fel-Nâya any more than Rowen was ready to wield it, and the only other option—dealing with Fadarah herself—felt impossible.

She thought again of her jump from the inn window. She had the odd feeling that, had anyone been watching, they would have seen ghostly dragon wings materialize from her body, guide her gently to the earth, then vanish. She tried to calm herself by listening to the music and the waves, but a knot of panic was already growing within her.

The moment she had delved into Namundvar's Well, drawing on the raw power of the Light to magnify her own, she had ceased to be a Shel'ai. She had become a Dragonkin of sorts. But that was hardly the only change she had undergone during the past year. She had betrayed Fadarah, a man who was like a father to her. She had betrayed Kith'el, her own husband. Blinded by wrath and unfamiliar magic, she had killed fellow Shel'ai—more than she could count or recall.

And that was only the beginning. In the prisons of Lyos, El'rash'lin had used magic to share some of his memories with Rowen, in hopes that they would make him more understanding of and even more sympathetic to the troubled past of all Shel'ai. For a time, it had. But she felt Rowen growing more and more distant of late. And her actions on the plains had not helped.

How long will it be until he's as much a stranger to me as Kith'el? That was inevitable. Sometimes, she felt as though she were gaining control over the awful power within her, but she admitted to herself what was probably more likely: she was losing herself, gradually merging with the Dragonkin within her. She looked around at towers and people, knowing that if she let go, she could utterly destroy them and leave not even ashes behind.

The feeling both thrilled and terrified her. She gazed down at her hands, conjuring wytchfire. It danced and played on her open palms as though alive. Only then did she realize she was no longer invisible.

The woman nursing her infant had recoiled, paralyzed with fright, clutching the bundle so tightly that the child began to wail. "Please," the woman cried. "Please, don't..."

"I won't hurt you," Silwren said. She held up her hands, intending it to be a gesture of peace, but the wytchfire roiled around her.

The young woman found her strength, stood, and fled. Silwren called out to her, begging forgiveness. But in her panic, she spoke in the Sylvan tongue. She watched the young woman flee and wondered what her voice must have sounded like to the woman. *Did she think she was being cursed?* Silwren thought of Lyos and how its citizens had gone from reviling her to greeting her as their savior.

That will not happen here. Never again. Not anywhere... unless I make my decision. She straightened.

The great sprawling structure in the distance was the Scrollhouse. She knew it would be heavily guarded, but steel and Human eyes had not stopped Shel'ai from entering before. Years ago, El'rash'lin and she had slipped unseen into the great library, seeking information on Namundvar's Well, and none of the clerics had been the wiser. And Fadarah had gone in there undetected so often, some joked that he must have memorized half the scrolls in Atheion.

She thought of one scroll in particular. A new purpose filled her. She faced the Borrowed Crown. Unseen, on wings of mist, she glided across the skiffs, bridges, and lamp-lit walkways. She had to act fast. If she delayed even an hour, she would lose her nerve.

She found Rowen and Jalist asleep in their room. She approached Rowen's bed and woke him with a touch to his forehead. She pressed one finger to her lips. He sat up, strong and bare-chested, his red hair unkempt. His green eyes widened. She realized that to him, she did not look like herself. Instead of pale skin, violet eyes, and delicately tapered ears, he must have seen mist, violet fire, and dragon-like wings of faint light that unfurled behind her, swaying like silk in a nonexistent breeze.

He sees what I am becoming... She forced herself to be a Shel'ai again. She felt her heart beating in her throat. She panicked, wondering if her old body could contain her. Then she shook herself.

"Meet me outside. Don't wake Jalist. Leave your armor, but bring the sword."

Rowen rose hastily, unsure at first if he was dreaming. He heard Jalist snoring across the room. He considered waking him then eyed his heap of kingsteel armor and decided to trust Silwren.

He emptied his bladder in the chamber pot, moved to the water basin, and rinsed his face with cold water. As he dressed in plain clothes and girded Knightswrath, he wondered if Silwren had woken him because of Igrid. *And why did Silwren appear not as a Shel'ai but a Dragonkin?*

Pulling on his boots, he thought back to legends he'd heard on the Lotus Isles, about Dragonkin who leeched so much power off dragons that they went mad. He wondered if they resembled how Silwren had looked on the plains and when she'd woken him just before: blazing white but ghostly, as though she were more magic than flesh, with clouds of mist that might have been wings unfurling behind her.

He toyed again with the idea of waking Jalist then left, one hand on his sword hilt. The common room was nearly empty. A few drunken patrons glanced up at him, but without his armor and tabard, he didn't earn a second glance.

The night air was colder than he'd anticipated, and a chill swept through him. He wondered if the coming winter or his own fears had caused it. Then he spotted Captain Reygo's guards. They were slumped against the outside of the inn, fast asleep. Rowen frowned. He doubted they had gone to sleep of their own volition.

He glanced around, looking for Silwren. He half hoped not to find her. Then he saw her waiting across the street in a slant of moonlight, very much flesh and blood. Her long platinum tresses hung past her waist, and her simple gown seemed as thin as a whisper.

He felt his pulse quicken. He approached her quickly, whispering, "What in Jinn's name are you—"

"Time for answers, Knight. Walk close behind me. Say nothing, and we will pass their guards unseen." She turned and began walking, nearly gliding over the cobblestones.

Rowen followed, feeling as if he were trailing a ghost, her lithe body outlined by moonlight. Anticipating questions from a squad of guardsmen, he tried to ready some kind of excuse, but a fisherman passed them without even looking up. A moment later, a stableboy stepped out and pissed in the street, only a few yards away, then scratched himself and went back inside without so much as a nod.

Silwren led him over a walkway, carefully weaving around a young couple kissing on the bridge. Despite the late hour, clerics and guards were milling about the Scrollhouse, sitting on the steps or leaning and chatting against the ornate pillars.

Even invisible, I bet they'll notice if I run into them. He turned sideways just in time to avoid colliding with a passing scribe. As he hurried after Silwren, he considered the fact that she must have cast some kind of spell on the guards left at the inn. When the guards woke, they might very well suspect what had happened. That meant he would have to leave Atheion that night—once Silwren had completed whatever task she had in mind.

And what about the Iron Sister? Do I still mean to save her? He squelched that thought for the time being.

Luckily, the doors of the Scrollhouse were open. Still, Rowen and Silwren had to slip past four Noshan guards who were speaking in whispers. Rowen cursed himself as he bumped into one of them, but the man only mistook him for one of his comrades. He slowed, hoping to eavesdrop on their conversation after he caught the word *Dhargot* and saw the guards grimacing and shaking their heads, but Silwren hurried him on.

Inside, they passed through an antechamber that smelled of tea and lamp oil. Long oaken tables were crowded with clerics of Armahg. Even so late, dozens were busy studying. Despite the number of people around, the chamber was so eerily quiet that Rowen found himself holding his breath as they passed through.

Silwren led him up a broad stairwell lit with ornate candelabras wrought of silver and gold, down a hallway lined with doors and tapestries, through an archway, and into the greatest library he had ever seen. She navigated the building with such ease that he wondered if she had been there before. He wanted to ask, but he did not know if the magic that prevented people from seeing them concealed their voices as well, so he followed in awed silence. The chamber sported huge, vaulted ceilings and pillars of carved marble. The books were what he found stunning, though. Hundreds upon hundreds of shelves were each denoted with great brass plaques covered in writing he did not recognize. The shelves were heaped with stacks and rows of books, plus countless scrolls bound in leather and ribbon. His mind reeled at all the knowledge the library must have contained—including knowledge of the Isle Knights—but again, Silwren hurried him on.

They passed through another chamber, where more clerics studied at long wooden tables, into a second fantastic library, every bit as huge and well stocked as the first. Unlike the first, though, the second also contained a great many artifacts set on pedestals, some enclosed in glass: suits of ancient-looking armor, curiously shaped pottery, and devices whose origins and purpose he could not guess. Then they passed broken iron statues. Though most stood, dull-glinting shards of them lay scattered at their feet. They appeared to be warriors, but some had horns; others were ghastly and contorted. One had bronze sickle-swords melded to each hand. He noticed that all of those that still had their heads intact had dark, eerily hollow eye sockets. He stopped in his tracks.

These were Jolym... living men made out of the stuff of the earth, fashioned by the Dragonkin.

He reminded himself that whatever life spark had been cast into them had withered or been destroyed at least ten centuries ago. Still, all those blank eye sockets and cruel expressions made him reach for his sword, as though they might come back to life at any moment.

"They cannot harm you. They are just relics now." Silwren spoke directly into his mind.

She stood just a few feet away, her eyes fixed on him. Despite Silwren's assurance, Rowen turned his back on the statues only with the greatest difficulty.

She led him off the main pathway, through a maze of aisles and shelves, to a simple wooden door guarded by a huge, fierce-looking man who wore the sigil of Armahg on his armor. There was a chair next to him, but he stood as straight as a statue, a spear in hand and a shortsword at his belt. Rowen tensed. There was no way they could open the door and get past this guard without him noticing. *What does she mean to do to him?*

Silwren approached the towering guard, reached out, and gently pressed her fingertips to his forehead. The man stiffened. Then he tumbled backward, eyes closing. Rowen rushed to help her but, with surprising strength, Silwren caught the giant guard and lowered him soundlessly into his chair. Rowen feared that the guard's spear would clatter loudly to the stone floor, but to his surprise, it hovered in mid-air until Silwren seized it and leaned it against the wall. She approached the wooden door. It was sealed by an intricate lock, but when she touched it, the door swung open, creaking slightly. Rowen glanced about, still fearing they would be discovered, but he saw no guards rushing to inspect the noise.

Silwren caught Rowen's arm in an oddly powerful grip and half guided, half pushed him through the door. As she did so, her voice rang out in his mind. *"He isn't hurt. Neither are the guards outside the Borrowed Crown. But we must finish this before they wake."*

Rowen nodded dumbly. Silwren closed the door behind them. He found himself in a narrow, claustrophobic corridor lit by only a single torch bracketed to the wall.

At the end of the corridor, Silwren led him down an equally narrow stairwell. Rowen remembered that the Scrollhouse was built upon a skiff floating on the sea. Momentarily puzzled, he wondered if that meant they were underwater. He had the dizzying thought that the skiff might extend below the waterline like the hold of a ship. He wondered if other skiffs throughout Atheion were built likewise and what might be hidden in them.

At the bottom of the stairwell stood another locked door, carved with symbols too worn to be recognizable. She touched the lock, and it sprang with a click. The rusty iron hinges grated loudly as she pushed the door open. Rowen winced, expecting to find startled clerics and armed guards on the other side. Instead, he saw only darkness.

Silwren raised one hand, and wytchfire coursed the length of her forearm, casting an eerie purple glow on their surroundings. The new chamber was almost completely empty, save for a few old tables and chairs as well as dusty shelves piled with tattered pages. The dust was so thick that Rowen had trouble breathing.

Silwren said, "We are visible now. There is no one down here, but we should still be cautious."

Something in her voice chilled him even more than the thought of all the swords he might have to face when it was time to leave. Part of him wanted to run and face them right away, but he forced himself to follow, half afraid of what Silwren might do if he stalled.

Silwren led him through another door, down another narrow staircase, and into another gigantic library even larger than the other two. Unlike the others, the room filled him inexplicably with a mixture of sadness and dread.

Aside from the illumination offered by Silwren's wytchfire, the space was utterly dark. He fought the impulse to draw Knightswrath or follow her closely as a frightened child would follow his mother. *I am a Knight of the Crane*, he reminded himself, only to jump a moment later when the waving illumination of Silwren's wytchfire caused the shadows to move.

Silwren led them through another maze of bookshelves, deeper and deeper into the chamber. Rowen had the odd feeling that he was passing farther back in time with every step. Fear quickened his pulse, but he fought to keep his breathing in check, less out of pride than a dislike for how the sound echoed in the vast chamber. Rowen thought back to how large the Scrollhouse had appeared from the outside, but he had the feeling that inside, somehow, it was even larger.

Finally, Silwren stopped before a shelf heaped not only with scrolls but with ancient jewelry and scraps of armor as well. She waved, and a sphere of wytchfire rose from her hand to hover in the air above them, casting its magical light over the shelf, stretching their shadows across the cold stone floor. Silwren chose a single great scroll bound in leather with ornate brass clasps. Oddly, it bore no dust. She gazed at it a moment, as though she were reading it without unrolling its contents, then passed it to him with slow reverence.

"To you, Rowen Locke, Knight of the Crane, I entrust this scroll, penned by Fâyu Jinn himself, detailing the lost history of the Shattering War and the founding of your Order."

Rowen wondered if he should respond. His mind raced, but he could think of nothing fitting for the occasion. He stared down at the priceless scroll—a thing that, like Knightswrath, he did not deserve—then back at Silwren. Her expression was unreadable, as stony as the faces of the shattered Jolym he had passed earlier.

She said, "The scroll will tell you many things, Knight, not the least of which is why I have to die."

CHAPTER TEN

THE SORCERER-GENERAL

THE DHARGOTHI ARMY SPREAD ACROSS the Simurgh Plains like a cloud of silk and steel. From his vantage point on a hill, Fadarah stared, shaking his head. He saw men, horses, and chariots by the thousands, milling near siege engines that bristled in the morning light. In the distance, a great column of war elephants waited. Fifty strong, fitted with gigantic plates of armor on their heads and massive legs, they wore saddles the size of chariots that could hold half a dozen archers. White tusks glinted in the sun like massive sabers of bone.

"So many," said Shade.

Fadarah nodded, momentarily speechless. The whole of the Dhargothi empire seemed to have been emptied onto the plains. And they had been busy. The massive corral below was filled with prisoners, all women and children, taken from the western cities. From time to time, a Dhargot would swagger toward the pens, select a woman from the crowd, drag her out, and rape her in full view of everyone.

Fadarah winced, trying to block out the screams. "How far have they gone?"

"Hesod. They've left a garrison at Syros, too." Shade pointed, just as the wind rustled the crimson greatwolves sewn into his bone-white cloak. "That was Quorim."

In the distance, visible only to eyes enhanced by magic, a forest of stakes swayed with bodies beyond the walls of a fallen city. Fadarah's scowl deepened at the sight of the smoking ruin. "I said they could have the cities. I didn't say they could do this."

"I reminded Karhaati of that just three days ago... *before* he marched on Hesod and Quorim."

"And what was the Bloody Prince's response?"

Shade's voice brimmed with revulsion. "He said I was not his liege. He also said that the harsh treatment of enemies is required by the Way of Ears and boosts Dhargothi morale."

Seated on horseback next to Shade, Brahasti chuckled. "So it is."

Fadarah turned to face the tall, frightfully thin Dhargot. "My orders are orders, Brahasti. Not suggestions. I remind you that you're lucky to be alive. If you want to earn back our good favor, you will remember that."

The Dhargot's expression sobered, though his eyes still glinted with malice. "You need not worry, Sorcerer-General. One lifetime has not enough years to forget your kind instruction."

Fadarah heard the derision in the man's voice but chose to ignore it. He straightened in the saddle of his gigantic bloodmare, using magic as well as the reins to control the beast when it tried to turn and bite Shade's mount. Fadarah was weary of the giant horse's moods, but he had little choice in terms of mounts. No other horse could support the weight of an armored half Olg.

Fadarah sighed, tapping his finger idly on the hilt of a massive two-handed sword strapped to his bloodmare. He had no taste for what he had to do next. He glanced over his shoulder. A dozen Shel'ai followed him, all in bone-white cloaks matching Shade's. He studied their faces, freely reading their thoughts. He sensed their loyalty and their trust, as well as their loathing for what was happening below.

He raised his voice, addressing them all. "There are no clean wars. Fix your mind on our plan, our purpose. We are not monsters. Though we do what we must, we will preserve all the innocent blood we can—"

Brahasti laughed. Fadarah turned, raised one eyebrow, and urged his bloodmare so close that the Dhargot's horse recoiled. Lightning fast, Fadarah backhanded Brahasti from his saddle. The Dhargot fell hard onto the grasslands, wide eyed, blood pouring from his face. Shade smiled, stifling laughter. Fadarah glowered at Brahasti as the horrified Dhargot gingerly touched his nose and sagging broken jaw, then lifted his gaze to meet his followers again.

He could tell, as their violet eyes met, that they all applauded his actions but wanted him to go further, to conjure wytchfire from his fingertips and scour the fallen Dhargot to cinders. But Fadarah would not go that far. Brahasti still had his uses.

"I'll say this again," he addressed the crowd. "We will kill and burn when we must. We will forgive when we can. But the time for forgiveness has not yet arrived." He turned to Shade. "Heal him." He pointed at Brahasti, who was shaking, though Fadarah could not tell if it was pain or laughter. "But leave his robes and face bloodied."

Fadarah rode slowly down the hill, into the sprawling tent city that was the Dhargothi camp. Everywhere, warriors in scaled armor and black silk fell to their knees as soon as they saw him. The prostration spread like wytchfire through the camp. Soon, thousands of armed men were kneeling in the mud. Fadarah ignored a sudden rush of exhilaration and led his column of Shel'ai through the camp, to the gigantic crimson tent of Prince Karhaati. Brahasti followed, slumped in his saddle. Though Shade had healed him, blood still covered Brahasti's face and the front of his clothes as a reminder for not only Brahasti, but also for the so-called Bloody Prince who commanded him.

The Bloody Prince's tent was wreathed in armed men, but all stood aside and fell to their knees at Fadarah's approach. Shade and Brahasti dismounted. Zeia dismounted as well, removing a helmet that revealed her close-cropped hair, which was black—a rare thing for her kind. Fadarah stopped her with a look.

"No, Zeia. Things could get heated in there. If the Bloody Prince calls for his guards, see that we aren't interrupted."

The fierce young woman nodded hesitantly. Fadarah stalked into the Bloody Prince's tent. Shade followed, with Brahasti in tow.

The tent's interior reeked of burnt sulfur and uncooked meat. Fadarah's eyes watered from the stink. He spotted the prince on the ground. The only thing separating the Dhargothi prince from the cold earth was a bearskin rug and the body of a slave woman. Fadarah tensed. Fadarah had not hesitated to intervene after walking in on Brahasti abusing some slave or prostitute. But Karhaati, the Bloody Prince, son of the Red Emperor and commander of the thousands of armed men outside, required a different tack.

Fadarah glanced at Shade and saw both disgust and warning. He did not look at Brahasti, fearing he would see a sadistic glint in the man's eyes. Fadarah hesitated before he stepped forward, waved his hand, and used magic to wrench Karhaati off the crying woman's body. The burly prince blinked in surprise but made no sound.

Fadarah knelt beside the woman. She was young, so young. He hesitated, though he knew what had to be done. He touched the poor woman's breast and sent a shock of wytchfire through her trembling heart. He straightened and faced the Bloody Prince.

Karhaati stood, arms folded, making no move to cover himself. His face was livid. "I wasn't done with her yet. Why did you kill her?"

"So there would be no witnesses, no one to tell how the Bloody Prince was burnt to cinders for disobedience." Wytchfire sprang from Fadarah's hands, coursing the full length of his body, further blackening his armor. Catching his own reflection in a shield leaning against a weapons rack, he saw his own eyes flare like white fire wreathed in violet flame.

Karhaati recoiled. "I am the emperor's son—"

"You are my servant. So is your father. If you doubt this, die now. I'm sure your father would be glad to send another to do our bidding."

Karhaati opened his mouth to reply then thought better of it. He stood in silence.

Fadarah scrutinized the man, wondering if he was even worth sparing. Like all Dhargots, Karhaati was tall. About thirty winters old, he was thickly built with a bloody, impaled dragon tattooed over his shaved chest. His eyes were painted, and he had the traditional shaved head and braided goatee of a Dhargothi warrior, though he wore no necklace of human ears.

Fadarah turned slightly and saw it nearby, resting on a pile of clothes. "Dhargots have a strange habit of testing the patience of their rulers." He turned and waved. An invisible gust of magic drove Brahasti to his knees between them. "I grow tired of this trait."

Karhaati's expression darkened. "What is *that* doing in my camp?" He pointed at Brahasti as if the man were a rotting corpse.

Brahasti snickered but said nothing.

"He is here because I wish it. And because, for all his crimes, he obeys far more readily than you do."

Karhaati's expression did not soften. "My father banished him. To breathe the same air as him is—"

"A disgrace you will bear, just as you will bear another." Wytchfire continued to roil at Fadarah's fingertips, tiring him, though he made sure he showed no sign of weariness. He pointed at Brahasti, and the Dhargot struggled to his feet. "Henceforth, Brahasti el Tarq will command your legions."

Karhaati's face went livid again. "The Dead God will breathe first!" The prince turned toward the weapons rack and reached for a sword.

Fadarah braced, deciding to wrestle the sword from the man's grasp. But before the Bloody Prince could act, Shade stepped forward and gestured, sending the sword flying out of the Bloody Prince's reach. Shade's other hand raised, awash in wytchfire.

Fadarah shook his head, stopping him, and took a step forward. Brahasti scurried out of the way. Fadarah dismissed his wytchfire a split second before he grabbed Karhaati by the throat and tossed him to the cold ground. The Bloody Prince cursed, rolled, and came up quickly. Fadarah was impressed, though he was careful to betray no sign of this.

"I'll not hand my necklace over to that simpering coward."

"I didn't say you'd have to. You'll still ride at the head of your legions. Take credit for Brahasti's victories, if you like. But if you wish to honor my alliance with your father, you will obey. And know that whatever disgrace you feel is *your* doing, not mine."

Karhaati blinked, appearing confused.

"I gave orders. Killing on the battlefield is one thing, but what I saw out there"—Fadarah pointed to the tent flap—"like what I saw in here"—he gestured to the dead slave girl—"has nothing to do with battle."

Then the Bloody Prince laughed. "You have power, Shel'ai. No one would deny that. But you have a child's understanding of war." The Dhargot picked up his necklace of ears and slipped it over his head. He donned a black silk robe next. His movements were slow and derisive.

Fadarah asked, "How soon can you march east?"

Karhaati shrugged. He stepped over the dead girl to reach a table, poured a goblet of wine, drained it, then poured another. "This is not a raid, Shel'ai. I have not left Dhargoth just to burn villages and gain slaves. I am trying to expand my father's empire—what will be *my* empire, in time." He drained his second cup of wine then poured a third. "That means I must fortify the realms I seize. Something *you* did not do." He gave Fadarah a derisive smile.

"I *gave* you those realms, Dhargot. I bought your assistance with them. Do not forget that."

"So you did." Karhaati took another drink. "I'm still undecided, so far as Atheion is concerned."

"I see no need for indecision. I gave you the Free Cities taken by the Throng, and I'm giving you time to claim and reinforce them, before you eventually help us take the Wytchforest. Atheion was never part of the bargain."

"So you said." To Fadarah's amazement, Karhaati yawned. "But Atheion is quite a prize. My father—"

"Is not here. I am." He took a step forward. "Atheion will not be touched... yet. Is that understood?"

Karhaati smirked. "Of course. Still, we need to shore up our southern flank. So I sent my cousin, Jaanti, to frighten them. He is a man of many skills. Diplomacy is not one of them."

"Fine. Leave Ziraari's host at Hesod, but march your own east, toward Cassica. You may take the city, but hold there."

Karhaati's smirk became a frown. "Why stop there? Lyos—"

"Lyos was not part of the deal. I have no intention of waiting months before we proceed to the Wytchforest. *If* I grant you Lyos, it will be later, when the time is right."

"Or perhaps you want revenge on them yourself?"

Fadarah thought back to the Battle of Lyos, which had seen the Nightmare critically wounded, his Throng decimated by internal revolt, and his Shel'ai—even himself—forced to flee for their lives. His pulse quickened, but he shook his head. "This campaign is not about revenge, Human."

"Isn't it?" Karhaati sat in his chair, drained his cup, and held it out. Brahasti grimaced but obediently fetched the pitcher and refilled the goblet. "As you say, Sorcerer-General. Our alliance shall be honored." He drank.

"So it shall," Fadarah said. He turned to go.

"One more thing," Karhaati said. "A surprise."

Fadarah tensed. He turned slowly to face the Bloody Prince again.

Karhaati laughed. "I bought you another ally. Some wild tribesmen from Nosh. Lochurites, berserkers, whatever they're called. Don't worry. They were cheap. But they're fey fighters... once they drink that poison of theirs. I've had them pestering the Noshans for a week now. I even have a force of them waiting to help Jaanti, if he decides to stay in Nosh and have some fun."

"The Lochurites are of no concern to me. You should have saved your gold."

"Not gold, just bronze. And you're welcome." Karhaati laughed again. "I confess, I was hoping we could work out a trade."

"A trade?"

"Say, a thousand Lochurite berserkers for... a mere four Shel'ai?" Karhaati sipped from his goblet again. The wine left his lips red. Some of the wine ran down his chin, staining his skin like blood. "I'm told you have thirty or forty left. Surely, you won't miss four."

Fadarah scowled, wondering how Karhaati had gained that information. He decided not to tell the Bloody Prince that in actuality, he only had twenty-eight Shel'ai left in the field. "No. My Shel'ai are needed elsewhere. Nor were they part of my agreement with your father."

"Agreements can be changed. Four sorcerers would make a big difference in a siege. They could slip in unseen, open the gates, save me maybe a thousand men."

"Your losses aren't my concern, Dhargot."

"They should be. The more men I have, the more help I can give you when it comes time to begin the wholesale slaughter of your kin."

Shade stepped forward. Though he glared at the Bloody Prince, his voice whispered in Fadarah's mind: *"He speaks sense, Father. Zeia and Avesha are anxious to fight. We could send them, maybe two or three more to—"*

"No. I told you, the Olgrym will not wait. We need to begin the attack on the Wytchforest soon, or the Olgrym will start without us. We'll need every Shel'ai we can muster. The Dhargots can join us later."

"But if their losses are too great or they decide not to honor our agreement—"

Fadarah gave his answer aloud, so that the Bloody Prince would hear. "Very soon, we will go west. Whatever remains of this army will join us, as will the hosts of your brothers, or I will personally see to it that the Red Emperor becomes childless."

For emphasis, Fadarah used magic to pluck the goblet from Karhaati's hands. Though he loathed drinking from anything that the Bloody Prince's lips had touched, he drained the cup. Then wytchfire flared from the fist that held the cup, melting it.

Karhaati smiled, took the pitcher from Brahasti's hands, and drank straight from the rim. More wine spilled down his chest. "You owe me a goblet, Sorcerer-General." He pointed at the dead woman then turned to Brahasti. "Get *that* out of here."

Brahasti gave Fadarah a questioning look. For the first time, Fadarah answered with a slight smile. "You command the army, Brahasti—in *my* name. In all other matters, so long as his orders do not conflict with my own, the Bloody Prince remains your liege."

Reluctantly, Brahasti went to drag the dead woman out of the tent. Fadarah gave Karhaati a final glance then left as well. They mounted their horses. As the column of Shel'ai rode out of the camp, thousands upon thousands of Dhargots knelt again. The camp was still hushed, save for the cries of the prisoners. Fadarah eyed the slave pens in the distance. He turned to Shade and whispered, "Go and gather up all the women and children. Send Zeia to search the camp. Make sure we have everyone. Tell the Dhargots we intend to sacrifice all of them to Zet, their dead Dragongod. Tell them we will mix the ashes in our wine and smear them on our weapons, as is the Dhargothi custom."

Shade stirred, visibly uncomfortable. "I have no love for Humans, but—"

"Just tell them. Then take all the women and children east, give them provisions, and turn them loose. Do it tonight. Tell them if they have any sense, make for Quesh or the Lotus Isles."

"If the Dhargots find out—"

"A risk we can afford."

"What about the women and children they'll take at Cassica? Will we intervene for them, too?"

Fadarah gestured for Shade to proceed. Shade bowed, then turned and whispered the orders to Zeia, who raised her eyebrows in surprise. But both hurried to obey, the crimson greatwolves on their cloaks rustling as they moved.

Fadarah glanced around, eyeing the kneeling Dhargots. Even if they believed his story, many would chafe at the loss of their prizes. Still, even Fadarah would not be able to prevent them from despoiling whatever prisoners they took from the next city.

We must show mercy when we can. He urged his bloodmare onward, anxious to be gone. Only when he had ridden from sight did the camp bristle back to life. Thousands upon thousands of Dhargots rose, as tense as lions in the afternoon sun.

CHAPTER ELEVEN

ESCAPE

JALIST WOKE AND KNEW AT once that something was wrong. The room was dark and silent. Trusting his instincts, he grabbed the shortsword he'd kept drawn beside him and held it in a guarded position before his face. He slid his feet out of the bed and rose slowly, careful to make no sound.

He listened for breathing but heard nothing. "Locke?" he called softly. No answer. Cursing, he fumbled with flint and tinder and relit the lamp. His sharp eyes scanned the shadows. He was alone.

He spotted Rowen's armor lying in the corner of the room. He frowned. *Why would Rowen leave his armor?* That seemed as unlikely as him attempting to rescue Haesha by himself.

Jalist dressed quickly, donning not just his plain clothes but his brigandine and boots as well. Then he girded his shortsword, slid his knife into his belt, and grabbed his long axe. Before leaving the room, he pressed his ear to the door. He heard muffled voices outside, probably coming from the common room downstairs, but that was all. When he was certain no one was waiting outside to knife him, he opened the door, still crouching, and stepped into the hallway.

He considered knocking on Silwren's door but decided that if she was gone or asleep, she could stay that way. He approached the stairwell and glanced over the railing at the common room. It was mostly empty, and the few people he saw appeared to be asleep in their chairs, the innkeeper among them. Rowen sat well apart from everyone else. Silwren was not with him.

Doesn't look like a trap. Still, he searched the shadows and held his long axe at the ready as he cautiously made his way down the stairs. Rowen glanced up at his approach. The Knight's eyes were red, either from weeping or from exhaustion. Then Jalist saw the scroll in Rowen's hands.

It was yellowed with age but different somehow from those old scrolls he'd seen in the libraries of Tarator. Those were often so brittle and fragile that only the most trusted monks dared handle them. It looked more resilient than paper or vellum. "Since when did you pass the wytching hours with poetry?"

"At least I know how to read."

"So do I." Jalist sat down and glanced at the scroll again. "What language? Doesn't look like Common, and it sure isn't Dwarr or Old Ivairian."

"Shao," Rowen answered, his voice breaking.

He can't wait to tell me something. "So I wake with my guts telling me something's wrong, and I find you reading a Shao tome I'm pretty sure you didn't have six hours ago." Jalist looked around. "I don't see Silwren. Something tells me I won't find her up in her room, either."

"Do you know what this is?"

"I just told you I didn't." Jalist glanced at the inn door, hoping to make out whether Captain Reygo's guards were still stationed outside, but the smoke-fogged glass obscured his view.

"It's a history of the Shattering War, penned by Fâyu Jinn himself."

"Is it now?" Through the glass, Jalist saw a dark shape standing in the street. He couldn't make it out but gripped his axe anyway.

"I always wondered why the Dragonkin didn't just come back. This explains it. Fâyu Jinn and his allies drove the Dragonkin north, off the shores of the Wintersea, and his allies—Shel'ai and some other Dragonkin who changed sides—they cast some kind of spell around the whole continent. They call it the Dragonward. They *can't* come back! And I understand what drove the Dragonkin mad. Jalist, it's the same thing that's affecting Silwren. Too much power. Only they were used to it. But they stole their power, their magic, from the dragons. Eventually, they stole so much that the dragons died off—at least, Jinn *thinks* they did. Nobody knows for sure. That was"—he unrolled a portion of the scroll that he'd already read—"two or three thousand years before the Shattering War. But... gods, Jalist..."

"Calm down. Does this have anything to do with the Shel'ai, or is this just an interesting story about dragons?"

But Rowen did not seem to hear him. "The *sword*, Jalist! Silwren was right. Nâya... I thought that was the Shao word for *knight*... and now, it is. But before that, Nâya was a person. A woman. Jinn's *wife*! And she was a Dragonkin. But that's not all." Rowen was shaking as he spoke, as excited as a child, though the enthusiasm made Jalist oddly frightened. "She was Nekiel's daughter. Nekiel... do you know that name?"

Jalist peered into Rowen's glass and found it half full. The Knight did not sound drunk. "Only as a curse. Some disciple of the Undergod, right?"

"Yes... and no. Jinn was never really sure what he was. But he ruled the Dragonkin. And Nâya was his *daughter!* Can you imagine that? Jinn married the daughter of his enemy..."

"Fine, finish your story before it kills you. But keep your damn voice down." Jalist scanned the common room, but no one was awake enough to eavesdrop, regardless of the excitement in Rowen's voice. The Knight continued as though he had not heard the warning, and Jalist had a bad feeling that Rowen had not exactly come by the scroll honestly.

"Nâya made the sword." Rowen drew Knightswrath and laid it on the table between them. The snowy swirls of its kingsteel blade glinted in the lamplight. "She made it because she knew Jinn was no match for the Dragonkin, no matter how many warriors he got to follow him—and he got a lot as the revolt spread. But she knew if she tapped directly into the Light, she'd make Jinn into... into something like the Nightmare. So she sacrificed herself. Gods, Jalist, he begged her not to do it, but she *gave* herself to the sword. She took the blade in her hands and shoved it through her heart... while Jinn watched! Then she washed herself in wytchfire. She *burned* herself into it—"

Jalist glanced at the blade. For a moment, he thought he saw a woman's face in the snowy swirls of the metal but decided it was just his imagination. "Just a story. This is *steel*, Locke. Big difference between steel and a woman. You're old enough to know that."

Rowen shook his head. "That's what I thought, but the scroll is right. It *must* be! Jalist, when I found the sword, it was rusted through. Kingsteel doesn't rust. It can't. But Knightswrath was ruined. And now it's not. That *has* to be magic!"

Jalist shrugged. "If only there were another explanation. Say, a powerful and deceptive sorceress leading you around by the nose hairs."

"It started *before* I knew her."

"Fine. I believe you." Jalist kept a wary eye on the inn door. "Just tell me where Silwren is and what happened to those guards outside."

Rowen continued, talking quickly, glancing rapidly from Jalist to the scroll. "She didn't just put her *own* magic in the sword. She tied it to the honor of the Knighthood. And not *just* the Knighthood. She tied it to the Sylvs, too. She made the sword into a kind of lens. The greater the honor of the Knights and the Sylvs and all those other realms fighting alongside Fâyu Jinn, the greater the sword's power would become. That's how Jinn, a mere man, beat the children of gods. But after Jinn, the Order withered. That's here, too." He unrolled the scroll farther and pointed. "One of Jinn's descendants finished the scroll, I think. He doesn't give his name, but the handwriting's different. He says how Jinn's whole alliance fractured. The Sylvs turned on the Shel'ai and started killing them... and the Knights refused to stop it. Nobody wanted to have anything to do with magic, and the Knights and Sylvs didn't want anything to do with each other. *That* must be why they concealed the legends of the sword and the Oath of Kin.

"Everything fell apart," Rowen continued in a rush. "The line of kings eventually got so bad that the Knights killed the last king and threw out the monarchy. *That*, at least, I heard about when I was on the Isles. I still don't know how Knightswrath found its way to Hráthbam. It *should* have stayed in Jinn's tomb, in Sylvos. But"—he shook his head—"I guess that doesn't matter now. What matters is rekindling the sword. Silwren knows how. She says *my* honor is helping—that's what got rid of the rust—and so did absorbing wytchfire, but it isn't enough. And there isn't enough honor left among the Knights or the Sylvs to finish it. She could restore the sword herself... but she'd have to sacrifice herself to do it." He hesitated. "*That's* what she's been hiding. She's afraid. But she doesn't have to be. If we can kill Fadarah and get the Sylvs and the Knights to fight together, we won't even need—"

Jalist slammed his fist down on the table, loud enough to startle some of the patrons from sleep. "You're not actually *believing* all this nonsense, are you?"

"Seems I'm believing a lot of crazy things these days."

"Skip to the part where you stole something from the Scrollhouse and brought half the city watch down on our heads."

Rowen blinked. "No one saw us."

"And Silwren? Where in the hells is she?"

Rowen was silent for a time. Then he stood, picked up Knightswrath, and sheathed it. "The jailhouse."

Jalist's eyes widened. "That's it. You've killed us. You were prattling on about fairy tales when we should have been running for our lives."

"We'll make it. Silwren says so. We just… can't be near her, in case something goes wrong."

"And the guards outside—do we have to kill them? Or do you think they'll just let us go without reporting back?"

"They're asleep. Silwren recast the spell. She said they'll stay that way until—"

Jalist waved him off. He rose, too. "When this is done, remind me to have a conversation with the two of you."

Rowen blinked. "There wasn't time—"

"To tell me what you were planning?" Jalist snorted. "No, I think there was. But I'll throttle you later. Right now, we need to start running."

Silwren stood before a squat, plain, one-story building with arrow-thin walls. The doors were closed, locked, and guarded. *No matter.* Another spell allowed her to pass through solid stone walls as though they were made of air. Still, it felt like wading through porridge, and she had the awful feeling that if she lost her concentration, she would materialize in solid rock.

She finished passing through the wall. Magic flowed through her blood, so intoxicating that she reeled. She grabbed a table to steady herself. Noshan guards filled the jailhouse, though none saw her. Here and there, a few played dice, ignoring the groans and protests of the drunks and brawlers occupying the cells. She slipped past the guards like a shadow. She found the former Iron Sister asleep in a cell apart from the others. She stopped for a moment.

The woman's mind was an open scroll. She read it—an entire life, all the woman's memories in an instant. Silwren wept. Then she walked through the bars as easily as she'd passed through the walls of the jailhouse. She felt a tug of weariness at yet another expenditure of magic, in addition to what it kept to maintain her invisibility, but she could not stop.

Rather than waking the woman and risking her making noise that might alert the guards, Silwren found her in a dream. In the dream, the woman was nude and unarmed, struggling against a host of leering Dhargots. They swarmed over her, tearing at her clothes.

Silwren burned the men away. She pulled the stunned woman to her feet and spoke to her there. It took only a moment to explain what was about to happen, though Silwren doubted the woman understood. Silwren touched her. The former Iron Sister vanished, as though her body had turned to mist.

Silwren reeled again. The magic roared within her, more violent and intoxicating than ever. She felt as though she were being alternately stabbed and kissed all over her body. She fell to her knees, still in the woman's now-empty cell. She forgot why she was there. She forgot the faces of everyone she had ever loved. She even forgot her own name. She saw herself as though she were still in someone else's dream, watching from a distance. She saw the guards scream and reach for weapons as something filled the jail cell. She rose through the ceiling: translucent and mist born, but huge and horned with violet eyes and six wings. Dimly, she realized she was seeing herself. She saw herself made of light.

Then she saw no more.

"Well," Jalist said dourly as he and Rowen stood outside the city, watching the winged visage evaporate from the night sky above Atheion, "do you think they know what we did?"

Rowen sensed it was a jest, but he answered anyway. "They'll put it together quick enough. Turns out, we'll have Noshans hurling spears at our asses after all."

Jalist held tight to the reins. Like Rowen, he was having trouble controlling his mount. All the horses, save Silwren's, were still frightened by magic; the dragon-like visage rising from Atheion, even at this distance, had left the very air charged so that it prickled their skin like a storm of tiny, invisible needles. "How long do we wait for her?"

"As long as it takes."

"Better brace for a fight, then." Jalist pointed.

Men were amassing at the squat half-moon wall near the outskirts of Atheion. Rowen wondered if Captain Reygo had already been roused from slumber and told that the disappearance of a prisoner coincided with a magical visage rising from the jailhouse.

He imagined Silwren trying to control all that power, to keep herself from killing again. A rush of cold chilled his blood. If she had not joined them yet, perhaps the power had been too much for her. "Silwren's not coming."

Jalist asked, "Is she dead?" His blunt tone made it hard to tell whether the Dwarr wished it so.

"I don't think so. I think she's... staying away from us." Rowen felt Knightswrath's hilt and found it so warm that he had to take his hand away.

Jalist raised one eyebrow. "Then it's time to go."

"Good idea," a voice said. Igrid materialized out of the shadows, a crooked smile on her face. "Is that third horse for me?"

Rowen tensed. Despite the distance, he could hear shouts coming from Atheion. They had not been spotted yet, but that made no difference. It would not be hard to track two—let alone three—fleeing on horseback. "You're not coming with us. Take Silwren's horse and ride south. Quesh is your best bet. They're kind to women." He paused. "I don't expect thanks, but if you have half a shred of honor, you'll say a prayer for the wytch who spirited you out of there. You have no idea what she risked doing it."

Jalist eyed the armed Noshans in the distance. "Locke, finish your farewells and set your spurs, for gods' sake!"

Igrid met Rowen's gaze. "Save your stern words, Knight. I'm coming with you." She went to Silwren's horse, pulled the reins from Rowen's grasp, and swung easily into the saddle.

Jalist turned. "We're not going on a pleasant little ride about the country. You come with us, you'll likely end up with a dozen Sylvan arrows in your tits."

"I know. She told me—though her phrasing was a bit more eloquent." Igrid faced Rowen again. "Your wytch told me where you were going. And she told me why. I thought it was just a dream, but then I opened my eyes, and here I was."

Rowen regained his senses and shook his head. "This is no joke. We're bound for the Wytchforest. And by the Light, the hells, and every other damn thing I can swear on, I don't want you anywhere near me."

Igrid made a pouty face that evaporated back into her crooked, mocking grin. "And here I thought we were getting along so well." Her expression sobered. "Listen, Knight. I don't understand half of what you're planning, but I know it has something to do with the Dhargots. Your wytch told me as much. So if helping you means more Dhargots dying—whether it's Sylv or Knights or gods know who kills them—then I'm with you."

Rowen scowled. "No. That's my final answer."

"Good. I'm tired of arguing. Besides, do you really want me at your back or up front, where you can see me?" Before Rowen could answer, Igrid snapped the reins and took off.

Jalist said, "If you want to kill her, I'll loan you my knife."

Rowen looked over his shoulder. The Noshans had organized. Their spearheads glinted in the white glow of Armahg's Eye. "I might take you up on that."

He gave Snowdark full rein. Jalist followed. The two men uttered a stream of curses as they hurtled after the former Iron Sister, melting into the cold western darkness.

CHAPTER TWELVE

THE CHASE

ROWEN LED THEM WEST AS fast as they could ride, given the supplies burdening their horses. They rode through the night and considered stopping at dawn for a few hours of rest, but they chanced upon a drovers' village, and a warning of Lochurites in the area persuaded them to stop at an inn. Rowen half hoped that when he woke scant hours later, Igrid would already be gone. But they found her in the stables, already dressed and ready.

They rode southwest, hoping to circle the mountains and approach the Wytchforest from the south. But they stopped at sundown when Jalist spied riders pursuing them.

Rowen said, "Noshans, probably. If we ride hard, we can stay ahead of them."

Igrid produced a spyglass, without explanation of where she'd gotten it, and looked. Frowning, she lowered it. "Sorry, Knight, but those aren't Noshans. I see dark armor and red horses. Seems I've gotten you into trouble." She sounded almost sorry.

Rowen snatched the spyglass from her and raised it to one eye. "Damn." He passed it to Jalist.

Igrid said, "The southern road has too many hills. You can see them from here. We won't outrun bloodmares that way. Better we go north."

Jalist scoffed. "And risk not only berserkers and these bastards following us, but even more Dhargots when we pass by Hesod?"

Rowen took the spyglass from Jalist and looked again. He counted four dark figures but six red horses. Rather than sell the bloodmares of their two slain comrades, the Dhargots had brought them along. A horse carrying only its own weight would not tire as easily as one carrying a rider. That meant the Dhargots could rotate mounts and stop less often for rest. "We can't outrun them, no matter which direction we go." He turned to Igrid. "I don't suppose I can talk you into leading them away from us."

Jalist hefted his long axe. "If you can't talk her into it, maybe I can."

Igrid reached behind her and drew a knife she must have stolen from the same village where she took the spyglass. "Feel free to try, Dwarr."

Rowen touched Jalist's arm to stop him. He checked the position of the sun. Dusk, a great blue-black wall of shadow, was creeping along the eastern horizon. "They're expecting us to keep riding southwest. We'll keep that way for now then turn north once it's too dark to see our trail. Night will be on our side."

Jalist said, "Good! Gods know nothing else is."

Igrid said, "No need. You two have bows. Give me one of them. I'm a good shot. If one of you is half as good as me, we might kill all four before they get close."

Rowen shook his head. "They're wearing armor. Besides, they have crossbows. Big ones. I saw them in the stables." He passed the spyglass back to Igrid. "Southwest then north. Let's go." He snapped the reins and took off, half hoping once again that Igrid would choose her own path.

They pressed on as hard as they could. When darkness swallowed them, they turned north. Instead of galloping, Rowen led them in a quiet, stealthy canter. No one spoke. They rode until dawn then stopped in a thin copse of trees to rest. When they set out again, still half exhausted, Rowen took Igrid's spyglass and scanned the southern horizon.

Jalist asked, "Did it work?"

Rowen lowered the spyglass and rubbed his eyes. "No."

Jalist swore. "No way they could have seen us change direction!"

119

"They didn't. They just guessed." Igrid turned to Rowen. "You're too predictable."

Rowen said, "Enough talk. All we can do now is ride hard and hope they're just as tired as we are." He patted Snowdark's neck in sympathy then snapped the reins.

When they stopped again, it was not to rest, though their horses were lathered with exhaustion. Rowen cursed.

Jalist asked, "Is this good or bad news?"

Ahead lay a Noshan village. A few thatched huts were nestled against a small lake, a nearby cattle pasture, and a squat adobe temple dedicated to Armahg. A few small naked children played in the shadow of a windmill. Then someone spotted them. Parents rushed to grab their children while a few farmers formed a ragged line, armed with shovels and dung forks.

Jalist said, "We could ask for help."

"No, we'll ride on."

Igrid said, "Good idea. If we're lucky, the Dhargots will think we hid here. While they're busy torching and butchering, we'll get away."

Rowen glowered at her. He could not tell if she was joking. But she had a point.

Jalist said, "Don't go getting any grand notions, Locke. These people are under the protection of their king. The Dhargots won't want an incident. They might just poke around a while, then go."

Rowen glanced at his friend. *You don't sound like you actually believe that.* He sighed. "Jalist, find us a place to set up an ambush. Igrid, help him." Before Jalist could object, Rowen spotted an old man who looked like a cleric. He rode toward him, holding up one hand in a gesture of peace.

The cleric met him halfway, smiling uncertainly. "An Isle Knight! I've not seen one of your Order in years, not since—"

"We're being chased, Father. Four men, bent on murder."

"Lochurites? Fear not, my son. We have hunters who can—"

"These aren't Lochurites. These are Dhargots."

The cleric's eyes widened. Rowen wondered which ghastly story the old man was playing over in his mind. "We... have no quarrel with Dhargots. This land is full of hills. Better you ride on."

Men spoke in hushed, angry tones. "Ride on!" someone shouted from the crowd. Others seconded him.

Rowen held up his hands again. "Better for you if we don't. The Dhargots will think you're hiding us, whether we stop or not."

The crowd fell silent.

"I promise, you won't have to fight. This is our battle, not yours. But you need to seek shelter right away!" Rowen gazed out at the sea of angry stares. He could not blame them. He had brought these troubles down on them. If the Dhargots got past him and harmed any of the villagers, it would be on his head. "Just get out of sight!"

He whirled Snowdark about and rejoined Jalist and Igrid, who were engaged in a heated argument over how and where to establish their defense. Jalist wanted to fashion wooden stakes and create a palisade. Igrid preferred to take refuge with their bows on the temple rooftop.

"Not the temple." Rowen pointed to where the old cleric was frantically gathering the people and herding them inside. "That's where the villagers are hiding."

"It's also the best place for an archer," Igrid countered.

She was right, but they had to keep the Dhargots away from the villagers. "No time for a palisade, either. We either catch our breath and take up positions here or else we turn around and charge the Dhargots on the field." Rowen grimaced. Neither option sounded good.

Jalist said, "These shortbows probably won't pierce that scale armor of theirs. We'll have to aim for their horses. That's riskier but better done from the ground."

Rowen pointed to a cart loaded with hay. "We'll use that to block the street. If we have to, we can light it on fire. Bloodmares are afraid of fire, just like any other horse."

"I remember," Jalist grumbled.

"We should spread out," Igrid insisted.

Jalist said, "These are trained Dhargot warriors. Not berserkers. They'll attack as one. If we don't do the same, they'll gang up and pick us off one at a time."

Igrid frowned as if she meant to argue.

No time for this! He dismounted and approached Igrid's horse. Drawing his dagger, he offered it to her. "You better be as good with a blade as you say, Iron Sister."

Igrid took the blade with a sour look, deftly twirling it between her fingers. "Watch and learn." She dismounted, gesturing for Jalist to do the same. Igrid gathered their horses, led them behind an adobe hut, and tied them off while Rowen and Jalist dealt with the cart.

"Nicely done," Jalist muttered.

They hauled the cart to block the village's only street, then Jalist set about lighting torches. He used his knife to sharpen the butt of each so they could be thrust into the ground when they weren't needed. Rowen surveyed their position. They stood near the heart of town with a row of squat buildings on either side. The Dhargots could only come at them out in the open, from the east or the west.

Rowen heard the cries of the villagers—some scared, mostly angry—as they took shelter in the temple. The temple doors thudded shut. He listened for the click of a lock or the woody scuff of a crossbar but heard neither. He glanced at Jalist and saw that the Dwarr was thinking the same thing.

"Damn village can't afford a lockmaker?"

Rowen shrugged. "Won't matter. They won't get past us."

"You sound more confident than I feel." Jalist leaned his long axe against the cart, within easy reach, and nocked an arrow. "Never was much good with a bow…"

"Don't worry. Just aim for the big red blurs with four legs."

Jalist turned and cursed him but grinned despite himself. The thunder of approaching hooves had replaced the angry, frightened din from the villagers.

Igrid rejoined them. "You any good with a bow, Knight?"

Rowen handed her his shortbow and his quiver of arrows. "Not as good as you said you are. Let's hope you weren't just boasting."

"Lucky for you, I never boast when it pertains to bloodshed." Igrid nocked an arrow and faced eastward.

Four riders slowly crested the nearest hill, two more crimson horses trailing them. The men looked neither tired nor surprised. One pointed. Rowen heard laughter.

"Smug bastards," Jalist muttered.

Rowen frowned. "Pretty confident for men with three sheltered archers blocking their way."

Igrid took careful aim. "They'll pay for that."

Rowen said, "Don't fire yet. That's at least five hundred yards. They're too far."

Igrid snapped, "This isn't a tilting yard, and you aren't my wise, grizzled teacher, Sir Knight." Despite her biting tone, she relaxed her arm and held her fire.

Jalist scowled at their still-unmoving enemies. "Their crossbows will have better range. If they start firing, we'll have to just duck down and wait for them to get closer."

Rowen said, "They'll taunt us first. Let them get close then—" He stopped himself. Isle Knights were honor bound to let their enemies make the first move.

Jalist said, "We aren't writing poetry here, Locke. Kill them however we can and brood about it later."

Rowen hesitated. "Don't fire until I say."

Jalist nodded, and Igrid said nothing. Rowen was about to remind her that it was largely her fault they were in this predicament, but at that moment, the Dhargots started forward at a slow trot. The bloodmares tossed their heads with restless anger, clearly uncomfortable with the pitifully slow pace.

Jaanti led them. The Dhargothi ambassador swayed derisively in the saddle, not even bothering to draw his sword or nock an arrow into the crossbow hanging from his saddle. The three warriors behind him had already nocked their crossbows and carried them in the crooks of their arms.

Jalist whispered, "Almost close enough."

"Wait for me," Rowen hissed through his teeth. He kept one hand on Knightswrath and his gaze fixed on the approaching riders. Only two hundred yards separated them—close enough for shortbows, though the aim would be difficult. Two hundred yards shrank to one hundred, fifty, then twenty. Finally, the Dhargots reined in directly in front of Rowen and Jalist then stopped at the outskirts of the village.

Jaanti raised one mailed fist in a sign of deference that did not coincide with the cold smile beaming beneath his half helm of blackened steel. "Parley," he called out. "Can I trust your honor, Isle Knight?"

Rowen flushed then cleared his throat. "Approach." Out the corner of his mouth, he said to Igrid, "He'll try and goad you, but let me do the talking."

The Dhargots drew closer and closer, towering and steely on their huge bloodmares. The painted eyes of the ambassador's guards narrowed murderously as they regarded Rowen and his companions.

"Close enough," Rowen called.

The ambassador laughed. "We are well within range of your little bows now. Good thing you Knights are men of honor. My name is Jaanti, in case you've forgotten. I am nephew to the Red Emperor and cousin to the Bloody Prince." He pointed. "I just want her."

This sadistic bastard is Dhargothi royalty? "I don't think she likes you," Rowen answered.

"Such things have never stopped me before." Jaanti settled back in his saddle, idly taking in the scene before him, as though daring Rowen and his companions to strike first. "I see a village without people. Are they hiding? Either way, I'll have to put them to the sword unless you give me a reason not to."

Rowen seethed. "These people have nothing to do with this."

Jaanti urged his horse a little closer. Spittle dripped from its red jaws, landing on the cart that separated them, soaking into the straw. "I believe you. Give me the woman, and I swear on Zet's burning corpse, no one else will be harmed. I'll even toss you a handful of coins, if your honor will let you accept them." The Dhargot lifted a heavy coin purse and shook it with a metallic jangle.

Rowen said, "I wouldn't take them if I was starving."

"Oh, I doubt that. I've seen starving men gnaw on their own children." Jaanti gave Igrid a wolfish grin. "Maybe I'll gnaw on that one when I'm finished with her. Jaanti feels hungry when he looks at her." He turned back to Rowen. "Take the coins. Keep them, give them to the villagers, throw them in a lake. I don't care. But we take the woman. Agreed?"

When Rowen did not answer immediately, Jalist spat out the

words, "Go fuck your horses. You'll not get her, in this life or the next."

Surprised by his ferocity, Rowen cast the Dwarr a sidelong glance.

Jaanti bristled at the insult, but the cold smile quickly returned. "We'll bargain, then. I'll trade you a dozen slave girls for her. Is this pretty whore so special to you?"

Jalist said, "She means even less to me than you do. But I wouldn't hand Fohl over to a Dhargot if I could help it. Sorry, friend. Just a little rule of mine."

Rowen said, "You can't have her. And we both know that if this comes to bloodshed, most of us here will die." *Unless I forget about honor and have them shoot you full of arrows right now...* He remembered what he'd said to Jalist about Knightswrath, what he'd read in the scroll about how the dishonor of the Isle Knights, the Sylvs, and the other races had left the sword rusted and tarnished. If he killed Jaanti after swearing his safety, how long before Knightswrath began to rust again?

Jaanti tapped the hilt of his broadsword. Despite his precarious position, he seemed completely at ease. "Listen, Knight. Either one woman dies, or many die. The choice is yours."

"There's another way." Rowen drew Knightswrath. "Single combat. You win, you take the woman—"

"The hell he does!" Igrid spat. She started to lift her bow, but Jalist grabbed her arm.

Rowen said, "You win, you take her. I win, she stays. And your men ride north and leave us in peace."

Jaanti's painted eyes narrowed. "I don't think the woman will come quietly after you die. I think we'll have to kill your friends, no matter what. I think you know that as well as I do. But I'm happy to start with you."

The Dhargothi ambassador tossed aside his crossbow, letting it land heavily in the grass. He dismounted, turned, and passed the reins to one of his guards. "Don't interfere." He circled the cart and drew his sword.

Rowen barely sidestepped in time. Jaanti's broadsword struck the straw cart, biting deep into the wood, but the big man wrenched it free before Rowen could counter. Rowen sidestepped again. He waved Jalist and Igrid back. Jalist lifted his shortbow.

Rowen shouted, "Stay out of this! Watch his guards, not me!"

He expected Jaanti to charge, but the Dhargot hung back, smirking, idly twirling his broadsword in slow, lazy figure-eights. "I haven't fought an Isle Knight in years. This will be fun."

Before Rowen could reply, the Dhargot pounced, unbelievably quick for a man his size. He swung at Rowen's greaves then angled the blade up and hammered Rowen's spaulders before Rowen could even bring his own sword into play. He slashed twice, but Jaanti had already backed off.

The Dhargot gave him a wolfish smile, lazily swinging his sword again. "If it weren't for that swirly armor, I'd have lopped off your leg and arm by now. Better pick up the pace, Knight."

Rowen cursed and held Knightswrath in a high guard. *I have to do better. Fâyu Jinn held this sword. He won a war with it. I can beat one dung-hearted princeling... or else I don't deserve to wear this armor.*

Jaanti stared at him, amused, and made no effort to counter his advance. Darkness had fallen, but Rowen saw the light of Armahg's Eye wash down their swords. As he and his opponent circled each other, Rowen tried to keep from looking at the torches stuck in the ground, knowing they would ruin his vision. He braced himself and brought his sword down with both hands, angling for the gap between the Dhargot's helm and spaulders.

Jaanti shrugged one great shoulder so the blow met his armor. He drove the pommel of his sword toward Rowen's face. Rowen ducked, stepped back, lost sight of his opponent, then felt Jaanti's blade drive into his cuirass.

The blow drove the wind out of him, but Rowen managed a quick stab at the Dhargot's chest, gouging out a shard of his scale armor. Jaanti withdrew his blade, nearly slashing Rowen's tabard in two. Rowen gasped for air and thought oddly of the tear that Igrid had inflicted the first time they spoke.

Can't seem to keep my knighthood in one piece...

Jaanti stabbed for Rowen's groin. He reacted on instinct, hammering the blow aside. The edge of the Dhargot's sword scraped his greaves instead. Were it not for his armor, the Dhargot would have already hacked him to pieces with nearly every swing.

I must be faster. I must be—

Jaanti came at him again, a smirking, steely blur. The man might have been royalty, but he clearly knew his steel. Rowen blocked a flurry of fast, accurate swings. Then he saw an opening and countered, gouging another scale from Jaanti's cuirass. Jaanti turned, offering him no target. The proper recourse was to step back, but Rowen swung again, leaving a bright scratch on the Dhargot's armored hip. Another slash cleaved a silk tassel from the man's armor. The visage of an impaled dragon floated to the ground.

Jaanti laughed. "Are you finally awake now, Isle Knight? Good. I'll quit being so gentle." The Dhargot came at him, using both his blade and the quillons of his sword hilt to rain blow after blow on Rowen's armored chest, legs, and shoulders, faster than he could counter.

Rowen gave ground, sweat in his eyes. Still wheezing for breath, he wondered if the Dhargot ever meant to stop. He flushed, thinking he was about to die with Jalist and Igrid watching.

His back struck something solid. The temple. Jaanti had driven him all the way back to the temple! Rowen ducked. Jaanti's blade sparked off the temple walls. Rowen rolled free. He came up fast, Knightswrath held before him, but Jaanti did not charge.

The Dhargot leaned on his sword. Only a slight sheen of perspiration on a bit of exposed throat gave any indication of his weariness. "Catch your air, Knight. We both know I could finish you now, but to be honest, I'm enjoying this."

Rowen's lungs ached for another moment's rest, but he hefted Knightswrath and charged anyway. Jaanti parried one swing, took a second off his spaulders, and countered with a blow that nearly drove Knightswrath out of Rowen's grasp. Before Rowen could recover, Jaanti drove an armored knee into his cuirass, followed by a hard shove that spilled Rowen onto the ground.

Rowen saw stars just beginning to shine through the blue-black haze of twilight. He thought he heard Snowdark whinny then Jalist shout and Igrid curse, but those sounds seemed miles away.

Then a dark figure blotted out the stars. "Do you yield, Isle

Knight? You'd make a fine addition to the Bloody Prince's harem. Can you dance or juggle? Can you sing?"

Rowen remembered where he was. He tensed his fingers. He tried to flex them around Knightswrath's dragonbone hilt and realized the sword was no longer in his grasp. He looked up. Jaanti had it. The Dhargot slung his own broadsword over his shoulder like a woodsman's axe and held Knightswrath with his other hand, prodding Rowen with the adamune's curved tapered point.

Rowen looked past him and saw Jalist. The Dwarr's face was blanched. Both he and Igrid were still holding their bows, but the other Dhargots had circled the cart and loomed over them, crossbows at the ready.

"Should I repeat my offer or cleave your skull on the temple lawn?"

Rowen answered by rolling closer, right up against the Dhargot's legs. He wrapped one arm around the man's knees then rolled the opposite direction, pulling the Dhargot down on top of him. Rowen had the pleasure of hearing the man curse.

They grappled. In such close combat, swords were no use; Rowen had already thrown two elbows into Jaanti's face before the Dhargot realized that. Jaanti released his grips on both swords and answered with a punch of his own. Rowen reeled. Then he saw Knightswrath lying on the ground. He reached. Before he could grab it, Jaanti kicked him in the chest. Rowen staggered.

Jaanti was on his feet. The Dhargot had lost his half helm, and blood streamed from his broken nose. He laughed nonetheless. He made no effort to wipe away the blood. "Is this what you meant by splitting me crotch to throat? Well, at least you made some small reckoning for yourself." Jaanti bent and retrieved his broadsword, kicking Knightswrath out of reach.

Rowen went for his dagger, realized he'd given it to Igrid, and searched frantically for anything he might use as a weapon. He saw nothing. He risked a quick glance at Jalist and Igrid, hoping one of them might throw him a blade, but Jaanti's men had already moved to block the way.

Rowen heard the sound of a crying infant and faced the temple again. He was only a few yards from the temple doors. The doors were still closed, but he could see the villagers watching through the windows, which were simply gaps in the adobe. Some of the people held blades. He wondered if they would come to his aid.

What am I to them? Then he asked himself a new question: *What are they to me?* He realized Igrid was right. They should have simply taken up position on the temple roof, hidden until the Dhargots got close, and rained arrows on them. As Jaanti circled him, clearly taking his time, Rowen remembered something his brother used to say: *Better to live with guilt than die without it.*

Jaanti stopped. He tipped his head, as though listening for something. Rowen heard it, too: the sound of footfalls coming from the western edge of the village. For one wild moment, Rowen thought Captain Reygo and a company of Noshan guards were hurrying to his aid. Then he noted Jaanti's smile.

Ragged, filthy figures emerged from the shadows. A few wore furs. Most were naked. Each one appeared gaunt and half starved. He saw women as well as men, though all looked more like animals than people, from their long nails to their sickly yellow eyes. "Lochurites..."

Rowen did not even realize he'd voiced the thought until Jaanti shrugged. "Odd times call for odd alliances." He faced the berserkers. "About time you caught up."

The Lochurites swaggered into the moonlight, their eyes wide, as though they were incapable of blinking. Rowen saw a fearful listlessness in the Lochurites' movements. He realized they were all probably drugged by whatever poison they ingested, supposedly to become immune to fear and pain. He counted at least a dozen appearing from the shadows.

Rowen heard screams from within the temple. Jaanti snapped his fingers. A tall, hairless, sickly-thin man with two bronze hatchets separated from the rest of the Lochurites. He approached Jaanti as a hungry dog might and half knelt, growling and muttering incomprehensibly.

Jaanti pointed at the temple. "People. Inside. Kill. Understand?"

The Lochurites' leader nodded his shaggy head. He gestured to the hissing, muttering shadows behind him. They started toward the temple.

Rowen cried, "Wait, we had a deal—"

"What deal? Neither of us said shit about the villagers. And don't offer me your life for these others, because I already have it." The Dhargot started toward him again, broadsword glinting. "Be a good loser and give me your throat."

Rowen backed away. *Everyone's about to die because of me.* He knelt. His fingers fought the straps to one of his greaves. He hardly realized what he was doing.

Jaanti frowned but did not slow. Rowen finished unbuckling his greave and rose, just as Jaanti was swinging. Rowen gripped the armor plate with both hands and swung, too, batting Jaanti's sword out of the way. Then he leapt forward and stabbed the edge of the greave into Jaanti's chin.

Jaanti jerked. Rowen gripped the bit of armor with both hands and drove its blunt edge into Jaanti's throat—once, twice, three times. Jaanti's eyes widened then glazed over. Blood gurgled from his mouth. His broadsword wavered. Rowen raised the greave over his head and smashed it down. Jaanti crumpled. Rowen knelt, snatched up the dead man's sword, and turned.

Still seated on horseback beside the cart, twenty feet away, the other Dhargots gaped at him. Then they remembered their crossbows. One shot at him, but the bolt glanced off Rowen's spaulders. The others turned toward Jalist and Igrid. One jerked as Igrid's arrow caught him in the thigh, between his armor plates. Jalist fired half a heartbeat later. His arrow struck the wounded Dhargot's bloodmare. The beast reared, tossing its rider to the ground.

The third Dhargot aimed his crossbow for Igrid, but the former Iron Sister ducked, rolled beneath the Dhargot's horse, stabbed, then came up as this animal reared, too.

Jalist had taken up his long axe. He grunted and cleaved one Dhargot's head from his shoulders then swung and shattered the sword of another. The second man reached for another weapon but stiffened as Igrid drove a dagger into the back of his neck.

Only one Dhargot remained. He tried for a moment to span his crossbow and fire again, but upon seeing that all his companions were dead, he gave up. He wheeled his bloodmare to flee. But Igrid screamed in defiance and scooped up a fallen shortbow.

Rowen sprinted toward the temple. The Lochurites had already forced open the temple doors, and some had pushed inside. Screams of panic and battle told him that the villagers with weapons were trying to fight off the Lochurites, despite being outnumbered. Those Lochurites still outside shoved toward the temple doors. They did not see him coming.

Rowen thrust Jaanti's broadsword between the shoulder blades of the nearest Lochurite, gave the blade a twist, then dragged it free. Another Lochurite pounced at him. Her yellow eyes roiled with rage and madness. She slashed at his face with a bronze knife, but Rowen cut her down. She fell with just a look of mild surprise.

Knightswrath lay in the grass, just a few yards away. Another Lochurite stood in the way. Rowen barreled past and let Jaanti's sword fall atop the corpse. He snatched up Knightswrath and turned just in time to slash another Lochurite who was hurtling toward him. The mad warrior hardly slowed. A bronze shortsword wobbled toward Rowen's face. He sidestepped, turned, and cut off the man's head. Then he ran for the temple door.

He smelled blood as soon as he got inside. Beside overturned stools and braziers, hot coals pulsed in the darkness. The old cleric lay dead on the floor, along with a few men who must have been hunters. Villagers fleeing toward the rear of the temple overturned an altar that was little more than a table heaped with carved wooden stars. Mothers were trying to wedge their children through the temple windows. A few men were trying to fight off the Lochurites. Those without weapons had armed themselves with candelabras or wooden stools.

Rowen counted eight berserkers. He knew he should wait for Jalist and Igrid. Instead, he howled and charged. Chaos surrounded him. Ragged men and women fought, their foul breath seeming to mingle with the shadows around them. Bronze weapons hacked at him. He answered with steel, sometimes parrying a blow with his vambraces, bashing foes with his armor. He howled, too—the dreadful sound echoed in the cramped temple. He slashed and slashed. He did not stop until his sword passed thrice through empty air. Then he stopped and stared.

All the Lochurites were dead. One, less drugged than the rest, had attempted to flee. Jalist wrenched his long axe from the fallen man's body. The Dwarr's eyes widened. "Dear gods, Locke!"

Rowen realized his armor and tabard were so splattered in blood that he might as well have bathed in it. He thought strangely of Namundvar's Well, of gazing momentarily into the Light. But, far too tenuous to hold, the peaceful memory slipped away. Then the chaos rose, swirling around him, and he fell into darkness.

CHAPTER THIRTEEN

THE HEALING

S HADE FOUND HER ON THE plains, unconscious and trembling like a wounded animal. She lay in a gigantic patch of scorched earth. Though her flesh remained untouched, pale and beautiful in the starlight, the fire had burned away her clothes. He felt a familiar arousal at the sight of her nakedness, remembering how they used to make love at night on the open plains, with no one else around for miles. She was so beautiful. He still wanted her, still needed her. She *had* been his wife once.

He squelched the thought. That had been practically a lifetime ago. Besides, he had not sought her out for that. "Silwren, my love…"

She did not answer.

He knelt before her. "Silwren!"

She looked up, though she stared at him without comprehension. Her eyes brimmed with wytchfire.

He started to pull back, sensing the unbridled power. Then he stopped himself. He reached out, brushed one platinum curl from her eyes, and gently touched her cheek. "I'm here. It's all right. I'm here."

She cocked her head, clearly not understanding, though he saw a spark of trust in her face. Just a spark. *That's more than I deserve.* He cleared his mind.

He took her face with both hands, holding her gaze. Slowly, he extended his consciousness into hers. He nearly recoiled when he felt the raging storm that was her mind. But he found his courage and moved forward, filled with resolve.

He closed his eyes and envisioned her madness as a thick jumble of knots, thousands and thousands of them. He moved among them, joining her consciousness with his own, slowly unknotting them one at a time. He felt the storm ebb, replaced at first by fear then sheer exhaustion.

Hours later, he finally opened his eyes. She was asleep. He lowered her to the grass, felt her breasts press against him, and was tempted again, but he unclasped his cloak and laid it over her like a blanket. He hesitated and kissed her forehead. "Sleep, my love. Goodbye."

She turned her face toward him, though her eyes remained closed. She whispered, "Kith'el..."

His name dissolved into the night air like a wisp of smoke. Shade's heart leapt. He lingered a moment, but she did not open her eyes. He rose and backed away from her. He did not think she would hurt him, but he could not say for sure.

Yet he hesitated. "Fadarah will know I sensed your pain," he said at last, then his voice broke. "He will know I came to help you. He will be angry. We are supposed to kill you now, if we can. Since you will not help us. But I think... I think he will understand."

Suddenly, he realized that the gigantic patch of scorched earth and burnt grass in which she lay was shaped like a dragon with many outstretched wings. He backed away again. He whispered, "Goodbye, my love. Sleep. And when you wake... run!"

Jalist helped the Noshans bury their cleric, along with three men and two women, in an apple grove near the village. Following the Noshan custom, they were buried without markers, in a silent ceremony held just before dawn.

Afterward, the villagers somberly collected the Lochurite weapons, for bronze could still be melted into coins, but left the lice-ridden clothing alone. They hauled the berserkers' corpses to a wretched pit used for burning trash. Jalist was heartened when smoke removed those staring yellow eyes from the world.

The villagers burned the corpses of the Dhargots and the dead horses as well. They had debated whether to haul the bodies before

King Hidas as proof that the Lochurites and the Dhargots had formed an alliance, thinking the information might earn them a reward, but Jalist cautioned against that. After all, one of the slain Dhargots was a royal. Though the villagers had not been involved in the killing, King Hidas might blame them for whatever diplomatic tensions might arise. Still, the new cleric of the town—a young man who had served as the old cleric's neophyte for years—insisted on carrying word to Atheion. Two men went with him, armed with the dead Dhargots' weapons and horses.

Livid, Igrid turned to Jalist. "You gave *them* the bloodmares?"

Jalist shrugged. "They'll need their speed if they meet any more berserkers on the road."

"I don't care if they meet ten thousand berserkers between here and Atheion!" Igrid's cry drew angry stares.

Leaning against the straw cart, sharpening his long axe, Jalist gave her a warning look, which she ignored.

"Those horses could have gotten us to the Wytchforest twice as fast."

"Or fetched a purse full of silver at the market. Maybe that's what you really had in mind."

Igrid snorted. "Sure... once this is over. I meant what I said—if this fool's errand will bring harm to the Dhargots, I'm for it."

"You better be. Because that Dhargot you let get away will be glad to tell everybody about us."

"I didn't *let him get away*, Dwarr! I put an arrow in his back. Not my fault his armor kept him alive."

"Doesn't matter. They won't just be looking for a sharp-tongued woman who insulted a Dhargothi royal by knifing some of his guards. They'll be looking for the people who killed the Bloody Prince's cousin. Gods help me, I'm starting to think the Wytchforest might actually be safer than here!"

Igrid glanced at the huts behind them. "The Dhargots might torch this place out of spite. I doubt the king will send a whole garrison to protect one village. These people should flee."

Jalist shrugged. "Some will. We warned them." He saw something— was it pity?—in her green eyes, but she shook it off.

"When do you leave?"

"Without Rowen? Never. Unless you want to take that pretty sword of his and try and do this yourself." He saw a spark in her eyes and glowered at her. "But if you try, I'll cut the head off your shoulders. You've been warned, woman."

"How protective you are. I wonder, is this the loyalty of a sellsword talking?" Igrid paused meaningfully. "Or the pining of a lonely man lover?"

Jalist stared at her for a moment. Then he laughed. "If you want to wound me with words, you'll have to come up with something fresher. I know what I am, woman. And crueler mouths than yours have failed to reduce me to tears."

He turned his attention back to sharpening his axe. Eventually, Igrid turned and stalked away, cursing under her breath. Jalist smirked. Then he tensed as a new figure approached the village.

Her white cloak concealed her face, but the platinum hair countered his dread. He pocketed his sharpening stone, hefted his long axe, and went to meet her. "So there you are."

Silwren eyed his long axe but did not flinch. "So here I am."

Neither spoke for a moment. Jalist gave in first. "Some kind of explanation would be most welcome."

"I'm sure it would. But I have none to give... aside from what you should have already guessed. I left to save Rowen's life. And yours."

She looked as pale as her cloak. "You left because you lost heart. Or control. Or both. And as usual, others had to pay for your weakness." He nodded toward the fresh graves in the distance. "You promised to help Rowen get to the Wytchforest. You swore—"

"So I did. And I will."

"Well, you're a little late. Rowen is dead."

Silwren shuddered. All the light left her eyes. "Dead..."

Jalist gathered his courage and took a threatening step toward her. He spoke through his teeth. "That's what I said."

"How?"

"Killed by some crazed berserker—*after* he took wounds fighting to protect these people, I might add. And where were you? Cowering somewhere?"

Silwren trembled, steadied herself, and faced him. Her unblinking eyes sent a chill down Jalist's spine, but he refused to break her gaze.

After a moment, her expression changed to relief, tinged with anger. "Your mind is an open scroll to me, Dwarr. You lie. Rowen lives."

"So he does. No thanks to you. But I trust I've made my point."

Silwren eyed him. "So you have."

"Good. Now get in there and heal him. I was telling the truth about his wounds. He's hardly opened his eyes for days, and a couple slashes look infected. Unless you can do something, he might lose his arm—or his life."

"He'll lose neither." Silwren moved toward the temple where Rowen and the other wounded were resting. Though she did not touch Jalist, he felt as though a torch had brushed past him, close enough to singe his skin.

Jalist grunted, shaking his head. Igrid stood outside the temple, staring at him. He expected to see mockery in her expression; instead, he saw surprise—or grudging admiration.

Not every day you see some damn fool pull a Shel'ai's tail. Jalist tried to go back to sharpening his long axe, but his hands were shaking. He pocketed the sharpening stone again and decided to take a walk.

CHAPTER FOURTEEN
DREAMS AND SOFT STONES

THE VILLAGE WAS MORE THAN a day behind them when Rowen realized he had not even thought to ask what its name was. This troubled him. Despite the initial rebuke of the village's ill-fated cleric, the other villagers had fed Rowen and his companions and allowed them to stay while Rowen recovered.

Some had reached for weapons at the sight of Silwren, but Rowen told them about what she had done at Lyos. A few had already heard the story. Whether they believed it or not, once she kindled her magic to heal the injured right before their eyes, most granted her their wary trust. Silwren had healed a sleeping woman's broken arm, but the old woman went so far as to slash her own arm in the same place to show her contempt for magic. Rowen thought it best that they not linger.

They set out the next morning. Riding was difficult but not impossible. He did not know how many wounds he had taken from the Lochurites. Supposedly, he had been near death. After Silwren's healing, he was just sore, and his skin bore no indication of the fight.

They continued northwest. Rowen had considered taking them south again, so they could circle the mountains and approach the Wytchforest with less risk of encountering Dhargots, but Silwren had vetoed him. She insisted that she could get them past the Dhargots. Though he was not sure he believed her, Rowen did not have the strength to argue.

As he rode, Rowen thought of his fight against the Lochurites. Memories of the battle blurred in his mind. He remembered the thick, bloody darkness, the weight of his sword, and the scrape of metal off rib bones. His stomach turned. He tried to fix his eyes on the road, a simple path worn by time and hooves, and enjoy the morning breeze on his cheek.

As though in answer, the breeze picked up, stirring his tabard. He glanced down. The villagers had resewn his tabard as best they could, but the thread, too thick and oddly colored, clashed with the rich azure silk of the tabard. He smiled to himself. He liked it. His tabard looked scarred.

His armor bore echoes of the fighting, too. Though kingsteel could not rust, Jaanti's blade had left several dents and scratches. He touched them as he rode, as though inspecting his wounds. Had Rowen not been wearing armor, Jaanti would have killed him in seconds. Rowen's eventual victory seemed less like a testament to his skill than a blend of lunacy and sheer luck.

I have to be quicker, stronger, smarter, or I'm no use to anyone.

He rested his hand on the dragonbone pommel of Knightswrath. The faint swirls of color in the bone caught the sunlight. Studying them more closely, he thought they appeared more purple than crimson. On impulse, he drew the sword and examined the blade again. The sword's name, written in ancient Shao script, glinted next to the silver inlay of a dragon in flight. He appreciated the snowy swirls left in the metal as the blade was forged.

Is Nâya's shade in there somewhere? He imagined Jinn's wife trapped in the folds of the metal, for centuries, screaming. A fresh surge of nausea pushed the thought from his mind. Like the armor of the Isle Knights, adamunes were immune to rust and rarely needed sharpening, but every sword had limits. Knightswrath had met Jaanti's broadsword edge on edge. He'd sliced at Jaanti's armor, too. The blade should have been chipped. Rowen peered closely but could not find a single blemish on the blade.

Is that part of the magic, too? If so, he hardly deserved it. He hadn't even beaten Jaanti with the sword. He considered what Nâya had given up, what Jinn had lost. Surely, despite all the corruption on the Lotus Isles, other Knights—like his old teacher, Aeko Shingawa, or Grand Marshal Bokuden—were more deserving of such a weapon.

He shook off the thought and shifted his attention to his companions. Silwren and Igrid were keeping their distance from each other. Silwren had saved Igrid's life. Rowen did not understand the source of the strange tension between them.

He thought of El'rash'lin and how the late Shel'ai had shared his memories with Rowen. He had seen evidence that the peaceful use of magic joined people somehow. Perhaps in spiriting Igrid out of the jailhouse, Silwren had come to know the former Iron Sister better than she intended—and vice versa. Perhaps neither woman especially liked what she saw in the other.

At the moment, though, Silwren gave no indication of ill will. She traveled in the plain clothes the villagers had given her, though she still wore the bone-white cloak she'd arrived in. When Rowen asked her about it, she refused to answer. As disconcerting as it was to see her in the cloak of Fadarah's Shel'ai, he reminded himself that the Dhargots were Fadarah's allies. If Rowen's group was spotted, Silwren's cloak might come in handy.

Rowen turned and focused his gaze on the towering, blue-green blur spanning the western horizon. For better or worse, they would reach the Wytchforest in two days. His pulse quickened. He could not discern the outline of the World Tree yet, but Silwren promised him that he would be able to soon. He felt tired and scared at the same time. Whatever was going to happen—better to get it over with.

He nudged Snowdark along, ahead of Silwren, quickening their pace.

They made camp at dusk near a pond shaded by a crescent of poplars. The air surrendered its warmth as evening fell, a sure sign that autumn was upon them. While Igrid and Rowen cared for the horses, Silwren conjured a fire in a circle of wet stones that Jalist had carried from the pond. They had only dried rations, which were adequate but tasteless. The bland meal was sweetened by a wineskin that Rowen had thought to purchase while in Atheion. The heady red wine, flavored with a spice he had never tasted, relaxed him a little. He stared into the fire as darkness deepened around them.

They passed the wineskin around the fire, saying little. Rowen had stripped off his armor, but like Jalist and Igrid, he kept his weapons nearby. They had left Nosh and were skirting the Simurgh Plains. Rowen did not think they would encounter any Lochurites so far north, but he still feared running into Dhargots since Hesod was nearby.

Encountering highwaymen was always a possibility, too. Shortly after Rowen's return to the mainland from the Lotus Isles, a cruel man named Dagath had nearly killed him on the road. Dagath was still alive, as far as Rowen knew. He wondered for a moment if he might one day meet his would-be killer again. Dagath would surely be surprised to learn that the unkempt, common traveler who had momentarily been under his knife had become an Isle Knight.

Rowen's gaze strayed to Igrid, who was sitting opposite him. The glow of the campfire played off her red curls and green eyes, not to mention an immodest amount of cleavage bared by her current outfit. He wondered if that was a deliberate ploy to arouse him into carelessness so she could rob him in his sleep. His hand strayed for Knightswrath. History aside, kingsteel was worth a fortune. So was dragonbone.

No, if she wanted to rob us, she could have done it after the battle in the village, while I was out cold. Still, he had no intention of trusting her with his life. Not yet.

Before Rowen could turn away, Igrid looked up and followed his gaze. Smirking, she looked about to make a biting remark, then apparently thought better of it.

Rowen blushed. He lowered his eyes, prodding the fire with his boot. "We should stand watch. I'll go first."

Silwren said, "No need. I've already charmed this area to wake me if someone approaches."

Rowen and Jalist exchanged glances. Rowen wondered if that was a Shel'ai or a Dragonkin ability.

Jalist said, "Just how great an area are we talking about? If we don't know a cutthroat is here until they're standing over us, the warning won't do much good."

Silwren faced Jalist, her mist-white pupils shining in the purple firelight. "I charmed the ground and water from the tree line to the far bank of the pond." She paused. "We'll reach Sylvos soon. We need rest. The spell will keep a more reliable watch than any of your eyes."

Igrid said, "Her magic lifted me clean out of a jail cell and dropped me outside, gentle as a baby. If she says she'll hear chimes or trumpets or whatever if somebody approaches, I believe her."

In place of gratitude, Silwren gazed at Igrid so sternly that the Iron Sister looked away. For one long moment, the only sounds were the chirping of insects and the distant screech of an owl going after a mouse.

"Fine. Agreed. We sleep. No watch." Rowen pulled off his boots and lay down, using a cloak for a blanket. He kept his sword and dagger nearby, resting one hand on Knightswrath's hilt. He told himself he did so in case he needed to arm himself quickly, should cutthroats approach the camp.

I hope you aren't a heavy sleeper, Silwren!

He closed his eyes and pretended to sleep until the myth finally became a reality.

Kayden Locke turned to face him, confident and smirking, his spear and armor splattered with blood. A band of Olgrym, sellswords who had left Godsfall to seek their own fortune, had spotted them crossing the Wintersea and sprinted toward them, howling. They'd already killed half the merchant's guards. The merchant himself had abandoned his crossbow and was hiding in the wagon. Only Kayden, Rowen, and Jalist remained.

"Better draw that sword, little brother. I'm not being paid to save your ass!"

Kayden had already speared an Olg about to split Rowen's skull. Rowen nodded dumbly and drew his Ivairian-style shortsword. He turned.

The setting sun spread like blood across the white face of the Wintersea. The snap of the remaining caravan guards' crossbows mingled with the crazed howls of Olgrym and the Dwarr oaths uttered by Jalist as he swung his long axe with both hands. But the bloody sunset caught his attention.

Then he heard an Olg charging him from behind. He whirled, slashing. He saw Kayden stiffen, wide eyed, as his throat opened.

"No… Kayden, I thought you were a…" Rowen caught his brother and lowered him to the ice.

Blood bubbled from Kayden's mouth. He could not speak, though his eyes blazed with rage and accusation. Kayden had dropped his spear, but he fumbled for another weapon and drew a long knife that gleamed wickedly in the setting sun.

"Kayden, wait—"

Kayden stabbed at him. Rowen recoiled. He felt a shudder race up his arm and looked down—he had thrust his shortsword through a chink in Kayden's armor. He had stabbed his own brother. Kayden's gaze met his, then it went dark.

Jalist approached him, bloody and disheveled. He pummeled Rowen with an accusing stare. "Well, he meant to kill you. I guess you had no choice." He paused. "Should be *you* lying on the ice like that, though."

"No, it was an accident…"

"Like hell. You wanted him dead. You've *always* wanted him dead. You—"

Rowen felt that awful shudder snake up his arm again. Jalist's eyes widened. The Dwarr slid off Rowen's shortsword and collapsed, bleeding on the white face of the frozen sea.

Rowen stared. "No, this isn't how it happened. This isn't right. Just a dream."

The Olgrym, the wagon, and all the other guards disappeared. For miles, only blank whiteness surrounded him. All he saw were the two corpses. Blood ran down the blade of his shortsword. He cast it away. Its weight made the Wintersea crack. The crack became a maw. Cold water rushed up and snatched him.

He flailed, trying to pull himself out of the water, but the ice crumbled every time he touched it. The entire Wintersea was melting, deliberately pulling away from him, insisting he drown. *This isn't real. This isn't real. This isn't—*

Rowen coughed as water entered his lungs. He spotted Silwren standing on the far bank, beautiful, naked, and ablaze with wytchfire. Hope surged through him. Silwren would save him. With supreme effort, he dragged one hand out of the water and reached for her. The water had turned red, but he hardly noticed. He fixed his gaze on Silwren. The raw power of her violet eyes drove back the coming night.

He called out to her for help. She faced him, expressionless. Then she turned and walked away. Rowen's limbs went stiff. He sank deeper into the cold.

Rowen woke from the nightmare, shivering. The campfire had burned out. Not even cinders remained. Cursing, he pulled his cloak tighter. He guessed it must still be hours before dawn, when the night was at its deepest.

Silwren was sleeping soundly, so still that she might have been carved from painted stone. He reasoned that must be why the fire had gone out. The sight of her frightened him for a moment, before he reminded himself that he'd just been dreaming. He considered waking her so that she could use magic to reignite the fire. He glanced up. Armahg's Eye was obscured by a palm of blue-black clouds, but the full moon was bright in the cold sky.

He heard Jalist snoring then realized Igrid was gone. He cursed again, in panic, but found Knightswrath lying on the ground next to him. The hilt felt strange to him, though he could not say why. He relaxed a little, figuring she had only gone off to relieve herself in privacy. He lay back down, using his pack as a pillow, and closed his eyes. He felt supremely exhausted, but his weariness felt like a thick quilt drawn over his face. He could not give in to it. Besides, Jalist's snoring roused his nerves as much as the echoes of his nightmare did.

He tried staring at the moon, focusing only on its gleaming craters, hoping the process would weary him—he'd learned the trick as a sellsword. But the light seemed oddly hollow. Finally, cursing, he sat up.

Igrid still had not returned. He wondered for a moment if she had left them—he would almost welcome that, though he would miss the sight of her. However, the pack containing her few possessions, mostly stolen, was still in the camp. Igrid would not have left anything behind.

Sitting up, he girded Knightswrath over his plain clothes. Again, the weight of the sword did not quite feel right, but he shook his head. He heard a faint rustle from below, by the pond. He headed toward it. The walk was a short one, but by the time he arrived, his heart thumped in his throat. He had some idea what he might find, but he could not stop himself from peering through the trees.

Igrid was bathing in the pond, thigh deep in dark waters lit by a sheen of moonlight. Her smallclothes were piled on the bank. Her back was to him, arched beautifully as she combed her fingers through her wet red hair.

Rowen blushed with shame and arousal, knowing he should leave. But she turned, naked and moonlit, and flashed him a crooked smile. "If you're going to stare, Sir Knight, at least come down and talk to me."

He tensed then shuffled forward awkwardly. "I'm sorry. I just... saw that you were gone and..."

"And you dashed off to rescue me from cutthroats, Olgrym, and sorcerers." She squeezed water from her hair, making no attempt to cover herself. "Naturally, you left in such a hurry that you didn't bother waking the others."

"I'm sorry..."

"Don't be. Glad I could distract you from the Dwarr's snoring."

Rowen smiled despite himself. He spotted a flat, mossy boulder sunk into the bank of the pond and leaned against it. It was soft, almost like a bed. He shook himself, vowing to look only at Igrid's eyes, but she had turned again. Water and moonlight cascaded down her backside.

"Feel free to join me," she called over one shoulder.

Rowen's heart leapt again, but he did not move. Suspicion blocked his excitement. "You're rather forward for a woman who tried to knife me less than a week ago."

Igrid cupped water in her hands, arched her back, and let the water run down between her shoulder blades. "I'm a woman of many moods. Tonight, I feel like apologizing." She turned sideways. Moonlight glittered off the jewel in her navel. "While you were asleep in the village, the Dwarr spoke of you. He said you'd been an orphan in Lyos. He even told me about your brother…"

Rowen shifted, suddenly angry. "Get to it, Igrid."

Igrid winced and folded her arms across her breasts. "You aren't what I thought you were. I'm sorry. That's all I wanted to say."

Rowen could not gauge her sincerity in the darkness, but he forced himself to laugh. "Well, Iron Sister, it seems you know more about me than I know about you. Is that a line you intend to hold?"

She turned her back to him and stirred her finger through the water. "What would you know of me, Sir Knight?" The sarcasm in her voice was unmistakable.

"For starters, how a thief and a whore became an Iron Sister." As soon as he spoke, he regretted the words.

Igrid dipped her hands in the water again. "I was an orphan, like you."

"Where were you born?"

She shrugged. "Cassica, maybe. I don't remember… except that wherever it was, I hated it."

Rowen watched the shadows of branches pass over her body like dark spears. "I'm sorry. I shouldn't have pressed. You don't have to tell me a damn thing if you don't want to."

The crooked smile returned. "Save your chivalrous apologies, Sir Knight. If I can face Dhargot steel without flinching, I should be able to mumble some honest words when called for. Still, there isn't much I can tell you about where I started out. Maybe my parents died. Maybe they just abandoned me. Either way, I was living on the streets by the time I was four or five. Some women at the local Temple of Dyoni took me to Phaegos, along with about a dozen other dirty brats. That wasn't too terrible until the Knights sacked the city for not paying taxes."

Rowen blushed. "I didn't have any part in that."

"Didn't say you did. Anyway, the clerics gave me my first name. At least, the first one I remember."

"What was it?"

"Anza." She shrugged. "Never cared for it. By the time I was eight or nine, I was back on the streets. Lived like that for a while, then a brothel owner took me in." She smirked again at Rowen's expression. "It wasn't like that. He just wanted to recruit as many pretty orphans as he could, so he'd have a fine roster once they grew up." She struggled with a tangle of hair then ripped it through without wincing. "I didn't have to... *entertain* for a few years yet. But he gave me a new name—Ilreeth—and took me to his brothel in Lyos."

Rowen smiled sadly. "We might have been there at the same time. I don't remember you, but I was down in the Dark Quarter. I couldn't even get into the real city without risking my life."

She continued as though she had not heard him. "I was... a whore until I was sixteen. The owner was worse than some, better than others. But I had food and clothes, not so many bruises, and the few coins he let me keep now and again." She shrugged. "It was what it was."

"What made you leave?"

She continued bathing as she spoke. "At the brothel, I entertained women as well as men. One was this delegate from Hesod. An Iron Sister. Some kind of officer, a captain, or something. She told me about their order." Igrid's lips formed a rare, slight smile, genuine and free of sarcasm. "An order of women who fought as well as men, who were free, well paid, and answered to no one but their queen. That sounded nice. I asked her to take me with her. She said she would. I snuck out that night to meet her at the gates. Only when I got there, the bitch had already left." She massaged a crick in her neck. "I actually thought she'd take me to Hesod. Gods, I was dumb! But I had brains enough not to go back to that brothel. I had a knife, some food, and a pouch of coins, so I set off on my own."

Rowen's eyes widened. "You traveled by yourself from Lyos to Hesod? That's—"

"A tough road. Merchants hire a half dozen guards to make that journey. But I had sense enough to travel at night and hide during the day. I got lucky."

She started toward the bank. Rowen's pulse quickened, but she was only getting her clothes. He forced himself to divert his gaze while she dressed. When he heard her moving again, he thought she was returning to the camp, but she joined him on the boulder.

"So there I was in Hesod—just another dirty orphan girl clamoring to join the Iron Sisters. There must have been two hundred of us, most just looking to get away from empty bellies or abusive husbands. But the Sisters aren't a charity. You have to prove yourself to get in. Then you have to work twice as hard to stay there. But I did it. They accepted me. I became an Iron Sister."

Rowen heard the pride in her voice. "Did you ever see the woman again, the captain?"

Igrid laughed. "Thank the gods, no! Maybe she got killed traveling from Lyos. Wouldn't have mattered anyway. I wasn't the same person. I was Igrid. That was my new name. That's who I was for two whole years."

"Before the Dhargots, you mean." Rowen instantly regretted saying it.

Igrid crossed her arms over her chest again. "Gods, it's cold! I thought I was used to it."

Rowen gave her his cloak.

She accepted it without comment. "The Dhargots sent an ambassador first—if that's the word for the kind of man they sent. Same kind of man as that bastard you killed. Only, unlike Atheion, we don't take kindly to threats. We killed him and returned his head to the empire."

"They killed a Dhargothi ambassador? Didn't they think there would be some kind of reprisal?"

"As I recall, Sir Knight, you beat a Dhargothi ambassador to death with a piece of armor. Turns out he was royalty, too. Were *you* worried about reprisal?" When he did not answer, she continued. "We were far from the empire, so close to the midlands that even the Throng hadn't troubled us. We were fortified. We thought we'd be all right."

But you weren't. Rowen could guess easily enough why Igrid of the Iron Sisters had become Haesha, a priestess of Dyoni, and fled southward. He knew he should let the matter drop. Instead, he heard himself saying, "There's no shame in what you did."

148

Igrid gave him a chilling look. "I asked for no absolution, Sir Knight. Least of all from a fellow orphan who carved the life out of his own brother."

Rowen tensed. With great effort, he pried his fingers off Knightswrath's hilt and forced a smile. "Good point." He stood. "I've intruded enough. Good evening, milady." He started to go.

Igrid grabbed his wrist. "Wait—"

Rowen broke free, but she grabbed him again. She was on her feet. Rowen tried a third time to pull away from her, terrified that she would see the tears in his eyes, but she kept after him, unrelenting. Dimly, he heard her apologizing over and over again. He kept trying to get away, then his strength failed him, and he wept. The air around him seemed to turn to ice, as cold as his nightmare.

He felt Igrid pulling him close, opening her borrowed cloak to let him in. The heat of her embrace startled him. He was even more startled when she kissed him. He hesitated a moment, oddly afraid, then gave in. She led him back to the mossy boulder, somehow laying him down without breaking their kiss. His cloak covered them both, blotting out even the moon.

"Igrid..."

"Shut up, Sir Knight."

And for a time, nothing separated them.

CHAPTER FIFTEEN
THE RED STEPPES

I GRID LAY ON THE MOSSY boulder, appreciating whatever act of chance made it curve to fit the shape of her back. She stared up at the moon then at the starry swirl of Armahg's Eye when the blue-black clouds parted. The latter made her shudder, considering what she was about to do. She lay there a moment longer, listening to the Knight's slow, even breathing. Then, very carefully, she untangled herself from his embrace.

She dressed quickly. She considered going back to the camp to retrieve her possessions first or to take a horse, but she decided against it. A horse could be tracked too easily, and she had no possessions really worth keeping. She eyed the sleeping nude figure of Rowen Locke a moment longer. She had to admit he was attractive—though not enough to make her stay.

"Sorry, Sir Knight." She stooped and drew his sword, leaving the scabbard behind. She was surprised by its weight. Its curved blade was as long as that of a longsword, but it felt lighter than any bastard sword she'd ever held. She took a moment to study the violet swirls and intricate carvings in the dragonbone hilt. She smiled. Even without the hilt, a true adamune from the Lotus Isles was worth more than most families saw in a lifetime. *With* the hilt, she would have more coins than she could carry.

Of course, she was breaking her word, but that didn't matter. She'd come with the Knight to get revenge on the Dhargots. They'd killed a handful of them in that Noshan village, including a Dhargothi royal.

That was enough for the time being. If she desired more revenge down the road, she could always track one or two and kill them in their sleep.

Still, guilt clawed at her as she girded the stolen sword. She considered circling the pond then changed her mind and waded across it, half hoping to rinse away her memory of the Knight's touch. She emerged from the waters and paused by the tree line opposite the campsite.

She remembered Silwren's spell, wondering if the Shel'ai would wake once Igrid crossed over. She doubted it. The stolen sleeproot she'd slipped into the wineskin, which she'd only pretended to drink from, should have been enough to make all three of them sleep like the dead. She might even have pried Rowen's fingers off the sword hilt and taken it while he slept had his nightmares not been enough to wake him.

I should not have told him so much. Why did I do that? She had even allowed herself to get angry, nearly driving him away and spoiling everything. Those were concerns for another day. She braced herself and ran. Stealth was no longer necessary. The trees blurred, shimmering past her in an odd trick of moonlight. She did not slow or turn around. On the grasslands, she broke into a sprint. The grass was cold and damp beneath her bare feet. In addition to her boots, she'd also left behind the bow Rowen had given her and the knife she'd stolen from the village. She had no weapons, save his sword, which she was not accustomed to wielding.

No matter. She could hide the sword, steal enough coins to buy shoes and another dagger, then make for Lyos and sell her prize. If the sword was really so precious to the Knights, surely they were willing to pay a tidy ransom for it.

Of course, she was not so foolish as to take it to the Lotus Isles directly. Once she set foot in one of the Knights' temple keeps, they would simply take the sword and likely kill her. But Lyos was a protectorate of the Knighthood, practically a part of their kingdom. She might find a delegate there who could take word of her bargain back to the Isles then return with the necessary price.

She considered the price as she traveled east, walking through grasslands lit by moonlight. The Isle Knights would deal in cranáfi, but coins were coins. A good sword cost fifty silvers—a fortune to most farmers and simplefolk but less than what that brothel owner in Lyos had made off her intimate labors in a single night. An adamune, on the other hand, might cost thrice that. One with a dragonbone hilt would fetch at least double that again. But Rowen's sword was also supposed to be the Sword of Fâyu Jinn, a powerful symbol and relic from ancient times.

Igrid doubled the figure twice more, for good measure. *Twelve hundred silvers...* She grinned. That was more than enough to open her own tavern or a brothel—maybe both—and plenty of bodyguards besides.

Then she had a new thought. Rowen Locke was a Knight of the Crane—the lowest of the three orders, sure, but he wore the Sword of Fâyu Jinn. If he survived his foolhardy mission into the Wytchforest, surely he would be promoted to Knight of the Stag. Perhaps he would even be a Knight of the Lotus one day. That meant he would have an entire temple and a garrison at his command. The wife of such a man would be powerful, too...

No, that won't do. With or without the sword, Rowen was a crusader. If the Sylvs didn't kill him, surely the Olgrym, the Dhargots, or the Shel'ai would.

The thought of the Shel'ai sent a chill down her spine. Silwren wielded an even greater power, reminiscent of the ancient Dragonkin. Surely she would help Rowen pursue Igrid. She wondered if she had acted too hastily. But they would have arrived at the Wytchforest soon, and she could not have stolen it then.

I could have taken it while we were still in the village, before Silwren returned, while Rowen was healing... but I didn't. Why?

She decided to fix her thoughts on her journey. Best she avoid the Dhargots, the Noshans, the Lochurites, and everyone else, for that matter. That meant traveling only at night, as she had when she left Lyos for Hesod, so long ago. She shuddered. As before, if cutthroats and rapists set upon her, no one would come to her rescue.

Won't matter. I'm different now. Stronger.

She hugged the sword to her, drawing strength from its weight.

She lowered her head and pressed on, toward Lyos. When the knot in her stomach felt like two interwoven serpents—one guilt, the other fear—she blamed it on hunger and quickened her pace.

Shortly before dawn, she came upon a village in the distance, which was little more than a cluster of shacks near a sheep pen. A cord was strung between one shack and an empty storehouse whose door was simply an open wall. Someone had carelessly left drying clothes splayed out on the cord. She hesitated, glancing down at her own attire. The low-cut tunic and tight britches had been successful in catching Rowen's eye, but they were not so good or practical for a woman traveling alone through lands giving way to autumn.

She saw no guards or dogs, but she still moved stealthily as she crept up to the clothesline and took what she wanted. She scouted around and even found a woman's boots, left outside the door of a shack. They were unimpressive, dirty and weakly sewn from poorly tanned leather, but Igrid took them anyway.

Ducking behind an empty storehouse, she stripped off her old clothes. She shivered as the morning air chilled her skin, but her new clothes were warmer. She used her old clothes to fashion a crude scabbard for Knightswrath and made a belt from strips of cloth. She'd even found a plain cloak that would give her a little more warmth and help conceal the sword girded about her thin waist.

She was about to set off again when she remembered her hunger. Though she knew she was pressing her luck, she searched the hamlet's storehouses until she found one that wasn't empty. All it contained were a few sacks of paupers' root. She grimaced. Paupers' root tasted only a little better than urusk meat, but it was better than nothing. She took what she could carry and set off again.

As she was leaving, she heard an angry shout behind her. She flashed a coy smile over one shoulder and ran. When she was well away, she slowed to eat. Her stomach tightened as she chewed and swallowed the bitter roots, but she felt better once her belly was full.

By then, the rising sun cast a red-gold sheen over the hills and grasslands before her. She felt the muscles in her legs turning to stone and knew it was time for her to sleep. She had to find a place to hide first. But all she saw for miles were more hills and grasslands.

Cursing, she trudged on, then eventually surrendered to her weariness and chose a place where the grass grew higher. She lay down, covering herself—and the sword—with her new cloak. She closed her eyes and was asleep almost instantly. She slept lightly and woke often, often clawing the sword hilt and half drawing the blade as she looked around.

Better this than nightmares. She stayed there as long as she could bear it then rose at midday. She forced down the last of the stolen paupers' root and pressed on. She felt horribly thirsty. She headed east, hoping at least to find a stream or a better place to hide. She tried to remember the last time she had looked at a map, wondering if any cities were nearby. She would be foolish to take the sword anywhere it could be seen, but she could always hide it, slip in and cut a few purse strings, then return for the sword and be on her way.

She traveled for hours and met nothing of consequence—no cities, not even a farmhouse or another little hamlet. Late in the afternoon, she froze in her tracks and looked down. The grasslands seemed to wilt into rougher soil spotted with thick deposits of red clay. She frowned at the eastern horizon, realizing that the distant hills looked faintly crimson, too. She cursed.

The Red Steppes. Gods, no wonder there's nothing here! She shook her head. She'd veered too far south. The Red Steppes were barren, practically uninhabited save for a few exiled tribes of Dwarrs. South of the steppes were the Stillhammer Mountains, the Dwarrs' ancestral homeland. Neither place would offer her any help or hospitality.

Wait, this can't be... The Red Steppes were almost directly south of Lyos. That meant she could not be more than two or three days from her destination. But she had only been traveling one day. She could not have crossed so much of the sprawling Simurgh Plains so quickly.

She knelt and examined the soil. The red clay was unmistakable. No other realm in Ruun had it. She straightened, turned, and even thought she could see the gray-white blur of the Stillhammer Mountains, far to the south. She trembled.

How could this—"Silwren..."

154

The Shel'ai must have bewytched her somehow. Igrid rubbed her eyes. She remembered the way the trees had blurred as she raced from the camp and how suddenly quiet everything had seemed. Silwren must have used the same kind of magic that had spirited Igrid out of her jail cell to move her farther east, nearly all the way across the plains, far from Rowen.

"You weren't asleep at all," she whispered to the empty air. "You watched him bedding me. Then when you saw your chance, you spirited me as far away from him as you could." Knightswrath still hung from her waist. She touched the sword. Her frown deepened.

"Why let me keep the sword?" She puzzled over that until her grumbling stomach captured her attention. She turned north and started walking again. *I suppose I should thank you. You shaved a week off my journey when you should have turned me to cinders!* She tried to laugh, but the sound died in her throat. She found herself shaking. She clasped her cloak with one hand and kept the other on her sword hilt as she started running.

Not long after, Igrid stumbled upon an orchard of wild fruit trees. She was so hungry that she nearly wept with gratitude. She did not recognize the small blue-black fruits, but they were pleasantly sweet. She ate all she could, wiping the juices from her chin. She knotted up her cloak and filled it with more fruits to take with her. The juice from the fruits had helped sate her thirst, too, but she was still grateful when she came across a stream.

It was barely a trickle, but she drank thirstily. Glancing around to make sure she was alone, she stripped off her clothes and bathed as the sun set. When she was done, she waded out of the red water and wrung the water from her hair. Then she turned and realized she was not alone.

A wide-eyed girl stood on the banks of the stream, staring at her. Igrid did not think the girl could have been older than fourteen, though her belly was round and obviously in the late months of pregnancy. The girl was quite homely and wore dirty patchwork clothes. One hand carried an empty wicker basket.

155

Igrid saw Knightswrath on the bank of the stream, still covered by her cloak, and rushed toward it. She knew she had nothing to fear from an unarmed pregnant girl, but she had no desire to chase after her should the girl decide to steal her possessions.

Igrid brushed aside the cloak and snatched up the sword. It fairly leapt from the crude scabbard, gleaming in the setting sun. "Get out of here," Igrid told the girl.

The girl did not move. "I didn't mean to stare at you with no clothes on. I's just going to pick berries when I saw you. Haven't seen anybody else here for ages, years probably." She hesitated. "You're prettier than Ma."

Igrid frowned. She wondered if the girl was feebleminded. She sheathed the sword but kept it close at hand. Then she dried off with her cloak and dressed. The girl's eyes did not leave her. Igrid was accustomed to being stared at—she even used it to her advantage whenever possible—but the girl's stare made her uncomfortable.

"Your clothes are wrong for you," the girl said finally. She tugged at her own clothes, as though Igrid simply did not know what the word meant. "They're too big. I got clothes you could have. They's Ma's, but she won't mind 'cause she's with the gods."

Igrid knew she could use a different outfit, but the girl made her uncomfortable. "I don't want your dead mother's clothes, child. Now run along." Igrid tugged on her boots, wincing as she did so. The girl was right. The boots were too big for her, too, and had shifted oddly as she walked, blistering her feet.

"We gots spare boots. You can have thems, too!"

Igrid considered shoving past the girl and heading on her way, but she eyed the girl's empty basket. "Are you from a village nearby?"

The girl cocked her head, confused.

Igrid sighed and tried again. "Who do you live with?"

"My Da. That's it. Nobody else this far south. Or north, I guess, if you's lived in the south." She paused. "I had a little brother, but he died coming out of Ma. That made her die, too."

Igrid doubted such wretched people had anything worth stealing. Still, if there was a house nearby, that might prove a better shelter than the grove of fruit trees. She gave the girl her best charming smile. "Do you think your father would shelter me for the night if you asked?"

"Ain't sheltered nobody for years. No travelers here. Closest village a ways north, but they don't come down here. Plus the roof leaks when it rains. But it likely won't rain tonight. You should stay. But I gots to fill my basket first, or he'll beat me awful." The girl headed for the orchard without awaiting a reply.

Igrid bit back a curse and followed her.

CHAPTER SIXTEEN

BRAHASTI'S PLAN

B RAHASTI EL TARQ REINED IN his horse and smiled. The
scouts had been right. The citizens of Cassica—conquered
only months ago by the Throng, only to have their conscripts
returned when the Throng was disbanded—had learned from its
mistakes. It was said that Cassica had been a mighty stronghold in
ages past, rivaling even Lyos and Syros. But its defenses had fallen
into disrepair over the years, especially after Fadarah's legions swept
in.

Since then, the people of Cassica had repaired the gates that the
Nightmare had smashed, along with all the damaged sections of the
wall. They had even reinforced the gates with a heavy iron portcullis.
A steep mound of earth surrounded the city, making it more difficult
for an enemy to tunnel beneath the walls or approach them with siege
towers. Furthermore, the Cassicans had built wooden platforms draped
with shields and animal hides that extended from the battlements,
emboldened with arrow-slits. Thanks to the additional fortifications,
no attacker could approach Cassica's walls without coming under
heavy crossbow fire from all sides.

And that has the Bloody Prince worried—though he'd never say so.

Brahasti lifted his gaze over the distant city's battlements and
saw that Cassica had its own engines of war: catapults, ballistae,
trebuchets, and steaming cauldrons likely already filled with boiling
water—maybe even boiling piss—ready to be up-ended on the heads
of attackers. He turned to face the roiling legions behind him.

The Bloody Prince rode ahead of his cavalry and gave him a scathing look. Brahasti had deliberately ridden ahead of the Bloody Prince as they neared the city, in full view of the rest of the Dhargothi legions, usurping Karhaati's place of honor. Brahasti had been exiled from the empire for years, but not so long that he failed to recognize the insult he had just dealt. Surely that insult was made worse by the fact that Brahasti looked nothing like a Dhargothi warrior.

In place of armor, Brahasti wore silk robes sewn not with the sigil of the dragon impaled on a spear but the crimson greatwolf. Unlike other Dhargots, who shaved their heads and grew braided goatees, he was clean shaven with a full head of dark hair. He was not even wearing a sword.

Brahasti knew that the Bloody Prince wanted to kill him, but the prince did not yet have the courage to disobey Fadarah's orders. Still, Fadarah's commands did not prohibit Karhaati from angling his armored destrier frightfully close to Brahasti's horse, leaning, and backhanding him with one mailed hand. Brahasti accepted the blow, spat blood, and concealed a grin. He knew he'd made his point.

The Bloody Prince removed his half-helm, an extravagant thing of steel and brass crowned with the visage of an impaled dragon, and scowled at the city. Even as the Dhargothi legions unfurled before the city, Cassica's gates and portcullis slammed shut. Dark figures manned the battlements, crowned in glinting half-helms of their own.

Brahasti considered the reports they had received from spies: Cassica had a thousand defenders, less than one-twentieth of the force he commanded. But well-provisioned, well-fortified cities had been known to last for months against equally dismal odds.

Karhaati said, "Fadarah should have lent us magic. I want to be washing my sword in the blood of Noshans or Islemen, not overseeing some tedious siege!"

"May I remind you, Sire, that Ivairia is directly north of us. You may not wish to show the Ivairians your backside for that long."

The Bloody Prince glowered at him. "I fear the Ivairians even less than I fear you. Every report says they're holed up in their keeps, frightened and hungry."

"Every report but the last one."

159

Karhaati shrugged. "Fifty lancers, maybe another fifty squires. A scouting force, nothing more. The Ivairians are too sickly and scared to care what happens—"

"On their own border?" Brahasti laughed. "They might have minded their own business when it was the Throng razing their neighbors to the south, but your army consists of flesh and blood, not magic and Nightmares. If they think they'll have to cross swords with a Dhargothi host sooner or later, they might decide to do it while your back is turned."

Karhaati scowled. "Fadarah never said we would have to fight the Lancers."

"Why should he? You battle his rivals in the northlands while he deals with his own in the west. Do you think he cares whether you lose ten men or ten thousand?"

The rage melted from Karhaati's eyes. "But he needs my help to take the Wytchforest—"

"So he does. But he doesn't want you so strong that he can't keep you under his boot."

Karhaati grunted his agreement. Nevertheless, he eyed Brahasti with mistrust. "Am I to believe that *you* care how many Dhargots die in the name of the empire?"

"Fadarah makes enemies the way your elephants' shit draws flies. Should he one day end up dead, I would avail myself to the great man left standing."

Karhaati turned, scrutinizing the deployment of the aforementioned war elephants that were, in fact, leaving a trail of shit and flies behind them. "If you aim for my friendship and loyalty, Earless One, you're an archer in dire need of practice."

"I aim for neither. I'll settle for grudging appreciation for my talents."

"So far, the only talents you've displayed involve drinking my wine and raping my slaves."

Brahasti smiled. "Then I shall prove myself right now. This is what you should do. And instead of ordering the men myself, I'll let you do it and claim credit." He paused. "Send three hundred men to ride down the Ivairians. Tell them to take prisoners, drag them north, strip them naked, and leave them impaled on the Ivairian frontier. The Ivairians know a warning when they see it."

Karhaati stroked his goatee idly. "A warning… or a challenge?"

Brahasti gestured to the massive host behind them. "You have over twenty thousand swords here! Your brothers have thousands more, just a few days behind us."

Karhaati bristled at the mention of brothers, whom he, in true Dhargothi fashion, viewed as competitors. "We still have this city to contend with. My elephants and chariots won't be much use against those walls. We could sling battering rams between the elephants, but—"

"Even their armor won't protect them from ballistae. Besides, elephants panic at the sight of fire."

Karhaati's painted eyes narrowed. "Then what does Fadarah's lapdog suggest?"

A great orchard growing against one of Cassica's walls drew Brahasti's attention. The boughs were thick with songbirds. From his vantage point, he could see over the walls, to a sea of wooden rooftops. Many more songbirds had roosted within the city. He imagined the Cassicans found the birds quaint, charming even, though to Brahasti's ears, the beasts sounded hungry.

"Dear prince," he said with deliberate slowness, "I suggest you prepare slave pens. And a tent full of wine and whores for me. Cassica will be yours by nightfall. But first, I need raw meat and fifty men with nets."

Karhaati frowned. "You've piqued my curiosity, Earless One. I don't know what you're planning, but choose your men and be on with it."

Brahasti moved quickly, filled with dreadful excitement. He chose his men, pointed at the orchard, and issued his orders. Then he turned to another man. "Fetch twigs, small ones, and string. Then prepare a fire."

By sundown, half the rooftops of Cassica were ablaze. Brahasti's men were still tying burning twigs soaked in pitch to the feet of the songbirds they had caught. Once released, the frantic, burning creatures screeched up into the sky. They arced over the walls then either shuddered from the impact of crossbow bolts or succumbed to the flames and plummeted onto the wooden rooftops.

While the city's frantic defenders were busy battling fires and trying to shoot birds from the sky, Karhaati's siege engines rolled forward, battering the gates and flinging even more fire over the battlements. Within two hours, it was over. A horn sounded, signaling Cassica's surrender. The gates of Cassica swung open. Brahasti watched. Beside him, Karhaati shook his head. For the moment, grudging admiration had replaced the Bloody Prince's loathing. "I misjudged you, General..."

Brahasti said, "The city is yours. I trust you've already filled my tent with the appropriate awards?" He waited for Karhaati to nod then turned his horse and rode off.

CHAPTER SEVENTEEN

THE FIRST LANCER

IGRID RELUCTANTLY FOLLOWED THE GIRL to the orchard, helped her fill the basket with fruit, then volunteered to carry it back to the farmhouse. When she asked the girl's name, the girl did not answer, so Igrid asked again. After two more attempts, Igrid began to wonder if the girl's parents had ever even bothered to name her.

Igrid's pulse quickened. She began to suspect what she would find at the farmhouse. She wished she weren't carrying the basket so she could loosen her sword.

Twilight darkened the road before her. Igrid felt her unease grow with each step. The girl seemed eager to ask her questions about her travels—what she did and what realms she had seen—but she clearly lacked the vocabulary to phrase her questions. Igrid strained to understand her and to keep from losing her temper. She reminded herself that a night's shelter from the wilderness was well worth the sacrifice.

Gods, the girl stinks, though! Igrid considered setting down the basket and tossing the girl in the stream, pretending it was some kind of game, but the girl hinted that her father was waiting and would be angry if she did not return home as quickly as possible.

When they reached the girl's home, Igrid stopped in her tracks. It was a small, simple dung hut with one uneven hole where a window should have been. The patches of dead grass that served as a yard were scattered with the bones of dead animals, probably the rabbits, urusks, and wild dogs they'd turned into suppers. A turnip garden was nearby, shabby and ill tended, but no privy. Flies and a putrid smell hung over the place like a funeral pall.

"You... *live* here?"

Before the girl could reply, her father appeared in the doorway. He was a small man, but the dung hut wasn't much taller than he was, so he had to stoop to exit and glare at her. When he saw that his daughter was not alone, he leaned back into the dung hut and withdrew a rusty hatchet. Igrid could not understand the curse he spat at his daughter. The girl took the basket from Igrid, gave her a warning look, and hurried inside. Igrid bristled when the man patted the girl's rump as she passed. Then the father turned to face Igrid.

One of the man's eyes was a sickly milk-white color, but the suspicion in his good eye was obvious. Forcing herself to smile, she opened her cloak. The man's suspicion give way to arousal once he'd studied her more closely. Though Igrid was no longer sure she even wanted to stay in the hut, she concealed her revulsion and smiled again.

"Good evening. I met your daughter by the stream. She said I might have your hospitality for the night."

The man either did not understand or was too preoccupied by staring at her bosom and wet, clingy clothes. She fought the impulse to close her cloak. She repeated herself, simplifying her phrasing. "Can I stay the night?"

The man scratched an unkempt beard. "You want to stay *here?*"

No. But Igrid realized, unexpectedly, that she did not have the heart to leave the girl. "Just for the night. I can pay you in the morning," she lied, but she intended to be gone before he woke.

The man was silent for a moment, wobbling a little as he stood there. She wondered if he was drunk. She had known many simplefolk to make their own wine out of fruits, usually putrid stuff that could be poisonous but succeeded at least in numbing the dreariness of their station. The man's lips cracked into a toothless grin, and she guessed what was coming next.

"You want to stay the night, you lay with me."

Igrid could not suppress a shudder of revulsion. She was glad her hands were free, though she managed with great restraint to keep from drawing her sword and cleaving the vile man's head in two. Instead, she crossed her arms and shook her head firmly. "No."

The man spat on the ground and brandished the hatchet. "Then go."

The girl appeared again. She squeezed her father's arm and whispered something in his ear, casting Igrid a sidelong glance. The man relaxed, and the hatchet came down. He pushed his daughter back inside the hut and gestured for Igrid to follow.

Igrid took a step backward, then the girl's face peeked out of the hut. The child's imploring gaze was so desperately lonely that tears sprang to Igrid's eyes.

Maybe the girl doesn't want to stay here. She can't. Maybe I should kill the bastard and take the girl to some temple in Lyos. She flexed her fingers on the dragonbone hilt of Rowen's sword. She wondered what the Isle Knight would do in her place.

The man stared at her. She turned her back on him and started walking. She listened carefully, in case he charged her. When she heard a heavy rumbling sound, she spun and drew her sword, but the man was still standing in the doorway. He looked as confused as she felt. She listened.

Horses... She thought for one fearful moment that Rowen had caught up with her. But no, the hooves sounded more like an army. She turned west, in the direction of the sound, but trees blocked her view. She hurried forward to get a better look. Out of the corner of her eye, she saw the man and his daughter join her, but she paid them no mind. "Gods..."

At least a hundred riders thundered across the grasslands. The first half of them wore full armor. Some wore bright, colorful tabards over their armor. They were unmistakably knights, but not Isle Knights. They looked nothing like Rowen. Their armor was heavier, and each armored man carried a long wooden lance tipped in steel, a bright pennant tied at the end. Squires dressed in brigandines and armed with shortswords worked to keep pace with the knights. Most hauled two or three more lances under one arm.

Igrid squinted, trying to discern a sigil in the waning light. She saw a profile of a rearing horse topped with a crown. She almost could not believe her eyes. *What are Ivairians doing this far south?* They were obviously in a hurry. The hooves of their horses kicked up a fierce cloud of dirt and grass as they tore across the plains. In the Lancers' wake, a second column rode in breakneck pursuit. These men wore the distinctive scale armor and black silk of Dhargothi warriors. She even thought she spotted a force of chariots some distance behind the riders. She could not see them very well through the chaos, but she imagined the horse-drawn carts were crowded with archers and spearmen.

This is going to be bloody. The Lancers and squires were outnumbered. Even slowed down by their weighty armor, they might outrun the Dhargothi chariots—especially if they sacrificed their heavily laden squires as a rearguard—but they would not escape the cavalry nipping at their heels. The Lancers seemed to sense that.

The column abruptly whirled about. Lancers and squires expertly regrouped into one fierce knot of muscle, leather, and steel then thundered down on the advancing Dhargothi cavalry. Igrid felt the pregnant girl draw close to her. Unthinking, Igrid found her hand and squeezed it.

Both winced as the Lancers and the Dhargots met in a head-on collision of wood and steel. Horses screamed. Lances splintered. Men fell on both sides, cleaved and bloody, dark flailing shapes in the twilight. But even outnumbered, the main force of Lancers drove clear through the Dhargots' center. Meanwhile, the squires closed in with shortswords drawn, hacking at wounded Dhargots or dismounting and stabbing them while they were still dazed. Others utilized the extra lances they were carrying for their lords, driving them through scale armor and flesh.

Igrid resisted the impulse to run out and join them. Meanwhile, rather than wheel about and clash once more with the Dhargothi cavalry, the Lancers tightened ranks and continued their charge against the chariots. Igrid realized their mistake at once. Had the Lancers pressed their assault against the Dhargothi horsemen, the archers in the oncoming chariots would have been hard-pressed to find a clear target in the swirling chaos. But as a single group, the

Lancers were easy targets. A few were still couching lances, but most relied on swords and shields.

Igrid heard the snap of bows over the din of battle. She winced again, expecting to see the Ivairians cut to ribbons. To her surprise, though, the Lancers' heavy plate armor protected them from most of the arrows. A few fell, but most hurtled on, shouting, and crashed into the line of chariots before the latter could steer clear.

The pregnant girl covered her eyes, even as her father stared through the trees, grinning wildly. Igrid watched anxiously.

The Ivairian squires were in trouble. The Dhargothi cavalry had regrouped in force and was having little trouble cutting down the lightly armored boys assailing them. Moments later, the squires attempted to flee, some on horseback, others on foot.

Three Ivairian squires, all on foot, raced in the direction of the hut. Even in the thin light of dusk, Igrid could make out the terror on their faces. She counted five Dhargots on horseback bearing down on them. Two of the squires threw away their swords, perhaps thinking that would dissuade their pursuers, but the Dhargots continued on.

Igrid gauged the distance—the squires would be dead long before they reached the shelter of trees. That meant the Dhargots would not see Igrid, the girl, and her father watching. "Look away," she told the girl, who was still clinging to her.

Then she heard a new rallying cry. Most of the Lancers were still clashing with the Dhargothi charioteers, but a handful had regrouped and were rushing to aid their embattled squires. One rode ahead of the rest to intercept the Dhargots pursuing the three squires. He had a fresh lance under one arm, though she had no idea how he'd gotten it. Unlike the other Lancers, his armor was finely enameled. She suspected he was their leader. He shouted, challenging the Dhargots to face him.

The Dhargots reined in. If they pressed on and slew the three squires, the knight charging from behind would have the advantage. They could turn and kill the madman first then slay the rest.

The Lancer never slowed. The Dhargots had barely turned before the Lancer angled his horse to the Dhargots' right flank, urging even more speed from his mount. The Dhargots tried to angle around his lance, but he swept it in a carefully controlled arc and drove it clean through a Dhargot's chest. The lance splintered. He let it go and drew his sword.

Steel flashed, flushed with blood. The Lancer blurred by, gracefully cleaving another Dhargot from the saddle as though the latter were standing still. Then the Lancer turned, swinging wide. Igrid thought he was leading them back to the rest of the battle. Instead, the Lancer wheeled so sharply that he nearly collided with his pursuers.

As Igrid lost sight of the man, another chorus of screams and clashing steel rang out, seemingly just as furious as the larger battle. The fleeing squires, meanwhile, raced back to help the embattled knight who had saved them.

Igrid's hand strayed to Knightswrath's hilt. *No, this isn't my fight.* She thought for certain that the lone Lancer had been cut down, but she spotted him... on foot, hacking with his broadsword through a forest of Dhargothi horse legs. The Lancer broke free, turned back to the screaming mass of Dhargots, and resumed hacking. The three squires joined him a moment later.

Igrid turned her gaze back to the larger battle. The Lancers had reinforced their squires. The Dhargots still had superior numbers, but their thinner scale armor could not withstand the Lancers' bastard and two-handed swords. The Lancers' heavy armor could, however, withstand a flurry of blows, though its weight made it harder for them to maneuver. The thick, swirling chaos of the battle also made it impossible for them to withdraw and launch another devastating charge.

She glanced west. The last curve of sunlight had dipped below the horizon. It was so dark that she wondered how any of the fighting men could tell friend from foe, yet still the screams and metallic reverberations echoed across the bloody grasslands.

The father grabbed the girl's arm. "We go." He pulled the girl after him. They disappeared through the trees, presumably returning to their wretched hut.

Igrid stayed where she was. She knew it wasn't safe at the hut. If a few Lancers or Dhargots broke off or fled the fighting, there was no telling what they would do. She had seen what the Dhargots had done at Hesod, and she had no reason to believe the Ivairians were much better.

She touched Knightswrath's hilt again. She had never wielded an adamune before, but she figured the basic principle with curved blades was the same as the basic principle of straight ones: carve up the enemy before getting carved up.

Then, in the distance, a line of shadowy figures slipped away from the battle and weaved through the trees. She was relieved when she saw the deserters follow the tree line and head north, away from the dung hut. But they changed their minds. She wondered why until she heard the pregnant girl's voice echoing, sharp and shrill, from the dung hut. She was arguing with her father.

The others had heard it, too. Igrid cursed. She could not make out the distant figures, but she guessed by their dark silhouettes that they were Dhargots. She glanced at the battlefield. The Dhargothi charioteers had been massacred by the Lancers early in the fighting, maybe two hundred yards from where she stood. Surely, bows and spears had been left on the field.

Ducking low, Igrid crept out of her thin cover of trees and began to circle the field, giving it a wide berth. Luckily, the fighting had mostly shifted northward, away from her destination. As she drew nearer, she tried to block out the whimpers of dying men. She spotted a Dhargothi archer lying prone on the grass. Heart pounding, she dashed toward him and snatched up his bow. She tried to take his quiver, but the strap was hopelessly tangled with his body, so she grabbed a handful of arrows. Then she ran back toward the tree line.

Once she reached the trees, she glanced north. The battle raged on in the field. Eerie moonlight revealed only brief glimpses of glinting steel and desperate, struggling figures. Igrid turned toward the dung hut.

What am I doing? Why risk your life here?

Nevertheless, she nocked one arrow and slipped the rest into her crude belt. It was nearly pitch black beneath the swaying darkness of the tree limbs, but she knew she would have no trouble finding the dung hut. All she had to do was follow the screams.

She resisted the impulse to make a mad dash toward the sound. If she was going to be of any help to anyone, she would need the element of surprise. She spotted the dark outline of the dung hut just ahead. She slowed even further, crouching low, and tested the draw of her bow.

She felt morbidly relieved when she saw that the men were raping the girl on the ground outside the dung hut, rather than inside. That meant they were easier targets. She leaned against a tree and lifted her bow. She took a moment to study her targets.

They were not Dhargots after all. Two Lancers loomed over the girl. They had stripped off most of their armor. Three eager squires were assisting them. A third Lancer milled in the distance, fuming with disapproval but clearly unwilling to intervene.

Igrid wondered for a moment if the father could assist her, or had the vile man fled for his life? Then she spotted him lying motionless near the doorway of the dung hut with a bloody stain on his back. Igrid relaxed her bowstring. As much as she pitied the poor girl, she could do nothing to help her. Even if Igrid fired at one of the rapists then ran, hoping to lure them away, she couldn't be sure all the men would follow or even if she could get away from them. Best she focus on safeguarding her own skin.

She repeated that reasoning to herself, certain of the logic, even as she raised her bow, drew back the arrow, and let it fly.

The Lancer on top of the girl suddenly howled and straightened, an arrow between his shoulder blades. Igrid snickered, nocked a second arrow, and fired.

The wounded Lancer toppled, a second arrow in his side, near the liver. Igrid fought down a surge of panic as the other men spotted her. She aimed and fired a third time as they turned. One of the squires staggered and fell to his knees. He was hurt, but not mortally wounded. Igrid backed up, reaching for a fourth arrow. The disapproving Lancer charged her, sword drawn.

She swiveled the bow and fired, but the arrow rebounded harmlessly off the man's gorget. The Lancer swung. Igrid had no time to draw her own sword. She swung the bow instead, knocking aside the blade. Then she used the bow like a quarterstaff and gave the charging knight a resounding blow on his chest. Still, the man did not slow. The sword flew again. Igrid ducked and rolled.

She hoped for a clear line of escape, but the others had cut her off. She was surrounded. A squire, half naked, lunged at her. Igrid sidestepped, drove her bow into the man's privates, then kicked him in the head when he doubled over. Another man, the other raping Lancer, charged her. He swung his fist at her.

Igrid sank, hooked one hand around the man's waist, and used his momentum to topple him over her knee. She shoved her last arrow into his neck as hard as she could, wrenching it from side to side for good measure, carving a ghastly hole. "Fuck *that*, you bastard," she hissed in his ear.

The final squire tackled her. The man had her by the arms. He was strong, but Igrid managed to stretch out one leg and use it for leverage. She put her shoulder under his chin and drove him to the side. He lost one of her wrists. That was all Igrid needed. She thrust her fingers into the man's eyes. The man howled, releasing her other wrist. She stepped back, snatched up her bow, gripped it like a spear, and went for the fallen squire's throat.

But the final, disapproving Lancer stepped between them. Moonlight flashed off his sword as he cleaved her bow in two. Igrid backpedaled, reaching for Knightswrath. The Lancer followed, too close. He held the sword at her breasts, close enough to prick her clothes.

"Yield," he grunted in a low voice.

"Go fuck an Olg." She sidestepped and started to draw the sword, but the Lancer was faster. He drove the pommel of his sword toward Igrid's face. She managed to duck, but the blow struck her forehead.

The next thing she knew, she was lying on the ground. A crescent moon hovered over her, floating next to Armahg's Eye. Both began to darken. *No. If I sleep now, I die.* She tried to rise.

Then a man was on top of her—the squire she had just injured. Blood poured from his nose. He gave her a horrible look, all murder and amusement, and began tearing at her clothes. She tried to fight him, but her hands felt leaden. Too slow, too weak.

Dimly, she saw the disapproving Lancer draw closer. The knight scowled and shouted for the squire to stop. The squire either did not hear or had no intention of obeying. Igrid turned her head the other way. The other two squires, wounded but still alive, were approaching. One had withdrawn the arrow from his side and pressed one hand to the wound. The Lancer shouted something at them, but both squires had armed themselves and shouted back.

Igrid fumbled at her waist. Her fingers closed over the hilt of her sword. Her enemy was right on top of her, breathing right in her face, but she thought she might at least bash his face with the pommel. The squire realized what she was trying and slapped her. He said something she could not understand. She felt cold night air on her skin.

You know what to do... Igrid retreated within herself, falling and falling. She imagined she was dressed and armored, behind high walls. She would stay there, safe, until they were finished. But the squire did not touch her again. One gauntleted fist grabbed the man by the throat and hauled him away. The squire's eyes widened, and he gasped. Igrid blinked. She watched the squire slowly slide off a blood-stained bastard sword, as though the steel were blossoming from his chest.

She looked up. The disapproving Lancer had not saved her. The knight she had seen before, the one in gilded armor, had dismounted. His helmet was gone, and his horse waited restlessly in the distance, along with a dozen more armored men. He was middle-aged with sandy, sweat-damp hair. He glanced at her before turning his attention to the others.

The final Lancer and the two squires stood at attention, eyes and weapons lowered. The man in gilded armor took a menacing step toward them. He gave the squires a cold look then turned to the final Lancer. "Sir Geoffrey, will you assist me in rendering justice on these men?"

The Lancer hesitated. "Sir Arnil, please—"

The man in gilded armor silenced him with a stern look. "You know the penalty for desertion... not to mention the *rest* of this." He pointed at the corpse lying in the doorway of the dung hut and the grubby girl, who was sitting up, dazed, pulling weakly at her torn clothes. "I dare you to say otherwise."

The remaining squires looked at each other, panic in their eyes. Neither made any attempt to deny the charges. One fell to his knees and began pleading for his life. Another opened his mouth, but before he could speak, Sir Geoffrey cleaved the head from his shoulders. Sir Arnil approached the pleading man and beheaded him while he was still kneeling.

Arnil faced the final Lancer. "Sir Geoffrey, by all rights, you should die for this, too."

The shamefaced Lancer glanced at Igrid. "Pardon, Sir Arnil, but I didn't kill the father, and I laid no hand on these women. I just watched." When Sir Arnil did not answer, Geoffrey said, "We're well beyond Ivairia's borders. There are no laws—"

Arnil slapped the man across the face. The gilded knight was of average build, smaller than Sir Geoffrey, but Igrid could tell at once that the latter feared him. Sir Geoffrey took the blow and bowed, making no effort to raise his sword.

Sir Arnil stepped back. Igrid followed his gaze to the pregnant girl. She had crawled over to her father's corpse and was shaking him. Then she stood and kicked him. She looked confused when he did not answer.

The gilded knight turned to Igrid. "I am Arnil Royce, First Lancer to the King of Ivairia. You have my apologies. This should not have happened."

She had prepared to give him a biting remark, but the sight of the girl kicking her dead father had driven the words from her mind.

Arnil continued. "It is forbidden to strike a Lancer, let alone kill two of them. My men would probably rather I kill you, as well. But as Sir Geoffrey says, this is not Ivairia. And it seems there are… extenuating circumstances here." He removed a rag from his belt and wiped the blood from his blade.

He faced the other Lancer. "You may not be a killer and a raper, but you *are* a deserter. However, the Dhargots are still out there. They'll regroup and attack again. I offer you a chance to redeem yourself."

Sir Geoffrey glanced past his commander, at the other scowling knights, then bowed again. "Thank you, sir. Should I survive, I will submit myself happily to the king's justice."

Igrid was about to ask what that entailed and protest if she found it inadequate, but Sir Arnil scoffed. "May you live so long." He gestured for the Lancer to rejoin the others then turned back to Igrid.

Before he could speak, another knight tore through the trees and rushed toward Arnil. The man dismounted in such a hurry that he hardly acknowledged the scene before him before whispering in the First Lancer's ear.

The Ivairian commander blanched. He returned to his horse and quickly hauled himself up into the saddle. "Another squad of Dhargots has reinforced the survivors of the first. They are bearing down on us. We must gain a better position and prepare for a countercharge, or we are all dead men!"

In an instant, the other Lancers forgot all about Igrid, let alone the dead man lying on the grass and the stunned, bloody girl standing over him. They wheeled and rode on through the trees, vanishing in the night. Igrid edged toward the girl, keeping her eyes on Arnil Royce, who remained behind.

The First Lancer faced Igrid. She followed his gaze to the exquisite dragonbone hilt of the adamune at her side. His eyes widened.

She braced herself, expecting the First Lancer to demand answers: How had a peasant woman come by such a weapon? Had she stolen it? Perhaps he would even try and take it for himself. Surely, he recognized that it was worth a fortune, perhaps even beyond his station, let alone hers. But the First Lancer merely sighed, withdrew a pouch from his belt, and tossed it at the pregnant girl's feet. It burst open. Gold and silver coins spilled onto the grass. "For your father. And your child." He turned his horse and rode away.

Motionless, Igrid watched as the entire company of men and horses wheeled north, thundered across the darkening grass, and disappeared into the night. Everything seemed impossibly dark and cold. Her head throbbed, and she was having trouble standing. The pregnant girl made no move to gather the coins. So Igrid stooped and gathered them herself, groping in the darkness, careful to leave none of them behind.

As Igrid straightened, she saw the grubby girl looking at her. The girl still had not spoken. Her dead father lay at her feet like a lump of misshapen wood. The bloodstains on the girl's clothes looked like shadows.

I should leave her. Igrid tucked the coin pouch into her torn tunic and considered what to do next. She had no desire to set foot in the wretched dung hut, nor could she expect the girl to go inside with her father's corpse still blocking the door. She started toward the stream. When the girl did not follow, Igrid went back, took her by the fist, and pulled the girl after her.

"First things first, girl. We have to wash you up. Then we have to give you a name."

CHAPTER EIGHTEEN
THE SORCERER-GENERAL

FADARAH STOOD IN HIS WAR tent and listened as Brahasti concluded his report. Despite the great chair behind him, Fadarah did not sit. Brahasti's voice, as usual, brimmed with arrogance. Not even Fadarah had been able to cure him of the irritating insolence. But for once, it was justified.

Cassica belonged to the Dhargots. The Red Emperor's sons had retaken all the Free Cities lost to Fadarah's army less than a year before, surging across the Simurgh Plains with thirty-five thousand Dhargots, a storm of chariots, and a herd of armored war elephants. Moreover, the Dhargots had shored up their lines with stunning efficiency, actually expanding the borders of their empire by a factor of three while simultaneously allowing virtually no foothold for a potential enemy seeking to challenge their recent acquisitions. Come spring, they would be in striking distance of both Lyos and Atheion.

The feat should have been impossible, but they'd done it—and the thanks went chiefly to Shel'ai magic... plus the cruel brilliance of Brahasti el Tarq. The man's reputation for strategy was well earned. He had exceeded even Fadarah's wildest expectations.

Of course, I'm still going to kill him when this is over. The thought made him smile. After all, Fadarah was no monster. A sorcerer, yes, and part Olg, but Brahasti was the true sadist. And the Dhargothi general's death was a long time coming.

He glanced across the impressive war map at Kith'el. *Shade.* It had been years since the change, but his son—for Shade was his son in everything but actual birth—still confounded him with the new name. Kith'el had renamed himself another word for *ghost* after he nearly lost his wife to the sorcerous machinations wrought in the depths of the Dragons' Graveyard. Of course, Silwren had survived—only to betray them.

But those were concerns for another time. Fadarah could tell what Shade was thinking without the need for mindspeak: the Dhargots had proven to be eerily capable pawns. Perhaps *too* capable.

Fadarah cleared his throat, interrupting Brahasti's report of troop movements and captured slaves. "You have done well, General," he said. "I am glad I decided not to kill you."

It was not a joke, and Brahasti did not seem to take it as such. But the Dhargot did not blanch or tremble, either. He merely bowed. "As you say, Sorcerer-General."

This one has no fear. Only malice. "I am told that you wish to leave the front. An odd request for so ambitious a conqueror."

Brahasti nodded. "I have agents in Atheion, but not enough to take the city from within. The Noshans are well provisioned. It will be a long siege, unless they choose to join the empire willingly. In the meantime, Ziraari will mass at Hesod and await your orders. Karhaati can hold the line at Cassica and keep making the Lyosi and the Isle Knights nervous. Meanwhile, the youngest prince—Saanji, the fat one—can guard their supply lines. All is as you intended. So, with your permission, I would like to retire to my estate in Dhargoth—the estate *you promised me*—until I am needed again."

Fadarah scowled. *He's hiding something.* "So you think the Dhargots will honor the terms of our alliance and help us claim the Wytchforest?"

"Without a doubt."

Liar. Fadarah was impressed, though. Brahasti had learned to clear his mind and, in so doing, shield his thoughts. Fadarah considered using magic to uncover the truth, but that kind of invasive use of magic could cause side effects. In case they needed Brahasti again, he thought it best to leave his faculties intact. "You have a request for me."

For half a second, Brahasti looked surprised. Then the Dhargot wisely bowed to conceal his smirk, though Fadarah saw it anyway. "If it pleases you, Sorcerer-General."

Fadarah grimaced, remembering some of Brahasti's more ghastly requests from the previous campaign. "Speak."

"The Bloody Prince has amassed a great number of slaves. While I am entitled to a portion of—"

"Take this up with Karhaati. I have no stomach for slavery and no interest in discussing it."

Brahasti bowed. "Your gentle disposition does you honor, my lord."

Fadarah conjured a tendril of wytchfire and let it crackle and writhe at his fingertips. He hoped the Dhargot got the message, though he suspected that Brahasti's eyes widened less out of fear than surprise and curiosity. "Don't mock me, Human. I could burn the flesh from your bones and use them to brace my litter if I wished."

As usual, Brahasti bowed at the threat but nothing more. After a requisite moment of silence, Brahasti said, "I prefer my bones and muscles attached, so I shall endeavor to get to the point."

Fadarah saw Shade tense and knew his son wanted nothing more than to burn the tongue out of Brahasti's jaw.

Brahasti said, "I fear I misspoke a moment ago. It is not slaves from the captured Free Cities that I desire. My lords have already been generous in that regard. But I was hoping for something a bit more exotic." Brahasti continued, an awful gleam in his eyes. "I am told that your Olgrym are massing at Godsfall, preparing for a major offensive against the Wytchforest. They've already taken some Sylvan prisoners. I'd very much like to obtain some. Female, preferably young—"

Shade made a sharp gesture, as though to slap Brahasti across the face. The Dhargothi general was ten feet away, but he flew backward, crashed against a table, and slumped to the dirt floor. Blood bloomed from his nose and a cracked lip.

Shade followed, wytchfire crackling from his fists. But Fadarah sent his voice into Shade's mind, as sharp as an arrow and louder than anything mere ears could suffer. Shade winced. Another man might have doubled over in pain, but Fadarah could tell that Shade had no intention of giving Brahasti that satisfaction.

I trained him well. Fadarah felt a pang of pride—tinged with guilt at having to strike his own son—but he forced a withering scowl onto his face and glared at Shade until the man stepped back. Fadarah stood before Brahasti. Instead of offering the fallen general a hand, he gestured and wrenched him to his feet with magic. Fadarah pressed one great, tattooed hand to Brahasti's face.

I could kill him. I could send raw fire into his eye sockets and burn that cruel brain of his into scalded porridge.

Fadarah conjured healing energies to repair the wound inflicted during Shade's magical assault. "I trust you will forgive my second-in-command. Young men often act rashly. If you will repeat your request, I will listen."

Brahasti felt his now-unbroken nose. "If it pleases you, Sorcerer-General, I would enjoy acquiring a number of female Sylvs. All young, all able—"

Fadarah slapped the man so hard across the face, utilizing the full brunt of his half-Olg strength, that the general collapsed to the earth again, momentarily unconscious. Fadarah saw a glint of elation on Shade's face but silenced it with a scowl. He turned back to Brahasti. He gestured, and a wisp of magic jolted the man awake.

Brahasti pushed himself onto his knees. Though blood streamed down his face again, he smiled. "It seems I owe you an apology. I should have been more sensitive to your condition."

Fadarah raised one eyebrow. "My... *condition?*"

"I hear that Olgrym routinely rape Sylvan captives. Your own mother—"

Fadarah gestured, wrenching Brahasti onto his feet. Fadarah's fists became maelstroms of wytchfire. "To the hells with your usefulness, Human! I will make candles of your fat before I let you speak to me that way again."

A spark of fear flickered in the general's eyes. The rush of satisfaction was enough to calm Fadarah. "You want Sylvan prisoners. Sylvan *women*. Why? Is it just to warm your bed?"

Brahasti's smirk chilled Fadarah to the bone. "Not quite. I've lowered my guard, Sorcerer-General. Feel free to pluck the answer from my brain, if you like."

Fadarah did just that. What he saw left him momentarily speechless. "Is that... is that truly possible?" he asked when he finally found his voice.

Brahasti's smirk broadened into a wolfish grin. "I believe it is. You, yourself, are my proof. I merely ask your permission to test my theory."

Shade tensed, as though he meant to invade Brahasti's mind, as well. Fadarah stopped him with a look then faced Brahasti again. "You will have what you ask. But tell no one. And check your cruelty, Human. I'll not have them suffer more than is absolutely necessary."

"As you say, Sorcerer-General. I am moved by this compassion for your enemies."

Enemies... "The Sylvs are merely those born without magic. In that sense, we Shel'ai are their cousins. We fight them, yes, but only because we must. Rape and torture are *Human* sins—ones we abhor." Fadarah felt his own face flush as he spoke. *By the Light, who am I trying to convince—him or me?* "Enough of this. Leave."

The Dhargot bowed and went on his way. Fadarah saw the question on Shade's face. "Brahasti has a lust for commerce now. He wants to sell Sylvan women to... certain like-minded parties in Dhargoth." Though it pained him to lie to Shade, he knew his second-in-command would object if he knew the truth.

"We must prepare to assist the Olgrym in their great offensive. Afterward, I will trust you to see to it that Doomsayer's female prisoners are transferred to Brahasti. Enemies or no, I'll sleep better with them under the care of anyone but the Olgrym."

Shade hesitated. "The Olgrym already have *some* prisoners, I believe. If he's going to take them, Brahasti will need guards."

"He can hire his own. Like that new sellsword captain. What's his name?"

"Dagath. He's no better than a Dhargot. Worse, if truth be told."

Just the kind of man Brahasti wants, anyway. "Release him from our service, but make Brahasti pay him. Gods know he can spare the coin."

Shade said, "It will be done."

"Doomsayer won't like us taking his prisoners. But he's not stupid.

180

If he challenges you on it, it will just be to save face with the other chieftains."

"So don't kill him, you mean."

Fadarah touched the tattoos on his face—the names of Olgish warriors and chieftains he'd killed—and wondered if he should add Doomsayer's name as well. While he intended to be close by when the Olgrym launched their ultimate attack on the Wytchforest, for the moment, he left the actual command of the Olgrym in Shade's hands. "No, don't kill him. We need him. He's the only chieftain who can unite all the clans. But if he protests, you can't let it go unanswered. If you have to, choose one of his warriors, the biggest you can find, and burn him alive—right in front of everyone. Tell Doomsayer and the other chieftains that's what happens when someone questions your orders."

"And Silwren?"

Fadarah sighed. Since Lyos, he had hardly thought about her. "If she and her pet Knight truly mean to carry Fel-Nâya before the Sylvan king, they will be in for a surprise."

"Perhaps. But Fel-Nâya is still a great prize. Maybe we should take it now, rather than let it fall back into the hands of the Sylvs."

Fadarah scrutinized Shade's stony expression for a moment before he sat down. "You're asking me for permission to approach your wife, even though you didn't ask my permission the last time you went to her."

Shade flinched but made no effort to defend himself.

"No," Fadarah said after a moment. He drummed his fingers on the armrest of his chair. "I know you still love her. So do I. But she's our enemy now."

"But she's getting stronger. She's probably even stronger than the Nightmare was by now. If—"

"If we don't help her, she'll destroy herself. Or our enemies. Or us." Fadarah shook his head. "There's nothing we can do. I know it's hard, but put her out of your mind... at least for now."

Fadarah felt a wash of guilt. *So much wasted... and all my fault. I should have known that what we'd unleash would be too hard to control. El'rash'lin warned me. But I didn't listen.*

Shade said, "Something else, Father. A piece of good news I've been saving."

Fadarah glanced at the war map again. *Strange. So many victories, yet I feel like I haven't heard good news in years.* "Tell me."

A slight smile tugged at Shade's lips. "Another Shel'ai has been saved. A child. She fled Sylvos two nights ago. Zeia found her and took her to Coldhaven."

Fadarah forced a smile. "Good. Good. See that she is taken care of. I'll speak to her soon."

He sensed that Shade was about to divulge more details—the child's name or perhaps something of her story—but Fadarah did not want to hear it. He waved again, and Shade left without protest.

Another one saved, but how many killed? How many infants left to starve or killed outright? How many unnamed? And all because Loslandril refused our offer of peace!

That, he knew, should have filled him with wrath. He sat back down in the great chair and stared at the map. He stared for a long time. Then he cursed. He touched the map and sent a spurt of wytchfire racing across the dry parchment, burning it to cinders.

I should stop this, he told himself. But he knew he would not.

CHAPTER NINETEEN

THE TOMATO PRINCE

S AANJI SPUN THE BLACK OPAL ring on his finger as he read
the letter a third time. When he finished, he scowled and held
the letter over a fat tallow candle. Fire curled the parchment,
sending black tendrils of smoke toward the angled silk roof of his war
tent. He glanced up and realized that the messenger was still standing
there, awaiting instructions.

Karhaati will want a reply. Saanji dismissed the messenger with a
wave. The messenger bowed before he left, though Saanji could read
the disdain on the man's face.

*No surprise there. Messenger or no, judging by the number of ears
hanging around his thick neck, he's one of my brother's ilk. The fact that he
didn't walk in and find me raping some poor, sobbing plainsgirl probably
makes me half a traitor in his eyes.*

Saanji was sitting before a table scattered with maps, scribbled
troop statistics, and unwashed wine cups. He chose the least dirty cup
and held it out. His slave, a wispy blond lad spared the rapes and fires
of Quorim, filled it. Saanji had marched from Imperian with a dozen
casks of fine Dhargothi wine, but Saanji detested sobriety almost as
much as he detested the sight of blood, and he knew there couldn't
be more than one or two casks left. This upset him as much as his
brother's correspondence did.

The other inhabitant of his tent, the camp steward whose goatee
had turned white with age, cleared his throat. "Foul news, milord?"

"I've never known my dear brother to send otherwise." Saanji drained the cup, let the slave fill it again, and took another sip before continuing. "Karhaati has taken Cassica... or Brahasti took it, more likely. They're going to stay there for the winter."

"Then on to Lyos?"

"Maybe. My dear brother made a deal with the Shel'ai to help them take the Wytchforest, but I think he'll saddle that duty on Ziraari. As for me, I've been ordered to join Karhaati at Cassica and help him keep the city in line."

The steward's jaw dropped. "We are... to go to Cassica?"

Saanji snorted with laughter then regretted it when he got wine in his nose. "Don't look so glum! Perhaps my brother has had a change of heart. Perhaps the gods visited him in a dream and convinced him to abandon all the barbaric rituals that have corrupted our people." He paused. "No, you're probably right. He's going to kill me."

"Then... why go, milord?"

"Everybody has to go somewhere." Saanji drained his second cup and was halfway through his third when he remembered they had been discussing something before the messenger arrived. "By the Dragongod, what were we talking about?"

"Foraging," the steward said. Though he had been standing the whole time, he showed no signs of weariness.

Saanji looked down at his round belly. His silk britches smelled faintly of urine and stale wine. "Ah, yes. Foraging. What of it?" He hiccupped.

"It is proving most ineffective. Your brothers' hosts burned much of the forests and croplands as they marched from Dhargoth, and from what I hear, these lands didn't grow much but turnips and bastards, anyway."

Saanji laughed. Though he liked the steward, for the life of him, he couldn't remember the man's name. "Are our stores exhausted already?"

"As I explained, Sire, we remain heavily supplied. But at Prince Karhaati's request, we have been reserving the bulk of our foodstuffs to resupply the fighting men to the east."

But not the wine. Karhaati and Ziraari can have the salted beef. They can have the vegetable gruel. They can have horses to ride and girls to rape—or the other way around, for all I care. But by Zet's steaming corpse, they won't get my wine!

To prove his point, he drained his cup and held it out again. The slave flushed. The pitcher was almost empty, and the servant poured what remained into Saanji's cup. He whispered feverish apologies before rushing off to find more.

He apologizes like he thinks I'll flay him just for giving me what I want. Then again, what was it that my dear father used to say about randomly violating a slave from time to time, just to keep the rest in line?

Saanji shrugged. The sadistic advice of the Red Emperor did not interest him, especially so far from Dhargoth. He looked up and realized the steward was still there.

The man cleared his throat. "Foraging, milord. Your orders?"

"Oh." Saanji hiccupped again. "What do you suggest?"

"There are some untouched towns to the south. We could raid them easily enough."

Saanji nodded. "Take what they have. Kill all the males, take the boys as slaves, but notch their ears. Rape the women and girls, and hang the corpses from trees before we go. Oh, and have anyone who opposes us impaled for a slow, agonizing death. That's the Way of Ears, yes?"

"As you say, milord."

Saanji stared at the steward, trying to tell if the man was serious, but there suddenly seemed to be three of him. Saanji was not sure he liked this man anymore. He waved his hand. "Fine. Do it. Send Captain... Captain..." He swore. "Send whoever you feel like. Send the whole bloody host for all I care." He tried to remember how many men he had. *Five thousand?* More than enough to raze a countryside in usual circumstances, but his host was as different from those commanded by his brothers as night from day. While it was customary for deserters to be strangled or impaled as an example to the other fighting men, rich households often frowned upon their beloved sons being executed for cowardice or timidity, even if the accusations were true. Those men had been given to Saanji, ignobly tasked with guarding baggage carts and burying the dead.

Saanji the Soft. The Tomato Prince. Cock o'Wine. He smirked, mentally reciting the long litany of nicknames his brothers had given him. They would be surprised when they found out he'd actually gotten his halfhearted men to bloody their steel and dampen their cocks off innocent, crying shepherd girls.

My father will be pleased. He tried to drink from his cup and found it empty. He cursed. At that moment, the slave returned with a full pitcher, sloshing some of the wine as he moved. As the slave filled the cup, his hands shaking, he spilled a few red drops on Saanji's robes. Saanji might have struck him or had him flayed, but he had more important matters to attend to. He gulped down the cup and had it refilled.

Then he turned, thinking the steward had left, but found the aged Dhargot still standing there. He had been talking—probably asking and repeating a question. Saanji blinked. "What?"

"The *other* matter, milord."

"What other matter?" Saanji remembered the message that had arrived only two days earlier, also from his brother, conveying a report from midland spies that their cousin had disappeared. "Ah, yes. Sweet Karhaati wants me to send torturers to pluck the toenails of some Noshan villagers and see if they know what became of our gentle cousin, Jaanti."

The steward nodded patiently, though he clearly already knew all that.

"It seems Jaanti was chasing a red-headed whore and an Isle Knight who irked him. I wouldn't want to be in their sandals!" Saanji laughed, spilling a little wine on his robe. He looked down and frowned at the stain. "Then again, if he's missing this long, he's probably roasting in Fohl's hells by now. Somehow, though, I think the world will persevere."

"So... you do not intend to send torturers to the Noshan Valley?"

"No point. But tell Karhaati I did, if he asks." Saanji's head was spinning. *Too much wine. I need some food to soak it up.* He dismissed the steward and turned to his slave. "Bring my supper. Spiced duck, sweetbreads, charred bacon, and anything else you think I'd like. Be quick about it." He glanced toward the opening of his tent and realized it was still the middle of the day. But his stomach was growling, and there was no one to chide him so far from the royal city.

He patted his stomach. *I'm the only Dhargothi prince who comes home from war fatter than when he left!* That thought made him laugh. He reminded himself to be cautious, though. His army was on strict rationing, and even those consigned to serve under the Tomato Prince might be irked by his constant feasts while they made do with vegetable mash and tepid ale. He doubted anyone in his complement had the nerve to attack him and risk drawing the ire of his brothers, though. Not yet.

Not that Karhaati and Ziraari would really give two shits if I turned up with my guts opened, but it's an issue of pride. My death would warrant a bloody revenge. Impalements, slow roasting, et cetera. He hiccupped before he could swallow, spilling wine down his goatee. He mopped his face with the sleeve of his robes.

I could throw a feast for the men. Give them some slave girls to violate. Let them wager on wild dogs fighting over bones. Isn't that how you make fighting men love you?

Of course, that was impossible. His brothers did not want to be slowed with baggage trains, so they'd left the bulk of their supplies with him, squatting on the plains south of Cassica. If Saanji squandered foodstuffs meant for the *real* fighting men of the empire, his father would hear of it. But what choice did he have?

"Raiding..." He thought of his steward. He'd said something about villages. Saanji tried to remember. When it came back to him, he cursed. Then he shouted until the slave boy appeared.

"Begging your pardon, milord. We're fixing your supper now, but it's not ready yet. Should I bring you more wine while you wait?"

Saanji glanced at the pitcher, which was still mostly full. The wine was sweet enough to draw flies. Still, he intended to drink it all before the sun went down. He smiled at the thought. Then he shook himself. "No. That's not..." He rubbed his eyes, trying to think straight. "My steward. Get my steward back here. His name is... whatever his name is. I just have the one. Tell him I was just joking. Forget whatever I said about the villages. No killing. Tell him to break into the reserve supplies. If Karhaati doesn't like it, the bloody bitch knows where to find me!"

He laughed. He tried to refill his own cup and spilled wine all over his table, soaking his scribbled figures and maps of conquest. "Boy, bring a towel." Realizing the lad had already left, he cursed and sopped up the wine with his sleeve instead.

CHAPTER TWENTY

THE OATH OF KIN

ROWEN DREW SNOWDARK TO A stop and gazed at the towering
trees in the distance. "By the Light, I had no idea…"
He realized he should have, but how could anyone be
prepared for such a sight? He had heard stories about the Wytchforest,
which the Sylvs and the Shel'ai referred to as Sylvos. Its trees were
so tall that they scraped the clouds, and the forest held the greatest
tree in all of Ruun. He had also listened to Silwren describe the
World Tree that blossomed from the heart of the forest, as ancient
as the world. Even though he had not quite doubted her, he had not
completely believed her, either. He saw that the stories had not been
exaggerated.

In the thinning mist, he saw wytchwood trees thrice the height
of the tallest towers, as thick as castle keeps, wrapped in vines and
leaves from top to bottom. But even the wytchwoods paled before
the World Tree, incomprehensibly huge, rising into the clouds. Its
massive trunk, thicker than all of Saikaido Temple, was stark white
against the dark surrounding trees.

Jalist sat beside him, wide eyed, stunned silent.

Lights and gigantic platforms spiraled up the part of the World
Tree's gigantic trunk that was visible through the surrounding
wytchwoods. He turned to Silwren. "Is that…?"

Silwren answered with a faint smile. "Shaffrilon, the Sylvan
capital, built on daises joined to the living trunk of the World Tree."
She laughed. "What we could reach, that is. King Loslandril's palace

sits on the topmost platform, crowning the spiral walkways. That's as high as anyone has ever climbed, and even that's nowhere close to the top." She pointed. "Can you see it?"

Rowen squinted but shook his head.

Silwren laughed again. "Such is the vision of Humans."

He wondered if she was mocking him, but her smile was all kindness. He marveled that she could be so calm while so close to a homeland from which she had been exiled. But Silwren's mood had improved greatly once Igrid was gone.

Igrid... Rowen blushed, momentarily forgetting the awesome sight before him as he remembered once more how her bare skin felt against his, their lips and bodies joined. He ached for her in a way that angered and baffled him, but he had tried for two days to accept that he might never see her again.

He still could not understand what had compelled her to lie with him one night, only to vanish by morning. She had left her meager possessions in the camp. He thought first that she had been abducted or had wandered off and been injured, but Silwren insisted that no one could have approached the camp without her knowledge. With a twinge of heartbreak, Rowen realized that Igrid had left them—left *him*—for good.

Unless Silwren's hiding something. But how does one tell if a Shel'ai is lying?

Especially after what he'd seen at Atheion and how simply she'd rendered them invisible to all the Dhargothi patrols when they rode past Hesod, he had to stop thinking of her as a Shel'ai. She was a Dragonkin. He shook his head. The situation was maddening. A year ago, he could barely have explained the distinctions between Sylvs and Shel'ai, let alone Shel'ai and Dragonkin. Since then, he'd learned far more than he wished to know. Still, he always seemed to have more questions than answers.

Rowen fixed his gaze on the World Tree again, hoping to rekindle that sense of wonder to squelch his sudden anxiety. But the gigantic, mist-gowned tree seemed even more surreal, like an illusion that would shatter the moment he touched it. "Well, we've only got about a day's ride left. We may as well get this over with." He flicked the reins and started forward.

Jalist said, "Are you mad? We can't just ride in there like we're out for an afternoon stroll. Those trees must be swarming with archers." He turned to Silwren for confirmation.

She nodded. "Just as Shaffrilon is built into the trunk of the World Tree, many Sylvan archers make their homes in the surrounding wytchwoods. Their mission is to guard Sylvos against all intruders. Normally, that means Olgrym and Wyldkin, but we will be no more welcome than they are."

Rowen frowned. "I've heard of Wyldkin, but I thought they were just Sylvs living outside the forest."

"They are. But only the Shal'tiar can come and go as they like. The Wyldkin live on the Ash'bana Plains either by choice or because they've been banished for crimes. They often fight the Olgrym, alongside the Shal'tiar."

"And now I suppose I have to learn who or what the Shal'tiar are."

Silwren opened her mouth to explain, but Rowen cut her off. "Another time. Just tell me how to get to the World Tree without getting my guts cut to ribbons by arrows."

Silwren hesitated. "If you want to invoke the Oath of Kin, you must reach King Loslandril. But the archers in the wytchwoods will never let you pass. The Wyldkin might be sympathetic to your cause, but only the Shal'tiar are allowed to enter and leave Sylvos at will. If you want to reach Loslandril alive, you will have to convince them to escort you in."

Rowen rubbed his eyes. "I'll pretend for now that I understood at least half of that. Where do we go first? The Ash'bana Plains?"

"There's a Shal'tiar garrison at Que'ahl, a Wyldkin village just north of the trees. We should go there first. The Wyldkin do not hate Shel'ai as much as their woodland kin. But even they will not welcome me. Best you do the talking once we arrive."

Rowen nodded. The late El'rash'lin had magicked some of his own memories into Rowen's mind in an effort to make Rowen understand the sorcerer's plight. As an unexpected consequence, Rowen could slip into those memories as though they were his own and speak a smattering of the Sylvan tongue. He hoped that would be enough to impress their would-be guides into not feathering him with arrows.

Silwren touched his hand. "You'll do fine. Remember, you are a Knight of the Crane. These people are your allies... even if they need to be reminded of that fact."

Silwren led the way as they veered north, skirting the tree line, far out of longbow range. Rowen followed her, trying to look stoic, deliberately avoiding Jalist's disapproving gaze. As they rode, he heard the scrape of rock on steel and realized that Jalist was sharpening his long axe.

Rowen lowered his hand and loosened Knightswrath in its worn scabbard. He decided it was a good thing the sword never needed to be sharpened. At least he wouldn't go to his death with a dull blade.

Rowen had no idea what to expect from a Sylvan village, though his first thought was that Que'ahl appeared to be more of a fortress than a village. He saw crops and huts, but the village itself was surrounded by three wooden palisades, each built a little higher than the last and joined by guard towers crowded with lookouts and archers. He even saw a few ballistae glinting in the afternoon sun.

The village appeared to have only one gate, and that approach was scattered with a maze of trenches. Rowen immediately recognized why, and he felt a swell of admiration for whoever had fortified the place. With so many trenches and pitfalls zigzagging across the grasslands, any army seeking to assault the village would likely lose its footing. Frequent and necessary changes in direction forced them to slow their pace, making them prime targets for archers.

Rowen felt a stab of fear in his gut as scores of archers trained their arrows on him. He guided Snowdark with his heels and raised both arms to shoulder height, palms open. He hoped that Jalist and Silwren were doing the same and that Silwren had raised the hood of her cloak. He led the procession, forcing a smile that he hoped the archers could see. He saw longbows shift. Tense, steely arrowheads patiently followed his every move.

Well, they haven't killed me yet... They were within earshot. He started to call out in Common, but his voice had gone hoarse. He cleared his throat and started again. "We're friends. Do not fire. I beg an audience with your commander." He braced himself, mentally rehearsing the words, then presented the same proclamation in Sylvan. "*I'jan hatosh! Ní mirkátu. Sivo hal'halashi.*"

Even as he spoke, he realized his inflection was wrong. His Human accent must have made the words almost unintelligible to Sylvan ears. He steadied himself and repeated them, more slowly. His pronunciation was still far from perfect, but he felt a mild satisfaction when he saw the archers raise their eyebrows, Sylvan-blue eyes wide with surprise. An archer disappeared from the tower, and Rowen hoped the man had gone to fetch an officer.

Rowen lowered his hands, making sure to keep them away from his sword hilt. Fifty yards ahead of them, the gates into Que'ahl lay open, but he decided to wait until his group was invited to enter. As he sat restlessly in the saddle, he whispered over his shoulder to Silwren, "Do I even want to know how badly I messed up the pronunciation?"

"No," Silwren whispered back. Her voice was even, and he could not tell whether she was amused, disappointed, or afraid.

Moments later, a squad of mounted fighters, all Sylvan, appeared at the gates of Que'ahl, armed with bows and blades. Some wore black brigandines while others wore plain clothes and had feathers braided into their hair. He saw women as well as men. Each fixed him in a dangerous gaze.

Rowen dismounted. Silwren and Jalist did the same. Jalist led Igrid's horse, which carried only their supplies. Rowen eyed the approaching Sylvs, trying to pick out the leader. They all looked nearly identical, and none wore a sigil. He decided to address them in Sylvan again. "*Sivo hal'ha—*"

"Spare us, Human," one lean, stern warrior interjected, speaking near-flawless Common Tongue. He stepped ahead of the others, resting one hand on the hilt of a curved shortsword, though Rowen could not tell if the gesture was a habit or meant to be menacing. "I suspect we speak your language far better than you can speak ours, although"—the Sylv smirked—"you are the first Human I have ever heard even attempt our speech." The Sylv looked past Rowen at

Silwren, and the smirk vanished. The Sylv's fingers tightened around his sword hilt. "Perhaps you had an instructor."

"Indeed, though not in the way you think."

The Sylv looked at him questioningly.

"We aren't here to fight," Rowen said. "I need to speak with your commander at once. I am Sir Rowen Locke, a Knight of the Crane. My companions are Jalist Hewn and Silwren—"

"A Shel'ai," the Sylv finished as Silwren offered a stiff nod.

Rowen tried to gauge the man's tone, but like his Sylvan features, it was too foreign to him. He could not even tell if the man before him was young or old. He began to tire of formality. "And your name?"

"If you are so eager to know the name of the man who is going to kill you, so be it. My name is Briel."

Rowen moved his hand for his sword but forced himself to smile. "I know little of Sylvan customs, it's true. But among Humans, it's bad luck to kill a man who comes in peace."

The Sylv pointed at Silwren. "*They* do not come in peace! Not now, not ever. If she is your ally, then I doubt you come in peace, either. And neither do *your* kind. If it's a parley you seek, I suggest you get to your point."

Jalist cursed. A dozen longbows trained on them, and still more Sylvs gathered in the foreground. Beyond the gates, parents ushered their children inside, just as the Noshans had in their village. However, the Sylvan parents returned a moment later with weapons in their hands.

He wondered if he should ungird his sword belt and surrender. Instead, he steeled his nerves and slowly drew his sword, facing the Sylvan leader. The Sylvs tensed.

Rowen was glad that none lost their grip on their bowstrings. He doubted even kingsteel armor could protect him from longbow arrows at close range. "I did not come here to be threatened. If you have eyes, use them now. What am I holding?"

Briel gestured as though to delay the archers. He frowned. "I see a sword. I see an Isle Knight and a Dwarr who are far from home. And I see a Shel'ai who should have gone farther."

"Then you are blind," Rowen said. He took a single step forward.

Sunlight caught Knightswrath's blade as he lifted it. He gripped the sword by hilt and blade alike, praying his bold move would not be answered by a dozen Sylvan arrows. He stretched out his arms, presenting the sword to Briel.

"Are you lending me your cutlery, Human? No need. I have some of my own." Briel drew his shortsword, holding it with loose grace that spoke of the deadly skill of its owner.

Rowen hesitated. He had not been under any delusions that he could gain an audience with the Sylvan king without first telling some lower-ranking Sylv the purpose of his arrival, but he had hoped at least to save his words for some kind of chieftain or general. He suspected that Briel was merely a junior officer.

He steeled himself again. "This is Fel-Nâya, also called Knightswrath, the sword entrusted to King Fâyu Jinn during the Shattering War." He tilted the blade so the gilded lettering carved into the swirling steel glinted. "On behalf of my Order, and in the names of Fâyu Jinn and Shigella, the kings of old, I hereby invoke the Oath of Kin." He paused. "Gather your steel, Sylvs. You are needed in the north."

Rowen's words hung in the heavy silence that followed them. Rowen fought back a smile. He had been mentally revising and rehearsing those words for weeks, fearing he might make a mistake, but their bold sound filled him with excitement. Rowen turned his gaze from face to face. Sylvan eyes stared back at him. He wanted to turn around and look at Silwren and Jalist, but he kept his eyes on the Sylvs.

Rowen could hear his own heartbeat. Snowdark and the other horses restlessly pawed the ground. He even thought he could hear the shifting of Sylvan armor and the creaking of longbows. But still, the Sylvs did not answer.

Rowen fixed his gaze on Briel. He waited in unbearable silence. Then, off to the side, someone laughed. Another joined in, then another. Before long, nearly all the Sylvs were laughing. Rowen flushed.

Briel grimaced as though he had just been conversing with a

lunatic and feared that the madness might infect him, as well. He stepped back. Then he pointed with his shortsword. "Kill them."

And before Rowen could move or speak, the air shuddered with the snap of longbows.

CHAPTER TWENTY-ONE
ANZA

"Anza," Igrid said.

The girl stared, uncomprehending.

"Your name is Anza. You have a name now. Do you understand?"

Igrid peeled off the girl's bloody clothes and led her into the stream. Though Igrid wanted to get as far away from there as possible, in case the battle between the Dhargots and the Lancers shifted south again, Anza was covered in her father's blood.

Igrid cursed as cold water soaked her britches. She palmed water over the girl's body, washing her like an infant. The girl grabbed Igrid's shoulders with wet, grubby hands and leaned on her, but she did not speak.

"Can you hear me? Gods, girl, say something!"

Anza moved one hand from Igrid's shoulder to her own belly. Her voice was barely a whisper in the night. "One of them hit me here. My baby…"

Igrid's eyes widened. She pressed carefully on the girl's belly, checking her as she'd learned to do in the brothels of Lyos. The girl winced.

"Your baby's fine," Igrid lied. "And so are you. Do you understand?"

The girl mumbled, "My baby," into the darkness.

Igrid washed the girl as best she could then led her out of the stream. They both shivered in the cold night. Igrid heard the faraway sound of men screaming.

"I hope they kill each other. Dhargots, Ivairians—all of them."

Igrid considered stopping by the dung hut so she could warm the girl and grab whatever meager possessions she had—including the clothes that the girl had promised—but the thought of going back there made her shudder. Besides, she had the coins that the Lancer had given her. She could buy whatever they needed.

She tried to lead the girl northeast, but in the dark, she tripped over an exposed tree root and nearly pulled the girl with her. Wiping her muddy palms on her britches, Igrid cursed again. She considered going back to the dung hut to look for a lantern, but she decided to keep going.

"You said there's a village to the north. If the Lancers and the Dhargots don't destroy it, we'll sleep in a bed tonight. I bet you've never slept in a real bed your whole stinking life. But you will tonight." Igrid forced herself to laugh. "After that, Lyos. You ever heard of it? It's a great city north of here. There are temples there. I'll find a nice one and leave you with some priestesses. Hells, I'll give them so many coins, they'll treat you like a queen!"

The girl stopped so suddenly that Igrid lurched, still holding her hand. The girl stared blankly at Igrid. Then her eyes widened. Igrid was just able to make out the girl's expression of terror. "Who are you? Where is…"

"My name is Igrid. I'm your friend. I helped you pick fruit from the orchard. Remember? I'm taking you north, somewhere safe. Do you understand?"

The girl stared at her a moment, blinking, then turned ungracefully and ran.

Igrid stared, stunned. Surprise became anger. She decided she'd had enough. She had better things to do than act as nursemaid to some addled girl. Patting the coin purse again, she started north. Then she stopped.

"Damn." She turned and went after the girl.

Anza had not gotten far. Igrid found her kneeling on the dark grass, her face blank, stroking her belly. Igrid approached her cautiously, but Anza hardly seemed to realize she was there. Igrid helped her up, firmly gripped her hand, and started north again.

198

"Where we going?" the girl asked finally.

Igrid just said, "North."

"North. To a real bed." Anza took a few more shuffling steps. "Can I have my baby in a bed?"

"Fine by me, though I don't know if the innkeeper will appreciate that." Igrid glared at the darkness before them and wished she could trade a fistful of coins for a single lit torch.

They walked until dawn and still they did not see any village. Twice, Igrid heard whimpers and cries of pain in the distance. She figured they belonged to fighting men abandoned on the field. She steered Anza away from the sounds, walking until they faded in the distance.

She tried asking Anza how far the village was or if they were even walking in the right direction, but Anza seemed to periodically forget how to speak. She held Igrid's hand and followed her meekly, though. As tired and sore as she was, Igrid was grateful for that, at least.

When sunrise finally unrolled across the grasslands, Igrid looked in every direction. Her heart sank. She saw no village, no city, not even a stream where they could stop and drink. "Keep walking. I know you're tired, girl, but we have to keep walking."

Luckily, Anza seemed to have lost all will of her own. She followed Igrid, limping along until her legs gave out. She pitched forward and might have fallen facedown or belly first onto the ground had Igrid not caught her. She lowered the girl to the earth as gently as she could.

"It's all right, Anza. It's all right. We'll rest a moment." Igrid took off her cloak, covered the girl, then lay down beside her. She closed her eyes and fell fast asleep.

Igrid woke to screams. She sat bolt upright, drew her sword, and looked around. Anza was gone. Igrid leapt up, turning this way and that. Panic filled her, but she spotted the girl a hundred feet away, crumpled on the grasslands.

Igrid ran to her. Anza had taken off her clothes. Then she saw why.

"It's all right." Igrid hugged the girl and kissed her grubby forehead. "It's all right."

Anza held up her hands. They were slick with blood. "My—"

"It's all right. Just lie down. Just rest."

But Anza convulsed. Then she screamed and pulled away, though Igrid could not tell if she was trying to escape or had been struck by a spasm of pain. She wrapped her arms around the girl and tried to hold her again, but the girl's strength was incredible. Igrid's arms went numb with the effort.

Then, all at once, Anza went slack. She stared up at Igrid with foggy eyes, her pupils wobbling back and forth. Igrid felt Anza's stomach. She moved down to Anza's thighs and forced herself to look. She winced. Though Igrid had no doubt that the baby had already died inside her, it had not come out. Anza was bleeding from the inside. Igrid knew how to help her, but she needed herbs, thread, hot water, and a sharp, clean knife. But she had none of those things. Then she remembered Knightswrath.

She'd dropped it when she knelt to inspect the girl, but she picked it up. She inspected the blade. It was too long and cumbersome for what she had to do, but at least it was sharp. "Gods, girl, this is going to hurt. I'm sorry. I'm so sorry."

She positioned herself, felt with her fingertips, and found the place where she needed to cut. She eyed it as she held the tip of the bare blade with one hand and leaned forward. The blade touched Anza's skin. Then blade and hilt vanished. In their place, Igrid held a thick, gnarled branch.

Igrid blinked, staring at the branch. She dropped it and wept. "Damn you, wytch." She looked up. "I'm sorry, Anza. It's not my fault."

The girl screamed, dug her nails into the grass, then whimpered and went still.

Cradling the girl's head, Igrid said, "Listen, I want you to lie here. I'm going to go and take a knife from one of those dead bastards we passed. They might have something else that can help you, too. Hells, I can sew you up with thread from their tabards, if I have to." She kissed the girl's dirty forehead, winced at its bitter taste, and stood.

Anza turned and gave her a blank look. The girl's mouth opened as if she were trying to form words, but Igrid backed away and ran. She wondered first where she should go, then she thought to scan the sky for crows. A dark murder of them circled to the southwest, not far from where she had heard screams during the night. Igrid broke into a sprint.

She intended to run the whole way, but it was far and she was already exhausted. Again and again, she had to stop. When she finally reached the body, she saw that it belonged to a dead horse—no sign of the rider. Igrid swore the names of every god she could remember and scouted the area. Crows scattered as she approached. She spotted a dark, unmoving shape on the plains, maybe fifty yards away.

She gathered her strength and ran again. The figure was, in fact, two men joined in a deadly embrace. One body belonged to a Dhargot with half a broken lance in his side. The other, an Ivairian knight, had a dagger of Dhargothi steel in his throat. Both men were wide eyed and staring. Another horse, alive and draped in Dhargothi vestments, lingered in the distance.

Igrid approached the horse first. She feared it would run away, but to her shock, her fingers closed around the dangling leather reins. She saw a necklace of dried ears caught on the saddle horn. She grimaced, seized it by the cord, and threw it away. She soothed the horse and pulled him back toward the bodies.

Igrid feared letting go of the reins, but the horse pawed idly at the grassy earth and did not run. She pried the dead men apart, fumbling in the bloody wreckage for a weapon. She found an Ivairian shortsword and claimed it, along with the Dhargothi knife. She used the latter to slice off the dead Lancer's tabard, which she planned to take with her. Then she spat on them.

She mounted the Ivairian horse and urged it to a gallop. She feared that her new fortunes in finding a horse would turn again and she would be unable to retrace her steps. She spotted Anza in the distance. The girl was sitting up, her back turned. Igrid urged more speed from the horse and reined in just a few feet from the girl.

"I'm sorry, Anza. I ran as fast as I could. But we're in luck. I found a horse. We can ride from now on. I'll do what I can for you, but we'll be able to ride and find a cleric who can do the rest."

She dismounted then took the girl by the shoulders and lowered her gently onto the grass. The girl was smiling. Igrid frowned then smiled back. "You're an odd one! Just what—"

Then she realized how pale Anza's face had turned. Igrid felt for a pulse. She felt the girl's belly, pressing here and there. Finally, she took the tabard she'd cut from the dead Lancer and used it to cover Anza's face.

"Sorry, girl." Igrid slid the knife into her homemade belt. Only then did she think of the coin purse. Cold panic flooded over her. She scanned the thick grasses and spotted the purse lying on the ground.

The coins had spilled out again. They glinted beautifully in the sun, all gold and silver. She gathered them with shaking hands. Then she caught sight of the simple length of rope that Anza had worn around her waist. Igrid undid her belt of rags and let it fall. She hesitated then unknotted the rope from Anza's waist and tied it around her own. She turned away quickly, securing the coin purse, dagger, and shortsword. Then she mounted her new horse and set off.

She refused to look back.

Igrid found dried rations in the saddlebags of her new horse. Despite her hunger, she had to force herself to eat. As she rode north, toward Lyos, she passed more bodies. Both men and horses lay motionless in torn earth scattered with slashed standards, discarded steel, and broken lances. She passed each with her new shortsword drawn in case any of the figures were still alive, but none moved. She took in the scene, trying to imagine what had happened.

It looked as though a massive, swirling cavalry battle had been fought for miles, swinging this way and that, as the Ivairians struggled desperately to break through the Dhargothi lines. There were more dead Dhargots than Lancers, though it appeared as though the Ivairian squires had been the easiest prey.

Why were they fighting in the first place?

Igrid cut a strip of cloth from a fallen Lancer's tabard and pressed it to her face, trying to block out some of the smell. Crows were everywhere, tearing at the dead, though they scattered at her approach, screaming and cawing into the sky. She squinted, fearing they might attack her or her horse's eyes, and waved her sword in front of her face.

As bad as this place was, it would look and smell ten times worse in a few days. She had expected to find a few stragglers from the surviving side probing the grasslands for survivors, but she saw no one. She began to wonder if the battle had continued elsewhere. She listened but heard only crows.

So much armor and steel, just lying there... Surely it was worth hundreds, perhaps even thousands of silvers, but she had no way to carry it. Before long, mud and blood would tarnish it, and all of it would be useless.

Such a waste. Igrid tried not to think about it. She touched the coin purse, reminding herself that she already had more than she needed for a fresh start. But touching the coin purse reminded her of Anza.

"Where's that damn village?" she grumbled to herself. If she could find it, perhaps she could lead the town blacksmith back to the field and help him claim all the metal in exchange for a share of the profits. Or, at the very least, she could find an inn, get a room and some hot food, and drown herself in as much wine as she could hold. The thought made her smile.

But she trudged on and still saw nothing. No village, no farm, nothing but torn grasslands scattered with dead men. Then she heard running water. She realized how thirsty she was and how much she wanted to wash the stink of the past day from her skin. Her pace quickened. She followed the sound to a river. There, she stopped.

The river was choked with dead men and horses, though the current had washed away the blood. On her side of the bank, Sir Arnil lay against the body of his horse, unmoving. He was surrounded by dead Dhargots. He must have tried to lead them away from his men or stayed behind and gave his life to cover their escape.

The First Lancer's gilded armor was stained all over, his tabard slashed to ribbons. His plain face was splattered with mud. The grip of a broken lance lay at his feet. The rest of the lance was thrust through the body of a Dhargot just a few feet away, pinning him to a tree.

A glint of light on metal drew her eyes to the First Lancer's sword. It was an Ivairian-style broadsword with a brass handle. The handle resembled a man with splayed limbs, so that the blade took the place of his phallus. The sword had three fullers and a waisted blade, but the blade itself had the distinctive glint and swirl of kingsteel. The Ivairian knight was still holding the sword, but his eyes were closed.

Not as fine as Rowen's sword, but kingsteel is kingsteel. Still, she moved cautiously. When she was ten feet away, Arnil's eyes opened. His stern look made her back away. Then his gaze softened a little. "Ah, the Iron Sister who carries the blade of an Isle Knight. Well met." He smiled at the look on her face. "Oh, I understand that women may become Isle Knights, but you don't seem the type. You don't strike me as a camp follower who goes around looting corpses, either." He eyed the Ivairian shortsword and Dhargothi dagger she was carrying. "Of course, I could be mistaken."

"You aren't." Igrid edged a little closer. "The Isle sword is gone, though."

"As is your city, Iron Sister." The First Lancer coughed. "And your companion... the girl carrying her father's child?"

"Dead."

"At your hand?"

"No." Igrid considered flinging her shortsword at him.

Arnil held up his hand. "The wrongfully accused often display anger while the justly accused feign hurt." He paused. "I believe you. And the child was stillborn?"

"Yes, thanks to your men."

"I feared as much. But those men are dead. Even Sir Geoffrey." Arnil eyed her. "Well, what now, Iron Sister? Will you knife a wounded man for his steel when there are plenty more blades just lying about, waiting for you to scoop them up?"

"Plenty of blades, but none as fine as yours." Despite her bravado, Igrid hesitated. She had the Lancer's coins, but even if she didn't sell his sword, it would make a good weapon to carry herself. But if the bodies strewn around him were any indication, he was not to be trifled with. Then again, he was obviously wounded, though she could not tell how much of the blood on the First Lancer's armor belonged to him and how much to his enemies.

She edged closer still. "Perhaps a trade? Your steel for a drink of water."

Arnil's hazel eyes brimmed with amusement, despite his pallor and sweating face. "I had to win fifteen tournaments to afford this sword, Iron Sister. I think I'll keep it, though you're welcome to try and take it from me if you think you can."

Igrid studied the man, thought it over, and decided not to press her luck. She was tempted to walk away and just leave him to bleed to death, but an image of Anza's pale face made her shudder. She stuck her shortsword in the earth, picked up a dead man's half-helm, filled it with water from the river, and carried it back to the First Lancer.

"I've drunk from my own helm before, but never the helm of an enemy." He accepted the helmet anyway and drank. Water ran down his chin, spilled onto his armor, and washed away some of the blood. A tremendous dent in his breastplate made the sigil of the crowned rearing horse look like a grinning face.

"There are bodies in the river, you know. You'll likely catch the rotting sickness and die."

Arnil drank without pausing then set the half helm on the ground beside him, letting the last of its contents spill onto the bloody grass. "You might be surprised, woman. I have a stomach of wrought iron."

Igrid surveyed the Lancer's dead opponents. She wondered if she would run into more Dhargots as she headed north. "What happened here?"

"What always happens when men with swords and sharp sticks have nothing better to do." He laughed, coughed, and tugged at his armor. "Supposed to be... scouting the borders, having a look at the Dhargots besieging Cassica. That's it. But the bastards came after us. Cut through my squires like paper, then my Lancers. They had a little more trouble with me." He laughed again, his eyes rolling.

"Where are the Dhargots now?"

"Dead. Gone. Fled. Who knows? You're the first living face I've seen since last night. And my Lancers?"

"Feeding miles of crows between here and there."

Arnil closed his eyes. "I was hoping some got away."

"If so, I didn't see them."

Arnil kept his eyes shut. He was quiet for so long that Igrid wondered if he'd died. She edged a little closer, and his eyes opened again.

"Change your mind about my steel?"

"I'll help you take off your armor. I'll clean and sew your wounds—for a price."

Arnil eyed the coin purse tucked into her belt. "I seem to be without my coins, Iron Sister."

"You're an important knight sworn to a king. He should be able to reward the woman who saved his champion's life."

Arnil's smile became a frown. "Indeed." His eyes closed. When next he spoke, his words slurred. "Best hurry, woman. I seem... to..." He sagged to the ground.

Igrid rushed forward, drew the Dhargothi knife from her waist, and sliced the straps securing the First Lancer's armor. She carefully opened his cuirass and gasped. Beneath the breastplate, the knight wore a leather jerkin, which was soaked in blood. She peeked under it and cursed.

Another fool set to die in front of me... "No." She had seen enough death of late. One man, at least, would be saved. She ran to search the heaps of dead men for the things she would need.

CHAPTER TWENTY-TWO
ARROWS AND ASH

J ALIST REACHED FOR HIS AXE when he heard the longbows fire, though he knew he had no time to defend himself, let alone attack. For one split second, as a black hail of arrows descended on them, he thought of Leander, the Dwarr prince he'd loved—the reason he had been banished from Tarator in the first place. He wondered if the stories were true: that in death, the gods or the Light would reunite him with the dead ones he'd loved.

The air before them turned to a broad, blazing curtain of wytchfire and swallowed the arrows, leaving nothing behind. Not even ash. As the wytchfire continued to hover in the air, Silwren stepped forward. Only she blazed with white light—or white-hot fire?—save for her eyes, which were slits of furious, violet flame. She still bore the body of a woman, though superimposed over her was a gigantic scaly thing with horns and a serpentine neck. Six wings of white fire unfurled from its body. Jalist stared. Rowen tackled him, knocking him out of the way.

The fiery wings spread, and Rowen rolled away. Jalist sat up in time to see the Sylvs manning the guard towers leap to the ground, as though fearing they were about to be incinerated. But the fiery wings stopped just short of the timbers. Silwren took another step forward. She waved, and the curtain of wytchfire poured back into her like water flowing backward up the waterfall to its source.

She faced Briel, for all the other Sylvs were fleeing. Then she spoke, and Jalist had to cover his ears. The booming voice seemed to come from both her and the fiery visage superimposed over her, the two speaking in unison.

"I am not a Shel'ai. I am not a Sylv. I am not a Dragonkin. I am none of these, yet I am all of them. I am the weapon forged by Fadarah to turn all of you to cinders. I am the vengeance of every Shel'ai you ever murdered, hundreds and thousands of them, echoing down through the ages. I could kill all of you. And I should."

All at once, the white fire disappeared, and she was Silwren again. She stood there, naked and trembling. Her clothes had burned away, though she did not seem to notice. "But I won't," she said, weakly. She started to fall.

Rowen caught her, his expression stoic, though Jalist could not fathom how the man had found the presence of mind to act.

Silwren slumped for a moment, allowing Rowen to wrap her in his cloak, then she pulled free and took a step forward on her own. "If I can swallow my wrath, you can do the same. And you will. This Knight has words to say. You will hear them. Or by the Light, I will burn the World Tree before your eyes and scour your seed from the face of the realms." She swayed again, and Jalist feared she would fall, but she held her ground.

Everyone else stared, paralyzed. Jalist retrieved his long axe, marshaled his courage, and strode to Silwren's side. Along the way, he retrieved Knightswrath—Rowen had dropped it in the chaos—and pressed it into the dumbfounded Knight's hands. As he did so, he noticed the handle was blazing warm, as though it had been brushed by Silwren's wytchfire.

Jalist fixed his gaze on Briel. He admired the Sylv for holding his ground when the others had run, though he looked as though he might be sick. Jalist said, "No more pleasantries. As my friend said, we have words for your commander. Fetch him now."

Briel trembled then seemed to wake from a dream. "I will—"

"No need," a voice said. "I am here."

A new figure strode through the open gates of Que'ahl and approached the group. The middle-aged Sylvan warrior wore a black brigandine, like the rest, though the sternness to his demeanor transcended even the chilly fierceness of his ice-blue eyes. He was unarmed but faced Silwren as though her display had been nothing but a parlor trick.

"I am Essidel, Captain of the Shal'tiar. If you have words, speak them to me."

Rowen moved forward, taking Silwren's place. "I am Rowen Locke, Knight of—"

"I heard. I was approaching when my sergeant ordered the archers to fire." Essidel cast a scathing look at Briel. "That is not the order I would have given." He faced Rowen. "We should find somewhere else to talk. If the Dwarr and your wytch promise to behave, you may come inside. I vow on my honor that no Sylv will harm any of you."

Rowen said, "She's not *my* wytch, Captain."

"Fine. We'll talk about it in the barracks. Follow me." Essidel led them through the gates toward a squat structure. Once inside, they faced rows of tables and a handful of Sylvs. The Captain of the Shal'tiar dismissed the other Sylvs with a quick word in his own tongue. Only Briel remained, though he stood at the rear, one hand on his sword.

Essidel gestured to a long table. No one sat. Rowen laid Knightswrath on the table. Its blade rocked gently, gleaming in the lantern light. Essidel, who had been fetching a pitcher of wine, paused for a moment and stared at it. "Is that really Fâyu Jinn's sword?"

Rowen nodded firmly.

"It's pretty." Essidel picked up a goblet from the table, filled it with wine, and handed it to Rowen. He filled another for Jalist. "Perhaps you would be so kind as to explain two things. First, how you stole Fâyu Jinn's sword, and second, how anyone—even a Human—could be dumb enough to bring it back here and ask an enemy for help."

"The sword came to me honestly," Rowen said. "I didn't steal it. And the Sylvs aren't my enemies."

"Yet you are an Isle Knight." Essidel set the wine pitcher down without filling a cup for Silwren. "One of the very order who have been plaguing our borders for weeks."

Rowen said, "I don't know what you mean."

"Then I'll explain. I'm talking about a company of Isle Knights riding around the Ash'bana Plains, attacking Wyldkin villages. I'm talking about the company of Knights who charged my men just moments after we'd finished fighting for our lives against a host of Olgrym."

Rowen was speechless, but Silwren stepped forward then gripped the table for balance. Jalist saw that she was still reeling from her display at the gates of the village, though he marveled that she had kept her powers in check at all. She said, "You claim those were Isle Knights you were fighting?"

Essidel nodded gruffly, keeping his eyes on Rowen.

"How do you know?"

"Because they were Humans dressed up in the same kind of swirly armor worn by this fool."

Rowen said, "How many of them did you fight?"

If the question caught him off guard, Essidel recovered quickly. "Fifty attacked my men, just a few miles north of here."

Silwren said, "And they fought you to the death?"

"No. They charged us. We rained arrows on them. Then they wheeled and ran for their lives."

"And these other raids?"

"A few Knights here and there. Usually, they just shoot crossbows, though a Sylvan child has more skill than the best of them."

Silwren continued, "Captain, how many dead Isle Knights have you actually examined?"

"When they charged us, we wounded half a dozen, probably mortally. But they limped off." Essidel hesitated. "They always take their dead with them…"

Jalist spoke up next. "Have these Knights ever actually killed anyone? Think hard, Captain."

The rage slowly faded from the Sylv's face.

"Odd. These men spend years learning how to kill, but they haven't managed to kill even one Sylv yet—or wound one, I'll wager. Not one old man, not even a child scurrying for cover." He took Essidel's silence for an answer.

Silwren said, "You see steel and scowls and thundering hooves, but were you to actually touch these illusions, they would fade like mist before a quickening sun."

Essidel filled another goblet and straightened. "You ask me to believe that the Shel'ai are trying to turn us against the Isle Knights. For what purpose?"

Rowen answered, "The Dhargothi hordes are claiming the northlands for themselves. Sooner or later, they'll unfurl their empire all the way to the Lotus Isles. We might not be able to beat them." Rowen blushed with shame as he said the last.

Essidel gave Rowen a curious look. "I could believe in the existence of an alliance between the Shel'ai and Dhargoth. Both have malice that eclipses their honor." His ice-blue eyes flicked over Silwren. "But the Shel'ai have no need to poison an alliance between the Sylvs and the Lotus Isles. We have our own war to fight with the Olgrym. We can't help you, Human."

Rowen winced. "But the Oath of Kin—"

"Was made ten centuries ago. We Sylvs are long lived, Human. I myself have seen two hundred summers. We remember things you do not."

"I have a scroll from Atheion, written during the time of the Shattering War. It says—"

"I don't care what it says. The Olgrym are massing. Fadarah appears to be their ally. If the Dhargots are their allies, too, we'll be fighting all of them before long. We can't send men to liberate your precious Free Cities when we're fighting for our lives here." He paused. "If you'd come with a few thousand Isle Knights to help us, things might be different. But you're alone." He picked up Knightswrath, his movements eerily fast, and passed the sword hilt-first to Rowen. "I'm supposed to kill any Isle Knight I see. But your story makes sense. So take your heirloom and go home. I'll forget I ever saw you."

Rowen returned the sword to the scabbard at his side. His green eyes flashed with defiance—or perhaps mere stubbornness. "I came to speak with King Loslandril, not one of his captains."

"Then go, Human. If you know what a tree looks like, you should be able to find Sylvos. This king's captain will not stop you. But those archers in the trees definitely will."

"How about you help us reach Shaffrilon alive?" Jalist asked.

Essidel took a sip of wine. "Sorry, Dwarr. I'm busy."

Rowen set down his cup. "I am not here for my health. I swore on my honor to carry this sword before your king. If it can be done, then I will do it. And if your race have as much need as mine to be reminded of their oaths, then I will remind them."

Essidel snickered. "And how will you do that, Knight? We Sylvs are not so easily swayed by flowery words. King Loslandril will not be easily swayed, either. I told you, we have our own people to fight for."

Rowen scowled. "It doesn't take honor to fight for your loved ones. Even an Olg would do that. Honor means swearing your sword to the people who deserve it. In the Codex Lotius, it says that prudence leads to death, but honor leads to a *good* death. In other words, Sylv, courage is not prudent. Neither is honor. But whatever they are, they're worth more than gold, more than kingsteel, more than my own blood."

A flutter of emotion passed over the Sylvan captain's face, but Jalist could not tell what it meant. Essidel said, "Words. Just words, Human."

"Maybe. Maybe not. But here I am."

A hint of surprise touched the captain's face, perhaps even a flicker of grudging respect. "Indeed. Here, you are. Well, you have no sense, Knight. That's plain. But it could be that you have courage."

Essidel turned to Silwren. "And you. What is your tale? You have the eyes of a Shel'ai, but no Shel'ai I've ever seen or heard of could do what I saw you do to my men's arrows."

When Silwren spoke, her voice was barely a whisper. "I was *born* a Shel'ai. But I sought to become something more. I tried to strengthen my magic so that I might defend my people."

Jalist tightened his grip around his goblet. *And the process nearly turned you into another Nightmare. It also drove you mad enough to kill the other Initiates...* Something told him she would leave out that part of the story.

Essidel's ice-blue eyes narrowed. "So use that power to kill Fadarah. And wipe out the Dhargots and the Olgrym while you're at it."

Silwren flushed. "I... cannot."

Essidel sighed. "So, not content with a Shel'ai's already-impressive capacity for murder, you somehow turned yourself into a Dragonkin.

Now, you say you've changed sides. But you can't actually *do* anything. Is *that* what you're asking me to believe?"

Jalist smothered a grin. *I hope she doesn't kill you for that, Sylv. I'm starting to like you.*

Silwren faced Essidel in silence. Then she gestured, and wytchfire sprang in a bright, deadly orb about her fist. Briel cried out a warning and drew his sword. Rowen moved to block the Sylv's path, though he looked just as surprised as Jalist felt. But Silwren did not attack, and Essidel gestured for Briel to step back.

Silwren said, "My parents were killed by a mob. A mob of men like you. Their crime was not killing me when I was born... when they saw that I was a Shel'ai. The mob would have killed me, too, but I ran. And Fadarah found me. He saved my life. He kept me safe. And I have turned on him." She opened her hand. The wytchfire sputtered, surged up again as though she were having trouble dismissing it, then vanished. "I turned on him to protect *you*, when for all I know, you fired the arrow through my mother's throat."

An awful silence filled the room. *A fair point*, Jalist conceded.

Finally, Essidel said, "How long have you been gone from Sylvos?"

"Years."

Essidel said, "I'm guessing you fled during the reign of King Rhil'thys. Things were different then. Loslandril is nothing like his father. The mobs—"

"Still exist, just as surely as Shel'ai infants are still abandoned on the plains, left to starve or die in the cold. Do you deny it? Can you name even one Shel'ai living peacefully in Sylvos?"

Essidel hesitated. Then he shook his head. "But I can name a dozen men and women who were executed for their murders on King Loslandril's orders. I killed two of them myself."

I wonder if he's telling the truth. If anyone could read the captain's mind, it was Silwren. When seconds passed and she did not call the Sylv a liar or burn him to ashes, Jalist figured they had their answer.

Indeed, Silwren's expression softened a little. "Look to your histories, Captain. Once, Sylv and Shel'ai fought side by side. Now, each lives in fear of the other. Once, the Knights of the Crane were a force for honor and goodness in the world. Now, most are no better than the warlords they were founded to oppose. True power must be given, not stolen. Otherwise, it is self-defeating. That is the lesson we forgot. That is the lesson all must relearn. Including your king."

Essidel regarded her for a moment, a grudging agreement in his eyes.

Well, that's a start. Despite himself, Jalist fought back a slight smile.

CHAPTER TWENTY-THREE

KNIGHTS OF THE LOTUS

AEKO SHINGAWA SAT AND LISTENED to Crovis Ammerhel's ringing indictments.

"And lastly," Crovis's voice boomed through the vast circular Hall of Council, "I accuse Sir Rowen Locke of thieving the greatest symbol of our Order—namely, the Sword of Fâyu Jinn, Fel-Nâya, also called Knightswrath, a sacred relic from the days of the Shattering War." Crovis paused for effect then resumed his seat.

A relic most of you didn't even know existed until recently. Despite this, many of the assembled Knights murmured their agreement. She rose to her feet, calling for attention. "I remind this assembly that Sir Locke is not here to defend himself against these allegations, nor is there any evidence of theft." She seized a scroll off the table before her and brandished it. "Perhaps Sir Ammerhel has forgotten this signed testimony, sent from the Soroccan merchant who came by the sword honestly and gave it freely to Sir Locke in exchange for saving his life."

Some Knights seemed to side with her, though more had agreed with Crovis. He faced her with a cold smile. His jet-black hair had been pulled back into a tight braid, giving him an especially fierce look. He did not rise, though it was customary to do so when speaking in the Hall of Council. "Lady Shingawa is quite correct. However, I remind her that our laws prohibit squires and those whose Knighthood has been revoked from owning or carrying adamune. Fel-Nâya is, at the very least, an adamune. It is, therefore, the sole property of the Order."

Aeko spoke through her teeth. "Perhaps I nodded off during these proceedings, but not once in the past few hours did we vote on whether or not Sir Locke's Knighthood should be rescinded."

A wolfish smile touched Crovis Ammerhel's face. He rose before he spoke. "Again, Lady Shingawa is correct. I move that we take such a vote immediately." He turned in a slow circle, eyeing all one-hundred-odd Knights seated on tiered stone chairs in the great hall. "We have here the proper number of representatives from all three ranks of the Order. Let us vote now and put this matter to rest."

Some of Crovis's supporters cheered.

Aeko turned to face Bokuden. The Grand Marshal sat in a plain wooden chair in the center of the hall, dressed in the armor of a Knight of the Lotus. Though the ancient chamber had been designed so that speakers had to stand in an open area at the center, surrounded by Knights seated on progressively higher rows, Bokuden was permitted to sit. His face scarred by age and battle, he wore an adamune at his side, though he seemed to favor a gnarled cane crowned with a visage of an intertwined crane and dragon. His knuckles were as white as his hair. Bokuden met her gaze, sighed, and rose heavily to his feet. He gestured for silence. The assemblage took longer than it should have to grant him that respect.

"I admire Sir Ammerhel's devotion to the expediency of our laws." He gave the Knight a strained smile. "However, the Codex Lotius clearly states that no Knight can be judged without first being granted the right to defend himself. Sir Locke is not here. While Sir Ammerhel would no doubt remind us that the vote can be taken in special circumstances in which the accused cannot be summoned, I remind this assembly that no attempts to summon Sir Locke to the Lotus Isles have yet been made. Therefore, any attempt to revoke his Knighthood is premature." He faced Crovis, smiled, and added, "And morally questionable."

Another uneasy grumble swept through the hall. Aeko could tell by the number of scowls versus the number of smiles that Bokuden's support had waned of late. But he was still their Grand Marshal until he either died or was voted out of office, and not even Crovis dared attempt the latter. Yet.

Aeko said, "If Sir Crovis wishes to call for such a trial, he may do so. I move that we send an envoy to locate Sir Locke and invite him to appear before this council. I stress that this should be a request, *not* an arrest, in keeping with the spirit of our laws."

Crovis stood and faced her, making no attempt to smile. "And if this kind invitation is refused?"

Aeko knew she was trapped, but that came as no surprise. Crovis was nothing if not cunning. She cleared her throat. "If Sir Locke will not appear before this esteemed council to speak in his own defense, then, in keeping with our laws, he must be stripped of his sword, armor, and title. But I have every confidence that he will agree to appear. After all, I remind this council of the courage he showed at Lyos... courage even his accuser has conceded."

Crovis nodded, the hint of a smile forming on his lips. "It takes more than courage to be a Knight. It takes reason, temperance, humility—and obedience to our founding principles. Of these, Locke has none. That is why he stands accused. But I am a servant of the law. If this council wishes to have Locke present when his Knighthood is revoked, so be it. I will see it done." He sat, pretending not to hear the cheers around him.

Aeko seethed. She knew that at best, she had only delayed the inevitable. Either Fel-Nâya would be taken from Rowen when Crovis found him in the wild, probably in or around the Wytchforest, or it would be taken when Crovis brought him back, found him guilty, and likely had him killed. And once Crovis had Jinn's sword, he would become a living legend. Crovis would replace Bokuden, or kill him, and nobody would object.

Unless I ride ahead and find Rowen first. But that was impossible. Laws decreed that whenever possible, a Knight of the Lotus must oversee the apprehension of another accused Knight. Aeko was only a Knight of the Stag. She could ride out ahead of Crovis, but she would have little hope of traveling through the realms alone with the Dhargots abroad.

She faced Bokuden and found him staring back. She realized they were thinking the same thing. Bokuden called for attention again.

"The Codex Lotius also states that the verdict comes at the end of a trial, not the beginning. Sir Ammerhel has clearly made up his mind as to Sir Locke's guilt. That is his right. However, to maintain fairness, I call upon this assembly to choose another Knight of the Lotus to lead the envoy." He stared down the glares from the dozens of Knights around him.

A disquieting silence swallowed the chamber. Aeko thought at first that one of Crovis's supporters would volunteer, but it quickly became obvious that none wished to claim a role they felt had been stolen from their leader. Of the ten Knights of the Lotus present within the hall, two or three were still loyal to Bokuden, but Aeko could tell by their meek expressions that they were in no hurry to openly defy the man who would almost certainly be Grand Marshal before long. Others might simply have been reticent to conduct such a mission through territories rife with Dhargots.

The silence wore on. Crovis eyed the Grand Master with open derision as he rose from his chair again. "Since no one else volunteers for this duty, I offer my own name and call for an open vote. That is my right."

Many Knights nodded their agreement, but Bokuden shook his head. "I am still Grand Marshal, Sir Ammerhel. I may choose whom to send, if I wish."

Crovis bowed. "Then we await your wisdom, Grand Marshal." He left the center of the chamber and resumed his seat in the lowest, closest row, which was reserved for Knights of the Lotus.

Bokuden, who had been standing since first he spoke, turned slowly, leaning on his cane. He seemed to take in the whole assembly before his gaze settled on Aeko. She saw his grave look and the faint hint of apology in his eyes. She started to shake her head, but Bokuden spoke, his voice booming so loudly that many of the Knights were startled. "Aeko Shingawa, Knight of the Stag, stand and be recognized."

She obeyed, though her armor suddenly seemed thrice its normal weight.

"In recognition of your unchallenged valor in the field, for temperance of thought and action, and for your steadfast loyalty to the precepts of both the Codex Lotius and the Codex Viticus, I hereby invoke my special authority as Grand Marshal to grant you the rank you deserve." He bowed. "I greet you, Aeko Shingawa, Knight of the Lotus."

Aeko felt the blood drain from her face. She'd sought the rank all her life... and when she finally received the honor, it was nothing more than a political maneuver. She forced herself to return the bow. For a long time, no one spoke. Then everyone was on their feet, shouting.

Crovis Ammerhel rose from his seat, as though he meant to charge Bokuden. Some Knights tried to restrain him, but he shrugged them off as though they were children. "This is an outrage. Ranks are granted by vote of the entire Council, not at one old man's whim!" Crovis had his sword half drawn.

Aeko stepped between them. She touched her own sword hilt but did not draw it.

Bokuden smiled, still holding his cane. "The Codex Viticus makes no such distinction, Sir Crovis. Indeed, in the early days when the Lotus Isles were still ruled by a king, such things were always done one Knight to another. No law forbids it."

"But tradition—"

Bokuden smiled thinly. "Fâyu Jinn had something to say about traditions that no longer serve their purpose."

Crovis glanced around. The other Knights had fallen quiet so they could hear the exchange. He straightened, stepped back, and let go of his sword. "You are within your rights, Grand Marshal. I apologize for my outburst. Nevertheless, I remind you that only two women have ever risen beyond the Order of the Stag, and the last was three hundred—"

"Again, no law forbids this. In fact, the legends say that near half of Fâyu Jinn's first battalion of Knights were women. Lady Shingawa has distinguished herself countless times... perhaps more than many of the old men in armor I see around me, myself included." He looked around the Hall of Council as though daring someone to disagree. A few older Knights blushed, but none spoke out.

Crovis cleared his throat. When he spoke, he was all formality. "So be it. I will accept the legality of your actions… though I believe they show contempt for this assembly and its traditions and do damage to the honor of our Order."

He turned smartly to face Aeko. "Lady Shingawa, I welcome you to the Order of the Lotus. Though I question the means of your promotion, I acknowledge your past courage. If it is the Grand Marshal's wish that you command the envoy sent to capture Sir Locke, then I will submit dutifully to your authority." His eyes cast daggers at her as he bowed.

As Aeko returned the bow, she wondered if Crovis's use of the word *capture* was deliberate. "Thank you, Sir Crovis. I look forward to serving the Light at your side, in Jinn's name."

Crovis straightened, stone faced, and stalked out of the Hall of Council. Nearly all the Knights of the Lotus left with him, followed by most from the Orders of the Crane and Stag, until only a handful remained. Some eyed her with respect, others with pity.

Aeko sighed. Bokuden returned to his chair. He looked tired. She had been about to rebuke him, but the sight of the cane wobbling in his grasp frightened her.

She approached him slowly and knelt. "Old friend, what have you done?"

He took her hand and kissed it. "I have saved the Order… for another month, at least. Beyond that, it's up to you. And Sir Locke." He squeezed her hand and settled back in his chair. "I hope you are right about him."

I hope I am, too. Aeko rose, bowed, and started to go. Then, on impulse, she turned back, bent low, and kissed the Grand Marshal's forehead.

He reached up and brushed his hand against the long dark braid hanging over her shoulder. "Goodbye, child," he said.

Aeko left, walking briskly so that no one would see her struggling to stave off her tears. Somehow, she knew that she would never see Sir Bokuden again.

CHAPTER TWENTY-FOUR

HEALING

FOR THREE DAYS, IGRID WATCHED Arnil Royce sleep. The Lancer remained feverish and shaking, even after she'd cleaned and stitched his wounds and rubbed them in a special Hesodi poultice she'd made from herbs she'd found growing north of the stream. Though he had not spoken directly to her after their first encounter, he mumbled incomprehensibly in his delirium. Igrid feared moving him, but for all she knew, Dhargothi warriors would return to scour the field for survivors.

So Igrid had fashioned a crude litter, bound it to a horse, and taken the wounded Lancer half a mile north, to a copse of trees beside a stream. There, she reasoned that she could treat his wounds and still keep a sharp lookout.

The Dhargots had taken such a risk in attacking the Ivairians. Who was to say the Lancers would let so gruesome an insult go unanswered? There might have been no love lost between the Lancers and the Isle Knights, but Ivairia could always ally itself with another of the remaining Free Cities.

Anything that involves more people killing Dhargots has my vote!

She squelched her memories of Hesod, thinking instead about her plan to move to Lyos and start her own tavern or brothel. The loss of Knightswrath had shaken that dream, but she still had the fat pouch of coins that Arnil had given her.

Not me. He gave them to Anza. But the girl was dead. And odds favored Arnil succumbing to his fever in the next day or so. Surely, she would be blameless in the gods' eyes.

Then why do I feel so damned guilty? She reminded herself that Arnil had not only saved her. Most commanders would have been practical and merely admonished the rapists or forgiven them entirely—especially amidst a battle, when all swords were needed. Others might have even killed Igrid and Anza outright to prevent them from speaking of it. But Arnil had dealt the sternest of punishments with his own sword while all his surviving knights watched.

Then again, his troops had done the deeds in the first place. Aren't commanders responsible for the actions of their men? She gave up on resolving such matters and checked on him again. He was tossing his head and mumbling. She felt his forehead. He was still frightfully warm to the touch. She sighed.

She had done her best, but she doubted any of her efforts would keep the man in Ruun for long. He had eaten little and drunk even less, and his condition seemed to be worsening. She eyed his kingsteel bastard sword again. She would take that once the Lancer was dead. *No sense leaving it behind.*

Igrid felt herself blush. *What's wrong with me? Gods, I'm just being practical. I tried to help him, didn't I? Just like I tried to help the girl. I could have left them behind, but I didn't. Not my fault. The gods saw fit to make them wither.*

She wiped the sleeping Lancer's forehead with a cloth dampened with cool water. "Not my fault," she muttered into the darkness.

A wolf howled in the distance, as though the night had decided to answer. She reached for a blade. She had seen plenty of wolves and wild dogs shamelessly feasting on the dead during the past few days, but thankfully, they kept their distance. After all, they already had plenty of bodies to satisfy them. Still, when she noticed that the fire was beginning to die, she gathered more wood. Fire, she knew, was her best defense against the wild.

Near dawn, rain began to fall. The campfire hissed, sputtered, and went dark. Igrid tied a cloth around her nose to block out some of the grisly reek and returned to the field of dead men. She gathered a stack of battered shields and propped two of them together to form a makeshift tent over Arnil's face, offering him a little protection from the storm. He continued to toss and mumble, completely unaware.

"You're welcome," she grumbled. She fashioned another crude shelter for herself. Then she stooped wretchedly in the cold, arms crossed, and waited for the storm to pass.

Igrid did not know when she fell asleep, but she awoke shivering and hungry. It was mid-morning and cold, but the rain had stopped. She checked the First Lancer. Though he trembled from cold, his fever had broken. She did not know whether to feel relieved or disappointed. Shaking her head, she set about finding kindling for a fresh fire.

The rain had rendered all the surrounding wood unusable. She'd had the foresight to prop a shield over her remaining firewood, but the storm had produced far too much rain, so thoroughly soaking the surrounding grass that the wood had become damp anyway. She tied a cloth around her face and forced herself to approach the dead again.

Days of rot plus the routine machinations of scavengers had done their work. The smell was terrible but not as bad as the grisly, open eye sockets. Her stomach tightened and turned, but she pressed on. She approached one dead Lancer, then another, using a knife to cut the straps and remove their armor, which was already beginning to rust. Holding her breath, she cut away the wool and leather padding the Lancers wore beneath their armor. She did the same for several slain Dhargots.

The cloth was stained in dried blood, but the armor had kept out the rain. She returned to the campsite with a grisly mass of cloth she could use for kindling. She sprinkled the cloth with liquid from a flask of strong flammable spirits she had found among the dead then used flint and tinder to start a fire.

The fire was smoky and foul, but the wind was in her favor. She stacked the damp firewood near the sickly blaze, hoping the heat would dry it out. She checked on the Lancer again. His shivering had ceased. She grabbed the waterskin and managed to get him to drink a little, though he still did not stir.

She contemplated what she would do once he woke up. He was

still an important man, and she might earn even more rewards for her assistance if she got him back to Ivairia in one piece. Her rumbling stomach reminded her of the dried rations she'd found. She ate her fill, forcing down the tasteless foodstuffs, and washed it down with a little sweet wine she'd also taken off the dead. Then she armed herself as best she could, taking up a crossbow in addition to her sword and knife, and went on patrol.

No one had returned to the field to claim the dead. Still, Igrid wanted to have a solid awareness of her surroundings. If any surviving warriors approached, she would see them long before they saw her, giving her time to flee, hide, or prepare to fight. She walked a broad perimeter of several miles and saw only empty grasslands scattered with trees and the remains of the dead.

Around early afternoon, she returned to the camp. She checked Arnil again, saw that his condition had not changed, and tried to feed him a little more broth. She ate a little more herself and rested.

She felt a familiar, tingling tightness in her abdomen, accompanied by a vague soreness in her nipples, and cursed. *This is a hell of a time for my monthly bleeding!* Still, it was something of a relief. The last thing she needed was to find herself with Rowen Locke's bastard child.

She stayed at the camp until boredom overtook her, then she went down to the stream to bathe. Late-afternoon sunlight sparkled off the water. She stripped naked and left her clothes—a mismatch of articles looted from the field—on the ground beside the water, next to her sword, which she'd thrust into the earth where it would be within easy reach.

She tested the water with her toes. Despite the sunlight glinting off the stream, the water was shockingly cold. She forced herself to wade in anyway, stopping only when the water rose past her thighs to her waist. She shuddered and swore loudly, but she was glad for the way the cold drove the lingering weariness from her body.

She washed her face, rubbing her eyes. She hadn't bathed since washing the blood off Anza. Igrid shuddered again, though it had nothing to do with the cold. She pushed the image of the girl's face from her mind, willing anything to replace it.

The Isle Knight had probably reached the Wytchforest. She wondered if he was still alive. Part of her even missed him. "Don't be a fool," she grumbled. "You betrayed him. He hates you now. You'd be better off falling in love with an Olg."

She knelt on the pebbly stream bottom, letting the water rise above her head. She stayed a moment in watery darkness, her eyes closed. The water did not feel so cold anymore. She could even feel the sunlight streaming through the water, caressing her. Despite herself, she smiled. She held her breath as long as she could then straightened. She combed back her wet hair with both hands, wiped her face, and opened her eyes.

She found Arnil standing on the bank, dressed only in his trousers, using his sheathed sword as a crutch. Arnil's pale face blushed. "Forgive me. I was just…"

"Being a man," Igrid snorted. She waded back to shore without covering herself and used an old cloak to dry off. Arnil turned his back as she dressed. *How is he even awake?* "You shouldn't be moving yet. You'll reopen those damn wounds I spent so much time stitching."

Arnil inspected his bare chest. "You sew well, milady. These should hold."

Igrid finished dressing, pulled her long crimson tresses behind her head, and tied them in a wet knot. "I'm no lady, Lancer. And I'm not an Iron Sister anymore, either." She grabbed her sword and started back to the camp. "You're probably hungry. There's plenty of bread and dried meat, though you're probably better off with broth and wine for now."

He reached to grab her wrist, wobbled, and missed. "How long—"

"Three days. Four, if you count today. I thought for sure you'd go to the gods."

Arnil traced his stitches with his fingertips. The skin was an ugly purple, and the stitches were seeping blood and pus, but that was not unusual. "You've cared for me all this time?"

For no reason Igrid could understand, she blushed. "Spare me your courtly gratitude, Lancer. I'm still keeping your coins, and whatever else your king gives me for keeping you alive."

Arnil nodded. As he hobbled back to the campsite, she looked at him more closely and realized he was balding. He was thin, too, and only a little taller than she was.

He looks like some dainty princeling exiled to the wild to reform him of his cravings for common whores and gambling. She smiled.

Then again, she had seen him charge five Dhargothi horsemen by himself. And when she'd found him by the river, he was wreathed in the bodies of slain foes. Spurred by sudden curiosity, she asked, "Why were you scouting the Dhargots? You don't really think they'd invade Ivairia, do you?"

The Lancer returned to the tree he had been leaning against and, with Igrid's help, sat down again. Igrid fed the fire and handed him a wineskin to drink from while she fixed his broth. When she looked at him again, the wine had left his lips red.

He took another drink, his face still expressionless, and said, "We'd heard how the Dhargots were sweeping east, claiming all the realms previously conquered by the Throng. Cassica is close to our borders. We trade with them for cloth and grain. When the sorcerers took Cassica, they never marched any farther north. They left us alone, but we didn't know if the Dhargots would do the same."

"If you just wanted to scout, you should have sent fewer men. You were too obvious."

Arnil laughed. "A scouting party of a hundred horsemen. We might as well have been blaring trumpets while we rode, for all the noise we made. Had it been up to me, I would have ridden alone, or nearly so. But courtly protocol requires that the First Lancer travel with an appropriate entourage."

She heard an unmistakable tone of bitterness and self-deprecation in his voice. "I've never known a knight to disparage his own precious Order."

"Any decent knight hates his Order, or else he's a fool. And anyway, I have a habit of voicing thoughts other men know to keep quiet. It's why the king listens to me... though he'd probably rather I shut my mouth half the time." He yawned and checked his wounds again. "What's your name, Iron Sister?"

She frowned. "I told you—"

"Then give me your real name so I can stop offending you."

My real name? She almost laughed. She thought of inventing a new one, or maybe using Haesha again. "Igrid. But I don't feel like telling you my story, so if you want to talk, tell me yours."

Arnil shrugged. "I was born into House Royce. My father is King Rodrick Whitetower's nephew. When I was five, they stuck a wooden sword in my hands, pointed at some sack men stuffed with straw, and told me I'd better learn how to kill. Not my fault I happened to be good at it."

Igrid scoffed. "So you were raised in a castle, or at least a keep of some kind. You probably had servants—women like me who had to do whatever you said, or else they'd be fighting the dogs for table scraps."

"Wolves," Arnil corrected. "Greatwolves, especially. Since the famine, there aren't many dogs left in Ivairia. But we have plenty of wolves."

Igrid's frown tightened. "Simplefolk sick and crying right outside your tower window while you ate your venison, smiled at your minstrel, and fucked your whores. And you want me to feel sorry for you?"

"Actually, I didn't ask for pity. But I would accept some of that broth."

She poured the contents of the pot into a wooden bowl and handed it to him. The broth was still thick and cold, but Arnil drank it without hesitation. When he returned the bowl, she filled it again and passed it back.

He nodded his thanks. "In my lands, peasants who talk like that would be flogged and stocked in the public square."

She reached for her sword. "Threaten me again—"

He waved his hand between swallows of broth. "No threat, milady. Call it surprise." He finished the bowl, set it on the grass, and turned his attention to the wineskin. "You talk like someone who has been wronged—and not just by my men."

"Is that your way of asking for my story?"

He lowered the wineskin. "If you like."

Her derision faded. She saw an earnestness in his eyes. She wondered if his curiosity was only the ploy of a man turned lustful by the sight of her bathing in the stream. She was all set to refuse him, then she changed her mind. "I wouldn't even know where to start."

Arnil took another drink then handed her the wineskin. "Start anywhere. Start with a lie, if you want. Just talk."

Igrid glanced at him. The moment seemed too much like her last encounter with Rowen, but she heard something in Arnil's voice that she had not noticed before. Grief? Guilt? She thought again of the bodies strewn across the plains.

He just needs to listen to something other than his own thoughts. That, at least, she understood. And before she knew what she was doing, she was talking. And even more surprising, she was telling the truth.

Once Igrid began, she could not stop. She felt a vague sense of disbelief when she saw sunset filtering through the branches of trees hours later, but still, she continued her story as Arnil listened. She spoke of being an orphan on the streets, of the brothels in Lyos, of her wish to join the Iron Sisters. She even spoke of Hesod's bloody fall and the Iron Sisters' slaughter, how she had turned craven when her order needed her most and fled, pretending to be a priestess. She tried to choke back her tears, but she gave in and told her tale as though she were alone, merely confessing her sins to the encroaching darkness. Much of the tale mirrored what she'd told Rowen. There was no longer a pretense, no secret agenda. She simply felt the need, finally, to speak without even the slightest lie.

She even spoke of her chance encounter with Rowen on the road to Atheion, how she had assaulted and humiliated him, only to have him save her from a fate worse than death. Arnil had been a rapt listener throughout her tale, but he seemed especially interested in the Shel'ai woman who wielded the power of a Dragonkin, for word of her exploits at the Battle of Lyos had already traveled north to Ivairia.

Igrid shared what little she understood of Fadarah's mad conquest and Rowen's and Silwren's far-flung attempts to thwart him. Though she said nothing about sleeping with him, after some shamed hesitation, she spoke of how she had repaid Rowen's mercy by trying to steal from him, only to have the illusion turned against her. She feared seeing rebuke in the Lancer's eyes, but he merely listened.

She spoke lastly of Anza, just another nameless wretch, one of thousands throughout Ruun, though her death had affected her strangely, unexpectedly breaking something inside her. When at last Igrid fell silent, she looked around, as though waking from a daze, and realized it was dark. While she talked, Arnil had tended the fire. She found him staring at her. He had not interrupted her once.

She flinched, suddenly self-conscious. "I don't know if I answered your question somewhere in all that... but if you want me to be clear, Lancer, it's not knights and noble lords that I hate. It's not even all the cutthroats and rapers, if you can believe it. They are what they are. No, it's those bastards who talk of honor like it's a real thing, then stab you in the back the moment you start to believe them. Better not to believe and rob them of their chance." She shrugged. "It's not a warm way to live, but at least you survive that way. Otherwise, you'd need a damn army to keep safe."

Arnil was silent for a time. "That Isle Knight you spoke of..."

"Rowen." Igrid blushed when she said his name.

"Had Sir Rowen been in my place, do you think he would have killed those squires for their crimes?"

Igrid was startled. "Yes," she said finally.

Arnil nodded. "Good. That's three of us. Find a few more, and maybe we'll put together an army someday."

CHAPTER TWENTY-FIVE
QUE'AHL

R OWEN STOOD OUTSIDE THE SIMPLE Wyldkin cottage that
served as both guest quarters and prison, glad that he had
been allowed a moment to wander. In contrast to the majesty
of the forest beyond, the fortress was stark and utilitarian. Buildings
were unadorned, with narrow doorways and even narrower windows.
While some Sylvs walked in the streets, others crossed raised platforms
joined by wooden bridges that, Rowen guessed, allowed defenders to
rain arrows on any Olgrym who succeeded in breaching the fortress.

The Sylvs had taken their weapons—including Knightswrath—
but so far, they had not been mistreated. After Silwren's dire
proclamation, Captain Essidel promised to keep them safe in Que'ahl
while he appealed to his general for further instructions. The general,
Seravin, apparently occupied a nearby fort. Essidel had ridden out at
once to speak with him, promising to be back by morning. Though it
was the middle of the night, the stronghold was more than adequately
lit by torches and lanterns.

Rowen had hoped to speak with Silwren, but the expenditure of
magic outside the gates had taxed her greatly, and she'd fallen asleep
almost as soon as they were escorted to their lodgings. Finally, unable
to sleep and irritated by Jalist's snoring, Rowen stalked off. Wyldkin
and Shal'tiar frowned when they saw him walking alone, but no one
challenged him.

In the captain's absence, their safety—and Que'ahl's defense—had
been entrusted to Briel. He seemed none too pleased with the duty

and was even less pleased when Rowen joined him on the wooden battlements. "Where is the wytch?"

"Asleep," Rowen said. At least, he hoped she was. He worried that her nightmares might conjure fire as easily as her hands did. "I keep thinking I understand her. Then I think I don't." Rowen was surprised that he'd spoken so bluntly.

"You'll get no sympathy from me, Human. If it weren't for Captain Essidel—"

A Wyldkin woman rushed up to the battlements and interrupted them. The two spoke in a rush. Rowen's patchwork knowledge of the Sylvan language was not enough to tell for certain what they were discussing, but he caught a certain word spoken again and again, always with a mixture of disgust and trepidation: *Olgrym.*

He felt for his sword before he realized it was gone. He wore plain clothes, too. His armor was in the cottage. Rowen turned, about to go back for his armor, but decided to talk to Briel first, who was speaking with a cluster of officers. Rowen waited until they dispersed.

Briel gave him a cold glance. "Go back to your wytch. You're in the way here."

"What's happening here?"

"Olgrym. They are moving south, hundreds strong."

Rowen made no attempt to conceal his disbelief. Everyone knew that due to constant fighting among the Olgish clans, no single clan could boast more than fifty warriors at a time.

Briel said, "I wish I were lying, Human, but I am not. There are at least sixty clans scattered throughout Godsfall, and it seems they've all united under one banner."

The thought sent a chill down Rowen's spine. "Are they invading the Wytchforest?"

"Not yet. Most Olgrym have no grasp of strategy, but this new leader, Doomsayer, is different. He knows better than to let us attack his flanks and rear. He'll have to wipe out the Shal'tiar and the Wyldkin before he can make for the World Tree." Briel turned, staring into the night. "There are six Wyldkin strongholds between here and Godsfall."

"How many are the Olgrym attacking?"

"All of them." Briel pointed.

Rowen squinted and saw a plume of fire on the distant, dark horizon. He detected the faint din of far-off battle. "Where is your captain?"

"Hopefully, helping General Seravin plan a counterattack. Or else he was caught behind the lines when the Olgrym advanced."

"Have you sent men to aid him?"

"Worry about yourself, Human. If any warrior could cut his way free of that"—Briel pointed at the horizon—"it's Captain Essidel."

Still, a trace of fear lanced the Sylv's voice. "Want me to wake Silwren?"

Briel's tone hardened. "Why in the Light would I want that?"

"Because her magic makes her more dangerous than your twenty best archers. If you're under attack, you might need her."

"Oh, I think we'll manage."

"I don't like the Olgrym any more than you do. Return my blade, and I'll fight beside you."

"I cannot command a garrison while worrying that you'll betray us the moment our backs are turned." Briel gestured to two Shal'tiar fighters. "Take him back to his lodgings and keep him there."

"You just said you can't spare the men. Forget it. I'm staying."

To Rowen's surprise, Briel smirked. He waved back the guards. "How good are you with a bow?"

"As good as any man here," Rowen lied.

Briel laughed. "I doubt that. But we'll see." He pointed at a nearby weapons rack. Some of the longbows were ornately carved and strangely curved, but Rowen selected a smooth, plain one, along with a quiver of arrows.

He tested the string. This Sylvan longbow had even greater draw weight than he was used to. He marveled that the lean Sylvs could use such heavy weapons. He figured he had the strength to draw one, but his aim would be shaky at best. Still, it was something.

Briel pointed. "Stand there. And if you so much as turn sideways with an arrow on your string, I'll cut your throat. Are we understood?"

Rowen nodded. He took up his position and looked out over the battlements, into the night beyond. "I don't see the Olgrym. Are you sure—"

"You will."

Rowen felt the Sylvs scrutinizing him as he drew an arrow and fit it to his borrowed longbow. Poison glistened on the arrow's tip, though he doubted any poison in the world could bring down an Olg. He hoped that, at the very least, the Sylvs would not notice how badly his hands were shaking.

Seems I have a knack for finding myself at the heart of sieges. He remembered the Battle of Lyos, which he had not expected to survive. Then, though, Silwren and El'rash'lin had been at his side, not to mention a whole company of Isle Knights, the men of the Red Watch, and a militia made up of gang members and citizens of the Dark Quarter. Right then, he was surrounded by Sylvs who most likely still considered him an enemy.

He thought of laying down his bow and fetching Silwren himself. But aside from Briel's mistrust, her display at the gates of Que'ahl had clearly drained her, drawing her perilously close to losing control and burning them all to cinders. Better they call upon her magic only as a last resort.

The Sylvs had lit beacon fires all over the plains, well beyond Que'ahl's walls, so that the yellow-orange flicker would illuminate advancing forces. Even without the fires, though, only the deaf could have failed to hear the approach of the dark-eyed, gray-skinned giants.

They marched like madmen out of the night, row upon row, their approach heralded by guttural shouts and cruel, challenging laughter. Once in view of the stronghold, still a few hundred yards away, they spread out. They seemed to fill the whole of the darkened plains. Rowen thought of how terrified he had been when, as a mercenary, he had seen just two or three Olgrym at a time. Those few had slaughtered thrice their number in battle. He tried to count the hulking figures advancing across the Ash'bana Plains, then he gave up.

Que'ahl had nowhere near the number of defenders it needed. *Still, we're fortified behind high walls. There are trenches and three palisades down there. We have bows. Even if our numbers are the same, we should beat them with ease.*

Then the Olgrym stopped. They formed a broad phalanx just beyond longbow range. Some of the Olgrym wore crude armor or furs, but most were naked. All were gruesomely painted for war. In addition to blades, spears, and axes, many carried boulders. These they wielded with ease, often using only one arm, though Rowen guessed that it would take half a dozen Humans or Sylvs to lift even the smallest of the Olgrym's stones. The Olgrym quieted for a moment, as though bracing themselves.

No matter. They're like wild boars. A few arrows and—

The Olgrym roared in unison. The din they had made before was nothing compared to the new noise. The beasts' voices tore across the grasslands like an avalanche. Rowen felt faint, though he took solace in the fact that many of the Sylvs—who had likely been fighting the Olgrym all their lives—betrayed signs of similar strain in their otherwise-grim expressions.

Briel's voice somehow carried over the Olgrym's roars. Rowen momentarily forgot he knew some of the Sylvan language, but he remembered in time to catch one word: *courage.*

Easier said than done. He wished again that he had Knightswrath or knew at least where the Sylvs had locked it up. The familiar feel of the dragonbone hilt would be as comforting to him as the implacable sharpness of its blade would have been, especially if the Olgrym began scaling the walls and got close enough to render a longbow useless.

But they can't scale the walls without ladders. Rowen squinted, studying the fire-lit figures in the distance. He searched for the dark shape of ladders, or even a few Olgrym toting grappling hooks fixed with rope, but he saw neither. He felt a surge of hope. "Briel, they have no ladders. Do you see? They'll have to try and hack through with axes. Even *they* can't do that!"

The Shal'tiar officer did not acknowledge his cry, though the other Sylvs around him sent him a few condescending looks. A moment later, he saw why. At least fifty Olgrym had moved ahead of the rest and stood shoulder to shoulder, tauntingly close to longbow range. All were naked and unarmed, save for what looked like gigantic wineskins. They roared in unison and upended the wineskins over their own bodies. Dark liquid poured out. They stood a moment, arms raised, then tossed aside the wineskins.

Rowen frowned. "What?"

More Olgrym came forward with torches. They raised the torches toward the dark sky, lowered them, and touched the torches to their comrades. The Olgrym burst into flames.

"By the Light!"

Those fifty-odd Olgrym roared again—the horrible cry rang with as much desire as pain—and sprinted toward Que'ahl.

The Sylvs had already fired once before Rowen remembered the longbow in his hands. He raised it, drew back the bowstring, and let it go. He could not track his own arrow's flight in the darkness, but he sensed at once that he'd missed.

The Sylvs were better. Arrows struck all the charging, burning Olgrym, though amazingly, only two toppled to the grasslands. The rest charged on, crazed, faster than Rowen would have thought possible. Then barely fifty yards separated them.

Rowen realized that Briel was calmly giving orders. All around him, the Sylvs were a blur, firing a second, a third, then a fourth volley while Rowen was still fumbling with his second arrow.

Rowen felt his heart in his throat as he chose a target and loosed his arrow. He knew he had not missed, though he could not be sure if it was his arrow or any one of a dozen others that sent the howling, burning warrior headfirst onto the grasslands. Rowen reached for another arrow.

A fourth of the burning Olgrym had been shot down, but the rest hurled themselves onward, some with a dozen arrows in their bodies. Some vanished into trenches and traps, only to claw their way out moments later, but others leapt clean over them. They were almost to the palisades.

That will slow them down. It has to.

He fired again and fumbled for another arrow from his quiver, just as the Olgrym reached the wooden stakes. He saw with relief that some of the Olgrym had rushed blindly forward and impaled themselves. He dared to hope that the rest would follow suit, if only to cut short the pain of burning to death. But most of the Olgrym managed to climb and claw their way past the earthwork defenses.

They flowed through the trenches and barreled past the second and third palisades, leaving more burning dead behind. But not enough. Only a few yards still separated them from Que'ahl's gates, which were right below him. Without intending to, he'd placed himself exactly where the fighting would be fiercest. The smell of burning flesh soared up into Rowen's nostrils. He winced, his eyes watering, and loosed another arrow.

Another furious twang resounded from the longbows of Shal'tiar and Wyldkin. A knot of arrows met the Olgrym's advance. Steely tips sliced organs and severed tendons. Six more Olgrym fell, burning and twitching on the grasslands. But the rest, shielded by those dying in front of them, sprinted the final few feet and flung their burning bodies at Que'ahl's gates.

Rowen heard and felt the stout beams shudder. *They're going to force the gates open. They're going to burn them and force them open.*

But Briel was already shouting a new set of orders. A squad of Sylvs upended fat cauldrons, pouring sand through a series of murder holes located directly above the gates. The sand spread over the burning Olgrym, suffocating the flames. Then the Sylvs sent a final volley through the murder holes, carpeting the area before Que'ahl's gates with arrows, killing anything left alive.

Rowen shook his head in disbelief. He leaned over the wooden battlements to get a better look at the tangled, bloody mess. His stomach lurched. "All that death, and they barely even singed the gates."

The archer next to him, a Wyldkin woman with feathers in her braided hair, gave him a sour look. Her grave expression belied the melodic beauty of her accent. "Wrong." She pointed.

Rowen's heart jumped into his throat again. The whole time they had been concentrating on bringing down the burning Olgrym, the rest of the host had been charging about fifty yards behind them. They had already reached the palisades and were either clambering over them or using gigantic axes to hack down the wooden stakes. The sound of splintering wood mingled with their guttural shouts.

Rowen stared. The Wyldkin woman loosed an arrow then kicked him. She shouted in the Sylvan tongue for him to wake up.

Rowen fumbled for another arrow. The Olgrym were so close that he hardly needed to aim. He could see their cold eyes, their gray skin stretched taut over bulging muscles and occasional protrusions of bone.

Then he saw the rocks. Those Olgrym who had armed themselves with boulders were heaving them over the stronghold's walls with the force of catapults. Rowen heard an awful, ominous *crack* to his right. He turned to see a guard tower struck by a flurry of boulders. The tower was crowded with archers. Some of the Sylvs managed to leap clear, but others burst in grisly showers of blood under the weight of the jagged rocks.

Rowen stomach lurched. He chose his target and fired again, putting an arrow three hands deep in an Olg's shoulder. The Olg paused to break off the exposed shaft and glance up. For one moment, their eyes met. Rowen had the awful impression that the Olg was memorizing his face. Then the Olg hefted his axe and hurtled forward. Rowen lost sight of him, but he could hear the sound of the beast's axe rending wood.

Gods, they're chopping their way inside! He nocked another arrow, but by then, all the Olgrym still alive had pressed themselves to the stronghold's walls and were tearing at the wood with their weapons. The floor quaked, and a few Wyldkin poured arrows through murder holes. Meanwhile, the dark-garbed Shal'tiar quietly left the battlements and massed in the courtyard below, blades and black brigandines glinting in the torchlight.

Rowen remembered Briel's orders, but the Sylv was nowhere to be seen.

The Wyldkin woman next to him said, "Safer here. Nothing down there but death." She fired an arrow through a murder hole, directly into the face of an Olg just a few feet beneath her.

The beast howled and swung up at her, but she was just out of reach. The Wyldkin calmly fit another arrow and fired, then another.

Rowen paused, peering through the murder holes at a heap of slashed and twisted corpses, all bristling with arrows. The archers were inflicting heavy damage, but for every Olg the Wyldkin killed, two more seemed to take his place. Rowen felt their odds of victory diminishing. Still, the woman was right. As close as they were to the Olgrym, the battlements were still safer than the courtyard would be once the Olgrym forced their way inside. Then he remembered Silwren and Jalist. Before he realized what he was doing, he left the battlements and rushed down the steps.

The Shal'tiar formed ranks with icy efficiency. Those in the front traded their longbows for swords and savagely curved polearms. A few seized ropes that Rowen had not even noticed before and pulled. To Rowen's amazement, the ropes were fixed to a wooden platform that covered a pit on their side of the gates. The platform was quickly dragged out of the way. As he hurried toward Briel, Rowen glanced down into the pit and saw wooden spikes protruding in the darkness.

Meanwhile, archers took up position on the platforms above. They were fitting three arrows at a time to their bowstrings. He also spotted two frightful ballistae designed to fire a dozen light spears all at once. The ballistae had already been loaded and aimed directly at the gates.

Briel stood at the center of the Shal'tiar line, scowling at Rowen. "You're supposed to be on the walls."

"I like it better down here," Rowen said, feigning bravado. As he spoke, though, he heard the dreadful sound of Olgrym axes chopping at the gates. "Let me get Silwren."

Briel hesitated. "If you like. You're a worthless archer, probably no better with a sword, anyway."

The change of heart surprised him. Rowen wondered if that meant their odds were even worse than he thought, and Briel knew it. He decided to press his luck. "My sword?"

"Go, Human!" Briel snapped. "If you want a blade, I'm sure there will be plenty lying on the ground before long."

CHAPTER TWENTY-SIX
AXES AND FLAME

ROWEN MADE HIS WAY THROUGH Que'ahl, back toward his lodgings. A mixture of guilt and relief filled him as he left the Shal'tiar to do what would surely be the worst fighting of the battle. He passed more Sylvan men and women rushing to reinforce the ailing gates, but they paid him no mind.

If Silwren can't help, we have to get out of here. The Sylvs did not seem to have even considered the option of retreat. But the Olgrym were clearly going to win the fight. Once they breached the walls, the stronghold would become a slaughterhouse.

He could not leave without Knightswrath. He ran in what he hoped was the direction of the barracks. He still had his bow, half wondering how he would respond if a Sylv tried to stop him, but the rear half of Que'ahl seemed all but deserted. Then he caught a glimpse of movement and saw three Wyldkin women armed with bows and swords, hustling a row of children into a small, wood-and-stone temple devoted to the Light. The Sylvan children's wide eyes were full of fright. The women gave him cold looks but quickly returned to their duty. When the last child was inside, the women followed, closing the doors behind them.

Rowen found himself wondering if they thought the gods would protect them there. He remembered the Noshans who had been slaughtered in their own temple. In his experience, the gods had no more interest in safeguarding the innocent than they did the guilty.

Granted, Sylvs worshipped the Light, but he had not known the Light to respond to prayers, either.

He shook his head and hurried on. He spotted what looked like the barracks and rushed in. To his relief, they were empty. He found an armory. His hope was short lived, though. He found dozens of blades and bows, but not a single rack contained the precious adamune. Then he spotted a chest in the corner. He opened it. Inside were the rest of their weapons. Still, Knightswrath was not there.

Rowen cursed. The sounds of battle had moved much closer than he would have thought possible in such a short time. He took the weapons, along with a Sylvan blade for himself. The blade was shorter and more curved than an adamune, though it seemed excellently balanced, and a test of its edge left a swell of blood on his thumb.

He ran back to their quarters. He was not surprised to see that the guards had already left their posts to fight alongside the other Sylvs.

Jalist stood outside, armed with a hatchet he must have found somewhere, but he cast that aside and took his long axe from Rowen's hand. "You picked a hell of a time to wander off."

"Olgrym," Rowen said, trying to catch his breath. "They're about to cut their way inside, if they haven't already."

Jalist paled. "That explains why you left your precious armor behind. And the sword?"

"Couldn't find it."

Jalist's expression was nearly sympathetic for a moment. He glanced around at the streets, which were empty except for rows of lit braziers. "Looks like everyone who can fight has gone to the gates. Just how many damn Olgrym are out there?"

"More than either of us has ever seen."

"Good to see our luck hasn't changed. Let's just get out of here while we still can."

"Where's Silwren?"

"Passed out. Pale as a bedsheet. I suppose we'll have to carry her... unless I can persuade you to leave her behind."

Rowen hurried into the cottage. True to Jalist's description, Silwren was lying on one of several beds lining the far wall. Her cheeks were as pale as the dragonmist of her eyes, though to his relief, she was awake.

She had pushed herself up on her elbow and was staring at him weakly. "How... many Olgrym?"

"All of them," Rowen answered.

Silwren stood then swayed unsteadily. Rowen moved to help, but Jalist shook his head.

"You keep watch. I'll carry her. She weighs two feathers, anyway." He wrapped one strong arm around Silwren's waist. "Sorry to treat you like a bag of potatoes, Sorceress, but we're out of options." Though he was a full head shorter than she was, he easily hoisted her over his shoulder.

Silwren did not protest, though Rowen caught her unmistakable grimace. He smothered a grin then sobered when he heard another surge in the battle. The cries of the dying Sylvs drowned out the clash of steel.

"Hurry," he said, rushing out. He looked around, trying to find some means of escape, but all he saw were the tightly lashed logs that formed Que'ahl's walls.

"What kind of damn town only has one entrance?" Jalist said. He gently lowered Silwren onto her own two feet.

"The kind that's probably used to repelling a host half this size." Rowen turned to Silwren. "Can you burn a way out?"

"I... I don't think so."

Rowen considered climbing over the walls, but there were no stairs or ladders nearby, and the highest rooftop sat well below the tops of the fort wall. He considered making a crude grappling hook with rope tied to a sword. They had no rope, but he'd seen coils of it in the armory. Or else they could try to dig under the walls, but the upright logs that formed the walls of the stronghold were likely sunken deep in the earth.

He turned to Jalist. "How long would it take you to cut through?"

Jalist started to laugh. When he realized Rowen was serious, he stepped forward and studied the stout stronghold walls. "Six or seven years."

Rowen fit an arrow to his longbow. "How about a few minutes?"

Jalist raised one eyebrow. Then he took a firm stance, his long axe in both hands, and went to work.

The Dwarr was fiercely strong, and the axe blurred in his grasp, sending a shower of woodchips in every direction. He sounded like the Olgrym hacking at the stronghold's gates, but Rowen saw at once that even Jalist could not work as quickly as necessary. He swallowed a surge of panic and turned, focusing on the still-empty streets.

Silwren joined him. A little of her color had returned, but she was shivering. She touched his arm. "I don't think I'll be able to help you. Not without... great risk."

Rowen heard the shame in her voice. He squeezed her hand. "You saved us at the gates. No way you could've known the Olgrym would attack tonight. Just bad luck."

Rowen listened to the steely chop of Jalist's axe on wood. The sounds were growing farther and farther apart. He fixed his gaze ahead. A bend in the streets of Que'ahl prevented him from witnessing the fighting elsewhere, but he could imagine how awful it was. He confessed to Silwren, "I made Briel think I was going to bring you."

She squeezed his hand but said nothing.

Surely, by then, the Olgrym must have hewn their way into the fortress. Soon, they would slaughter the rest of the stronghold's defenders and sweep through the streets, killing anyone left in hiding. He thought of the children and the Wyldkin women in the temple. He couldn't just leave them.

He started forward, but Silwren grabbed his arm. Rowen smiled thinly. "I take it you were reading my thoughts."

"The Olgrym are close. We'll never get away with a herd of children following us."

Rowen deliberately removed her hand from his arm. "Odd that a Human would have more concern for Sylvan children than you do."

Her wince told him that his words had wounded her.

"Stay with Jalist."

The Dwarr's face was slick with perspiration, but he continued hacking away. Rowen sprinted down the brazier-lit streets. He saw dark figures in the distance but could not tell if they were Olgrym or Sylvs. Mercifully, the temple was close. The Wyldkin stood guard outside. He called out to them in Sylvan, insisting he had a way out of the stronghold. Then he stood, catching his breath, and waiting for their answer.

He heard rustling from inside the temple, followed by stifled crying. The Wyldkin women glanced at each other. He could see they were skeptical, but they were also practical. If scores of bows and blades could not hold back the Olgrym at the gates, what hope did they have in the temple?

One said something Rowen could not hear then rapped on the temple doors. Wood scraped wood as a heavy crossbeam was lifted out of the way. The doors opened, and the third Wyldkin woman appeared. She gave him a cold look, but the three spoke in quick whispers. Two went back inside to gather the children.

Rowen kept a wary eye on the streets, flexing his bowstring. *Just a little longer...*

But time had caught up with him. A thick, ghastly knot of Olgrym appeared a hundred yards away, their bodies smeared with blood and gore. Rowen counted one dozen, then two. He hoped the Olgrym would not see them, but one pointed and howled.

The third Wyldkin woman cursed. She screamed a warning to her comrades. They appeared a moment later, dragging some children and pushing others. Some of the older children carried smaller ones. One girl had armed herself with a splintered makeshift spear she must have fashioned from a broken candelabrum.

Rowen pointed. "Around that corner, then three blocks away. My friends will guide you to safety." *At least, I hope so.*

He could see they still did not trust him, but that made no difference. Even a slight chance was better than none. The children ran, creating a ragtag column that still moved far too slowly for Rowen's tastes. One Wyldkin woman went with them. Two stayed behind. They said nothing but joined him, stone faced, longbows in hand.

The Olgrym, seeing the majority of their would-be prey escaping, howled again and broke into a sprint. They surged down the streets, knocking over braziers in a shower of cinders, sometimes tripping over and fighting each other in their haste.

Gods, it's finally about to happen. I'm going to die.

Rowen realized one of the Wyldkin women was talking to him. She repeated herself, speaking decent-enough Common Tongue despite her accent. "What is the battle cry of your people?"

Rowen's senses were so soaked with fear that it took him a moment to realize what she was asking. Finally, he answered, "*Singchai ushó fey.*" He was about to translate the Shao phrase—*No courage without fear*—then realized there was no point.

The first Wyldkin aimed down the shaft of her arrow and let it fly. The second followed suit. Rowen did the same. All three arrows found their marks, but the charge did not slow in the slightest. Fear quickened Rowen's limbs, allowing him to nock and fire another arrow nearly as quickly as the archers beside him. He saw an Olg draw an arrow from his gut, toss it away, and keep charging, but the Wyldkin arrows converged on the Olg next to him and brought him down. He fell, tangling the legs around them, slowing the charge.

I should have taken a spear from the armory. Rowen fired a third arrow but could not tell how grievously he'd wounded his target. The ground shook as the Olgrym approached. Sylvan bows twanged beside him. More arrows drew blood, but somehow, the charge quickened.

Rowen threw down the bow and drew his borrowed shortsword. He reached out and plucked a torch from a nearby brazier as well. As he did so, he realized numbly that this was his chance for one final, profound thought. But he could think of nothing.

Then the Olgrym were upon them. Rowen had the sudden feeling that he was dueling a gigantic boulder tossed in advance of an avalanche. The odd thought made him smile, giddy with fear, despite the panic knotting his muscles and nerves. He had hoped to stand his ground, but already, he was backpedaling as fast as he could, ducking beneath the bone-crushing swings of an Olg's axe. A little blood dripped off the tip of his Sylvan shortsword. He'd managed to cut the Olg's arm, though the beastly warrior did not seem to notice.

I'm still alive. So far, I'm still alive.

The Wyldkin women were not so lucky. One had fallen before she could draw her sword, an Olg's spear pierced almost completely through her body. The other had run—not out of cowardice, Rowen sensed, but the hope that she could lure the Olgrym off the children's trail. It had not worked.

Rowen felt his back strike something solid. He ducked. The Olg's axe rang off a brazier. Rowen swung blindly then sidestepped—directly into the path of another Olg who was driving a spear at his chest. With as much luck as skill, he managed to turn sideways and parry the thrust, though the force of the blow jarred his sword arm. The Olg's face was so close to his that he could smell his putrid breath. The thing seemed to be smiling. Rowen thrust his torch into the Olg's smile and pushed hard.

Cinders burned his hand, but the Olg howled. Then he backhanded the knight, driving him toward the one with the axe. The second Olg simply reached out, caught Rowen by the arm, and threw him to the ground. Rowen grunted as the air left his lungs. He looked up to find a gray mountain blocking out the starlight. He tried to stab the mountain, but it sprouted hands that wrenched the blade from his grasp.

Then Rowen heard the beautiful twanging of bowstrings. The Olg fell backward, away from him. Hail after hail of arrows poured out of the night, slashing into the Olgrym's ranks.

From the direction of the stronghold's gates came a squad of Sylvan archers. More filled the platforms above. Another squad of swordsmen, led by Briel, moved to flank the Olgrym. Somehow, despite how quickly they aimed and fired, they did not strike him by mistake.

Rowen might have cheered, but he thought of Silwren and Jalist, not to mention the Sylvan children. He clawed his way back to his feet and fumbled for a weapon. The first thing he saw was the dead Olg's axe. It was absurdly large and heavy for him, but it was better than nothing. He hefted it and ran to find his friends.

Luckily, the Olgrym were too busy clashing with the Wyldkin and Shal'tiar to notice him. There seemed to be more Sylvs than he would have expected, given that the Olgrym had already carved a path into the stronghold. He hoped he would not get tagged by a stray arrow.

He followed a trail of tipped-over braziers, considered picking up another torch, then realized he would need two hands to swing the axe. He heard the din of battle ahead, distinguishing Jalist's angry cry through the noise, and ran faster. He rounded the corner in time to feel a wave of heat wash over him. Purple fire flowed like water from a broken dam. A wave of sheer force followed the fire, knocking him to the ground.

Silwren! He fixed his eyes on the blaze, forcing them open despite the glare. Enormous bodies struggled in the violet wash, writhing and burning. Then they were gone. The fire vanished, too.

He expected to see Silwren standing there, madly triumphant, her body still washed in tendrils of light and wytchfire. Instead, a hooded man wearing a white cloak sewn with crimson greatwolves turned from the cinders of the Olgrym to Silwren, who was crumpled on the earth, stunned but alive.

Gods, who is that? Rowen could not see the man's face, but it made no difference. Aside from Silwren and El'rash'lin, Rowen had never met a single Shel'ai who had not promptly tried to kill him. He glanced past the cloaked man and saw the corpse of the third Wyldkin woman nearby, a longbow still clutched in her hands. Panting, Jalist stood in front of the Sylvan children, a dead Olg at his feet. Beyond him lay the portion of the wall that Jalist had been attempting to cut through, chipped but still largely intact.

Rowen caught Jalist's eye. They both looked at the cloaked Shel'ai again. Then they hefted their weapons and started forward.

The cloaked Shel'ai lowered his hood, revealing coldly handsome features and a vague, wolfish smile. "I was supposed to help them reduce this fort to ashes. Instead, I saved you again. I should not have done that, my love. Why do you think I did that?"

Rowen froze in his tracks. It was Shade, Silwren's one-time husband, the one sorcerer who had pitted Rowen in battle against his own brother. Raw anger filled him, enough to drive him mad. Rowen charged, heaving the axe over his head, howling for blood.

Shade turned, his face registering only the slightest hint of surprise. Slender wrists came up, igniting with tendrils of wytchfire. Rowen saw his doom in those tendrils, but he did not slow.

"No," Silwren said. She rose, a wisp of wytchfire sputtering weakly from one palm.

Shade frowned. Though his white pupils were fixed on his former wife, he waved his hand in Rowen's direction.

Rowen's legs flew out from under him. The fall drove all the air from his lungs. The ponderous axe flew from his grasp. Rowen cursed in his mind, lacking the breath to form the words, and tried to lift himself.

While the Sylvan children cowered or stared with wide eyes, Rowen heard the Sylvan fighters mopping up the remaining Olgrym in the distance. Shade had not yet seen Jalist. The Dwarr was crouched low and circling, moving through ash and cinders, his bloody long axe glinting in the torchlight.

"You won't kill me," Shade said confidently. Rowen feared for a moment that he was addressing Jalist then realized he was speaking to Silwren. She did not answer, though wytchfire continued to flicker weakly from one hand.

Shade began to circle her, never taking his eyes off her. Bright tendrils of wytchfire still coursed the length of his forearms. "How many times have I saved you, my love?"

"As often as you have tried to kill me, *my love.*"

"A vexed heart does strange things." Shade lowered his wrists, though he did not dismiss the wytchfire. "Enough. Had it been anyone else overseeing this attack, you would be dead now. But it wasn't. It was me."

Silwren retreated a step but smiled coldly. "I do not think the Light brought you here, husband."

"I healed you after Atheion. Even now, I'd welcome you back. So would the others. So would our father, if you would let him."

Jalist was close. *Just a few more seconds...* Silwren must have seen the Dwarr's approach as well. Rowen wondered for a moment if she would warn Shade.

If she does, I will kill her. Rowen rose to his feet, shaking with the fury of his own conviction. *Silwren, if you can hear my thoughts, hear this: let him die. Shade dies tonight, or by the gods, I will come after you. And unless you kill me, too, I'll cut out your heart and squeeze out the blood like water from a washrag. I swear it.*

He saw her shudder and wondered if she heard him.

Jalist broke into a mad dash. He raised his axe with both of his strong hands, a terrible fierceness in his eyes. The glinting axe fell. Rowen waited for the spray of blood.

It did not come. A huge, armored shape appeared, as though emerging from behind an invisible curtain, directly in Jalist's path. Fadarah caught the shaft of Jalist's axe and stopped it in mid-air. Before the stunned Dwarr could react, the armored figure flung him aside.

Shade jerked away, startled by the sound. "Father!"

Fadarah gazed down at the axe he had wrenched from Jalist's hands. Wytchfire poured from his grasp. Wood turned to ash. Steel melted. Fadarah turned and regarded Silwren. "Hello, my daughter."

Silwren retreated another step, her face pale. Aside from the din of battle still raging in Que'ahl's streets, the only sound belonged to the frightened, crying children. They had retreated and pressed themselves against the wall as far as they could go.

Rowen faced Silwren. He meant only to think his words, hoping she would hear them, but he shouted them instead. "End this. For gods' sake, kill them. *Kill them both!*"

Fadarah smiled. "What now, my daughter? Do we three kill each other?"

"Go," Silwren commanded, her voice breaking. Her wrists came up, wytchfire igniting at her fingertips. Weak at first, the tendrils brightened. Fire became light that flickered and pulsed around her body, forming the vague outline of a dragon.

They can't kill her. She's too powerful... but she can kill them! But she had not even called upon her magic to defend herself against the Olgrym, too afraid that she would lose control and kill everyone around her. What would happen when she did? *Do it, Silwren,* he thought, hoping she heard him. *Unleash hell. Gods, kill us all if it will end this. Do you hear me?*

She turned to him and shook her head. She turned back to Fadarah. "Go." Her voice did not break. She waved her hands. Both Fadarah and Shade disappeared.

Rowen yelled in furious disappointment, but a fresh chorus of screams reached his ears. He turned in time to see a handful of Olgrym driven into view, hard-pressed by a swarm of Sylvan swordsmen. Though many had already been slashed or cleaved by swords and arrows, they raged on as though the only thing that mattered to them was killing as many Sylvs as they could before they were finally killed themselves.

The Sylvs seemed happy to oblige. Even dwarfed by their enemies, each Sylvan warrior charged like a madman. Rowen got the impression that they would have done so even if the Olgrym had had the upper hand. Rowen had meant at first to join the battle, but he stood and stared, overwhelmed by the sheer ferocity of the fighting. He even forgot the sudden rush of anger he'd felt when Silwren let Shade and Fadarah go. He gaped as the two forces hacked themselves to ribbons.

"Gods, I've never seen anything like that..." Jalist said, joining Rowen. "Not even at Lyos. You?"

Rowen could not wrest his eyes from the scene. "No."

Only one Olg remained. The beast howled in defiance and swung his greatsword in a massive, two-handed swing. The Sylvs were too close to dodge the blow, and blocking it was impossible. Three Sylvs fell in bloody heaps. But the blow was costly. Before the Olg could recover for another swing, the Sylvs swarmed him, stabbing and slashing. They kept slashing, even after the Olg had fallen.

One Sylv lifted his head and spotted Rowen and Jalist. He gave them a ragged look, separated from the rest, and approached. Torchlight played off his chilling expression and black brigandine further darkened by blood. So much blood covered his face that Rowen did not recognize him. Then the Sylv wiped his face on his sleeve and regarded Rowen with ice-blue eyes. "Hello, Knight."

Rowen knotted his fingers into fists. "Captain Essidel, it seems you've borrowed my sword."

Essidel lifted Knightswrath and gave the adamune a critical glance. The curved blade glistened with Olgish blood. Essidel wiped that on his sleeve, too. "Damn thing's sharp. Good balance. And unbreakable, as far as I can tell. Too bad you're not selling it."

Rowen wondered if he would have to fight the Sylv for it. He risked a quick glance at Jalist, who had lost his long axe, thanks to Fadarah, but he touched the pommel of the shortsword at his belt.

Rowen glanced back at Silwren. She lay on the ground, crumpled and naked. Resisting the urge to run to her, he faced Essidel again.

He considered rushing the Sylv, but he sensed a lethal quickness in the man. He remembered what Briel had said on the walls: if anyone could cut his way out of a trap, it was Essidel. The captain had done more than that. He'd brought reinforcements and saved his stronghold, apparently without taking a single wound.

He'll cut me in half if I try. "My sword, please." Rowen held out his hand.

"Calm down, Knight. I'm many things, but I'm no thief." Essidel sheathed the sword but kept one hand on the dragonbone pommel as he surveyed the devastation around them. "Quite a night. Tell me, have you ever danced with Olgrym before?"

Rowen thought of the battle on the Wintersea, the one that still haunted his dreams. He nodded. "Nothing like this. What happened to the rest?"

"We drove them back. But it cost us. Four strongholds burned. The next time, they'll roll right over us." Essidel gave him a critical look then grunted, as though satisfied. "I'm about to do something very stupid, Human. I trust you won't make me regret it." He unbuckled Knightswrath and, with an edge of reluctance, handed it over.

Rowen girded the sword at once. "Don't worry, Captain. If I wanted to kill Sylvs, I could have joined with the Olgrym."

"I don't think they'd have you. You're a bit short. Besides, that's not what I meant. I didn't just come back here with reinforcements. General Seravin, my cousin, ordered me to kill you."

Essidel spoke so easily that Rowen needed a moment for the words to sink in. Jalist recoiled, trying to flank the captain, while Rowen's grip tensed on Knightswrath's pommel.

"If I wanted the three of you dead, I'd have filled your bodies with arrows long before now."

Silwren had gotten to her feet and was wrapped in a dead Wyldkin's cloak, comforting the Sylvan children she had done almost nothing to save.

"The last time your archers tried that—"

Essidel waved him off. "No need for threats, Knight. I'm letting you go. Just turn your back on the World Tree and keep walking until you reach the Isles. I want you gone before I've finished my bath."

Jalist nodded. Instead, Rowen shook his head. "I'm not going."

Essidel shrugged. "Fine. Grab a shovel and help us dig graves. Dig yours first."

Other Sylvan warriors were closing in, stone faced but visibly tense and bloody from fighting. Essidel took a step back. Briel appeared, bloody and wild eyed, a sword in each hand. He gave Essidel one of them.

Rowen said, "I *must* speak with your king. If your general won't take us into the Wytchforest, guide us yourself."

"I'd love to, Knight, but I'm in the middle of a war just now."

"Then give us an escort—"

"You have an odd concept of war for a man who seems fairly good at killing. The whole Olgish race appears to be sweeping down on us. I need thrice as many fighters as I have left just to sufficiently man this fort, let alone drive the Olgrym back. I can spare no one."

"Then we'll go alone. Give us a letter authorizing safe passage. We'll present it to the first border guards we see—"

"They'd fill you with arrows before you could pull it from your pocket. And if you're still here when my cousin arrives, he'll do the same. I might not agree with him, but he's the general, not me."

Rowen flushed. He could feel Jalist's eyes boring into him, but he refused to meet the Dwarr's gaze. "Then I'll talk to him myself. This general—"

"Seravin. And *no*, you won't talk to him. You'll die *in front* of him. But that's your business. Not mine. I wish you'd displayed this level of ignorance before I put a sword in your hands. Now I'll have to take it off your corpse." He began issuing orders to his men in their own language.

Rowen distinguished enough of the Sylvan words to catch the captain's intentions: he meant to have them imprisoned until General Seravin arrived, to do with them as he wished. Meanwhile, fuming, Jalist muttered a string of creative insults as he palmed the hilt of his shortsword and awaited Rowen's orders.

Finally, face burning, Rowen said, "Stop. Enough. We'll go."

Essidel gestured for his men to step back. "I'm glad we agree. My men will return your horses. Where you ride them is your concern, though I'd prefer you not take them south and get them killed, along with yourselves." He added, "It would make me feel better about my decision if your wytch could use some of that terrible magic to heal my men's wounds and keep a dozen or so of them from dying. Might even be enough to dissuade my cousin from chasing after you."

That's not likely. "I'll tell her."

"Do that. Either way, I want all of you gone in an hour." Essidel left without another word.

Jalist gave a low whistle. "Want to explain to me what in all the hells happened tonight?"

"Wish I could." Rowen glanced back at Silwren. Other Sylvs had gathered the children and were leading them away from her. She stood alone, shaking, staring at the ground. "We better hurry," Rowen said, heading toward her.

CHAPTER TWENTY-SEVEN

THE LANCER AND
THE IRON SISTER

I GRID SUGGESTED THAT THEY TRAVEL at night. Arnil Royce
agreed, so she returned to the battlefield, where riderless horses
still milled about, and found a stray Ivairian rouncey for him.
She helped him into the saddle. The Lancer voiced no complaint, but
in the moonlight, she could see the strain on his face. She was glad he
had agreed to leave off his armor, though he still wore the kingsteel
bastard sword at his side.

Glancing at the expensive sword, Igrid wondered how much use
Arnil would be in a fight. He needed more time to rest. She was
amazed his wounds had not reopened, let alone festered, but at the
same time, she knew they could not afford to stay there any longer.

It was clear that even if any other Lancers or squires had survived,
they had no intention of returning to the battlefield to search for
him. Given the sheer number of the Dhargothi cavalry, though, and
the chance that Dhargots might patrol the empty lands south of the
conquered cities, their best bet was to make for Lyos as quickly as
possible.

"I know what my plans are once we get there." Igrid patted her
purse of coins and glanced over her shoulder at the three additional
horses she had caught on the plains and intended to sell. "What about
you?"

Arnil warily scanned the darkness all around them as they rode.
"I'll ask the Lyosi king for safe escort back to Ivairia. Then I'll tell my

own king what's happened, in case he doesn't already know, and see if I can convince him to lend me a few thousand Lancers so I can repay the Dhargots in kind."

Igrid remembered the short work the First Lancer had made of the Dhargots she'd seen him fighting, and she smiled at the thought of what he might do with a substantial army at his back. "Do you think he'll agree?"

"Which king do you mean?"

"Either," Igrid said.

"I knew the old Lyosi king, Pelleas—at least, I knew *of* him. A decent man, if not a particularly bold one. But from what we heard up north, Fadarah's sorcerers deviled their way into the city during that last battle and slaughtered him and most of his family. I don't know the son who rules now." Arnil shrugged. "Gods know he has no great reason to help me. Ivairia has certainly never come to the aid of Lyos before. Then again, if this new king has any sense, he knows the Dhargots have taken nearly all the Free Cities. Soon, Lyos may be under its second siege in less than a year. And this time, I doubt the Isle Knights will be so anxious to ride to his defense. He could use all the friends he can get."

"And *your* king?"

Arnil scratched his chin. "Rodrick Whitetower could marshal three thousand lances and maybe four times as many footmen. Not enough to beat the Bloody Prince but enough to give him pause... especially if he forms an alliance with Lyos or the Lotus Isles. But..."

"You don't think he'll do it."

Arnil was slow to answer. "I don't know what they taught you of strategy, Iron Sister, but wars aren't as simple as they appear in brothel songs."

Igrid considered kicking him in his wounds. "Perhaps the good knight would deign to instruct me in such matters." She bowed in the saddle.

Arnil could not have missed her sarcasm, but he responded seriously. "The Bloody Prince has twenty thousand men and a herd of armored elephants at his command. I know. I saw them. There's another fifteen thousand reinforcing and supplying his rear, not counting however many thousands are still massed at Hesod. If that weren't enough, there's Fadarah and his sorcerers in the west and rumors of Lochurite wildmen running amok in the midlands. And the Olgrym, too, if they pick a side in this."

"All the more reason to join forces against them."

Arnil snickered. "Tell me, Iron Sister, did Hesod appeal to the other Free Cities for aid? Of course not. No one trusts each other. No one wants to fight for anyone else."

Igrid thought of Rowen's absurd plan to try to invoke what he called the Oath of Kin. "Maybe they will if they have to."

"Let's say they did. Let's say we slaughtered the Dhargots, killed Fadarah and his sorcerers, then set fire to Godsfall—a blaze not seen since Zet fell from the heavens. How many lives would that cost us?" He shook his head. "Death in battle is just the beginning, Iron Sister. Bodies rot. Crops burn or wither with no one left to tend them. That means plagues and famines, which means rats and greatwolves and highwaymen, worse than either of us can imagine."

I can imagine more than you think. "Then why tell your king what's happened? You could just lose yourself in wine and quim and let them think you're dead. Why fight the Dhargots at all?"

A shadow of surprise passed over his expression. Finally, he said, "Even that kind of destruction beats living under Dhargothi rule. Besides, they killed my men. Maybe Whitetower won't let me ride all the way to Imperian and shove my sword up the Red Emperor's cock hole, but he can at least let me bloody his sons' noses a bit."

The Lancer's bravado wore away her indignation and put a faint smile on her face. They rode on through the night, encountered no more signs of battle between the Dhargots and Arnil's Lancers, and made camp in a copse of dogblossom trees just as dawn was whitening the night sky.

Though Arnil had refused all offers to stop and rest, she could see that he was exhausted and pale. As she helped him down from the saddle, he swooned and clung to her like a child. "It seems... you have the advantage over me," he jested weakly.

Igrid tended the horses and built a fire. Then she helped him change the dressings on his wounds. Blood seeped through the bandages, but the smell was not overly putrid. *A good sign. He might yet live.*

Both were too tired to eat, but Igrid offered him strong wine, which he accepted with a grunt of thanks. She had a mind to talk to him more about his plans, anxious to hear about anything that involved the suffering of Dhargots, but he had hardly passed the wineskin back to her before he fell asleep.

He didn't even offer to take a watch... That surprised her. Though she certainly did not expect someone in his state to stand guard, she would have thought that his lordly sense of honor required he offer, at least. Then again, she could not begin to imagine how tired he must have been. The wounds he'd taken would have killed most other men.

She wondered if Rowen Locke would have survived that. She yawned. She did not know why that mattered to her, so she shook her head, trying to clear her mind. The night was cold, but the fire warmed her. She had half a mind to keep watch a while longer, but weariness sapped what remained of her strength. So she took another long swig of wine, tucked a drawn knife under her bedroll, and went to sleep.

She woke at midday to see that Arnil had already risen and was saddling the horses. Some of his color had returned.

He said, "We're close enough now that I figured we could ride straight there. I've already filled our canteens. There's a stream a little ways east if you want to wash up. I promise I'll stay away this time."

"You shouldn't be moving so much."

"And you have red hair."

She frowned. "What does that mean?"

He shrugged. "Nothing. I thought we were both just stating the obvious." He rubbed his side and grimaced. "I'll prepare food while you're gone. It won't be much, but at least it will taste bad."

She concealed a grin by frowning at him again. "You're in good spirits for a man whose insides might be bleeding to death."

"I jest when I'm nervous." Arnil girded his sword. "I've been known to laugh like a hyena in battle. Thankfully, my men took it for a sign of courage." He waved her on. "We can be at Lyos by sundown. Hurry, and I'll get you a room at the finest inn in the city."

"Not likely. I have all your gold." But she hurried anyway.

Through the bright haze of the midday sun, Igrid saw the great green swell of Pallantine Hill bustling with activity. Men and women in togas and sarongs moved amid carts and vendors in plain clothes. She smiled. She imagined the king's palace and that fine manicured city with its high walls, thriving market, and tiled roofs. She had to admit, her life as a prostitute in Lyos had not been all bad. Lyos was a better city than Hesod, provided one had the wealth to enjoy it.

Below the city, surrounding the hill and scattered on outcroppings of soil and rock, was the Dark Quarter. She shuddered to think of it. Mercifully, she had not been forced to work there as a prostitute, though she had heard plenty of stories of girls who had worked in the slums—none of them good.

Rowen had grown up in the Dark Quarter. He'd become a hero among the Lyosi.

Not sure what use that is to me, though. After all, even though the Lyosi could not possibly know that she had betrayed their favorite heroes, they also had no reason to trust her if she claimed to be Locke's wayward ally. Surely, others had already made such claims in the hope of advancing their fortunes in what, following the fall of Syros, was the greatest of the Free Cities. No, better to keep that to herself.

She thought of something else: though she could not say what had possessed her to do so, she'd told Arnil everything about her association with Locke. If he mentioned it to the Lyosi king, the king might punish her for betraying one of Lyos's champions. She glanced at the Lancer as he rode beside her, tempted to request his promise of discretion, but that struck her as akin to admitting a weakness. That was the last thing she wanted.

"You think the Dhargots are closing on Lyos already?"

"Not yet. Too early. They need to shore up the lands they've already taken, or else they'll lose them, just as Fadarah did." He looked around. "It's autumn, Iron Sister. No way the Bloody Prince can take Lyos before the snows come. Soon enough, he'll have to pull back and winter at one of the conquered cities. And that's if he doesn't decide to steer for Atheion and the midlands."

Igrid said, "You don't sound convinced."

Arnil answered by quickening his pace. They rode on in silence. Within an hour, they reined in before Pallantine Hill. The cobblestone road that was King's Bend gleamed red gold in the half light. In anticipation of introducing himself to the king, Arnil insisted on donning his armor, though he required Igrid's help to do so. She worried about the strain reopening his wounds but knew better than to argue with him.

They started up King's Bend. The path was crowded with traders, citizens, and prostitutes. *Not to mention pickpockets,* Igrid thought, making sure her coin purse was well hidden. Arnil led with a fierce look, though, and they went unchallenged. Igrid scanned the crowds with sharp eyes but saw far fewer thieves than she'd expected. She glanced at the reeking slums of the Dark Quarter and was surprised to see that they appeared less wretched than she recalled. *Exactly what did you do to this city, Locke?*

They rode up to the gates of Lyos itself, where Arnil boldly approached the watch captain, introduced himself, and said he had business with the king. Igrid followed, hoping she might be introduced to the king as well. Arnil's voice sounded unusually haughty.

The men of the Red Watch glanced at each other uneasily, but the captain immediately sent one to take word to the palace. "If you'll wait a moment, Sir Royce."

Arnil answered with a curt nod.

Igrid smirked then grew uncomfortable when Arnil did not even acknowledge her. *Has the smug bastard already forgotten the part where I saved his life?* She glanced at her attire, which was plain but a bit revealing. *No, the great knight just doesn't want to be mistaken for cavorting with a common whore.*

She considered grabbing the Lancer and shaking him but had the sudden feeling that he might respond by introducing her to that kingsteel bastard sword of his. Fuming, she waited. After what felt like hours, the Red Watch soldier returned with one of the king's ministers. The latter spoke with Arnil in a hushed voice that Igrid could not hear. Arnil nodded and followed the man into the city. A squad of Red Watch closed around him.

Igrid tried to follow, but when Arnil did not even look at her, the guardsmen blocked her path. "There's an inn down the street," the captain said pointedly. "I'll tell Sir Royce where you've gone."

Igrid bit back an insult and nodded. A man of the Red Watch took her horses while another led her to a modest two-story inn that did not appear nearly as extravagant as she'd hoped, but she reminded herself that it was better if people did not realize the wealth she had hidden under her cloak. She rented a room, hid her possessions, then left for the stables.

There, she found the stablemaster, a bored, gray-haired man in gilded sandals and a silk toga. She introduced herself, parted her cloak, batted her eyelashes, and sold all the horses for just a little less than the outrageous price she'd requested. While she had originally intended to keep one for herself, she decided against it. She had no need for a war horse if she truly intended to stay in Lyos. She could buy a palfrey or a pony later, if she liked.

As she headed back to the inn, she kept a sharp eye for thieves— even as she deftly cut the purse strings of a Noshan sailor, a Queshi merchant, and a Red Watch guardsman who tried to strike up a conversation but kept his gaze fixed on her cleavage instead of her eyes. She hid most of her new wealth under a loose floorboard and went back down to the Common Room. She made sure to sit facing the stairwell leading up to her floor, sitting at an angle so she would see if anyone tried to enter her room. The inn was crowded and boisterous, which suited her fancy. She ate her fill then cheerily shared wine and company with a Red Watch sergeant, a young priestess of Dyoni, and a middle-aged prostitute-turned-brothel-owner.

She also worked her way through the crowd, dodging gropers and stealing what she could, just to keep her hands limber. By the time she retired for the night, she'd appropriated a stiletto with a pearled hilt, a pair of sandals that looked to be her size set with gemstones, a handful of copper coins, a slim volume of poetry from the Lotus Isles, a gemstone ring, and most daring of all, a horned half-helm of enameled steel.

Igrid thought she had done her work unnoticed, but the aged prostitute who called herself Sheen approached her with a sneer and pointed to the bulge in Igrid's cloak where she'd stashed her stolen goods, except for the half-helm, which she had placed under her barstool and concealed with a dropped shawl. Igrid bribed her to say nothing. The old woman pocketed the coins professionally then praised Igrid's skill and offered her a job.

Igrid politely refused. "I mean to start a brothel of my own."

Sheen laughed. "Another dreamer! Well, Lyos is the place for it. Take my advice, girl: buy the favor of the Red Watch *and* the Temple of Dyoni as soon as you can, whatever it costs. For bodyguards, your best option is a few squires who failed training at the Lotus Isles. Good fighters. Plus they'll still have a sense of honor about them." She rolled her eyes. "Red Watch men might serve, but they're more likely to steal from you. Never deal with anyone from the Dark Quarter, if you can help it. And deposit everything you can spare with the Lenders' Guild. They're expensive but trustworthy." She added, "Oh, and leave that half-helm downstairs. It belongs to the son of the man who runs the Blacksmiths' Guild. He's not someone you want as an enemy, and there's nowhere you can sell the helm where it won't be recognized."

Igrid thanked the woman, handing her another coin. She was glad she had not mentioned the fact that she'd lived in Lyos before. Given the manner in which she'd left her last brothel over two years ago, the less these people knew about her, the better. She finished her wine, discretely depositing the half-helm under the barstool next to her, and went upstairs—just as the helm's furious owner was beginning his search.

She found her door shut, but she still entered tensely, one hand gripping the pearled hilt of her new stiletto. A would-be thief or rapist might break into her room but lock the door behind him then lie in wait. But her room was empty. She undressed, washed with tepid water from the basin on the nightstand, and lay down. She smiled. The bed had clean sheets. She expected slumber to steal over her right away, but she found herself thinking of Arnil.

By then, the First Lancer had surely spoken with the Lyosi

king. Because the Lancer had not already returned, she suspected he probably did not intend to. She wondered if the king had agreed to help him. He certainly had no great reason to. And the Lancer could not purchase bodyguards or supplies for the trip, since Igrid had all his money.

Maybe he'll try to slip through on his own. That would be foolish, though. Ivairia was at least three days north and west of the city, and thousands of Dhargots might block the way. Igrid felt a pang of worry then chided herself. After how coolly the Lancer had acted at the gates, she was uncertain why she cared what happened to him.

She thought of Rowen again, of the light on his armor and the dumb trust in his green eyes. Before she could stop herself, she began to cry. She cursed in the darkness, hugging the stiletto to her breasts, half hoping that someone would break into her room just so she could stab them.

CHAPTER TWENTY-EIGHT
PARTING WAYS

THEIR WOUNDED DON'T SCREAM... JALIST had taken a while to pinpoint the cause of his new unsettled feeling as he watched the Sylvs tending their wounded and dying. Some had lost limbs. Others had been pierced by great Olg blades that left wounds twice as wide as a man's palm. Many would die within the hour. Had they been Humans or Dwarr, they would have been screaming, crying, and shitting themselves. Courage made no difference. Jalist had seen the bravest Housecarls weeping and calling for their mothers. After all, a body and mind could take only so much, and the legends claimed that even Zet wept after the terrible torments inflicted by the other gods as punishment for making dragons.

But the Sylvan warriors, men and women alike, were almost completely silent. They did little more than wince and shake or, from time to time, offer a low whimper. And the children of Que'ahl, some of whom were surely watching their parents die, bore their grief in the same way. Jalist might even have mistaken them for Jolym if not for the wetness in the Sylvan children's eyes.

Moved by pity, Jalist approached the nearest child—a boy standing stoically near what surely was the corpse of his father—and squeezed his shoulder, thinking to comfort him. But the boy glanced at him, cold and uncomprehending, and moved away.

"Save your pity, Dwarr. To our kind, it is an insult."

Jalist turned to see Briel leaning heavily on a spear. His black brigandine was bloody and slashed in half a dozen places, yet the exposed flesh had been washed clean. Jalist saw no trace of wounds.

The Sylvan fighter followed his gaze and scowled. "You have your Dragonkin sorceress to thank for that. Had I been conscious, I would have refused her help."

"And died because of it."

"A return to the Light, far from all of this... I'd have welcomed it." He nodded after the boy who had just been mourning his slain father. "Wyldkin and Shal'tiar sometimes have to keep their children close by, even in battle. Against the Olgrym, most of the fighting is done at night. Knives and shadows. The children learn early on to keep silent. A cry at the wrong time could get everyone killed. It's a lesson we remember all our lives. Olgrym have literally ripped men to pieces and raped women to death, trying to illicit a sob of pain or a cry for mercy. Always, they fail."

Jalist stared at Briel, trying to discern whether the pride in the man's voice was a product of guts or madness. *Perhaps a little of both.* He glanced at the nearby corpse of an Olg, riddled with arrows. *Gods, if I had to fight them all my life, I'd go mad, too.* "I believe our hour has nearly elapsed. We should go before your captain has to make good on his threats. Where is Silwren now?"

"Other side of the stronghold, with the Knight. More wounded there. We thought she was done. She was beginning to look a bit... unraveled... but she insisted on continuing."

So she found the magic to heal dying men who hate her, but she couldn't bring herself to kill Fadarah, Shade, and an army of Olgrym threatening to kill us all? Jalist shrugged. "These are odd days."

Briel did not reply. The moon crested the smoking walls of the stronghold and glinted coldly off the blade of the Sylv's spear. Jalist glanced up. The skies over the forest looked so foreign. Even Armahg's Eye seemed so cold and unfriendly. *Not like home.* Not for the first time, he thought of lying on the grassy hills of Stillhammer, beyond the great fortress of Tarator with its bright banners and gray walls. He thought of Leander, strong and lean with breath like wine, lying with him. He started to smile, but the memory quickly left him feeling hollow.

He was almost glad when Briel's equally unfriendly voice interrupted his thoughts. "When the wytch is finished, I'll escort you out. Captain Essidel has ordered it."

"How kind of him. I doubt we could find our way out the gates without such a skilled guide."

"I am not your guide. I will wait for you on the plains, south of the stronghold."

Jalist frowned. *South?* "Save your energy, Sylv. We'll find our own way out."

Briel took a step closer, and Jalist tensed. Briel spoke in a whisper as sharp as arrows. "I was nearly cut to pieces, Dwarr. I should be dead. Even those few of us who have actually seen Shel'ai magic know that what your wytch did is far beyond what any Shel'ai can do."

Jalist heard a tremor in the Sylv's voice, uncertain if it was awe or fear.

"So understand, this was *not* my choosing. In this, I agree with the general. And I want nothing more to do with your wytch—now or ever. But I am a member of the Shal'tiar. I follow my captain's orders. And it seems the wytch impressed him enough to change his mind." Briel gave him a final icy look before he stalked away.

Jalist swore. Then he had an idea. Briel would be waiting south of the stronghold. Maybe Silwren and Rowen did not yet know that Captain Essidel had changed his mind. Maybe if he said nothing...

He shook his head. He had seen the look on Rowen's face—determination bordering on madness. He knew that look. Rowen would make his way into the Wytchforest, all the way to the World Tree, no matter how pointless or suicidal the task was.

But do I have to go with him? Jalist cursed himself. He might have been disgraced among his own people and a worthless sellsword besides, but he had given his word—or implied as much. He would see Rowen Locke safely to the legendary World Tree and the Sylvan city of Shaffrilon. After that, he was on his own.

And then what? Go back to Stillhammer and let them kill me? Or head south and die in some ditch for a few copper pennies?

"Decide that later," he grumbled and went to find the others.

The Wytchforest seemed to grow at their approach, stretching from the earth like an impossibly high wall glazed in moonlight. Jalist thought again of the legends of the World Tree. His pulse quickened when he realized he would see it soon enough. He thought of Leander again.

Strange. I've been thinking of you a lot lately, you beautiful gods-damned coward. Too afraid to stand up to your father, too scared to come with me. Jalist shook his head. He turned his attention to Rowen instead. The Knight had donned his kingsteel armor and tabard, both damaged and repaired, not unlike the Knight himself.

Rowen was trying to read from that scroll again in the moonlight. It must have been too dim, or else he was too agitated to concentrate, because he quickly gave up. He was trying his best to appear stoic, but Jalist knew him well enough to recognize the fear and excitement behind Rowen's steady gaze. He was anxious to reach his destination and deliver the speech he had been mentally rehearsing for weeks, but he was also afraid—and for good reason. If the Sylvs actually believed that the Isle Knights had allied themselves with the Olgrym and the Shel'ai, what would they do to Rowen, regardless of Knightswrath?

No, Briel will protect him. And so will Silwren. He studied the Shel'ai next. Moonlight mingled with the glow of Armahg's Eye and spilled through her platinum tresses as she rode beside him. He had to admit, she was beautiful. Still, he did not trust her. *But she will keep him safe. Everything has led to this. Besides, she's as much an enemy to the Sylvs as Rowen is. Best they stick together.*

Briel said, "We are close to Sylvos and far enough from Que'ahl. Best we camp here and enter in the morning. The forest guards will be… less apprehensive if we approach in daylight."

You mean less likely to fill us with arrows. Jalist watched as Briel set camp. It wasn't much of a camp. The Sylv slept on the bare earth, which suited Jalist fine, but he also forbade the building of a campfire. That irked him.

What, you think it'll spread all the way to the Wytchforest? It was said that the Wytchforest could not be burned down, though the Olgrym had certainly tried many times. In fact, some even said that some kind of ancient enchantment left behind by the Dragonkin guarded the Wytchforest and protected it from the ravages of winter. *That would be nice*, he thought, noting the chill in the air around them.

Rowen had drawn away from the others, sword in hand, and was busy practicing the martial dance of the Isle Knights. Jalist had seen him practice it often enough to tell that he was improving. Each movement was strong and quick, graceful in a way Jalist found alluring until he stopped himself.

The dance was difficult without armor; with the added encumbrance, it must have been grueling. Yet when Rowen finished, his face damp with sweat, he began again without pause. He completed the long series of movements, blending balance with speed and strength, then, to Jalist's surprise, rested only a moment before starting a third time.

Jalist approached him. "You're going to strain something—and *not* in a good way."

Rowen scowled but did not slow. "I need to practice more. I'm tired of almost dying. I need to be better."

"Seems you've been doing just fine for yourself."

Rowen turned on his heel, slashing upward, then down. He leapt about, disemboweling imaginary foes sneaking up behind him. Sweat flew from his face. "No, I haven't." He sank into a low stretch then leapt back up on his toes and executed a series of lightning-fast lunges and parries, ending in a full-body turn and slash that would have cleaved a foe's head from his shoulders.

Rowen finished the dance and leaned heavily on his sword. "I barely beat Kayden. Even though he wanted to die, he had to fight me as hard as he could. It was luck as much as anything. And that Dhargothi princeling could have killed me any time he wanted. Someday, if I live long enough, I might have to fight Crovis Ammerhel. And he's better than both of them combined."

Or just give Crovis the damn sword and be done with it. When Rowen began the martial dance a fourth time, Jalist shrugged and left him alone. *Let him sweat the melancholy out of his blood. Besides, he's probably right.*

As Jalist sat alone, his thoughts drifted back to Stillhammer.

Winters in the mountains were notoriously cruel, much worse than in the Free Cities or the midlands, but also exhilarating for how they tested one's mettle. Jalist remembered wintering in the deep vaults of Tarator with the other Housecarls, shivering in his brigandine and thick fur cloak before perpetually inadequate hearth fires, trying to appear fierce as he guarded the king and, from time to time, shared looks with the king's soft-eyed son.

There I go, thinking of Leander again. He cursed so sharply that Briel looked up. Jalist pretended to have stubbed his toe. Then he decided to busy himself with his new weapon, an elegantly curved long axe that he'd taken from the Sylvan armory. He straightened in time to accept the rations that Rowen handed him: spiced bread, plus some dried meats and fruits and warm wine to wash it down. The Knight seemed calmer, though half dazed from exhaustion. Jalist drank deep and passed the wineskin back.

Rowen said, "Want to tell me what's on your mind?"

"Plenty of things, like the fact that we could use a damn fire." He made no effort to lower his voice.

Briel said, "The Olgrym succeeded in getting suicide troops past our defense lines. They'd see our fire. Besides, even if they didn't, the archers guarding Sylvos might mistake us for Olgrym and send a squad to blanket the area with arrows."

Jalist gave the Sylv a look that was cold in more ways than one.

Rowen sat down beside him, though his eyes lingered on Silwren's cloaked figure standing alone in the distance. "You still don't trust her."

"Any reason I should?"

"She's going to keep me alive."

"Will that involve standing about and looking scared while Sylvs, Olgrym, Dhargots, demons, and gods know what else try to give your innards a suntan?"

Rowen scowled. "Lower your voice. We've talked about this. Every use of magic is a risk for her—"

"A risk she takes, and survives, when it suits her. And don't pretend you aren't thinking the same damn thing!" Jalist shrugged. "Listen, I'm not saying she's Fohl's concubine. She's done some good things.

267

But relying on her is like praying to the gods when somebody's got a knife to your throat. Trust yourself, not her."

Jalist saw Silwren tense in the distance. He wondered if she was using her magic to eavesdrop on their conversation. He tightened his grip on his new long axe, though he remembered how easily Fadarah had thwarted his attack—and Fadarah wielded only a flicker of magic compared to Silwren's.

Rowen put one hand on his, pushing the axe down. "She fought her own kind at Lyos. She helped us at Atheion. What more do you want from her?"

Are you trying to convince me, or yourself? "She could have finished this by killing those purple-eyed bastards. Instead, she spirited them away. Every day is another chance for her to end this, and she doesn't take it. But she's pretty, and you've seen her naked, and she acts helpless even though she isn't, so I may as well be talking to a wall."

Rowen winced at the insult then laughed. "You're wrong. At least, I hope you are." He sighed. "So are you going to tell me what's really on your mind? Who's Leander?"

Jalist tensed. "What—"

"I try to keep my distance when it's dark, but the fact is, you talk in your sleep." Rowen smirked. "Wouldn't have thought much of it, but the past few days, I've heard you mutter that name at least a dozen times while you were awake, too. So who is it? An enemy? Some old lover? A god I've never heard of?"

Jalist meant to deny it. Instead, he said, "Only a god to me."

Rowen grinned. "I thought so. Tell me about this living god of yours."

Jalist glared at him. "I like it better when you're stupid."

"Me, too."

Why haven't I told him before? Gods know Locke isn't like other men. He wouldn't give a piss what my lover has between the legs. Still, Jalist hesitated.

"We'll start simple. Alive or dead?"

"Alive. At least, he was when I left him."

"How long ago was that?"

Jalist went back to sharpening his axe. "Years and years. Before you knew me."

Rowen nodded thoughtfully. "Someone you cared about enough to still be thinking about them a good ten years later. But someone you can't go back and see because—"

"Because my people treat man-lovers like kindling for campfires. That clear enough for you?" Jalist's eyes stung as he spoke. He hoped that would conclude the matter, but Rowen persisted.

"So get him out of there. If he's... like you... isn't he in the same danger?"

Jalist scraped the whetstone down his axe, drawing sparks in the moonlight. "No. Not Leander. The mobs can get away with almost anything. They could butcher a Housecarl, and the king would give them a cask of wine as thanks for rooting out a traitor to our ways. But killing... even *accusing*... the king's son is another matter."

Rowen was quiet for a moment. Then he whistled softly. "You finally start to make sense, my friend. Why didn't you say something sooner?"

"Because I knew that you'd tell me to go off on some damn fairy-tale rescue. Only I'm no knight, and Leander isn't my gods-damned maiden. It's all over and done. It was done before you and your brother even met me. So drop it."

Rowen winced. Jalist made to work the whetstone again but slipped and dragged his knuckles down the edge of his axe. He cursed as blood swelled from a gash in his gray-tinged skin. Rowen tore a strip of silk from his tabard and handed it to him.

Touched, Jalist accepted it, but he said nothing as he wound the fabric around his fist and tied it. "I'm surprised you didn't ask your wytch to heal it for me."

"Didn't think you'd accept." Rowen sighed. "Stop being stupid and go to Stillhammer. I don't need you here. I'll be in the Wytchforest by morning. If the Sylvs mean to kill me, your axe won't make a damn bit of difference." He squeezed Jalist's shoulder. "You've done enough. More than I had a right to ask for. You helped get me here. Silwren and Briel will keep me safe now. Stop your bellyaching and get out of here."

Jalist blinked. "No. You may have mule dung for brains, but I'm not about to leave you with—"

"Go," Rowen repeated. He stood, smiling. "*My* war, Jalist. Not yours. Head straight east, travel at night, and you'll slip past the Olgrym and the Dhargots better than I ever could." He took a pouch from his belt and pressed it into Jalist's hands. Jalist felt coins inside. "That's all I have left, but it's more than I'll need in Shaffrilon. Keep the horse. I don't like how he's been eyeing Snowdark, anyway."

Jalist looked past him, to where Silwren still stood statue-still, and wondered if she'd heard their conversation. "Forget it, Locke. I've come this far. I'll finish it."

"Finish what? If the Wytchforest were any closer, I'd be leaning on it. Either the Sylvan king will kill me, or he'll laugh in my face. Probably the latter... meaning I'll just head north, try to keep ahead of the snow. Maybe I'll even go back to Lyos. They like me there."

Liar. Sooner or later, you'll go looking for Igrid. Or else you'll stay with that platinum-haired wytch until she gets you killed. He tried to smile. "You never were very smart."

"Never claimed to be." Rowen squeezed Jalist's arm again. "Get going, you dunce. If you make it, look for me on the Lotus Isles someday. I'll be the brooding bastard in battered armor."

And with that, Rowen Locke smiled and walked to the far side of the camp, apart from Silwren and Briel. He did not turn around as Jalist gathered his things, paused to wipe his eyes, and walked away.

CHAPTER TWENTY-NINE

MERCY

"SWEET GODS, WHAT HAS HE done?" Saanji sat in the saddle and stared at the grisly scene before him. He wished he were still drunk. But given the possibility that his eldest brother had summoned him simply so that he could kill him, Saanji had decided to stop drinking hours before he reached Cassica. He faced a moonlit field south of the city walls. Though the battlements of the city blazed with fires and resounded with laughter, the field caught his attention.

At first glance, the field had been planted with hundreds and hundreds of poorly stuffed scarecrows. But Saanji knew better. "How... how many, do you think?"

His steward, who looked as pale as he imagined he did, stammered a reply. "Maybe... three thousand, Prince."

Three thousand... Saanji was close enough to hear the creaking of wooden stakes amid the whimpers of the slowly dying. Their limbs waved feebly in the darkness. All the impaled, mostly men, were nude. They looked gaunt, as though they'd been starved and beaten long before they were impaled. Saanji realized he must be gazing upon the remains of Cassica's army.

Just then, the wind shifted, and an overwhelming reek washed over him: sweat, tears, and bodily filth. He covered his mouth to keep from retching. He drew some small comfort when his stern-faced steward leaned over his horse, shaking, and threw up his supper on the dark grass of the Simurgh Plains. Meanwhile, his host rolled to a stop behind him. Horses whinnied at the frightful smell. He heard other soldiers curse or retch. A few cried.

Moments later, the steward touched his arm and pointed back at the city. In the distance, the gates were opening. A squad of riders emerged from behind the dark walls. The steward wiped his mouth. Saanji straightened in the saddle. Some of the approaching riders held lanterns. By their glow, Saanji expected to see his brother coming. But the gray-haired rider leading the squad was smaller than Karhaati by half a foot, though just as broad-shouldered.

"General Umaari, where is my brother?"

The general scowled and narrowed his eyes. "He's gone north, Prince Saanji, to seek sport with the Ivairians. He was not expecting you for two more days."

That's why he isn't here to greet me himself. Should I be relieved? Saanji pointed at the vast field of suffering bodies. "The letter said Cassica surrendered. They *surrendered*, Umaari. Why were these men impaled?"

The Dhargothi general frowned. "These are the soldiers of the enemy. Your brother chose to make an example of them, to dissuade rebellion and disobedience among the remaining city populace."

Saanji touched the hilt of the ceremonial shortsword at his side. Though he had almost no real training or skill with weapons, he imagined drawing that sword and beheading the general. But he reminded himself that others were more deserving of blame. "Where is General Brahasti?"

"Dismissed, Prince. He's been released to the west until your brother needs him again." Umaari's curt tone made it clear that his use of Saanji's title was reluctant. To him, Saanji was merely the Tomato Prince.

Saanji felt his cheeks flush. He forced himself to smile. "My brothers have always had a good-natured rivalry as far as cruelty is concerned. I'm told that when Ziraari took Hesod, he impaled a thousand souls in the Dragongod's name."

General Umaari grinned. "The Bloody Prince has more than thrice-honored the Dead God."

Saanji glanced at his steward. "Well counted." He faced Umaari again. "When does my dear brother return?"

"By dawn, Prince. If you like, I am acquainted with his plans for you." Saanji started to reach for his sword, but Umaari said, "He wants you to take over the governance of Cassica whilst overseeing the supply lines for all Dhargots in the field." He spoke as though it were a trivial matter.

Saanji nodded carefully. "Until we march for the Wytchforest?"

Umaari answered with a thin smile. "I will leave the talk of such matters to your brother, Prince."

Gods, we're going to betray Fadarah, aren't we? Saanji turned back to the creaking field of impaled victims. His stomach quivered. "General, until my brother returns, I am in command, am I not?"

Umaari blinked. "Yes, Prince."

"Then here is my first order: send out squads of spearmen and put all of those people out of their misery. I want it done quick. But... give each one a drink of wine before it's done."

Umaari started to laugh, as did the squad of Dhargots behind him. The Dhargots massed behind Saanji did not.

Umaari's expression sobered. He touched the necklace of dried ears around his throat. "Prince, what you ask—"

"I ask nothing, General. I am a son of the Red Emperor. My every breath is a command. Now, will you obey, or would you prefer to join the impaled?" Acting on sudden impulse, Saanji drew his shortsword. To his surprise, an impressive chorus of scraping metal told him that the thousands of Dhargots massed behind him had done the same.

Umaari's horse reared, nearly dumping the general on the ground. Umaari regained control of his mount by cursing and raking its flanks with his spurs. Then he bowed. "I am yours to command, Prince Saanji."

At least, for the next few hours. "Good. Also, my men are tired. See to it that they're given food and lodging."

"I will." Umaari added with a toothy grin, "There are a number of young Cassican girls still alive. I could send those, too, if you like."

The wind shifted again, washing a fresh wave of Human reek over them. Saanji's eyes stung. "If I want them, General, I'll let you know." Snapping the reins, he rode past the general, into the city.

Rowen woke to see Briel hovering over him, his Sylvan features framed in darkness. He reached for Knightswrath, but Briel held up his empty hands and whispered, "I came to wake you, not cut your throat. Stand up. We have to move."

Silwren stood just beyond, wrapped tightly in a cloak. She said nothing but nodded toward the north. Rowen swore. He stood, fumbling with his sword as he glanced at the purple fire on the horizon.

"I thought your captain said the fighting was done for the night."

"Even Captain Essidel makes mistakes." Briel girded his sword, grabbed the reins of the horses, and brought Snowdark over to Rowen, leaving Silwren to get her own horse. "If the Shel'ai are attacking the strongholds, we can't wait until morning. I have to get you into the forest now."

"But you said the archers in the trees—"

"We'll have to risk it." Briel mounted his horse.

Rowen wondered if the violet glare on the northern horizon meant that Que'ahl was under attack again. Maybe it had already fallen. *Gods, Jalist, did you get far enough east, or did I release you in time to get you killed?*

Briel yelled, "Knight, we have to ride!"

Rowen patted Snowdark's neck and pulled himself into the saddle.

Silwren held out her hand, and her horse came to her. Silwren mounted and joined them. "The Dwarr lives. He made it far enough east before the next attack began."

"I'll ride ahead and tell the archers you're coming," Briel said. "Don't delay, but don't gallop after me, either. Give me time to convince them not to kill you." With that, the Sylv spurred his horse southward and rode off into the night.

Silwren said, "He's worried about his captain."

"I'd rather he were worried about us." Rowen glanced north one last time then faced south and snapped the reins.

An hour later, Briel found them. On foot, he materialized out of the darkness so easily that Rowen jumped, despite his best efforts to keep a sharp watch. He might have cursed, but the taut look on Briel's face told him to be silent. Shadows moved in the darkness behind Briel, each armed with a black bow. Rowen counted at least a dozen Sylvan archers, but a hundred more could have been lurking in the shadows.

Briel said, "Captain Essidel has vouched for both of you... as have I... but if you attempt to get away from us, we will shoot you full of arrows before you get ten feet. Also, you must surrender your weapons."

Rowen remembered being told the same thing outside the palace of King Hidas at Atheion. But poised to enter the Wytchforest, presumably to be taken before the Sylvan king, he hesitated. Then he unbuckled Knightswrath and passed it to Briel. Rowen was not surprised when the Sylvan archers did not seem to relax in the slightest. After all, they could not disarm a Shel'ai.

Rowen glanced at Silwren. He hoped that Briel had introduced her only as a Shel'ai. He hated to think what the Sylvs would do if they found out Rowen and Briel had escorted a Dragonkin into their kingdom.

A dark-garbed, green-hooded Sylv brought Briel's horse, and the Shal'tiar sergeant mounted again. "Stay close," he warned.

"Just take me to the king," Rowen said. He eyed the archers, who seemed to be retreating into the darkness. "Will they follow us?"

Briel said, "Yes, but you won't see them," and started riding again.

Despite the fabled size of the Wytchforest, the night was so thick that Rowen did not even realize they'd entered it until he rode past a dark, gnarled tree. When he craned his neck up and up, curious how tall they were, he was unable to see the top against the stars. Almost immediately, Briel cautioned him to keep moving. Rowen nodded, his heart beating faster. Already, thanks to El'rash'lin's memories, the darkness felt strangely familiar. The next time he rode past a wytchwood tree, he reached out, touched the gnarled bark, and smiled.

But El'rash'lin never went to Shaffrilon. Neither did Silwren, or Fadarah or Shade, or any of them, as far as I know. Rowen pushed the thought from his mind, took a deep breath of forest air, and tried to rehearse what he would say to the Sylvan king. Before long, the rising sun cascaded through the dense forest, and the majesty of his surroundings washed over him. Speechless, he stared at trees that seemed to rise higher than any tower or spire he'd ever seen. And for the first time, he realized he was surrounded not by a dozen hidden archers but by hundreds.

Some moved amid the trees, staring impassively with weapons in hand, but most watched from above. Great wooden platforms had been built into nearly every tree, about twenty feet up, and were connected by a seemingly endless network of rope bridges. Sylvs stood, statue-like, on every platform and bridge. Unlike the Wyldkin, they wore no feathers in their hair and wore brown and forest green, but their eyes shown with the same mistrust.

A short while later, he caught sight of a broad white wall beyond the trees. It rose so high that it faded into daylight, dominating the southern horizon, creating an implausibly huge span of polished snowy marble. He pointed. "I didn't think Sylvs built castles."

Briel's sour expression melted into a slight smile. "That's no castle, Human. You're staring at the base of the World Tree."

Rowen's eyes widened. "But you said we're still a day away!"

"But close enough to see the biggest, oldest tree in the world, Human."

Considering the armed, mistrustful Sylvs watching them from every angle, Rowen knew he should keep quiet, but he could not help himself. "If it weren't for the surrounding forest, would we have been able to see the World Tree from Que'ahl?"

Briel's smile broadened. "Human, if it weren't for the surrounding forest, and the clouds, you'd probably be able to see the World Tree all the way from Lyos." The grandeur of the Sylv's words overshadowed the mockery in his voice.

Rowen turned to Silwren, about to ask her why she, who had lived in the Wytchforest for a time, had never described something so wondrous. But the words died in his throat when he saw the tears in her eyes. He reminded himself that while Silwren had grown up in the Wytchforest—she was one of very few Shel'ai who could make that claim—her parents had been murdered.

Gods, I've never even asked her about her parents, her family! Until the previous night, he'd had no idea about Jalist's ill-fated affair with the Dwarrish prince, either. Guilt filled him, but it turned abruptly to worry when a squad of Sylvan fighters appeared before them. Unlike the others, they held drawn swords. Briel dismounted and went to meet them. When they argued, Rowen started to reach for Knightswrath—then realized he no longer had it.

He whispered to Silwren, "I can't hear them, but—"

"*I can,*" she said telepathically. "*These new ones want to know why we're here, why we're still alive. Briel says they're under Captain Essidel's protection.*"

Rowen hoped the Sylvan captain's influence was enough to keep them alive.

"*Don't worry, Knight. If they attack us, I can teleport you to safety.*"

"But what will that do to you?"

Silwren smiled, her eyes still damp. "Don't worry about me. Worry about anyone who would harm you."

The fierceness in her eyes so moved him that Rowen struggled to formulate a proper response. Before he could, Briel returned.

The Shal'tiar sergeant's face was flushed with rage. "Damn you, Knight. I should be fighting beside my brethren! Instead, it seems I'll have to follow you all the way to the capital."

"I'm sure there'll be plenty of fighting later," Rowen said.

Briel did not laugh. Leaning close, he whispered in Common, "I've told them that they'll have to kill me if they want to harm you. To harm a Shal'tiar is a great crime among my people. But I'm not sure that will be enough to save you. Do you understand?"

Rowen swallowed hard. "Just get me to the king, Briel. That's all that matters."

"I doubt they'll let you see the king, at least not right away. They'll probably arrest you as soon as we reach the capital. And they'll kill you if I leave. But I promised Essidel, so I'll do what I can."

Rowen marveled at the sergeant's loyalty to his commander.

He wondered for a moment if there was more to it than that, but Briel cast a cold look at Silwren. "They'll be watching you closer than ever—especially *you*, wytch. Keep your hands in sight. Work no magic, if you value your life."

Silwren nodded coolly. "I am not your enemy. Take us to the capital. We'll do the rest."

Briel raised one eyebrow. "Perhaps." He mounted his horse again. When they started out, the Sylvan swordsmen formed a tight circle around them, their blades flashing blood red in the light of sunrise.

CHAPTER THIRTY

DOOMSAYER'S HOUR

DOOMSAYER WATCHED SUNLIGHT SPREAD ACROSS the Ash'bana Plains and imagined it was a great bloodstain. The thought aroused him. Though he had no Sylvan captive to rape, he tipped his head back and howled. Then he tossed his head so that the animal skulls braided through his tangled dark locks shook about his bony gray face, and he thrust his great blackened sword into the sky.

The last Sylvan stronghold smoldered in the distance. Though his forces had been unable to press all the way to the Wytchforest during their earlier attack, the enemy had suffered greatly. The next time, his forces rolled over the last two Sylvan strongholds with ease. Now the Olgrym stood poised, at last, to strike at the very heart of the Sylvan nation.

Doomsayer howled again. The howl was echoed again and again by those behind him—scores, hundreds, even thousands. Tribe after tribe. The Skullshards, the Ash-Hands, the Felmauls. Dozens more, all united as never before. United under him.

Even as he had the thought, as though to mock him, a rider moved ahead of the Olgish host. Slight, cloaked, and shorter even on horseback, the man did not reek of fear.

"Shade." Doomsayer grimaced as he spoke the name. "You come to watch blood spill or spill some yourself?"

The Shel'ai's bloodmare balked at the smell of Olgrym, but the sorcerer controlled it and answered the Olg with a cold gaze of his own. "Guard your tongue, Olg. I come to command you."

Doomsayer laughed. "You talk like this in front of my tribe?" He waved his blackened sword that was easily as long as the Shel'ai was tall. "Maybe I cleave you in half for that."

Shade's violet eyes and bone-white pupils stared back, unflinching. The sorcerer smirked. Violet flames flickered to life, coursing the length of one arm while the other held the reins of the bloodmare. Doomsayer's pulse quickened. Despite the number of times he'd seen it lately, wytchfire still fascinated him.

"Maybe I burn you to cinders in front of your tribe. Maybe you die without tasting Sylvan blood. Is *that* what you want?"

Doomsayer's grin faded. "You kill me, they cut you to pieces. Your big general's too far away to help you." He pointed to a distant hill, where Fadarah sat astride his own bloodmare. Doomsayer hoped Shade would look in the direction he pointed. All he needed was for the sorcerer to turn, and he would cut him in half.

But Shade held Doomsayer's gaze, unblinking. The crimson greatwolves sewn into the sorcerer's white cloak stirred, rustling despite the dead-calm air.

Finally, Doomsayer laughed again. "You are lucky only I know your tongue, little man. If my warriors knew how you'd insulted me, one or both of us would have to die now." The Olg chieftain turned southward again. "Your fire, our muscle. By tonight, your whole army will be dead or thrown back. Olgrym will reach the big trees. We cut them with our axes. No swords, no bows will stop us."

The sorcerer winced. *Is that fear I smell?* Then it was gone.

"The Sylvs aren't my army." Shade's fists coursed with wytchfire. "*You* are my army." He nodded at the ranks upon ranks of Olgrym seething behind them. "They"—he nodded at the Sylvan legions in the distance—"are my enemies."

But you look like them. Doomsayer decided that did not matter. In moments, Sylvan men would feel his blade splitting them in half. By that night, Sylvan women would feel the same.

He waved his sword and howled again, calling to the tribes in the Olgish tongue. He told them of the glories awaiting them and of the lusts and dreams of conquests passed down by countless generations, finally set to be fulfilled. The Olgrym howled in reply, their frenzy growing by the second. Some of them began slashing their own bodies. Others set themselves on fire. When Doomsayer was sure the sound of their howling had carried across the grasslands and shaken the Sylvan legions so that the reek of their fear wafted like perfume off their paltry fortifications, he glanced at Shade.

The sorcerer nodded his approval.

Doomsayer gave the order. The Olgrym charged.

On a hill a half mile from the Olgrym's army, Fadarah fought back tears. *Forgive me, Kith'el. I should be the one leading the Olgrym.* But that, he knew, was impossible. Given the brutality of their culture, the names of dead chieftains tattooed to Fadarah's face—those he'd killed to avenge his mother—might actually earn the Olgrym's respect. But the thought of being near those creatures filled him with such loathing that he knew he could not directly command them himself.

For all I know, Doomsayer could be my father. The thought brought a sardonic smile to his face. That would certainly add further poignancy to the moment when Fadarah finally killed him. But that moment would have to wait. So he kept his distance and watched.

Nearly all of the Shel'ai were with him. Only the children had been left behind at their remote, northern stronghold of Coldhaven, along with a few trusted sorcerers to safeguard them.

We have too many enemies. It was good, at least, that a great many of those enemies were set to be culled from the list. He glanced at the other Shel'ai as they encircled him protectively, mounted on bloodmares. He did not have to read their minds to guess what they were thinking.

They had come to lend their strength and sorcery to the battle. None relished the thought of aiding Olgrym any more than Fadarah did, but they dared not wait for the Dhargots' help, if doing so would mean Doomsayer's defeat and the loss of an opportunity to breach the Sylvan realm. He took a moment to ponder the breakneck campaign of the past few weeks. To the north lay Brai-yl Run, the Ash'bana

Plains, a smattering of Wyldkin villages, and all the strongholds of the Shal'tiar. All were gone.

Their hour of triumph had arrived, the culmination of a campaign he had devised with El'rash'lin so many years before. They would vindicate so much sacrifice and loss. Yet the thought brought him no joy.

Memories of his encounter with Silwren, just days before, returned to him. Fearing Shade might encounter her during the attack, Fadarah told himself that he'd followed in order to ensure the safety of his second-in-command. He knew the truth, though: he needed to see Silwren, to try to persuade her one last time to join them. But her actions made it clear that she was as unreachable as she was fainthearted.

But she'd done enough. In teleporting him and Shade miles away, precisely when they were needed most, she'd helped stall an attack that would have surely seen all the Shal'tiar strongholds destroyed in a single night. Since then, though, she'd been absent from the battlefield. And as a result, the remaining Sylvs north of the forest had been decimated with ease.

Fadarah fixed his gaze on the dark tide of muscle and murder closing on the Sylvan lines. As much as Olgrym feared and worshipped magic, he had to admit that the alliance of the Olgish tribes was entirely Doomsayer's doing. And the Olgrym appeared only too willing to charge what remained of the Sylvan legions: a smattering of palisades and trenches dug hastily in front of the towering trees, crowded with exhausted, bloodied archers and swordsmen.

Within moments, a thousand Sylvan longbows would answer the Olgrym's howling with a deadly song of their own. Dozens of Olgrym would fall, their gigantic bodies feathered head to toe with arrows. Maybe a thousand Olgrym would die before the rest reached the trees.

But reach them they would. Fadarah closed his eyes, willing away the tears. *No other way.*

Opening his eyes, he imagined what would follow: the Sylvan legions falling back, drawing the Olgrym after them. The Olgrym advancing, reckless and crazed, certain of their victory. They did not even bother to look up at the countless platforms yoked to the wytchwood trees, swarming with archers. Sylvan longbows blurred, making a sound like music, forcing the Olgrym to pay in blood for their every step into the sacred land.

But that also brought him no joy. By sundown, the culmination of the first day of wholesale slaughter, the flower of the Sylvan army would be dead. Still, the Olgrym would have their foothold. For the first time in centuries, the Wytchforest would be breached—and there would not be enough Sylvs left to drive out the intruders.

They will slaughter each other by the thousands. Whatever Sylvs and Olgrym remain can be driven off by magic, or with the Dhargots' help, if necessary. And when it's done, Sylvos will be ours. We will finally have a home.

The first screams of battle reached his ears. He saw the morning sky darken with Sylvan arrows, watched the first trickle of what he knew would be a deluge of Sylvan and Olgish blood. *Enemies. Both are our enemies.* But before he could stop himself, he thought of his mother. He hardly remembered her, but she had cared for him. The others had killed her and driven him out. If she—a Wyldkin, a Sylvan woman forced to bear the child of her husband's killers—could love that child, even when it stared up at her with violet eyes stained by magic...

She had loved him, but her own people killed her for it. She was the exception that proved the rule. And his story was not so different from that of all the other Shel'ai he had saved—who had, in turn, saved him. Fadarah tightened his jaw. *Let them burn. Let them all burn.*

He straightened in the saddle and drew his sword, willing wytchfire to wash the length of its blade. Then he signaled a charge of his own.

CHAPTER THIRTY-ONE

ARRIVALS

ROWEN RECALLED A FABLE THAT constituted one of the few memories he had of his mother. It said that it would take a hundred men, linked arm in arm, to encircle the World Tree. But when they finally reined in at the base of the tree, he realized that multiplied by a factor of ten, that figure would still have come up short. Sundown splashed off the World Tree's white bark, which, unlike the gnarled wytchwoods, was silky smooth.

Before him lay Shaffrilon, the Sylvan capital. Though Silwren had described it a little, basing her descriptions on what she had heard from her kin, part of him had still anticipated a city similar to Lyos, crowded and sprawling. Instead, the capital appeared to be six different cities, and he presumed an equal number of cities existed on the other side of the trunk, each one built upon a massive platform affixed to the side of the World Tree. The platforms spiraled up the great trunk, all joined by a broad white walkway that rose higher than his eye could follow. People, looking no bigger than ants, moved along the platforms and walkways.

The base of the walkway hosted a broad, high wall of white stone, easily as large as the walls of Lyos, lined with battlements and archers. Though he was still fifty yards from the gates, Rowen saw ornate carvings of twisting tree limbs reaching toward a sky full of stars.

"The World Gate," Briel said.

Rowen wondered what would happen next. They'd ridden all day without food or rest, but his weariness evaporated at the thought of finally arriving at his destination. He glanced down at his attire. He smoothed his tabard and wiped at his armor, wishing he'd thought to polish it. Then a trumpet sounded. The World Gate opened. Riders dressed in green silk and armed with spears rode out to meet them.

Briel, along with some of the Sylvan swordsmen who had quietly escorted them all day, rode ahead to speak with the riders. The conversation devolved into shouting almost immediately. Rowen tensed, resisting the impulse to turn Snowdark and ride away. He eyed the Sylvan archers and swordsmen still massed around them, gauging his odds of successfully disarming one before the rest killed him.

"Stay calm, Knight. I told you, I'll keep you safe."

Rowen nodded, forcing himself to keep his eyes on Briel. The Shal'tiar sergeant rode back a moment later. The riders who had emerged from the World Gate came with him, their fine raiment rippling in the faint breeze.

Briel cleared his throat. "I'm sorry, Knight, but you're both being arrested. They're taking you to the House of Questions. I'll accompany you to see that you are not harmed. I advise you not to resist."

Before Rowen could answer, Sylvan hands grabbed him, unceremoniously hauling him down from the saddle. Someone put a bag over his head. Snowdark whinnied, but Silwren made no cry of protest. It took all his willpower not to scream or fight as rough hands dragged him back onto his feet, tied his hands, and dragged him forward like an unruly slave.

Brahasti reined in and grimaced when he saw the place. Far from the luxurious Dhargothi villa he had been promised, his new home more closely resembled a small winery that had lost its crops to drought and its owner to revolting peasants. The atrium was scattered with trash, including the wreckage of stone columns and the remnants of a ruined garden wreathed in diseased poplars.

He cursed. Judging from their reek, the stables had not been mucked in weeks. Still, the stone structures encircling the villa were mostly intact, and the wooden ones could be repaired. The fortifications would need to be improved as well. Brahasti was not as interested in keeping intruders out, though, as he was in keeping prisoners inside.

The trick will be making this place effective without making it look too much like a prison camp. Though the area was remote, with no cities or villages within a day's ride in any direction, he had his own aesthetics to consider. Luckily, Brahasti's talents applied to more than battlefield strategy, albeit with less pleasure. But he reminded himself that the end result would be pleasurable indeed. And profitable.

He turned to face the sellsword captain. "We must make this place livable as soon as possible. The first prisoners will be arriving any day now." He dismounted.

The captain, an unshaven and generally brutish northlander named Dagath, followed suit. He narrowed his eyes—his one good eye, at least. He wore a patch over the other. Brahasti guessed his reluctance had more to do with being so far from the front, faced with the prospect of grueling manual labor rather than battle.

Wait. Just wait.

As his train of servants, horses, wagons, and sellswords filtered into the villa, Brahasti toured the grounds with Dagath. Pinching his nose, he first ordered the stables cleared. Half of Dagath's sellswords were put on repair duty, to mend shutters and wooden walls and clear stones in anticipation of the stone masons' arrival in a day or two. The rest of the men were tasked with digging a trench, four feet deep and four feet wide, all around the villa. The makeshift moat would be filled with caltrops. The only way to avoid the fiendish spikes would be a single wooden bridge, which would be overseen by a guardhouse at one end and a wooden tower at the other.

Dagath adjusted his eyepatch, reminding Brahasti that until recently, the sellsword had preferred leaving the empty socket visible to everyone. Though Brahasti found that amusing, it was unappetizing. So he'd ordered him to cover it.

"And who the hell's going to build that?"

Brahasti smirked. In another time and place, he might have had the captain executed for that kind of insolence. However, Dagath's demeanor was well suited to Brahasti's ultimate ambitions. Ignoring the question, he said, "Both the tower and the guardhouse will be manned day and night. I want the men armed with spears and crossbows, in addition to whatever else they fancy. Also, I want two gates—one at each end of the bridge."

Dagath scratched a ghastly knife scar running the length of his cheek. "Begging your pardon, milord, but how long will we be staying here?"

"A long time. Years, unless I find someplace better."

Brahasti knew Prince Karhaati would not object to his absence; he despised Brahasti as much as he wanted to pretend the campaign did not need him. Of course, Fadarah would expect Brahasti to ride back to the front once the snows melted, but a lot could happen in so many months. Fadarah might die. Fortunes could change. Brahasti had no real desire to reign in the Free Cities pinched between Ivairia and the Lotus Isles. They were stubborn lands, and no matter how firmly or frightfully the Dhargots ruled, there would always be rebellions. As far as Brahasti was concerned, he had everything he wanted right before him—or he would, soon enough.

Dagath hesitated, and Brahasti imagined the uncouth man was trying to decide how far to press the matter. He concealed his amusement and waited for the question.

"Milord... is all this necessary? We're well in Dhargoth, good three days from the Simurgh Plains—even if the Free Cities were still free, which they ain't."

"Your point, Captain?"

"Well, kind of seems like we're prepping for a siege. Seems a bit odd for a country house is all."

Brahasti still had not decided how much to tell the captain. Of course, the mercenaries already knew that Brahasti would be keeping Sylvan prisoners there. The duty probably already seemed tedious, and Dagath's sellswords weren't exactly known for their temperance and reliability. Even though they were well inside the new boundaries of the empire, Brahasti had few friends there and no actual Dhargothi warriors to protect him. Unless he wanted to risk his sellswords' disobedience, perhaps even an outright rebellion like the one that had befallen this villa's previous owner, it might behoove him to hint at the future pleasures that came with Dagath's new post.

"Not a siege. More like… an orphanage." He enjoyed the bemused look on the sellsword's face. "Of course, in addition to children, there will be a great many Sylvan women coming here. I expect them to *stay* here. Beyond that, so long as you and your men obey my every command, I will leave these women to your… discretions."

A leering smile replaced the sellsword's irritation. Within moments, the uncultured brute's mind was probably awash in lusty thoughts of exotic, golden-haired maidens trembling and crying beneath him. So long as the Sylvan women were kept in ample and ready supply, Dagath would be the most loyal captain Brahasti could ever ask for.

The general decided to tell him nothing more right then. But as he continued issuing orders to the suddenly attentive mercenary, Brahasti could not suppress a wild grin of his own. More than the thought of the forthcoming crop of Sylvan prisoners pleased him. Brahasti was no stranger to exotic women—willing or unwilling made no difference.

Instead, he thought of Fadarah. Brahasti had been serving the Shel'ai long enough to learn a bit about how the sorcerers worked—and more importantly, how they were made. Once, he'd overheard Fadarah and Shade discussing how a Sylvan scholar had calculated that every child born to Sylvan parents had a one-in-a-thousand chance of being born a Shel'ai. Beyond that, there seemed to be no further rhyme or reason to the odds, except that they increased fantastically if one or both of the parents were Shel'ai. Except for a handful of children born to Shel'ai that Fadarah had saved, all those whom Brahasti had ever known had been born to Sylvan parents.

All but one. Fadarah was a half-Olg. It was so obvious. Yet so many men had completely missed the fantastic importance of that fact. Brahasti doubted anyone in all the long, bloody history of Ruun had ever stopped to consider the implications. Shel'ai could be born even when one of the parents was not a Sylv.

And before long, Brahasti would have hundreds of poor Sylvan girls at his disposal. All he had to do was let the sellswords have their way with them—as he would—and sooner or later, the girls' bellies would swell. After that, he need only be patient. Any child without violet eyes could be disposed of easily enough, and as he amassed more and more captives, the breeding odds would increase.

Brahasti felt the afternoon sun on his face, watching it turn his wretched villa into gold. He knew that Shel'ai powers did not manifest until adolescence, and Shel'ai aged more slowly than Humans. That meant it would take years for his crop to bear fruit, but eventually, he would have Shel'ai of his own, to raise in his service. They would protect him and magically extend his life, or he might sell them to whoever wanted them. In time, his wretched villa would become an empire.

Emperor Brahasti...

He continued giving orders to Dagath, but suddenly, he felt like laughing.

CHAPTER THIRTY-TWO

BREACH

B Y SUNDOWN, FOR THE FIRST time in as long as Essidel could remember, his men were running out of arrows. The earlier death tolls paled against what he saw. From great platforms not used since the days of the Shattering War, the Sylvs had rained death upon the advancing Olgrym, trying not only to slow the rampage but also to provide cover for General Seravin's routed men.

Armed with pikes and curved Sylvan swords, the general's men had attempted—against Essidel's repeated urgings—to stall the Olgrym's charge and hold them on the plains. By then, Que'ahl had fallen and Essidel's surviving host of Shal'tiar and Wyldkin had been fighting the Olgrym virtually nonstop for three days.

"Fall back to the forest," Essidel had pleaded. "Use the trees. Give every man and woman a longbow and have them attack from above. Arm the children, too. By the time the Olgrym reach Shaffrilon, they'll be in tatters. The Shal'tiar can attack them from behind while our reserves keep them out of the city."

Essidel had been proposing virtually that same plan for months, ever since the Olgrym had begun pouring out of Godsfall in unprecedented numbers. He had even written to King Loslandril and Prince Quivalen—as had the chieftains of many beleaguered Wyldkin villages, most of which had since been destroyed—trying to find anyone in Shaffrilon who would listen.

But Shaffrilon was practically another world. Majestically hewn into the living, incomprehensible heights of the World Tree, Shaffrilon was nearly as different from the Ash'bana Plains as Godsfall itself. Its citizens were soft, too accustomed to relying on the Wyldkin and the Shal'tiar to keep them safe, as they had for centuries. Even the hasty army of Sylvan fighters levied by General Seravin and sent to reinforce the front had been almost more of a hindrance than a help.

Like most Sylvan generals throughout the ages, Seravin was mostly a bureaucrat. And Essidel's cousin had no intention of being recorded in the history books as the general who allowed the enemy into Sylvos. Still, Essidel had appealed to him one last time, recounting all he had seen. He described the blood, the howls, the dying.

But General Seravin had merely eyed him with revulsion. "By the Light, cousin, are you truly proposing that we *let* the Olgrym into Sylvos? Is *that* your brave solution?"

Fighting to contain his temper, Essidel wiped the blood from his face and answered, "I am proposing that we save our realm through the only strategy left to us. I would think that would appeal to you as well."

That had been a mistake. Seravin's captains were there, and the general blushed at the public insult. "Need I remind you, Captain, that Sylvos faces these dangers because *you* have failed to hold positions maintained by generations of your predecessors."

Essidel continued arguing until the situation nearly came to blows and Seravin ordered the captain removed from his war tent. Left with no choice, Essidel had gathered what remained of his fighters and gone off to the Ash'bana Plains to fight and, presumably, to die.

As sundown bled through the trees, Essidel was surprised he was still alive. The Olgrym had crashed into General Seravin's lines of frightened, mostly untested men like a thousand battering rams assailing a fortification of twigs and twine. Essidel's remaining Shal'tiar hit the Olgrym in a flanking maneuver, inflicting heavy losses, but nothing could stop the inevitable. Soon enough, Seravin's forces fell back, and the Olgrym howled through the wytchwood trees. The general must have had taken Essidel's advice after all, except that by then, they'd lost too many men.

Essidel had thankfully had time to redeploy his remaining Wyldkin to the trees, and enough of Seravin's troops had reached the twenty-foot platforms before the ladders were hauled up. The Olgrym were too bulky to scale the trees and too impatient to chop down the huge trees, and everyone knew that wytchwoods were impervious to fire. So the Olgrym drove onward toward Shaffrilon, passing beneath a canopy of devastation.

Rope bridges allowed the Sylvan archers to keep pace with the Olgrym, maintaining a continuous hail of arrows, while Essidel attacked them from below. But their quivers were not inexhaustible; before long, runners were forced to go back to Shaffrilon for more arrows. But in a surprising act of cunning, Doomsayer ordered the Olgish tribes to scatter once they were in Sylvos. They spread out, too numerous to track, and descended like wolves upon the other Sylvan villages dispersed throughout the forest.

Bloody and exhausted, Essidel followed on the ground, shadowed by the now-empty platforms above. He slowed to catch his breath and scanned his surroundings. He heard the sounds of battle coming from a dozen different directions at once. He leaned against the nearest tree. Then he realized a dead Sylv had been pinned to that tree by an Olg's spear. He straightened. He turned and saw three Olgrym lying facedown in the leaves, their backs full of arrows.

"Captain, which way?" one of his men asked.

Everywhere. Essidel waved at the dead Olgrym. "Retrieve these arrows."

His Shal'tiar, the dozen men and women who had not been killed or scattered, rushed to obey. He was glad to see most still had their bows. Essidel sheathed his sword and checked his own quiver. He had three arrows left. Fitting one to his bowstring, he scanned his surroundings again.

They could climb the trees and follow the rope bridges all the way to Shaffrilon. Surely, the king needed them at the capital. Defending Shaffrilon and the king was their chief priority. He gritted his teeth. *But the Olgrym are too scattered now. We won't be able to kill more than one or two from that high up. And the Olgrym are still attacking villages—*

As though on cue, a fresh chorus of screams, the cries of the slaughter, reached his ears.

"That way," Essidel said. Then he ran.

By the time Essidel's party reached the Sylvan village, all its inhabitants had died or fled. But there were still Olgrym there, blood drunk and despoiling the dead. Essidel leapt over the bodies of a mother and child. He took aim at the nearest Olg and loosed his arrow. The tip passed into the Olg's brain through the ear. The Olg jerked, then his great bulk crashed to the forest floor, a bloody axe spinning from his grasp.

Essidel fitted another arrow and fired as his Shal'tiar fanned out behind him, their bows sounding the song of vengeance. Three more Olgrym fell. But six remained. Essidel put his last arrow in the throat of one of them then drew his sword and waited for the first enemy to come within range.

Two more Olgrym fell, their bodies feathered by arrows, but the rest were too close. With disciplined speed and precision, half his Shal'tiar backpedaled to keep firing their bows while the rest drew swords and formed a skirmish line.

The battle was brief but furious. The Sylvs slew the three Olgrym but lost four comrades in the process. Essidel dragged his sword from an Olg's jaw. He knew the names of each Shal'tiar who had fallen. They were his friends. He had fought beside them for years.

No time to mourn. We have to keep moving.

He saw no sense searching for survivors. They would find none there. His remaining fighters retrieved their arrows and pressed on, sprinting toward the next chorus of screams, hoping they would not be too late.

In a clearing, they encountered a knot of desperate Sylvan fighters locked in a pitched melee with an equal number of Olgrym. Unlike the Shal'tiar, most of the Sylvs wore the leather brigandines and forest-green cloaks of General Seravin's men, though some wore plain clothes and fought with weapons they surely must have taken off the dead. Essidel counted at least twenty Olgrym.

Too many. For a split second, he hesitated. If they tried to relieve their kinsmen, they would be killed. Essidel thought of Shaffrilon and King Loslandril. He pictured the Olgrym running amok through the ancient palace, painting the walls with the entrails of the royals. He knew he should press on toward the capital, still a full day's travel on foot. He could not save the fighters, anyway. Better he try to save the king.

However, Essidel raised his bow, drew back the string until the feathers touched his cheek, and let the arrow go.

For awhile, fortune favored them. The Olgrym, so intent on slaughtering the Sylvs right in front of them, did not notice the Shal'tiar firing hastily retrieved arrows into their backs until four of their number had fallen. Then they divided their force. Half charged the Shal'tiar, their long strides and powerful legs rapidly devouring the distance between them.

The Shal'tiar scattered. Some who had already hidden behind trees emerged, slashing or firing on the Olgrym from behind. Others ran, hoping to force the Olgrym to further divide their forces. Suddenly, Essidel found himself fighting alone. An Olg came at him like a mountain.

Essidel felt his pulse quicken but waited until the last possible second then tucked his shoulder and rolled, narrowly avoiding the powerful but clumsy thrust of the Olg's spearhead. He rolled closer to the Olg and swung his sword with both hands. He made contact just below the Olg's kneecap. Sylvan steel sliced through tendons and sinew, glancing off bone. Essidel wrenched his sword free and rolled. Howling, the Olg stabbed at him again.

The tip of the Olg's spear caught Essidel's leather spaulders, slowing him down. The Olg ignored the pain from his ravaged leg and threw himself forward. Somehow, the Olg had a dagger in his free hand. No time to dodge. Essidel lunged. The tip of his sword caught the Olg's wrist and sank deep. The arm kept coming, and Essidel wondered for a moment if the dagger would find him after all. Then it stopped a finger's span from his chest.

The Olg abandoned the spear and tried to punch him instead. Essidel lowered his jaw and raised his shoulder. The Olg's fist struck his shoulder—hard enough to shock all of his senses and drive him to the ground. Essidel's sword, its blade still buried in the Olg's other arm, broke with a shrill crack. Essidel threw the hilt blindly and groped for his own dagger.

But a Sylvan arrow struck the Olg's shoulder. Another struck his thigh. Then a daring Sylv charged and drove a spear into the Olg's throat, shoving the spear until it shattered. Essidel rose and turned. His savior was a woman. Her hair, a darker shade of gold than that of most Sylvan women's, was tied back in a long braid splattered with blood. She wore a brigandine and forest-green cloak. A pair of shortswords hung at her belt. She drew one and offered it to him. Essidel accepted it and turned to gauge the rest of the battle.

His heart sank when he counted three black-garbed bodies lying nearby, cleaved and still. A fourth Shal'tiar was badly wounded and being supported by two Sylvs in green cloaks. Essidel didn't see any more Olgrym. Most of the original group of Sylvs had been killed, but another force had arrived in the midst of the fighting.

Essidel could hardly believe his eyes. Before him were at least fifty green-cloaked fighters, some on horseback. Leading them was General Seravin.

The general was only twelve years Essidel's senior but looked twice his age. He sat low in the saddle, as though wounded, though Essidel saw no blood on him. "General."

"Cousin," Seravin answered tersely. "We make for the capital. You may follow us or conduct your wounded to the village of Jen'hanai." His tone made it clear that he hoped Essidel would choose the latter.

"Jen'hanai still stands? I thought all the villages—"

"It stood when we left. Two dozen wounded but capable archers were guarding it. They have clerics and healers there. Farewell."

He turned his horse as though to ride away, but Essidel grabbed the horse's bridle and held it, despite the general's scowl and the horse's cry of protest. "General, what news from the front?"

"All of Sylvos is now the front, Captain. How do *you* think we're faring?"

"I saw Shel'ai on the plains, fighting with the Olgrym. I lost two whole squads to their damn wytchfire. But I haven't seen any since. Are they all dead?" Though Essidel doubted that could be true, he'd ordered his men to target them first. He'd already personally cut down one while she was busy burning another Sylv to cinders.

Seravin shook his head. "About twenty of them ride with Doomsayer toward Shaffrilon. Even they can't burn the trees, but their wytchfire is wreaking havoc with my men. I sent a hundred riders to intercept them."

Essidel could tell by his cousin's tone that the general did not expect his riders to be victorious. He rubbed his shoulder and tested his arm. To his relief, he felt no errant shifting of bones. "They can't take Shaffrilon in a day. The Olgrym are scattered all over the forest. That means they'll have to set up a fortified camp somewhere. If we can guess where—"

"Guess all you like, cousin. We ride to Shaffrilon to protect our king."

The general jerked the bridle from Essidel's grasp and rode off, his riders trailing after. Most of his footmen followed, but some lingered, seeming uncertain. They made a show of gathering the wounded. Essidel wanted to curse them, but he understood. *They know he's leading them to a slaughter. If Shaffrilon is going to burn, better they not be there to see it.*

He shook his head. The Olgrym had broken through the Sylvan lines, but sprinting all the way to Shaffrilon would only leave them too exhausted to fight. He might expect that kind of brash action from Doomsayer or the other chieftains, but Fadarah was not that stupid. He had to realize that a realm as huge as Sylvos could not be taken in a single day. He would halt his forces somewhere, fortify his position, and recoup his strength.

Unless he just means to use up the Olgrym against us... He remembered what Silwren and Rowen had said about the Dhargots. *Could another army even now be marching on Sylvos? If so, when would it arrive?* He tried to remember the particulars of what had seemed, at the time, too implausible to believe.

As he helped one wounded man onto his feet and another bandage a slashed arm, he thought that, for the moment, it did not matter where the Dhargots were. The Olgrym and the Shel'ai were already in Sylvos. The Olgrym could not be driven out; they would have to be tracked and killed down to the last man. But the Shel'ai were another story. For all their scheming and murder, they were also cautious—perhaps to a fault. If he could deal them a serious blow, they might withdraw and leave the Olgrym on their own, trusting that they could always renew their siege of Sylvos once the Dhargots arrived to help them.

But how do I hurt the Shel'ai? He thought at once of Silwren. Briel had surely led her and the Knight of the Crane to Shaffrilon... but how had King Loslandril responded to them? He had received no word. Essidel trusted Briel to get them safely to the World Tree, but what happened after that was up to the king.

Of course, even if they were alive, Shaffrilon was still a full day's march, at the heart of the forest. And if the king *did* agree to accept their help—he had little choice—Silwren would be needed there.

No, I'm on my own... Essidel glanced down at his new sword. The woman who had given it to him knelt nearby, stone faced, holding the hand of a man whose belly had been opened. The man whispered something to her. She whispered back. He nodded. Then, with an iciness to put any of his Shal'tiar to shame, she drew her sword and stabbed him.

Essidel had seen fighters put their comrades out of their misery before, but the sight still unnerved him. He went to her.

Wiping off her blade, she glanced up at him. "A fine war you've lost here, Captain."

Essidel bit back an angry retort and scrutinized her garb. She wore her armor like a soldier, but most of General Seravin's host had little or no training. *Who is this woman?* "Why didn't you follow the general?"

She shrugged. "Plenty of blades and blows rushing back to Shaffrilon. Not many guarding the rest of the realm. Towns out there need protecting, too, what with a few thousand Olgrym marauding around our kingdom. Figure I can do as much good back here without all that running around."

She doesn't talk like a forest dweller. More like a Wyldkin. But if she is, what's she doing in the regular army?

"Then come with me," he said. He raised his voice, rallying those around him. "Our beloved king is in the hands of the general. We have another task. I mean to make for Jen'hanai, raise whatever force I can, and strike out."

The woman gave him a cold look. "You want to lead us against the Olgrym again? Seems you didn't do so well the last time."

Essidel saw his surviving Shal'tiar bristle at this insult of their commander, but some of the green-cloaked Sylvs nodded, seemingly preferring to blame him over General Seravin. "I don't mean to fight the Olgrym any more than I have to. I mean to find Fadarah and kill him."

Everyone stared, speechless.

Then the woman smirked. "That has a nice ring to it." She sheathed her sword, stooped, and retrieved a spear. "I'll take that sword back after he kills you. In the meantime, my name is Khi'as. And if you're serious about this, Captain, I bet I know where we can find him."

CHAPTER THIRTY-THREE
THE PRISONER

L ONG AFTER ROWEN HAD GIVEN up pounding on the locked
door and calling for the guards, he continued to pace his new
living quarters. Located in a squat structure the Sylvs called
the House of Questions, built high up in the World Tree, the room
had a single arched window offering a dizzying view of the forest far
below. He could gaze out the window, even climb out if he wished, but
there was nothing to cling to, and it was a sheer drop hundreds and
hundreds of feet, all the way to the forest floor.

Still, despite being a prison, the room contained more finery
than anything he had ever seen. The floor was glossy wytchwood,
and the walls were covered in murals depicting what he guessed were
key battles from the Shattering War. He saw no representation of
Fâyu Jinn and his Knights, but again and again, he saw one figure,
presumably King Shigella, leading a revolt against winged, fire-eyed
Dragonkin with burning hands. He thought that they looked a bit too
similar to Silwren for his comfort.

Then he noted with amusement that in a few murals, Shel'ai
appeared to be fighting alongside the Sylvs. Apparently, someone had
not taken kindly to those depictions. Unlike the others, which were
as pristine as though they had been painted that day, those depicting
the Shel'ai had been slashed with knives. Over one, he found potent
Sylvan slurs that—thanks to El'rash'lin—he was able to decipher.

Rowen had been in the Wytchforest for four days, locked in that
room for three. An old woman who refused to look at or respond to

him brought him food: whey bread, sweet fruits he had never seen before, a strange but delicious stew of spiced vegetables, and sweet Sylvan wine. He had a bed more comfortable than the one he'd slept on in Atheion. For light, his room contained a single luminstone. He was even given water to bathe with. In place of a chamber pot was actual piping that surpassed anything in Lyos.

Shelves held books—histories of Sylvos predating the Shattering War, mythologies of the gods and dragons, and stories from the days of the Dragonkin. Rowen tried to keep himself from going mad with frustration and boredom by delving into tales of the creation of the Sylvs, who were fashioned by the Dragonkin as slaves, coupled with the Dragonkins' slow descent into madness.

Gods, I need to get out of here! But the door to his room, locked and guarded, was as unlikely an escape route as his window. Besides, he did not know what he would do if he managed to escape. The Sylvan king had refused to see him. No prefect or general had bothered to visit him, either. Knightswrath had been taken and, like Silwren, could have been anywhere. Despite the initial awe he'd felt at the sight of the World Tree, his arrival at the Sylvan capital had been maddeningly anticlimactic.

He glanced out the window and wondered if they simply wanted him to kill himself. His jailors' animosity was obvious in their expressions, as well as the muttered curses they probably did not know he understood, but otherwise, they had not assaulted him. Briel had accompanied them at first. The stern Shal'tiar made certain that Rowen was not mistreated but coldly ignored his questions, refusing to say where Silwren had been taken.

Since then, no one had spoken to him. The guards in the hallway entered his room only to make sure he did not attack the old woman who brought in his provisions and changed his linens, but he could learn nothing else of what was happening in Sylvos. Still, Rowen knew something was wrong.

Even from his extravagant prison, he could hear commotion. Through the window, he saw crowds moving far below. They were too far to discern clearly, but he thought he saw what looked like refugees flowing into the city while what could only be soldiers marched out in column after column of forest-green cloaks.

The war must be going badly. He thought of Que'ahl and wondered if Captain Essidel was still holding the strongholds or if the Olgrym had finally broken through. If so, had they breeched the Wytchforest yet, or were the Sylvan legions still keeping them at bay?

Once, briefly, Silwren's voice had broken abruptly into his thoughts, but she'd said only that she was unharmed and that he must be patient. She counseled him not to attempt escape. Then she was silent. But at least Rowen knew she was alive.

But why doesn't she get me out of here? Frustrated, he stopped pacing long enough to deliver three powerful side kicks to the locked door. It caused an enormous racket and hurt his foot, but the door seemed unfazed. The guards outside offered no response. He wondered again why Silwren did not simply use her magic to liberate him from his prison and take him to see Loslandril, whether the king liked it or not. Surely, she could make them invisible, just as she had in Atheion.

But hours passed, and she neither appeared nor mindspoke with him again. He wished he could contact her himself, but from what little he understood of magic, it seemed that she could only read his thoughts when actively attempting to do so. So Rowen read, ate, paced, performed the sha'tala as best he could without a weapon, read more, drank wine, and tried his best to keep from going mad.

Finally, at sundown, he heard the great metallic fuss of his door being unlocked. He braced himself, and the door opened. Briel entered, gesturing for the scowling guards to stand down and wait outside. Briel closed the door behind him. The guards locked it again.

Briel wore his black fighting leathers, and a matching sword and dagger hung at his belt. A shortbow and quiver of arrows were strapped to his back. He was wearing fighting gloves. By the blue glow of the luminstone, Rowen saw something in the Sylv's expression that frightened him. His anger slacked. "How close are the Olgrym?"

"A day," Briel answered bluntly.

Rowen stared. "They made it—"

"Inside the forest. General Seravin's whole force has been routed. Que'ahl was burned to the ground, along with every Wyldkin village and stronghold left on the plains. My captain is probably dead." Briel blinked. "There are a few Shal'tiar reserves stationed in the city. Loslandril refuses to flee. So we're taking command of the capital's defenses." He paused, his face like stone. "I am not supposed to tell you any of this, but you'd guess it readily enough when you looked out your window and saw a few hundred Olgrym hacking their way toward you."

Rowen shuddered. Somehow, he suspected that defending Shaffrilon's broad, spiraling walkways would take priority over him. "Give me back my sword. I'll fight with you. Gods, at least give me a way to defend myself!"

He saw Briel consider it before shaking his head. "Some commands must be followed, Human. I just wanted you to know what was happening. You deserved that much." He turned to go.

"Briel, wait. This has gone on long enough. You have to let me see the king!"

"Human, there are thousands of Sylvs out there right now, dying to defend this realm. Do you really think one Knight of the Crane would make that big of a difference?"

"Not me—Silwren. You *need* her, Briel. She's a Dragonkin—or near enough. Her magic could mean more than a hundred Sylvan fighters. If I can convince the king—"

"Silwren stays where she is. She's lucky she's even still alive. Nearly everyone who knows she's here wants her dead. I've already had to disband a mob and replace six different guards who wanted to harm her. But Loslandril can deal with her when the fighting's done." He tightened his gloves. "Farewell, Human. The next time we meet, one of us will probably be a corpse."

Briel knocked twice on the door, and the guards unlocked it. Rowen tensed. For one mad instant, he considered charging them and trying to fight his way out, but he changed his mind. Briel left. The guards scowled at him and locked him in again.

Rowen sighed. *The Olgrym will be here tomorrow...* He wondered where Jalist was. Part of him regretted sending the Dwarr away. He could have used an ally right then. Still, he hoped Jalist had managed to get far enough east before the Olgrym launched their latest round of offensives. He hoped his friend would reach his homeland and be reunited with his true love, though he was beginning to wonder if those kind of things happened outside of fairy tales. Rowen shook his head. Then, not for the first time, he searched his room for something he could use as a weapon.

CHAPTER THIRTY-FOUR
THE GLASS KNIFE

Long after he had dismissed his advisors, his captains, his servants, his bodyguards, and even his worried son, King Loslandril continued to sit at the gigantic table in his council chamber and stare at the reports. Most were hastily scribbled messages from the elected speakers who presided over their respective villages. All spoke of the Olgrym's rampaging advance and begged for assistance. But Loslandril had no assistance to offer. By then, most of those people were probably dead.

The Olgrym had broken through General Seravin's lines, but the Sylvan armies were rallying to destroy the Olgrym once and for all. The attacks within the heart of Sylvos were sorrowful exceptions. *How could it be otherwise?*

Loslandril smiled wretchedly. That was what he was telling his people, anyway. He knew better. He stared into his empty wine cup. *My father was a tyrant. My grandfather was a fool. But I will be the king who lost his realm to the enemy.*

He grabbed a pitcher, filled his cup with thick, sweet-smelling wine, and drained it. Then he filled it again. *No, I need to keep my senses. I need to be strong for my people.*

But what was there for him to do? That Shal'tiar sergeant, Briel, had already mobilized the few hundred men in the reserves. His own city captains seemed only too happy to relinquish command to the young but seasoned veteran. Those reserves were massing at the base of the World Tree, at the mouth of the Path of Crowns, ready to defend the World Gate. Meanwhile, all the citizens of Shaffrilon who were not soldiers but were still proficient with a longbow were being armed and posted along the walkways, on the edges of the great daises overlooking the forest.

Briel had suggested that Loslandril make an appearance at the World Gate, as well, in order to bolster the men. But the rest of his advisors encouraged him to stay in the palace, citing the fact that Shel'ai had been seen fighting alongside the Olgrym. Surely, the sorcerers wanted Loslandril dead.

He drained his cup down to the last drop. As he refilled it, the hand gripping the pitcher shook. Loslandril wondered if the wine or merely his age were catching up with him. He wished suddenly that he had not dismissed Quivalen along with the others. But Quivalen's presence could have been as aggravating as it was heartening. Though no longer a child, he often behaved like one. Upon hearing that Silwren had been brought into the city, he screamed so loudly that she must be killed immediately that Loslandril had wondered for a moment if he would have to order his guards to restrain the prince.

He's always been sickly and hot tempered, ever since Chorlga touched him. Maybe he did something to him besides draining the dragonmist from his eyes.

Loslandril touched his hand to his chest, tracing the scars through his silk tunic. Still, they pained him. Of course, he had not been able to completely conceal their existence. Quivalen had asked repeatedly about the scars, but Loslandril had always refused to tell him the truth. Naturally, though, the prince had deduced that they were caused by magic, which seemed to make the prince detest Shel'ai every bit as much as his grandfather had.

Better he never learn the truth, especially if our kingdom is about to fall to his own kind. Loslandril chided himself for the thought. Quivalen was not a Shel'ai anymore. He'd never exhibited the slightest trace of magic. Whatever powers he might have wielded, Chorlga had taken. *No, not taken. Devoured.*

He remembered the legends of Dragonkin enhancing their own power by draining it from Shel'ai, long after their magical addictions had rendered dragons extinct. According to other stories, the Shel'ai woman held captive in his city was not a Shel'ai at all but some kind of self-made Dragonkin, like the infamous Nightmare. Surely that meant she could not be trusted, but perhaps Loslandril could use her to save the city.

Loslandril glanced across his table at the Sword of Fâyu Jinn. Loslandril could hardly believe his eyes. His father had showed him that sword, rusted and ruined, when he was a boy then entrusted it to one of his agents ordered to take it beyond Sylvos and give it away.

Now it's come back. And it's whole. A Knight of the Crane brought it to me. That has to mean something.

Despite Quivalen's insistence that the sword was a forgery, something told Loslandril that it was not. Still, even if the Isle Knights fighting alongside the Olgrym were merely an illusion, even if Loslandril were willing to strike an alliance with them, the Lotus Isles were on the other side of Ruun. The enemy was on his doorstep.

Perhaps Silwren could save them, but Quivalen and nearly everyone in the capital wanted the woman dead. But without her help, the city would fall. Quivalen would be torn to pieces, his entrails smeared like war paint on the muscles of some unconscionable Olg.

I can't let that happen. I've already lost Jalthessa. I won't lose Quivalen, too. He started to refill his wine cup then noticed the shadow of someone standing over him. He smiled. "I ordered you to leave me, my son," he said, not unkindly.

But the voice that answered was not Quivalen's. "You will find that I do not excel at obeying orders, great king."

Loslandril had not heard that voice in fifty years, yet the terror it produced made all those long years melt away in an instant. He dropped his cup, letting it spill and shatter on the floor, and rose shakily from his chair. He backed away. Then, on instinct, he stepped in front of Fel-Nâya, blocking it from view.

Chorlga smiled at him with dark, rotten teeth. His features, otherwise coldly handsome, had not aged a day. As before, he did not blink. He still appeared to be a blue-eyed Sylv, though Loslandril knew that was only an illusion. He wondered at once where Quivalen was, if he was safe.

Forcing a scowl, Loslandril said, "We had a deal. You said I would never see you again."

Chorlga nodded lazily. "You did not keep your word, so I saw no reason to keep mine."

Loslandril shook his head. "I rejected Fadarah's truce. I kept the Shel'ai as my enemies. Because of that, my kingdom has been invaded. What more would you ask of me?"

"All the Shel'ai dead. That was what your father wanted, isn't it? That was the legacy you promised to fulfill."

Loslandril stared at him, uncomprehending. "I've stood by my whole life and let them be murdered—"

"Then punished the murders, whenever you could. Because of that, Shel'ai that otherwise would have been killed at birth were simply abandoned outside the forest. I found some." Chorlga licked his lips. "And for that, I'm grateful. But enough escaped my attentions that you now find your kingdom in peril. In short, great king, this is your doing. Not mine."

Loslandril remembered the look of ecstasy on Chorlga's face when he had drained all semblance of magic from Quivalen's infant body. He imagined Chorlga wandering the outskirts of Sylvos, doing likewise to every Shel'ai child he found abandoned there, then leaving them to die when he was finished. Despite his hatred for the Shel'ai ruining his kingdom, Loslandril blinked.

Chorlga continued, his smile gone. "This kingdom is not yours, Sylv. Before you die, it will be taken back. By me. That can be delayed, though. I have come to offer you another deal."

Loslandril touched his chest, feeling the scars through his tunic.

Chorlga laughed. "Oh, nothing quite so dramatic. In fact, I assure you that neither you nor your beloved son will be harmed. In addition, I will see to it that the Olgrym do not invade Shaffrilon." He took a step closer. "And if the Dhargots come to help the Shel'ai, as they've promised, I'll drive them back as well. Shaffrilon and all of Sylvos will remain yours for..." He hesitated, as though contemplating. "Another ten years."

Loslandril frowned. "This kingdom has been under the guidance of my forefathers for over ten centuries. Now you ask that I relinquish it in a mere ten years?"

Chorlga turned toward a marble pedestal that contained a single glowing luminstone. He touched the stone. It went dark, as though his touch had absorbed the light. Then he touched the pedestal. The marble cracked. Chorlga faced Loslandril again, smiling. "Would you rather relinquish your kingdom now or after I singe the flesh off your son's bones and make you watch Olgrym rape his corpse?"

Loslandril considered snatching up Fel-Nâya and attacking, but something compelled him to keep the sword out of sight. Instead, he seized the wine pitcher and threw it. He had the satisfaction of seeing Chorlga's eyes widen in surprise before the man waved his hand and the pitcher flew sideways. The pitcher shattered, and the pieces skittered across the floor in the blue light of the chamber's remaining luminstones.

Chorlga smiled again. "Such tantrums are not kingly. But if it will make you feel better, you may throw as many pitchers at me as you like. We can make it part of our agreement."

Loslandril expected the guards to rush into the chamber, alerted by the noise, but no one appeared. He reminded himself that the sound of the cracking marble pedestal had not brought them, either. Perhaps Chorlga had already killed them. "What would you have me do—beyond surrendering my kingdom?"

"A simple thing. Hardly anything, really." He stepped forward, withdrew something from his cloak, and offered it to the king. When Loslandril did not accept it, Chorlga turned and laid it on the cracked pedestal.

The small black knife appeared to be made out of glass. Though it bore no markings or distinguishing characteristics, the sight of it oddly sickened him. He knew at once that there was something dreadfully special about this knife. "Who am I to kill?"

"You already know, great king. You need not do it yourself, but I want the wytch dead by morning."

"How do you even know she's here?"

"When one like her is close by, I feel it. Luckily, that is a skill she has not yet mastered. Nor will she."

Loslandril glanced at the knife. He could not move to take it without stepping away from the table. He decided to continue stalling. "She could kill me or whomever I send with a touch. How will one little knife do what whole armies could not?"

"My dear king, surely even a Sylv can sense the obvious. That is no mere knife. In ancient times, such blades were called *freyd*. They absorb magic like water into a washcloth. This is the last. With it, she will be helpless before you."

"Then why not use it yourself?"

"Face to face, she may sense what I am—and sense, in turn, what the *freyd* is. In the hands of a Sylv, she will not. And by the time she does, the blade will already be in her."

Loslandril considered using the knife on Chorlga but doubted he could move that quickly. "Or perhaps you're afraid that she's too powerful for you."

Chorlga's dark grin returned. "I have watched this one for quite some time, without her even knowing it. I even considered trying to make her my ally. But I do not think she would agree to such a thing, and though she is far weaker than I am, I see no need to risk facing her now."

Loslandril eyed the man carefully. He knew he should simply nod in agreement, but he had wanted to ask a single question for fifty years, though he doubted the answer would surprise him. "How is it that you are here?"

Chorlga touched the pedestal again. It cracked no further. "Another man would have asked what I was first."

"I know what you are. I think I knew the moment I saw you. But I thought all the Dragonkin were banished beyond the Dragonward."

"Perhaps I was just good at hiding. A better question would be to ask why I have shown you such generosity instead of simply reducing your bloodline to ash."

"I don't have to ask that. I already know. You're afraid the realms will form another alliance against you. If they do, you'll lose. For all your power, you're just one man. So, like the Shel'ai, you're hoping we'll all kill each other and save you the trouble." Loslandril feared he had gone too far. He expected Chorlga to curse him, taunt him, or even kill him.

Instead, Chorlga laughed. "Great king, you are an insect. The alliance you speak of could not happen, but even if it did, I would burn through it like a fire through straw. Your armies pose no more danger to me than a child's playthings. If you doubt me, send your fastest rider east, all the way to the Stillhammer Mountains, and see what I have done there. That is just the beginning." He paused. "But while you await his return, watch me burn the marrow from your son's bones."

Loslandril turned from the Dragonkin's unblinking gaze and stared at the glass knife. "Rid us of our enemies, and I will rid you of Silwren. And in ten years... Sylvos is yours."

He expected a response, but when he looked up, Chorlga was gone. Loslandril dared to hope it had all been a dream, but when he picked up the glass knife, it was so cold that he had to pry his fingers loose. The glass knife fell to the floor but did not shatter. He felt sickened, torn between weeping and vomiting.

He grabbed a letter off his table—a letter from a village pleading for help against the Olgrym—and used it to pick up the knife. He threw it on the table. By chance, it landed next to the sword. Their blades touched. The knife recoiled like a living thing, sliding across the table, nearly falling to the floor again.

Loslandril stared. Then he went to retrieve the knife again. But before he could pick it up, he saw Quivalen staring at him. His body went cold even though he had not touched the *freyd* again. "My son, how long have you—"

"Long enough." Quivalen choked. "Father, I heard..."

Loslandril shook his head, even as he realized that Chorlga must have known the prince was there. "Lies. Just lies, my son. He wants to trick us." He moved to embrace him.

Quivalen recoiled. "I heard the pact you made—"

"Another lie. I simply said what I had to say. I won't surrender the city. If I have to kill one wytch to save my people, so be it. After that, we can—"

310

Quivalen pointed at the knife. "You should use that on me. I am a Shel'ai..." He spoke the word like a curse.

"Not anymore. Do you understand?" Loslandril glanced past his son and saw an open door. Beyond the door, two guards lay motionless on the ground. One lay facing them, his face impossibly pale. His eyes had been burned away.

By the time Loslandril wrenched his gaze from the dead man's blackened eye sockets, Quivalen had picked up the knife. Unlike Loslandril, he seemed able to hold it without freezing pain. The prince held the knife for a moment, studying it, then raised it to his own throat.

For one moment, Loslandril remembered how he had very nearly carved out his then-infant son's eyes with a different knife. Shaking himself from his daze, he screamed his son's name and broke into a sprint. Quivalen looked up a moment before Loslandril tackled him. They crashed into the table, struggling for the knife.

Quivalen had always been frail, but suddenly, he fought with appalling strength. In the struggle, Loslandril slashed his own palm, bit back a scream, and lost his hold. Quivalen rolled away, rose to his feet, and held the knife to his own throat.

When he saw the blood welling from his father's fist, he blanched. "Father, you're hurt..." The prince seized a silk napkin, rushed to his father's side, and pressed it to the wound.

Loslandril accepted the help, waited until his son was close, then snatched the knife from Quivalen's grasp and tossed it away. Unnatural rage filled him, and he wanted to strike his son. Instead, he rubbed his scarred chest through his robes. Loslandril felt very old. He slumped to his knees.

"My son, you'll not harm yourself. Too much has already been given in your name. You'll not squander it. For me, for your mother, I'll have your word on this." He locked Quivalen in a fierce gaze. "Swear it."

Quivalen recoiled again. "Father, I'm sorry—"

Loslandril reached out with his wounded hand and grabbed his son by the tunic. He shook him. *Swear it!*

Quivalen nodded, weeping. "I'm sorry. Father, I swear it. I swear. I won't do that again. I won't."

Loslandril continued to clench his son's tunic of golden silk. Finally, Quivalen pried himself free. He backed away. Loslandril stared at him. The two embraced, weeping.

"No more," Quivalen gasped. "Don't sacrifice any more..."

"I won't," Loslandril promised. "Just this one thing. Just one last thing, and Sylvos will be safe." *At least, for now.*

Loslandril spotted the knife, lying under the table, and went to retrieve it. He hesitated a moment, but when he picked it up, it did not feel quite so cold anymore. He switched it to his wounded hand, clenching it tightly despite the pain. He refused to let it go. "One more death."

Quivalen touched his shoulder. "Father, let me do this."

Loslandril shook his head. "You have never killed before."

Quivalen shook him. "Yes, I have. I have, Father. Years and years ago... a Shel'ai baby, born in one of the villages. I heard, and I did what had to be done. And I can do it again." He seized his father's wrist, the one holding the knife.

But Loslandril did not believe him. "I don't want you stained by this."

"So you'd rather stain yourself?"

Loslandril almost laughed. "All kings murder, even if they don't actually wield the blade. You would learn that, in time. If there *was* time..." Before he could stop himself, he was weeping again.

Quivalen held him a moment then took the knife from his grasp. Loslandril moved to stop him, but he was too slow. Quivalen rose to his feet and stepped back. He looked down at the knife.

"Don't worry, Father. I can do this. I *have* to do this."

Loslandril stood. He braced himself, preparing to fight his son for the knife again. Quivalen backed toward the door, waving the glass knife to keep him at bay. "Stay here, Father. Please, just stay here. I'll come back when it's done."

Despite himself, Loslandril smiled. *Jalthessa, he has your stubbornness.*

Quivalen backed out the door, stepped over the dead body of a guard, and closed the door behind him. Loslandril moved to follow, but when he opened the door, he saw his dead bodyguards. Though all their eye sockets had been blackened, the rest of their bodies looked unburnt—as though the fire had been inside them, dragged out through their eyes. Loslandril thought once more of what Chorlga had done to his son when he was an infant. Shaking, he closed the door.

CHAPTER THIRTY-FIVE

HOMECOMING

JALIST WOKE JUST AS THE morning sun was rising off the distant blue of the Burnished Way. He had camped amid the crags of the Red Steppes, a day from his homeland. His small campfire had died while he slept, so he woke to see frost on the grass. He rubbed his cold legs, stretched, and rose quickly, anxious to get his blood flowing.

I should be used to this. Maybe I'm just getting old.

He had traveled light since leaving the Wytchforest, sometimes riding through much of the night, avoiding fire, and living off dry rations to avoid attracting undo attention. But the Dhargots ruled the Simurgh Plains, patrolling and looting at their leisure.

For a time, he had traveled farther south, hugging the Noshan Valley, thinking he would be safer there. The previous week, he'd spotted a band of Noshan warriors battling a crazed pack of Lochurites. The sellsword and tracker in him told him not to intervene. It was not his fight, and there was no profit in it. But when the Lochurites started gaining the upper hand, some of them so drugged and wide eyed that they kept fighting even after sustaining mortal wounds, the Housecarl in him won out.

A thrown sword brought down one Lochurite. A sweep of his long axe took out another. The remaining wildmen turned to face the new threat, which allowed the Noshans time enough to rally. They aligned their bucklers into a shield wall and closed in, finishing the fight with spears.

The Noshans had thanked him with a skin of wine and fresh news. Atheion, they said, was in turmoil. A great Dhargothi host led by one of the Bloody Prince's brothers was wintering at Hesod. That was not far from the mouth of the valley, and rumors had spread that the Dhargots were threatening to lay siege to Atheion by winter's end if the City-on-the-Sea did not voluntarily join the empire.

Jalist had already seen the host from a distance, a seething mass of tents, chariots, and loud, ponderous war elephants, but the news alarmed him. The Noshans further informed him that the Red Emperor's other two sons had hosts of their own shoring up their eastern positions on the Simurgh Plains, not far from Lyos.

Which is next for them—Lyos or the Wytchforest?

He remembered the stories of how the Wytchforest remained in eternal summer, regardless of the snows blanketing the outer lands. A Dhargothi host with ample provisions and a foothold in the forest might very well find the Sylvan kingdom almost as hospitable as one of their already-conquered cities. But would they help Fadarah, as they'd promised, or try to take the Wytchforest for themselves?

He worried for Rowen. But he reminded himself that Rowen must be safely in Shaffrilon by then. The Dhargots would be the least of his worries.

After parting ways with the Noshans, Jalist's journey had gone better for a few days. Then the Dhargots caught him. The scouting party, only five strong, did not seem anxious to fight the grizzled sellsword. But they demanded he surrender his horse.

Jalist had almost refused, but one of the men had a loaded crossbow. They took most of his supplies, as well, including his shortbow and the wineskin the Noshans had given him. Worst of all, they took his long axe. But they let him keep his shortsword after he convinced him that he'd fought for the Dhargots in the past.

Now, waking on the Red Steppes, cold and hungry, he could not wait to see his home. Still, he dreaded it. The Stillhammer Mountains were not likely to be friendly to an exiled Housecarl who had not only committed the ultimate male taboo of favoring men over women but had pursued their own prince besides. That Leander had reciprocated hardly mattered. It did not matter that Jalist had been gone for nearly ten years—Dwarrs had memories as perpetual as the stone on which they lived.

Jalist glanced down at the black wingless dragon tattooed to his right biceps—the mark of a Housecarl. *They might kill me. Then again, King Fedwyr was an old man. He could be dead by now. If Leander's on the throne, maybe things are different.*

He ate the last of his dried rations and continued on. He was out of provisions, but he had managed to conceal his coins from the Dhargots. By nightfall, he would be close enough to Tarator to find an inn and buy himself a mug of stout Dwarrish beer.

Of course, he would have to conceal his tattoo if he wanted to avoid questions best left unanswered. His brigandine and plain clothes were sleeveless, but he had a ratty cloak that he could wear until he found something better. In the meantime, he dirtied a rag with mud formed from the red clay of the steppes and knotted the rag around his arm so that it would look at a glance as if he had simply bandaged a wound.

Late in the afternoon, Jalist found a stream and refilled his waterskin. Then he followed the stream southward to a grove of trees. There he stopped and drew his sword.

The bodies had been picked clean by birds and greatwolves, but amid the bones and rusted metal, the sigils of the clashing forces were still discernable. The first, a bloody dragon impaled on a spear, was obviously Dhargothi. But the other, a visored helmet topped with a golden crown, astonished him.

What in all the hells were Lancers doing this far south? He rummaged among the dead for useable weapons, but as he suspected, rain and blood had left all of them rusted through. He did find a small pouch of iron crowns on a dead Dhargot and a handful of copper coins on the corpses of Lancers and their squires.

Wealth is for the living. Feeling a bit better about his fortunes, he followed the foothills as they gave way to the realm of the Dwarr.

Jalist remembered one particular village with the uncreative name of Stonehome, on the outskirts of the realm. Like most Dwarrish settlements, Stonehome was really just a loose cluster of adobe cottages, home to craftsmen and goatherds. But it had uncommonly good beer.

That had been almost ten years ago, but he doubted much had changed. His stomach growled at the thought of bread and tavern stew. Given his extra coin, he could afford to stay there a few days before pressing on for Tarator. That would also give him time to gather information and plan his next move—especially as far as Leander was concerned.

His father probably married him off to some nobleman's daughter. He may be no more pleased to see me than anyone else. This thought gave him a jolt of panic. He realized how naively hopeful he was—not to mention how lonely he'd been, especially lately. But if nothing else, it would be good to be back among his own people, eating Dwarrish food and conversing in his native language.

Jalist's steps quickened. He knew it couldn't be far. Then he heard the cawing of crows and saw their dark wings blackening the sky farther south. He cursed. *Some farmer must be slaughtering his livestock. A bit many crows for that, though…* He loosened his shortsword and slowed his pace. The hills ahead of him were scattered with boulders and patches of trees. He knew there was a lake nearby as well. Shepherds and goatherds would be there, perhaps even a few children splashing in the water. But when he reached the lake, no one was there. No people, no animals. *Moved on to better grazing land, maybe?*

When he reached the village, he could tell right away that something awful had happened there. There were no bodies, but the signs of battle were evident in the smashed doors and overturned carts.

He spotted the inn at the center of town. Rather than approach it directly, he skirted the village first, crouching low, listening. He expected to hear voices and laughter coming from the inn—if not Dwarrish voices, then maybe some company of sellswords that had taken up residence there.

He crouched outside one of the inn's windows and listened. Nothing. The door was open—hacked off its hinges, more like it. Jalist stared into the darkness, waiting for his eyes to change, then he entered slowly.

The inn's common room was in total disarray. Tables and chairs had been smashed. Bits of wood and shards of pewter mugs and bowls covered the floor. Though he saw no bodies, the floorboards had been stained too dark for spilled beer.

Jalist flexed his fingers around the hilt of his shortsword. He found the larders fully stocked, though the kitchens looked as though a pitched battle had been fought there as well. Meat had been left to rot, but he suspected wolves and wild dogs had already taken care of most of it.

Jalist searched the shelves and cabinets and found bread—stale but edible—plus some dried sausages. Untapped barrels of beer were stacked high in the cellar. His stomach rumbled again, but he did not eat. He had the wild thought that maybe everyone in the village had been poisoned.

Searching for clues, he checked each of the inn's rooms. More dark stains and broken furniture but no bodies. No discarded weapons or scorch marks left by fire.

Someone hauled off all the bodies. They took the weapons, too. But they left all the food behind. Dhargots wouldn't do that. They'd impale the dead... and the living.

Jalist wondered who else might dare attack Dwarrs in their own realm. His people kept to themselves, staying well out of the feuds of the other kingdoms of Ruun, but they had a formidable army and were famously protective of their own. An old adage often recited by Dwarr stated that an assault on the least of them must be answered with the same ferocity as an assault on the king himself.

He remembered the battlefield he'd seen earlier and wondered if that was connected somehow to the incident in the village. But he could not imagine Dhargots or Lancers doing such damage. And it did not seem like the Isle Knights' style. That left the nomadic Queshi, whose realm was southwest of here. But they were frequent traders with the Dwarrs, and Queshi always fought on horseback, firing their composite bows from the saddle. The attack had been done on foot, with blades. Face to face, eye to eye. *So who does that leave?*

He inspected the bloodstains again. They were old. He considered investigating every house in Stonehome, searching for anything branded with a sigil. Instead, he left the inn and followed the sound of crows. After only a few minutes of walking, he was forced to cover his nose. Even though he knew what he would find, he pressed on.

He found the bodies in a gorge. Dwarrs and livestock alike had been flung down and left there, tangled and uncovered. A great murder of crows swirled overhead. They screamed with frustration because the gorge was deep and filled with death but too narrow for more than a few of them to access at a time. The crows fought savagely for the remains, even though there was flesh enough to feed them all ten times over.

The bodies were slashed all over but dressed, with belts and pouches around their waists. He even spotted the glint of weapons in the gorge. Whatever force had wiped out the town had invested just enough effort to remove the bodies from plain sight without bothering to rob them.

Jalist shook his head. He had seen death before, even slain children. But the attack on Stonehome was different, done purely for pleasure, for sport. He doubted that even the Dhargots were that sadistic.

Whoever killed them could still be here. Jalist scoured the ground for a trail. He found it easily enough. As impossible as it seemed, the trail belonged to only a handful of killers, on foot. The trail led southward, toward Tarator. There were tears in Jalist's eyes, but those same eyes narrowed as he straightened, gripped his sword, and began following the trail.

An hour later, he found another town. Like the last, it, too, had been ravaged. But the dead had been left where they'd fallen. Jalist called upon all of his willpower to force himself to investigate the slaughter's aftermath. The Dwarrs had not been taken by surprise. He found both men and women armed with axes, bows, and shortswords. He saw shields and Dwarrish ringmail. What he did *not* see were dead attackers.

Jalist told himself that the killers might have carried off their own slain. He searched for clues about the invaders—a foreign weapon, a buckle off a dead man's armor, or a scrap of fabric with a sigil on it.

He found nothing. That frightened him. No matter how meticulous the invaders had been in hauling off their own dead, surely in all that chaos, they could never have completely cleansed the battlefield of their identity.

Jalist searched and searched. Gradually, he accepted the grim reality: the Dwarrs had not managed to kill a single enemy.

A chill raced down Jalist's spine. *Magic?* He remembered hearing that some forty or fifty years ago, a younger King Fedwyr had sent his Housecarls to attack Fadarah when he tried to settle on the outskirts of their realm. Perhaps the Shel'ai had come for revenge. But surely, the sorcerers had more pressing battles to wage. Besides, even if some kind of magic had been used to immobilize the Dwarrs, they had been slaughtered with steel.

Fine. Not the Dhargots, not the Shel'ai, not the Ivairians, not the Olgrym, not the Queshi, and certainly not the Sylvs, the Lyosi, or the Isle Knights. And not fellow Dwarrs, slaughtering each other. Who, then?

Jalist wondered why the killers had bothered to hide the corpses in the first village if they would leave others where they lay. His stomach clenched as he inspected the rotting flesh. He suspected this town had been attacked soon after the first. Hiding the dead in the first village wouldn't conceal the slaughter from the rest of the Dwarrs, since it was moving in their direction anyway. But it might conceal it from anybody passing through the Red Steppes.

Jalist clenched his fist. *So someone invaded the realm and started slaughtering Dwarr but didn't want any of the other realms to find out about it. At least, not right away.*

What kind of host could wipe out two whole villages of Dwarrs without sustaining any losses? Among the Dwarrs, boys and girls alike were taught to fight starting at an early age. Even the children could throw axes with deadly accuracy.

Maybe the attacks happened in the middle of the night. But he found no burnt-out torches on the battlefield and no characteristic smoke stains on the walls. The Dwarrs had died in daylight. There had been plenty of warning. It simply had not made a difference.

Jalist glanced in the direction of Tarator. Whatever had killed all those warriors could still be there. Besides, he was an exile. The

Dwarrs weren't even his people anymore. He considered fleeing then continued south.

The carnage only worsened as he traveled deeper into his homeland. Dead Dwarrs lay on the road, not just commoners but whole squads of Housecarls, too. The famed fighters had been mowed down in columns with no more difficulty than the dead sheep and goats scattered in the hills.

Impossible. But there they were, in cleaved and bloodied ringmail, near fallen banners depicting a black wingless dragon set against a golden mountain on a field of white. Jalist trembled. For the first time, he feared finding Leander's face among the fallen.

No chance of that. He never was much of a fighter. Besides, the Housecarls would protect him. If Tarator were in danger, they would move him farther south—all the way to the sands of Dendain, if need be.

But then what? Would they hurry him onto a ship and send him away? If so, where would he go?

Jalist shook his head. *One mystery at a time. But wherever you are, Leander, I'll find you.*

He fought the impulse to sprint as he continued south. He fought, too, the desire to call out in search of survivors. For all he knew, the enemy was just over the next hill. Better they meet him only when they felt his blade splitting their spines at the neck.

By sundown, Jalist still had not seen a single living thing, except for the crows. On foot, he was still a full day's journey from Tarator. That meant he would have to seek shelter. And, as much as the sight of so much death had turned his stomach, he would have to eat.

At the next ravaged village, he covered his nose and forced himself to enter an inn. Deciding that concealing his tattoo was the least of his worries, he removed his cloak and turned it into a makeshift sack, which he filled with dried meats, what little bread hadn't gone moldy, and a skin of strong beer.

As dark started to fall, the silence of the dead village frightened him all the more. He left quickly, frequently turning to look behind him. He had no intention of camping on the open road, so he went into the hills. He passed a field full of dead livestock. Nearby, he found a cottage with the family still inside, but he could not bring himself to haul out their corpses or force himself to sleep near them. So he moved on, his limbs heavy, his senses frayed. He knew he needed sleep, but he couldn't imagine stopping anywhere in the nightmare and closing his eyes.

Finally, he found a ditch without corpses and a hole partially overgrown with tree roots. He crawled inside. Just then, it began to rain.

"Perfect," he muttered. The sound of his own voice frightened him.

Shaking his head, he forced himself to eat. His stomach lurched, and he vomited up his first attempt. He drank half the beer, and once he felt his head swimming, he managed to keep down the rest of his food. He was tempted to finish the beer, but he knew he needed to keep his senses sharp. Cold and miserable, he wrapped himself in his cloak and tried to sleep.

The nightmares came at once. He saw Tarator burning. He saw Leander being hacked to pieces. Jalist tried to reach him, but his legs had stopped working. Finally, somehow, he reached him, but Jalist's axe did no harm to the shapeless demons tearing the Dwarrish prince with their claws. Then the shapeless demons turned to face him. They reeked of blood and sour milk. Terror filled him, and Jalist fled. He left Leander behind, and the prince laughed at him, screamed for help, and cursed him. And even in his dreams, Jalist wept.

CHAPTER THIRTY-SIX

ROYAL BLOOD

ROWEN WOKE FROM NIGHTMARES OF fire, battle, and his brother. For a moment, he wondered where he was. He groped in the dark and, by chance, touched the thick black cloth covering the luminstone that his captors had left on the nightstand beside his bed. He tore away the cloth. No longer concealed, the luminstone's soft-blue glow drove back some of the shadows. Rowen sat up, shirtless, and rubbed his eyes.

"You were dreaming about Olgrym again."

Rowen jumped. Silwren was sitting in a chair across the room. The luminstone's glow made her violet eyes look as black as night. She stood slowly and approached him. Her wispy nightgown was nearly transparent. Rowen felt his blood stir, even though her approach brought with it a pang of dread. He forced a smile to his lips.

"Next time you rescue me, feel free to wake me up soon as you get here." Rowen spotted his tunic and pulled it on. Blushing, he drew his trousers over his smallclothes, though Silwren did not seem to notice.

"How long till dawn?" He glanced at his room's three beautiful arched windows, but they were utterly dark. The sunrise was difficult to see through all those towering wytchwood trees, anyway.

"The Olgrym are still a few hours away. The fighters are massing at the World Gate."

Rowen glanced past her at the closed door. He wondered if she had incapacitated the Sylvan guards outside or merely ghosted into the room. Since she had not yet led him out the door, he figured it must be the latter. "Are you going to join them?"

Silwren gave him a look he could not interpret. "I have not been invited."

"Since when did someone need an invitation to defend themselves?" Rowen rubbed his eyes. A few frightful tendrils of his dream—dung-smeared Olgrym howling madly, setting themselves on fire before they charged—still clung to him. "Besides, you're a Shel'ai in the Sylvan capital, and they aren't trying to kill you. I think that's as much of an invitation as you're going to get."

Silwren stared at the luminstone as though she had not heard him.

Rowen resisted the sudden urge to shake her. He went to a basin and splashed cold water on his face, grabbed a towel, and dried off. "I take it they still haven't talked to you." When Silwren shook her head, he said, "I tried to talk Briel into asking you for help."

For the first time, Silwren smiled faintly. "What did he say?"

"More or less what you'd expect." Rowen tossed aside the towel. "Doesn't mean we can't march down to the World Gate and help them anyway."

Silwren raised one eyebrow. "You want me to fight on behalf of people who will probably fire a hundred arrows at me as soon as they see me?"

Rowen thought back to Que'ahl, where the Sylvs had considered peppering them with arrows, only to watch as Silwren turned all the arrows to ash. If she wanted to, she could turn the mighty World Gate to cinders along with the Olgrym and Sylvs.

But that might drive her mad... and a mad Dragonkin is even more dangerous than a sane one. If there is such a thing. Rowen reminded himself that she could very well be reading his mind, and he cleared his thoughts. "Well, if you're not going to side with the Sylvs, why in the hells are we here?"

"We are here because *you* insisted on it."

"The Oath of Kin?" He flexed his empty hands and looked around, again, for something he might use as a weapon. "I was wrong. We shouldn't have come here. Maybe we should just go."

"Go where?"

Rowen considered taking Silwren east, so she could help the Isle Knights fight the Dhargots. But he'd lost Knightswrath. Crovis Ammerhel would see him put to death for that. "The Free Cities. The Dhargots are burning them. I say we go to the closest one and burn the Dhargots instead."

The words quickened his blood, but as soon as he saw Silwren's droll expression, he knew she intended to refuse.

"We both know you aren't going to leave Shaffrilon, Human. And neither will I."

"But you still won't fight?"

Silwren turned to stare quietly at the luminstone.

"You still haven't chosen a side, have you?"

Silwren winced. "I've killed Shel'ai... my own kind. I've protected you against everyone who's tried to kill you. What more do you want from me?"

Rowen thought back to the scroll they'd stolen from Atheion, telling of how Fâyu Jinn's beloved had sacrificed her own life to ignite a terrible power within Knightswrath. That power had turned the tide of the Shattering War. Guilt filled him. What right did he have to ask that same price from Silwren? Besides, if Silwren could bring herself to kill Fadarah and Shade, then use her existing magic to help drive back the Dhargots, Knightswrath would not be necessary.

Rowen turned and poured a glass of wine. He poured another for Silwren and passed it to her wordlessly. She took it with trembling hands.

"Your people make good wine," he said. "A little sweet but strong as hell. Jalist would love this."

"You're worried about the Dwarr."

Rowen nodded. "Can you... use your magic to see him? Is he safe?"

"He's too far. And... I am not myself." Silwren took a long drink, nearly draining her glass.

Rowen wondered if Shel'ai could get drunk. *Might be she needs to.* He offered to refill her glass, but she shook her head.

"You had a knack for forgetting that Fadarah is my father," she said suddenly. "In virtue, if not in blood. My *father.* And you want me to kill him."

Rowen thought of Kayden again. "If you want to talk about family..."

Silwren gave him what he thought was an apologetic look. "I know our sins—his and mine. Still, what you ask—"

A shrill trumpet blast interrupted her. Rowen jumped again, nearly dropping his glass. "Olgrym?"

Silwren closed her eyes. A faint, violet glow flared about her body then dimmed. She opened her eyes. "Just a vanguard. Their main host isn't here yet. But there's fighting at the gate."

Rowen nodded. He had already seen how little concern Olgrym had for tactics. They seemed to relish the idea of dying in battle. He imagined the vanguard hurling themselves at the World Gate, braving an impassible storm of arrows and steel, reveling in any slaughter—even their own. Rowen's fist clenched around the wine glass. He drained it and set it down, fighting back the rush of blood that went to his head.

"Well, if you don't want to fight, we have no reason to be here. I say we leave before the Sylvs realize you aren't still locked in your room."

For a long time, Silwren stood motionless, breathing faster, like a trapped animal. "I feel... something strange. I've felt it before, but I thought it was just my own madness. It reminds me of how I felt when Iventine or El'rash'lin were close by... Iventine, especially."

Rowen thought of the Nightmare, all scaled and flaming before the gates of Lyos, and shuddered. "Are you sensing Fadarah and the other Shel'ai?"

"Maybe," Silwren said, though she sounded doubtful. "I have to face them, Knight. You're right. I haven't chosen a side yet. But I must try one last time to stop them with words. If that fails, I'll stop them with fire."

"You've promised that before."

Silwren looked up, hurt, then nodded. "So I have. But if you have faith enough for one last promise, I'll make you one. Before the sun sets again, either I die or Fadarah does."

Her body blurred, as though he were seeing her through a waterfall. Then she vanished altogether. Rowen glanced at the dark mouths of the windows, listening to the distant cries of alarm and battle. He wondered if he should pity her or be angry at her for not setting him free before she disappeared.

Finally, left with nothing to do, Rowen considered trying to sleep again. He covered the luminstone with the dark cloth again. But he'd hardly lain down in bed when he heard shouting outside his door. He rose and pulled the black cloth off the luminstone just in time to see the door flung open. A thin, wild-eyed Sylv lurched into the room, dressed in richly embroidered bedclothes. He had a knife.

Rowen moved to the far side of the room, thinking for a moment that some madman from the capital had decided to kill him. The Sylvan guards entered his room as well. He thought they would restrain the thin man and wrest the knife from his hand. Instead, they drew their swords and stood by the door.

The wild-eyed Sylv stabbed at the air in Rowen's direction. "Where is she, Human?" The Sylv spoke in heavily accented Common.

Rowen picked up a wine glass. He pretended to drink the last few drops, even as he rehearsed he motion that would allow him to break the glass on the nightstand and arm himself with a glass shard. "I have no idea what you're talking about, sir, but I like your tailor. Tell me, does he live in the capital?"

One of the guards pointed at him with his sword. "Speak with respect, Human! You address Quivalen, crown prince and son of the king!"

Rowen narrowed his gaze at the shaking, gaunt figure before him. "Apologies, Prince. I wish we'd met sooner. I've been hoping—"

The Sylvan prince charged him. Rowen sidestepped, dodging a wild stab from the knife, which seemed made of black, nonreflective glass. He broke his wineglass against the wall but backed up. "Wait, Sire, let me—"

The prince turned and slashed again. He missed by a foot, but Rowen felt a strange coldness glance across his chest. He feared the guards would rush to the prince's aid, but they stood in the doorway. The prince waved his glass knife in Rowen's face. "Where is she? She's not in her room. Tell me where she's gone or—"

Rowen tossed the broken wineglass at the prince's face. When the prince dodged, Rowen stepped forward, grabbed both the prince's wrists, and drove his knee into the prince's groin. He twisted the prince's limbs so that Rowen was behind him, even as the glass knife, still in the prince's hand, hovered dangerously close to the prince's throat. Rowen pressed his back against the wall, holding the Sylvan prince like a shield.

"I just ran out of patience. Get Briel, or I'll cut your damn prince's throat."

The prince whimpered. The guards had already started forward, but at Rowen's threat, they froze. They glanced at each other. One turned and rushed out the door.

CHAPTER THIRTY-SEVEN
WISDOM AND JUSTICE

B RIEL PULLED A STAINED RAG from his pocket and quietly
wiped the blood from his curved shortsword. Illuminated by
moonlight spilling through the branches of the World Tree,
some of the Sylvan warriors were doing the same. Others gathered
the hulking corpses of the few Olgrym who had managed to scale
the World Gate. Slashed by arrows and swords alike, the bodies were
barely recognizable. Rather than dispose of them by dragging them
down the steps, the Sylvs simply heaved dead over the battlements
so that their corpses created a grim testimony to what had happened
there—and a warning to the next band of Olgrym that attacked.

*A vanguard… this was just a vanguard, one hundred fey Olgrym with
ladders and hooks, and it took everything we had to kill them!*

Briel surveyed the fortifications. Most of the Shal'tiar had perished
days earlier in the fighting, but the World Gate had been reinforced
with Shaffrilon's reserves, plus nearly every man and woman who
could draw a bow. He saw a few children, too, and knew the need was
too great to dismiss them.

Technically, General Seravin was in command, though the man's
haughtiness had been replaced by a woefully discouraging timidity
that made Briel wish more than anything that Essidel were with them.
But Briel was certain that the legendary Captain of the Shal'tiar lay
among the slain—and with him, whatever faint hope they had for
victory.

He glanced up the Path of Crowns to the smaller but still imposing fortifications of the Moon Gate. King Loslandril was supposed to be up there, inspiring Shaffrilon's defenders with his presence, but the monarch had yet to make his appearance. Instead, they had General Seravin, pale and shaking, with a cup of strong wine sloshing in his sword hand.

I am in command—or near enough. Briel shuddered. He had never wanted to be in command. Only days before, he could have named a dozen men and women who would have been better suited for the task. But all of them were dead. *And I will be, too, in another day or so.*

A horrible, reeling thought came to him. He had long since ceased to fear his own death, but the image of the mighty World Tree burning, magical flames licking the platforms and scouring the bones of countless dead, forced him to steady himself. *No. Not yet. We'll find a way. Somehow—*

He heard a commotion and turned. A scout was pushing frantically through the ranks to reach him.

Something's wrong in the city. Fire? A riot? Or— He thought of Silwren and cursed. "Let him through," he shouted. He faced the scout. "Report."

The scout gasped for breath. "It's Prince Quivalen, Captain! The Knight is trying to kill him!"

Briel winced at his new title, even as a ripple of unease swept through the ranks, and scowled disapprovingly at the man's loud tone. "What are you talking about?"

"The prince found out that the wytch escaped, so he questioned the Human, but—"

Briel seized the man by his leather jerkin and shook him. "What do you mean, she 'escaped'?"

The scout looked ill. "She's not in the House of Questions. We're searching the city, but the Human said you have to come, or he'll cut the prince's throat! The king is safe, but three guards were found dead in the palace. Burned. The prince is... shouting something about a Dragonkin threatening the city. Does he mean the wytch or someone else? Have the Dragonkin come back?"

Gods, did Silwren turn on us? Did she try to kill the king? The man had lowered his voice, but Briel could already hear the alarm spreading. "Are they still in the House of Questions?"

The scout nodded. "The king has already gone there with more men."

General Seravin was descending the walkway from the Moon Gate, flanked by bodyguards. Briel glanced southward, over the battlements, at the already-bloodied field beyond. "Report this to the general. He's going to wonder what's going on when I walk right by him. Tell him I'm going to the House of Questions to sort this mess out myself."

As he raced up the Path of Crowns, Briel could see that the prince had already caused quite a panic. The citizens of Shaffrilon, those too young or old to fight, flooded the streets. Some had armed themselves with bows and makeshift clubs. They were joined by hundreds of refugees from the other settlements throughout Sylvos that had already been ravaged.

A few recognized Briel by his uniform, and soon, a throng of Sylvs surrounded him, plaguing him with frightful questions. Some asked if Silwren and the Dragonkin mentioned by the prince were one and the same. Others insisted that they'd heard from guards, who had heard the prince directly, that the Dragonkin was someone else—a man.

Ignoring the questions, Briel shook a young corporal of the city watch. "You want the king to see this? Rally your men and get these people back in their houses. If these streets aren't cleared in half an hour, I'll personally toss your severed head over the World Gate!"

The corporal blanched and nodded.

The guards outside the House of Questions appeared no less frantic than those outside. Pushing through two whole squads of guards crowding the hallway, Briel found the king in the doorway of the room where Rowen Locke had been secured. As the king turned, the glow of the luminstone highlighted the scar below the king's eye. Briel wondered how Loslandril had received that scar then pushed the thought from his mind.

The king entered the room, Briel right behind him. Despite all the guards outside, only three stood inside the room, swords drawn.

Briel figured that was the king's doing, and he was glad for it. The smaller the audience, the better.

The Isle Knight stood with his back against the far wall, both arms wrapped around Prince Quivalen, who was red eyed and crying. The prince held a strange knife with both hands, though Rowen had his hands over the prince's, using his superior strength to keep the edge pressed to Quivalen's throat. The Knight looked angry but composed.

The most dangerous kind of man.

Briel turned back to the hallway and pointed at the highest-ranking officer. "I'll handle this. The king is safe, and the prince will be, too, in just a moment. Meantime, there's a crowd outside. Go out and see that they return to their homes. Then help the others search the city for the wytch." The officer opened her mouth to protest, but Briel said, "I want this hallway empty before I turn around again, or Captain Essidel will know the reason why."

He turned his back on the sound of rushing footsteps. He gestured for the three guards inside the room to follow the rest. When they were gone, he glanced at the king, wondering if he meant to address Rowen himself. Though his face was taut and his unblinking gaze was fixed on the glass knife hovering at his son's throat, the king said nothing. Briel closed the door. The only sound was the prince's ragged sobbing.

"Want to tell me what this is about, Knight?"

Rowen said, "Silwren didn't kill anybody."

"Maybe. Maybe not. Tell me where she is, and I'll ask her myself."

Loslandril touched Briel's arm. "The Knight is quite correct. His wytch didn't kill my men, though, for now, that does not leave this room."

One of the king's hands was freshly bandaged. Briel gave Rowen a scathing look. "Sire, did this man—"

"An accident, nothing more. I am sorry we have not spoken sooner, Isle Knight. Perhaps one day, you will understand why. For now, release my son, and we can talk."

For a moment, Briel thought that the Isle Knight would actually lower the knife. Instead, he said, "Apologies, Sire, but your son seems intent on killing someone I care about. I think I'll keep him like this for the time being."

Loslandril's gentle facade fell away. "This is my city, Human! I command thousands of men—"

"But not the knife at your son's throat." Rowen shook the Sylvan prince for emphasis.

Quivalen whimpered.

"I don't want this any more than you do, Sire, but until I get some answers…"

For a long time, no one spoke. Then the king sighed. "Very well. I'll begin with tonight. My son speaks the truth. A Dragonkin *did* visit us this night. He killed three of my men, for no reason other than to demonstrate his power, I think. But *killed* is not the proper word. He drained them, as the Dragonkin used to leach off the dragons of old."

Briel wondered for a moment if the king had concocted the bizarre story to cover up Silwren's murders or in attempt to confuse the Isle Knight long enough for Briel to disarm him. He started to reach for his sword, but the king touched his arm again.

"This Dragonkin has visited us once before… though I will not speak of that. This time, he offered ten years of peace in exchange for driving off the Shel'ai, the Olgrym, and the Dhargots. And in return, all I had to do was stick *that*"—he pointed at the black knife—"into the wytch's body and turn it."

Silence filled the room again. Briel wondered if he looked as stunned as the Isle Knight did. Then Rowen said, "Silwren said she felt something, but she didn't know what it was."

"His name is Chorlga. Have you ever heard that name?"

Rowen shook his head.

"This one moves in the shadows, I think—scheming, sowing conflict. I think he has done so for centuries. But I'll say no more with a knife to my son's throat."

Rowen was still for a moment, then he lowered the knife but kept one arm wrapped loosely around Quivalen's neck.

Loslandril nodded slightly, pulled up a chair, and sat. "It seems you speak our language—probably the first man since Fâyu Jinn to do so. I'm told this is a result of a spell cast by El'rash'lin, Fadarah's one-time second-in-command."

Rowen said, "He turned on Fadarah and died saving us from the Nightmare."

But Loslandril hardly seemed to hear him. "I am told also that your Order is not our enemy, that the past reports of Isle Knights fighting alongside Olgrym were Shel'ai illusions. I am inclined to believe that. But it makes no difference. Chorlga is a bigger threat than Fadarah—or anything else, for that matter. I have to do whatever I must to protect my kingdom."

Rowen gave the monarch a derisive smile, even as Quivalen struggled feebly to escape. "As you've protected it so far?"

Briel tensed, but Loslandril faced his accuser, unflinching. "I have done far more than you know, Sir Locke. But I've not come to argue. I just need to know where Silwren has gone."

"So you can kill her?"

"Yes."

The king's honesty seemed to catch the Knight off guard. "I have a better idea. Let's all just wait here like good little madmen until Silwren returns. I'll keep the knife. Then, King, you can decide whether you want her to turn you into ashes or ask her to save your whole damn kingdom. If you're lucky, she won't make you give it up in ten years."

The king stood, fuming, but Briel touched his arm. Facing Rowen, Briel crossed his arms. "We both know you aren't going to kill him, Knight. So put down the knife. If you don't, I'll fetch a bow and put an arrow through your eye."

Rowen tightened his grip on Quivalen's throat, causing the young man to whimper again. "Careful. This one makes a good shield."

"Not good enough." Briel ignored the scathing look from his king and took a step forward. "What will it be, Knight?"

Rowen felt as if the muscles in his arm were on fire—though he had the odd sense that the glass knife was also slowly freezing him. He could not tell whether he had been standing like that for minutes or hours, pressing the glass knife to the Sylvan prince's throat, but he knew one thing for certain: he could not keep it up much longer.

Briel seemed to sense it, too. The Shal'tiar fighter still had not called back the guards or made good on his threat, but Rowen knew it was only a matter of time. As the minutes stretched on, Briel only grew calmer. His cold, unshakable gaze reminded Rowen of Captain Essidel's.

This one won't break. He's calling my bluff. He's sure I won't kill this squirming bastard—and he's right!

The Sylvan king was another matter, though. Loslandril glared and trembled while pacing the room, growing more agitated by the moment. Rowen considered issuing a fresh round of threats on the prince's life. But that opportunity vanished a moment later when two worried guards entered the room. One held a bow. Briel took it. With deliberate slowness, Briel took one long, dark arrow from the guard's quiver and fit it to the bowstring. In the unwavering glow of the luminstone, the arrow's steel tip gleamed.

The king opened his mouth as though he meant to stop it, then he turned away.

Briel said, "Time's up, Human. Make your choice." He drew back the bowstring until the fletching touched his cheek.

No courage without fear, Rowen thought. He remembered something his brother used to say: *Hard to fight when you're dead.* He cursed. Then he lowered the glass knife and shoved the Sylvan prince away. The king caught his son and helped him into a chair.

Briel trained the still-drawn arrow on Rowen. "Now the knife."

Rowen tossed it to the floor, hoping it would shatter. Instead, its blade left a crack in the stone floor. Briel kicked the knife away. Then he relaxed the bowstring and drew his sword. Both guards leapt forward, seizing Rowen by the arms.

King Loslandril retrieved the glass knife and came forward. "You attacked my son, despite being a guest in my kingdom. Whatever else happens in regards to Silwren, you must pay for that."

Rowen tried to fix a brave expression on his face. Then, in his most careful Sylvan, he said, "I surrender to your wisdom and justice."

King Loslandril regarded Rowen again. "Guards, step away from the prisoner but keep your swords drawn. Stab his legs if he makes any move other than what I order."

The guards reluctantly stepped back.

Loslandril stepped forward and offered Rowen the glass knife, hilt-first.

Stunned, Rowen took the knife. A chill raced up his arm. Over the king's shoulder, he saw Briel's eyes widen. Quivalen rose to his feet, opening his mouth to protest, but Loslandril stepped back, raising one hand to call for silence.

His eyes never left Rowen. "Draw that knife across your right cheek, deep enough to bleed like a battle wound."

Rowen looked from Loslandril to Briel. The captain had recovered from his shock. He met Rowen's gaze and nodded slightly. Rowen recalled something from El'rash'lin's memories: a rarely employed ritual wherein a person accused of a crime was allowed to harm himself in return for a commuted death sentence.

He's still going to use me to try to get to Silwren. But even if I had Knightswrath, there's no way I could get past Briel and the guards. The best he could do was play along. Still, he flinched when he raised the knife and felt the cold edge against his cheek. Reflexively, he moved his hand away. He saw Briel half draw his sword, moving to flank the king in case Rowen decided to attack.

No courage without fear. Rowen shut his eyes for a moment then opened them. *Gods...*

He fixed his gaze on the king again, watching for some reaction as he dragged the knife across his face—a rush of cold, then heat, then stinging pain—but the king did not so much as blink.

CHAPTER THIRTY-EIGHT

CRACKS IN THE WALL

ESSIDEL LOWERED HIS SHORTSWORD TO prevent a glint of errant light from splashing down the curved blade and giving away his position. He peered through the blue-black foliage. Ahead lay a scattering of stone ruins overgrown with grass and moss. He frowned. "You think Fadarah's in Ish'kana?"

Khi'as whispered, "Either here or the World Gate. If the latter, it won't make a damn bit of difference, because we'll never get there in time."

She's right. Essidel had never seen the place before, but he had read about it. Ish'kana, the City of Friendship, had been built during the twilight of Shigella's reign to commemorate the alliance between the Sylvs and the Isle Knights, intended to serve as both embassy and home to dignitaries from the Lotus Isles, Stillhammer, Ivairia, Atheion, and half a dozen other realms.

Essidel almost laughed, surveying the ruins. *See how well that turned out.* He wished Rowen Locke were there to see the sight, then he felt a pang of guilt, realizing the Isle Knight was probably dead. He took a deep breath and let it go.

He understood what Khi'as meant. Though relatively close to the capital, Ish'kana had been abandoned for centuries. No Sylv would come there. That meant that if Fadarah needed a home base inside Sylvos to plan his attack, the place was as good as any.

Still, Essidel saw no horses. "The Shel'ai were riding bloodmares."

"Maybe they abandoned them."

"Or they were smart enough to hide them." *Or they aren't even here.* He ordered the rest of the company to hold their positions while he crept ahead, alone. He moved as slowly as a shadow, crawling and creeping between toppled pillars and shattered temples. Though he heard nothing but the sound of wind through the trees beyond, he half expected to be burned alive any second. But no Shel'ai were in sight. He was about to give up when he peered into the remains of what might once have been a storehouse and found a herd of ruddy horses. A few turned to regard him with indifferent yellow eyes.

The Shel'ai must be close. Essidel fixed his gaze on a single structure that might once have been a great hall. The high, circular walls were relatively intact save for a web of palm-wide cracks and a few breaches big enough for a man to pass through. He saw a flash of violet light inside, and his pulse quickened. A wave of uncertainty washed over him. If Fadarah and the rest of the Shel'ai were in there, Essidel was facing the only place in all of Ruun that was even deadlier than the besieged World Gate.

This is madness! I should go back to the capital, tell Seravin, and come back with a thousand fighters. He thought of the platforms and bridges that connected the branches of the World Tree with the surrounding wytchwoods. Bypassing the Olgrym would have been a simple matter.

But that would take too long. In the meantime, Shaffrilon would fall. We'd have to abandon the city entirely... the king would never agree to that. Essidel studied the great hall again. *I could surrender. Hide a knife somewhere. Wait until I get close to Fadarah then—*

He dismissed the idea, reminding himself that Shel'ai could read minds. Even if they did not kill him on sight, they would never be so easily fooled. He considered other strategies that he'd employed against the Olgrym in the border wars: tactics built on diversion, surprise, and subterfuge. But Shel'ai were not Olgrym.

The clouds broke, and light glinted over the ruins. Essidel glanced up at Armahg's Eye. He considered praying for help then decided against it. He regarded the distant starry swirl for only a moment before returning to Khi'as and the others, who had taken shelter behind a low, ruined wall. He explained his simple strategy.

Khi'as looked doubtful. "We could surround the place, wait for him to stick his head out—"

"I counted six gaps in the wall, as good as doors. No telling where he'd come out. The longer we wait, the greater the chance that we'll be seen... or sensed." He glanced at the great hall's dark, open doorway and suppressed a shudder. "I'll go in alone."

Khi'as opened her mouth to argue, but Essidel saw movement and silenced her. He pointed. A figure in a white-and-crimson cloak had just emerged from the shattered doorway. Essidel tensed, but the Shel'ai moved slowly, without purpose.

Still, he's a sorcerer. And he's facing us. If those damned magical senses of his—

The Shel'ai glanced left and right then opened his cloak, loosened his britches, and started to piss.

Essidel glanced at Khi'as. "We wait," he said, using hand signs.

But a moment later, what little luck had graced them so far abandoned them. The Shel'ai turned sharply in their direction. Essidel could tell by the man's tense posture that it was no idle motion. The Shel'ai had heard something, but he had not seen them yet. Essidel grimaced. *That's it. No choice now but to run.*

Khi'as touched his arm. For a long time, neither blinked. Then they both nodded in silent agreement. Without taking his eyes off the Shel'ai, who was slowly approaching the ruined wall, Essidel extended one hand behind him.

One of the Sylvan fighters crouching behind him quietly placed a shortbow in Essidel's hand. An arrow followed. Essidel crawled sideways until he was behind a wytchwood sapling twice as broad and tall as he was, then rose to his knees and nocked the arrow. He had only seconds to act. Still, he took a deep breath and held it. If the Shel'ai heard or sensed the arrow, he would burn it in midair and warn the others. *We'll all die.*

He held the breath, cleared his mind, and drew back the bowstring. Squinting, he let the bowstring go with a snap. The arrow leapt into the darkness, narrowly missing the top of a toppled column, and caught the Shel'ai in the cheek. It sank nearly feather deep. The Shel'ai stiffened. His mouth opened. Wytchfire sprang to his fingertips, twirling violently. But Khi'as was on her feet, bow in hand. Her arrow sank into the Shel'ai's chest. Two more Sylvs fired. One arrow caught the dying man in the shoulder, another in the side. He took a step back toward the great hall, stumbled, and fell.

Wordlessly, Essidel retrieved his own heavy quiver of arrows and stepped out from cover. Khi'as followed, another arrow on her bow, her curved shortsword already loosened in its scabbard. The others followed.

Essidel smiled tightly. The Sylvs were not Shal'tiar, but they made no sound. With luck, they might slip into the great hall undetected. He had no way of telling how many Shel'ai were inside, but once the fighting started, numbers would make no difference. Essidel had no delusions that he or any of the other Sylvan fighters would get out of there alive. But he knew that Fadarah, because he was part Olg, would be easy to single out. So long as Fadarah died, nothing else mattered.

Still crouching, he ran as fast as he could while moving quietly, weaving through a maze of rubble and toppled structures. He and his band of archers were nearly to the great hall when another cloaked figure appeared in the doorway. Essidel swallowed a curse and loosed the arrow.

The Shel'ai's violet eyes widened a split second before she gestured. An invisible gust of magic batted aside Essidel's arrow. But Khi'as's arrow followed too quickly and caught the wytch between her breasts. She screamed and fell backward into the great hall.

That's it. They know we're here. Best we can do is run and hope they don't follow. He faced Khi'as. "Get the others out of here. I'll stay for Fadarah."

Khi'as answered by fitting another arrow and firing at the first figure who appeared in the doorway. A flood of wytchfire burned her arrow to ashes, but she reached for another.

The others had fanned out and taken cover where they could. They loosed arrows at the doorway as quickly as they could. The Shel'ai retreated inside, unleashing another storm of wytchfire in the archers' general direction before he went. Essidel crouched low and felt the fire pass overhead, singeing the back of his neck. One of the men behind him screamed, but Essidel knew better than to waste time turning around.

He loosed another arrow. Khi'as did the same. Only by then, they had no target. Essidel heard muffled shouts from within the great hall. Facing a gap in the stone wall, he glimpsed movement and loosed an arrow. The arrow missed by the width of a finger, rebounding off the stone wall.

"Nice shot," Khi'as said dryly.

"Save your breath for prayers. If one or two of them get out—"

Waves of wytchfire struck them from the flanks. Essidel heard screams and felt heat roiling all around him, whitewashing the night with awful brilliance. Pain stabbed all his senses. He reeled a moment before he managed to employ the mental discipline of a Shal'tiar and will away the worst of it. Still, unable to see, he fired on instinct then discarded the bow in favor of his shortsword.

How did they get around us so fast? He heard a muted cry to his right. *Khi'as.* He shoved past the sound and stabbed in what he hoped was the direction of her killer. His sword passed through empty air. Then he jerked. He felt as though a lance of molten steel had been thrust clean through his thigh. He staggered, turned, and threw his sword. He heard a scream. He managed a smile of grim satisfaction before another fiery lance opened his chest to the world.

CHAPTER THIRTY-NINE
MERCY

S HADE LOWERED HIS HANDS AND watched the final tendrils of wytchfire fade from the battlefield, leaving behind only corpses and blackened stone. He turned, about to order Avesha to lead a search of the surroundings, but she sat on the ground, leaning against a ruined wall. Three arrows protruded from her cloak, each one centered in a growing red stain.

Fadarah stood just outside the great hall, huge and armored, his fierce, tattooed face utterly expressionless in the darkness. But for a moment, Shade sensed from him a wild surge of grief.

Zeia stepped in front of him, blocking his view. Soot blackened her young face and clung to her dark, close-cropped hair. Tears glistened in her violet eyes. "We lost Hathia and Brinn."

"And Avesha." Shade pointed.

Zeia gasped. She started toward Avesha then stopped and turned back to Shade. "Three more dead, and still, the World Tree is not ours!" She cast a spiteful glance at Fadarah.

"Quiet your thoughts, sister. This was not his fault." Shade expected Zeia to nod meekly in agreement. In all the years he'd known her, she had never displayed any ferocity, save toward her enemies.

Instead, Zeia pulled away. "For one who calls himself the Sorcerer-General, our adopted father seems remarkably inept at both magic and strategy!" She pointed at Avesha's corpse. "She saved my life. Que'ann saved hers. Now they're both dead."

Shade winced at the mention of the grandmotherly old Shel'ai who had used her powers almost exclusively to heal. She had died at Lyos. "I know that. But Fadarah rescued her, just as he rescued me. He saved all of us—"

"We should have kept some of the Olgrym as bodyguards. You said that yourself."

Shade glanced past Zeia and saw Fadarah watching them, listening. "It was a risk. They crave bloodshed, not guard duty. If we'd kept them here—"

"Then *this* wouldn't have happened!" Zeia trembled, despite the wytchfire appearing in bright plumes from her clenched fists. Shade stepped back, wondering if she would lash out in her grief. Instead, she addressed those Shel'ai standing around her—all those left alive. She spoke words that, given her fury, must have been broiling inside her for quite a while, carefully hidden.

Shade glanced at Fadarah again. *"Should I stop her?"*

Expressionless, Fadarah crossed his arms and slowly shook his head.

The others listened. Some wept. A few crossed their arms and angrily turned their backs on her, but Zeia persisted. She spoke of every failure and every home they'd lost. Gradually, the weeping Shel'ai began to nod.

Shade moved so that he blocked the approach to the ruined storehouse where the bloodmares were stabled.

Zeia faced Fadarah across a field of ashes and blackened bone. "You've killed for too long from a distance, General. When was the last time you looked into the eyes of your enemy? If you did, you'd know the Sylvs will never surrender." She turned slowly, facing each Shel'ai in turn. "I'm going back to Coldhaven. I'm going to protect the children we left behind. I'm going to make sure they have nothing to do with this war... and I'll kill anyone who tries to stop me."

She backed away from Fadarah, wytchfire still roiling at her fists. But the Sorcerer-General continued to regard her in stony silence, arms crossed. Zeia continued to back away. Then she turned on her heel and strode off into the darkened forest.

For a long time, no one spoke or moved. Then one of the Shel'ai lowered his head and followed Zeia. Two more followed. Some of the others stared at them with contempt, but most looked away.

Shade hurried to Fadarah's side. "You can't let them go. The others will see it as a sign of weakness—"

"They thought it was weakness—not mercy—when I let the Nightmare die. When I released the Unseen. Even when I let that Soroccan merchant go after he tried to kill me, when killing him would have brought nothing but flies. All my *mercies*."

Shade frowned. "General, you should rest—"

Fadarah gave him a look so withering that Shade took a step back.

"Let me go after them," Shade tried. "Just to talk. It will be a kindness. When they get back to Coldhaven, the ones we left to guard the children will think they turned craven and abandoned you. It'll be a fight—"

"Let them go. We have other concerns." Fadarah's voice grew distant. "Zeia was right. I am not blameless. My sin is that I have hesitated. But no longer." He raised his voice. "Gather yourselves. We follow Doomsayer's hordes to the World Gate."

No one moved. Then Shade heard a faint whimper. Miraculously, one of the Sylvan fighters had survived. A woman, burned nearly head to toe, stirred. Her body too ravaged even to scream, she began to crawl feebly along the dirt toward the corpse of a Sylvan captain. Shade realized she might just have been trying to reach a weapon.

Shade started toward her, wytchfire gathering at his fingertips, but Fadarah grabbed his shoulder and stopped him. The Sorcerer-General drew his two-handed sword and strode toward her. He loomed over her for a moment. With supreme effort, the dying woman rolled over and faced him. Her mouth opened as though to speak, but only a pitiful, wet rasp emerged.

Fadarah knelt. He removed his gauntlet and pressed one large tattooed hand to the burned woman's face. The woman winced in agony as Fadarah's fingers probed her raw nerves. Then a soft violet glow began to drift like fog from Fadarah's hand. Her body drew it in like water soaking up a sponge. The woman gasped, as much in surprise as in pain, and arched her back, reflexively grasping the hand

344

that had touched her. She might have tried to shove it away, sensing what was to come, but Fadarah was far too strong.

The Sorcerer-General urged more and still more healing energies into her body, until at last, he withdrew. He looked pale and exhausted, as though he'd just returned from a great battle, but he stood, eyes fixed on the burned woman at his feet. The burns remained, but he had accelerated her healing by weeks, if not months. She was in far less pain, and her milky eyes had cleared. She even tried to sit up.

Shade frowned, surprised by Fadarah's act of mercy.

Fadarah helped her. "What is your name?"

The warrior woman tried to speak, choked, then tried again. "Khi'as," she managed. She eyed the nearby corpse of the war band's leader. The man's body was charred, his face fixed in a ghastly smile. Khi'as trembled. Then she fixed Fadarah in a defiant gaze. "If you mean to interrogate me, you're wasting your time. I know nothing."

Fadarah shook his head slowly, unblinking. "I'm not going to interrogate you." Fadarah held her gaze. Then he drove his sword through her breasts, clean through her body, and deep into the ground. The woman's eyes widened. She did not cry out. Fadarah stepped back, leaving his gigantic, dark sword where it was. He held her gaze until she died. Then he turned and swept his eyes over his final handful of cloaked disciples.

"I trust I've made my point. The time for mercy has passed. Now is the time for fire and blood. All who agree, let them follow." Fadarah stalked off toward the horses. One by one, the others followed, until only Shade remained.

As he heard his companions saddling and mounting their unruly bloodmares, Shade approached the dead Sylv. The smell of her charred flesh filled his nostrils. He held his breath, knelt, and closed her eyes. Then he stood and hurried after his master.

CHAPTER FORTY
FAREWELLS

IGRID WOKE TO KNOCKING ON her door and sat up straight, knife in hand. Her first thought was that it was the Red Watch, coming to arrest her for all she'd stolen over the past few days. But no one cut purse strings as deftly as she did. Besides, she'd taken care to dress differently and move to a different inn every night.

The knocking resumed, becoming louder and more insistent. She rose cautiously from the bed. Naked, she shivered in the cold, realizing she had forgotten to close the shutters the night before. A fine layer of frost had formed on the windowsill, and she could see her breath. She started to reach for her clothes then stopped herself. If the person pounding on her door was after her blood, the distraction might be a good thing. She reversed the knife in her hand so that the blade was concealed behind her wrist. She moved quickly across the room, unbarred the door, and yanked it open. Her right arm tensed, ready to plunge her knife between the neck and shoulder of whoever was standing beyond.

In the doorway stood Arnil Royce. Instead of armor, he wore a richly embroidered tunic covered by a plain cloak. His eyes widened. "You have a curious manner of greeting visitors, Iron Sister."

Igrid cursed. She considered shutting the door in his face and going to dress herself first, but she opened the door the rest of the way and returned to the bed to fetch her cloak. "I haven't seen you in six days, you bastard. I asked the palace guards about you, and they said they had no idea what I was talking about. For all I knew, Typherius threw you in a dungeon."

"The king's men were bound to keep my presence here a secret." Arnil entered her room and closed the door behind him. "I'm sorry I worried you."

"Who's worried? Do as you like, Lancer. I just—"

"Wanted to make sure you were properly rewarded for getting me to Lyos alive?" Arnil smirked, even as Igrid felt her cheeks redden. "If I may say, Iron Sister, it's hard to find you when you keep changing inns and hairstyles... though I'd wager I could have simply followed the wails of robbed merchants and broken hearts."

Igrid could not decide whether that was a compliment or an insult. "Well, Lancer, you've found me. May I ask your purpose in so boldly entering my room?"

Something flickered in his eyes, possibly desire, but he bowed. "I came to take my leave of you. I'm heading north within the hour."

The pit of her stomach felt hollow, though she could not say why. "The king granted you an escort, then?"

"He won't get involved. But a company of Isle Knights arrived in Lyos last night. There was talk at first that they'd come to reinforce the city, but the latest reports say the Dhargots have stopped at Cassica." Arnil hesitated. "I asked around, and it turns out the Knights are on a different kind of mission. They're trying to locate your friend, Sir Rowen Locke."

Igrid blinked. Her fingers tightened around the hilt of her knife. "Why? Do they think he needs their help? He must have reached the Wytchforest by now. They should have marched with him from the start if they meant to be of use!"

"You mistake me, milady. They do not mean to help him. They mean to arrest him." He paused, as though giving her time to reply, but Igrid was speechless. "I attended their meeting with the king. Two Knights of the Lotus lead the company, a man and a woman. The man thinks Locke is a traitor who stole Fâyu Jinn's blade out of vainglory."

Igrid's jaw tensed. "And the woman?"

"She's Locke's friend, I think. Officially, she commands the Knights, though you could cut the tension with your knife. She says she means to find Sir Locke and… reassess the situation. Though truth be told, based on the number of Knights who seem to side with this man, Crovis, I doubt she'll have her way on this."

Igrid followed Arnil's gaze and realized that she was white-knuckling her knife. She relaxed. "And how does this concern you… or me, for that matter?"

"The Knights have agreed to give me safe escort to Ivairia, since they're riding west anyway. That is, the *woman* agreed, though I doubt one in five of her Knights supports her decision. She's stalling. But it's to my benefit. As for you…" He shrugged. "You said Locke was your friend. I thought you'd care to hear what may become of him."

Igrid felt her heart in her throat. "You're wrong. I'm done with Locke. My business is in Lyos now."

"Then this should help." Arnil tossed her a small pouch of coins. "A gift from the king—that is, a gift to me that I won't be needing. Not as much as I already paid you, but you're welcome to it."

Igrid upended the pouch. She counted twenty cranáfi, each coin stamped with the balancing crane of the Lotus Isles. She returned the coins to the pouch and tossed them onto her bed without comment.

Arnil said, "Will it be a tavern or a brothel?"

"Perhaps one of each." Igrid turned her back and let her cloak fall to the floor. She dressed in full view of him—not as an act of seduction but out of the hope that it would make him forget whatever questions she sensed he had been about to ask.

The Lancer did not acknowledge her nakedness, though she thought she heard a slight tremor in his voice. "A fine plan, I am sure. In that case, perhaps you'd like to speak with Commander Shingawa on Locke's behalf. At the very least, I'm sure she could convey a personal message from you. After they've clapped him in irons, that is."

Igrid decided to dress Lyosi style. She wrapped a silk sarong around her breasts and fixed the clasp at her throat. She found her hands were shaking. She was glad her back was still turned. She slipped her feet into the fine stolen sandals lying beside her bed. Then she buckled her belt, with the knife on her hip. She took a deep breath to steady herself before she turned around. "Thank you, Lancer. I will consider your suggestion."

Arnil gave her a dour look. "Well, it's no concern of mine. Do as you like. I thank you once again for your assistance, though I'm sure my gold was the only payment you desire." He bowed again and started to go.

Igrid said, "You misjudge me."

Arnil shrugged. "As you say, milady." Stone faced, he turned to leave again.

Igrid crossed the room and took his arm, stopping him. "My relationship with Locke is... *was*... not easy to explain."

His frown said that he did not believe her.

She was not surprised. *Who am I trying to fool here? My relationship with Locke couldn't have been simpler. He saved me from the Dhargots, and I repaid him with treachery. I used him.*

Arnil gently removed her hand from his arm, though he did not reach for the door again. When he spoke, his voice was softer than before. "I need no explanation, milady. It is not my business. I see how this troubles you. And I think you are not quite so hardhearted as you pretend."

To her surprise, he pulled the glove from one hand and touched her face so gently that she barely felt it. She felt an odd ache when he pulled away. He bowed a third time. "Goodbye, milady. If you change your mind, you'll find us assembling on King's Bend within the hour." And then he was gone.

Igrid stood in her room as though carved from stone. She eyed some of the other goods she'd already bought stacked in the corner of the rented room: a good Lyosi shortsword, plain traveling clothes, and fine boots with dark, hardened leather on the outside and soft leather and velvet on the inside. She'd had them made special, and they were better suited for traveling in the wilderness than traversing the clean cobblestone walkways of Lyos. *Odd. Why did I do that?*

She touched the hilt of the shortsword. It had not been wrought of kingsteel—despite her new wealth, that was still far too expensive—but it was better than any other sword she had ever owned. Light, fast, and sharp, it had a waisted blade and an ergonomic wooden handle bound in leather.

Not well suited to the city, where daggers are easier to hide. But perfect for travel, she thought dourly. *Well, I've already entrusted my coins with the Lenders' Guild. I could buy a horse and ride west with the Knights. I could vouch for Rowen, tell them how he saved me, what he did for those Noshan villagers. And when they catch up with him, I could beg his forgiveness.*

Igrid winced. She would not beg—not in this life and certainly not for forgiveness from any man. Besides, Silwren's illusionary conjuring of Knightswrath still irked her. Rowen's forgiveness would be fair compensation for her letting his wytch live.

She felt a cold breeze. She turned and eyed the frost on the windowsill. Beyond, a few flurries flitted about. *It won't be long now.* She went to the window and closed the shutters. Then she undressed, shivering, and went back to bed.

CHAPTER FORTY-ONE

THE TOMB

U NSEEN, SILWREN ARRIVED IN SHAFFRILON as the morning
light spread across the Path of Crowns. She reeled for a
moment as the full power of a Dragonkin roiled inside her.
It flooded her senses, threatening to overwhelm her. She knew that if
it did, she might very well destroy all she'd come back to protect. She
fought it by focusing her mind on the image of Rowen's face.

I will not give in. I cannot. Not now.

The knowledge of what she had seen at Ish'kana gave her strength,
even as it filled her with despair. She had returned too late to prevent
the battle, but she had heard Zeia's accusations, sensed the others'
growing agreement, then watched in horror as Fadarah healed a dying
Sylv only to kill her as a demonstration of his newly hardened will.

Concealing herself from view of a man she had once taken as her
husband, Silwren had watched it all. Her plan to try one last time to
speak to them withered and died. But faced with the other option
of killing Fadarah and Shade—all of them, as she'd told Rowen she
would—her courage faltered. But it had been replaced by courage of
a different sort. If she could not bear to destroy Fadarah and Shade
herself, one way to help Rowen still remained.

Back in Shaffrilon, she faced the House of Questions. She started
forward then stopped. *If I tell Rowen, he will try to stop me. Better I do
what must be done then leave the sword behind. For him.*

But even then, Rowen might not be safe. Without her, he would
have no one to teach him how to use the sword's true abilities. He

would flounder. He would be hurt. Still, he would be safe from Fadarah and the others—safe from the sins of all the Shel'ai.

Nodding, she hesitated a moment longer, smiling in the darkness and wishing she could at least say goodbye. She started toward the palace. Though the walkway behind her was crowded with frightened Sylvs, a line of guards kept them from ascending any higher. She blocked out the cries, blocked out everything, and ascended the walkway in grim silence.

She had never seen the palace, but she'd seen paintings of it: a narrow, tall building topped in white spires, draped in green banners and wreathed in statues of the gods. The strain of remaining invisible became too great. She shimmered into view, startling the two smartly armored guards outside, but a touch on each of their foreheads made them tumble into unconsciousness. Silwren touched the locked gate, and it swung open easily.

She met three more guards and a handful of servants inside. All greeted her with wide blue eyes. Some reached for weapons, but at Silwren's gesture, all slumped to the floor. Though the use of magic did not tax her quite so much, a great weariness still built inside her. As she moved past them, Silwren had the odd feeling that she was becoming ethereal again, floating over the stone floor.

Not floating—flying. She fixed her gaze on a broad, ornate staircase in the distance. She moved quickly, knowing that to delay risked further erosion to not just her courage but her sanity as well. At the top of the staircase, she incapacitated another servant, wincing when the boy dropped a pitcher of wine that shattered on the marble floor.

Still trusting whatever inexplicable magical sense guided her along, she made her way through the maze of palace hallways and staircases. At last, she came to what looked like a blank wall. Sensing some kind of strong, ancient magic emanating from the wall, she touched it. To her surprise, the stone shimmered as though turning to water, then it vanished altogether.

Silwren faced a narrow corridor. Though the corridor was unlit, a pale white glow preceded her. She realized with a start that the light was emanating from her own body. With a mix of fright and elation, she hurried on.

The corridor narrowed further, bending this way and that. The floor inclined, and the stone walls gave way to wood. She had passed into the World Tree itself. All her senses tingled. She wondered how long it had been since someone had been there.

The corridor widened then came to a sudden dead end. She faced a breathtaking mural. Centuries old, it depicted a host of winged, ethereal figures leading an expressionless host of iron Jolym against a smaller, defiant host of Sylvs, Isle Knights… and violet-eyed Shel'ai.

Though she knew she was running out of time, Silwren felt her eyes drawn to a part of the mural depicting a dark-haired woman with tapered ears. Though flames and ghostly wings emanated from her body, she stood not among the Dragonkin but with those she'd been raised to despise.

Nâya… give me strength. Silwren wept. Unsure how to proceed, she touched the wall. It shimmered and disappeared. When it was gone, she stepped forward—alone—into the tomb of Fâyu Jinn.

Luminstones had been placed in the small tomb, and their blue radiance mingled with the white glow of Silwren's body. The first thing Silwren saw was a white-haired man in kingly garb, by the far wall, kneeling before an ornate stone sarcophagus. Next to a man she guessed was the Sylvan king stood Briel, his sword drawn. A figure knelt before the Sylvan warrior, bound and gagged, his face washed in blood. After a moment, Silwren recognized him. Rage and worry made her fingers flare with wytchfire. She pointed her fingertips at the king's back but restrained the fire. "Release him or your king dies."

Briel pressed his sword to Rowen's neck. "Lower your hands, wytch. Please."

Silwren could see by Rowen's wide, pleading eyes that he wanted to tell her something, but she extended her mind into the mind of the Sylvan warrior instead. She sensed Briel's reluctance. Still, he would kill Rowen if she threatened the king.

Silwren lowered her hands, though wytchfire continued to snake between her closed fingers, testing her control. Only then did the king rise, slowly, and turn to face her, his eyes drooping and bloodshot.

"Father always said only magic could open the doorway. But when he took the sword... when he sent it away... I realized he was lying." Loslandril smiled faintly, touching a scar beneath his left eye. "I came here after he died. I thought it would give me strength. But all I found was armor. Even Jinn's bones are gone."

Silwren looked from Loslandril to Briel. "Release the Knight, and Sylvos retains its king. Harm him, and I'll burn the palace around your ears. I will not tell you again."

Briel bit his lip, uncertain, but Loslandril said, "You came for this?" He tapped the dragonbone hilt of the sword clumsily girded about his waist. "You know I can't let you have it."

"I'm not asking." Silwren felt a surge of derision and considered making good on her threat. Then she remembered how Fadarah had killed that Sylvan woman. Derision became pity. "We don't have to be enemies. We are not the monsters your father feared."

Loslandril frowned. "My *father* was the monster, wytch. I've known that since I was a child. It's not *you* I fear. It's not the Shel'ai, either. It never was."

Silwren wondered what the Sylvan king meant. Despite the risk of using her magic, she extended her mind into his, far more deeply than she'd done with Briel. The tomb of Fâyu Jinn shimmered and vanished, replaced by the king's bedchamber. Through the king's eyes, she saw Prince Quivalen as an infant, staring up at her. She felt the king's panic as though it were her own then the cold metal of a knife as she briefly considered protecting the prince's life by cutting out those damning, violet eyes.

Then she saw *him*. The man radiated power and malice—far worse than any Shel'ai she had ever known. She realized at once what he was and recoiled from Loslandril's mind, tumbling back into her own body. For a moment, she could not speak. But as she fought to reclaim her own senses, a dreadful comprehension filled her. At last, she understood why the Shel'ai had never known peace.

The Sylvan king faced her. The white glow of the tomb filled the wrinkles in his face like snow in a cracked, ruined wall. Loslandril nodded slowly, as though he'd sensed her probing his mind. He undid the laces of his tunic and opened his shirt, showing her the ghastly wound that Chorlga had given him so many years ago. "Understand, wytch, I have no choice. He is stronger than you, stronger than anyone. I am sorry."

Silwren braced for his attack, but neither the king nor Briel made a move. Rowen screamed incomprehensibly through his gag, warning her before Briel could knock him down. Silwren turned, finally recognizing the trap.

A thin, wild-eyed Sylv lunged at her. He whispered, "I am nothing like you," and struck her breast. He started to step back, but Silwren caught him by the wrist. Wytchfire raced up his arm. The thin Sylv tried to break free, but the fire washed past his shoulder, spreading over his face like a mask. He screamed.

The king screamed, too. Something in his anguished cry caught her attention. She turned back to face him. The king had drawn Knightswrath and charged her, but a wave of her hand sent him tumbling backward, even as the magical expenditure sent a jolt of pain through her own chest.

Rowen surged to his feet. Though his wrists and ankles remained tied, the Knight grappled with Briel, punching him with his bound hands. Despite Rowen's fury, Briel had already cut him twice—once on the arm, once on the thigh. The Sylv stepped back to deliver the death blow.

Silwren gestured again, more harshly, and Briel's arm snapped. His shortsword clattered to the stone floor. The Sylv fell, hissing through clenched teeth. Rowen followed, groping for Briel's fallen sword. His eyes met hers. Though they were safe, Rowen's eyes widened with horror.

An icy chill swept through her. She looked down and saw the hilt of a glass knife protruding from her chest. For a moment, she could not believe it. She felt no pain—only cold. The chill deepened. She pressed one hand to her wound. She tried to summon more wytchfire to stave off the chill, but the knife drew in the fire as soon as she released it. The room tilted and shimmered around her.

"Rowen," she gasped.

Everything turned white and cold. She thought for a moment that she'd been transported to the Wintersea. That she was alone—and naked.

Nâya... oh, gods... please, just—

Before she could finish her prayer, the ice cracked. Silwren fell through, into miles and miles of cold, dark water.

CHAPTER FORTY-TWO

THE BRASS MASK

J ALIST WOKE, WET AND SHIVERING, hours before dawn. He knew there was no point trying to sleep more than the little bit he already had. He felt more exhausted and despairing than ever. But at least the rain had stopped. He cursed and drained the last of the wineskin. Then he crawled out of the ditch, checked the stars to make sure he was facing south, and started walking. Several times, numbed to the sight of Dwarrish corpses, he stopped at farms and searched for provisions. He claimed a warmer cloak, a pair of matching stilettos with black gemstones in the hilts, and the top half of a broken spear. He cursed himself for not taking one of the dead Housecarls' long axes the night before.

Jalist returned to the road and continued south. Around midday, he encountered what appeared to be a desperate, failed attempt at fortifications. A squad of Housecarls had dug a ditch and erected a wooden palisade to block the road. Scorched grass and stone, along with the lingering smell of oil, told him that the fighters had also tried killing their enemy with fire. Jalist passed easily through the shattered palisade and picked his way through the dead. He searched for a usable long axe, but all were rusted and unreliable.

The crows had either fled in fear or finally succeeded in sating their depthless hunger. Jalist considered saying a prayer to Maelmohr, pleading for the care of dead souls, but he changed his mind. *Where were you when your followers were being slaughtered, you divine bastard?*

After walking for an hour, he stopped in his tracks and wondered if he might be drunker than he thought. There, on the road before him, about a hundred yards in the distance, stood a man.

No, not a man. A giant! The figure stood at least seven feet tall. His back was turned. More remarkably, though, he was covered head to toe in gleaming brass armor. It was almost blinding. Still, he was the first living person Jalist had seen in days. He debated whether he should hide or call out to the man. Then the man turned and faced him.

Jalist decided not to run—it was only one man, after all—and raised a hand in greeting. The brass-armored figure offered no reply. But Jalist realized for the first time that he held a hatchet in each hand. The brass-armored figure started toward him, his movements quick and jerking.

Jalist drew back a step. "No need to fight, friend. I'm just looking for answers."

The brass warrior neither answered nor slowed his brisk, mechanical advance.

"Fair enough. Maybe you're one of the bastards I've been looking for, anyway." *If so, let's hope I fare better than my kinsmen!* Jalist drew his shortsword with one hand and gripped his broken spear with the other. As the figure closed in, Jalist saw the ghastly smiling facemask. Like the rest of the man's armor, the facemask was wrought of gleaming brass, though the eye holes looked hollow and wholly black.

In the back of his mind, Jalist guessed what he was facing, but he could not believe it. By then, the Jol was only twenty feet away. Jalist threw his sword. It struck the Jol squarely in the chest. The Jol rung like a hollow bell but did not slow.

"Gods..." Jalist picked up a rusted axe off the ground, but the Jol was on him before he could throw it.

The brassy demon made no sound but came at him with that ghastly smile fixed in place. Both hatchets blurred. Jalist dove to one side, narrowly missing them.

The Jol followed. The hatchets swung again. Jalist sidestepped and smashed the rusted axe down on the Jol's left thigh, which was nearly level with Jalist's chin. A jolt of pain swept up Jalist's arm, as though he'd just tried to chop a stone in half. The axe blade cracked. The Jol brushed off the blow and swung at him again.

Jalist backpedaled desperately, discarding the broken axe, stabbing the Jol's arm with his broken spear. The force of the blow jarred him, but again, the Jol did not slow. Jalist dove, came up, and thrust the spear between the Jol's hip and thigh, where there should have been a gap in the armor. Instead of passing through flesh, the spearhead scraped off brass, sliding into nothing.

Gods, the damn thing's hollow!

Jalist abandoned the spear and backpedaled, narrowly avoiding having his skull split open as the Jol turned and swung both hatchets at his face. As he retreated, Jalist got a better look at the Jol's hands. His opponent was not holding the hatchets—they were literally *part* of its arm.

Well, at least he won't be able to throw them at me. The hatchets were wrought of kingsteel, flecked with dried blood. Jalist retrieved his shortsword and tried to parry the Jol's next strike. But the force of the blow shattered the blade and sent a shard of steel into his face, gashing his cheek. A kingsteel hatchet, unhindered, continued on and might have cleaved him between the eyes had the sight of the shard of metal flying at his face not already caused him to recoil.

Jalist fought the impulse to stanch the warm flow of blood down his face and neck and threw the useless hilt of his shortsword into the Jol's grinning face, hoping to distract it. The quillons sparked off its nose, but the Jol charged without pause.

Cursing, Jalist drew both his stilettos and retreated again. He could tell that he was a bit quicker than his opponent was, and he thought about fleeing, but the memory of that body-filled gorge burned away all thoughts of retreat.

He continued to back up, trying to keep some distance between himself and his opponent, but the Jol was relentless. It was chillingly quiet, too, save for a slight grating sound when it moved. Its mechanical ferocity more than made up for what it lacked in skill. It followed him everywhere he went, always swinging, always grinning as it tried to hack open his skull like a ripe melon. Jalist thought to trick it, trying to lure it toward a corpse or a bit of wreckage so that it might trip, but it stepped around each obstacle as though it could see in every direction.

Jalist thought back to the legends, trying to remember some clue as to how to kill such a thing. But he had never paid much attention to those stories, convinced they were a waste of time.

Whatever gods are up there, I bet they're laughing at me. Jalist risked a quick, spiteful glance at the sky. *Savor it while you can. I'll be with you soon enough. Then we're going to have a little chat.*

The next time the Jol came at him, Jalist tried to sidestep, but the hollow demon anticipated this and moved to block him. It swung, carving a divot in Jalist's brigandine. Bits of leather and metal flew through the air. Jalist retreated, cursing.

I can't keep this up much longer. He eyed the Jol's sadistic grin and wondered what it was thinking. Even though its lips—if they could be called that—had not moved once, Jalist had the strange feeling that it was mocking him. Jalist slashed with his knives, leaving bright scratches on the Jol's brass forearms, but it kept coming. Finally, one of its hatchets sliced into his brigandine, going deeper than the first had. Jalist felt warm blood running down his stomach.

Howling with fury, Jalist leapt forward. He slipped under the Jol's blurring hatchets, stepped in close, and wrapped his arms around the Jol's smooth, cold waist. Jalist's arms flexed. His thighs buckled. Before the Jol could strike again, Jalist had lifted it clear off its feet and thrown it on the ground.

The Jol rolled and kicked, as awkward as a turtle flipped on its back. Jalist circled and kicked it in the head. It lifted its head to look at him. Jalist knelt and thrust both his daggers into its dark, hollow eyes.

He leapt backward, searching around for another weapon. His slashed cheek throbbed painfully as he tensed his jaw. He expected the Jol to rise, unhurt. Instead, it jerked wildly then went still. A faint hiss of smoke unfurled from its eye holes.

Jalist stared uncertainly, gasping for breath. He held one hand to his slashed brigandine, trying to stanch the flow of blood within. He picked up another rusted axe off the road, approached cautiously, and rained blows on the fallen Jol's face until the grin was dented and unrecognizable. Still, the Jol did not move. Jalist shook his head, threw away the axe, and sank to the ground.

"So that's how you kill them."

Before he knew what he was doing, he laughed. It sounded mad to him, but once he'd started, he could not stop. He laughed and laughed until tears ran from his eyes. At some point, the laughter became sobbing, but he hardly noticed. He only stopped when he heard a great metallic racket coming from behind him. He turned.

"Gods..."

A great host of Jolym was coming up the road from the direction of Tarator. Some were wrought of brass or bronze, others of iron. A few seemed to be made of pewter or wood. Row upon row, each had a blade, an axe, or a pike fixed to each of its hands and a different, equally grim expression carved into its face.

The great host shambled to a halt, facing him. Exhaustion and despair became terror. Jalist rose shakily to his feet. He turned and ran. And the Jolym followed.

CHAPTER FORTY-THREE

THE KNIGHT OF THE LOTUS

E SSIDEL, WHERE ARE YOU? SERAVIN could not remember the last time he had prayed for his cousin's well-being, but he did so as he watched the Olgrym pour out of the trees and throw themselves at the World Gate. Many of the bestial warriors had already smeared their hulking gray bodies with the entrails of their victims. Others had doused themselves in oil or tar and lit their bodies on fire, howling in a kind of raw, agonizing ecstasy as they charged the battlements. They came by the hundreds, by the thousands.

"Gods, we can't stop them..." Seravin realized he'd vocalized the thought and cursed himself. Luckily, the din of battle seemed to have prevented his officers from hearing him. Seravin raised his hand, clenching his fingers in a fist to conceal their trembling, and brought his hand down to signal the attack.

All along the parapets of the World Gate, Sylvan bowstrings twanged in unison. Arrows flew in fat, dark gouts. Trebuchets hurled jagged boulders or smoldering clay jars, which shattered on impact, spreading even more fire. Olgish bodies toppled and were trampled by the brutish tide behind them. Olgrym fell by the dozens, many of them burning and bristling with arrows. Yet the tide did not slow.

Though the Shel'ai had not appeared yet, Seravin wondered for a moment if they would even be needed. He spotted greataxes, grappling irons, and siege ladders amid his charging foes. All along the parapets, squads of swordsmen already stood prepared to hack down any scaling implement that successfully weathered the storm of arrows—as they had already been doing for hours, since dawn, turning back wave after wave.

But we can't turn them back forever. We can't—

Then, at last, he spotted cloaked and hooded figures pressing through the Olgish ranks toward the walls. Though the Olgrym towered over them, something in the sorcerers' cloaks made them equally fearsome—as did the wytchfire billowing from their fists in snapping, violet tendrils.

"Shel'ai!" he called, pointing. "Archers, bring them down as soon as they're within range!"

But even as Sylvan bows shifted, a wall of Olgrym closed in around the Shel'ai. Unlike the majority of the other Olgrym, who had been naked or dressed in crude furs, the Olgrym around the Shel'ai wore full armor and carried massive iron shields. They locked their shields, protecting their masters from the Sylvan arrows.

"Use the trebuchets!" Seravin swallowed a knot of panic. "I want more buckets readied over the gates. Water and sand, both. If the sorcerers try to burn them down…" *Can anything extinguish wytchfire?* With a pang of dread, he realized he did not know.

Then he spotted Fadarah at the heart of the advance. As big as an Olg and armored in black, he looked almost identical to his Olgrym bodyguards. But Seravin caught a glimpse of the Sorcerer-General's telltale tattoos.

They serve power and madness. No wonder—

A trebuchet fired. A boulder the size of a man's torso arced over the parapets, directed either by skill or sheer luck at Fadarah himself. Seravin had the impression that the entire roster of the World Gate's defenders held their collective breath. He dared to hope.

But the Olgrym tightened formation, pressing shoulder to shoulder, shields raised. Seravin lost sight of Fadarah in a crush of metal and a wild spray of blood. At least three Olgrym fell, but Fadarah remained. Seravin thought he saw the Sorcerer-General laugh.

We won't get a shot like that again.

Seravin glanced over his shoulder, up the Path of Crowns, toward the Moon Gate. A line of reserve archers manned the second gate, shifting restlessly beneath Sylvan banners. Seravin wondered if the king had arrived. Given the sour mood of Shaffrilon's defenders, he doubted it. He did not see Briel, either. He wondered again what was happening in the city, what had caused those mad rumors of Dragonkin, and why the king wasn't at his side.

The men need someone to inspire them. They need another Shigella. They need a king—or, at the very least, a great warrior. Instead, they get me. He almost laughed. He'd led the Sylvan armies on the Ash'bana Plains, but that role had been almost entirely ceremonial. Everyone had known that Essidel was in command. Seravin had resented him for that—but he had resented him from inside a fortified stronghold, safe behind the veil of Essidel's tactical brilliance.

In the end, even Essidel had failed. Or perhaps it was Seravin's fault for not listening. Either way, the fact remained: Shaffrilon was facing the greatest threat since the Shattering War, and Seravin had no idea how to stop it.

Gods, Essidel, where are you?

"Dead, probably," he muttered. He touched his sword hilt and faced his officers. "All right, call down all the reserves. And send a message up the Path of Crowns. Anybody who can't fight should flee. When the Shel'ai reach the gates, we'll hold them as long as we can."

His officers exchanged frightened, sheepish looks. Seravin guessed they were trying to decide which of them would deliver his message. That one, in so doing, might survive another day.

Whoever it is, it won't be me. Seravin tightened his gloves and drew his sword. He gazed out over the parapets. The Shel'ai were closer. He tried to remember the slogan of the Isle Knights—something about courage blossoming in the presence of fear—but then he spotted Fadarah wading through the carnage toward the gates, his hands streaming wytchfire. Seravin's mind went blank.

Briel's eyes watered from the pain, but he fought through it and got his bearings. He saw Rowen, wide eyed and half mad, use Briel's fallen sword to cut himself free then rush to Silwren's side. She had fallen in front of the stone sarcophagus. The Knight pressed both hands to her wound, whispering to her. Though Briel had dealt Rowen two shallow cuts, the Knight did not seem to notice. As for Silwren, despite the obvious depth of her wound, she hardly bled. The white glow had faded from her body, though.

Briel fixed his eyes on the glass knife between her breasts. He saw it stir. But Silwren's eyes were wide and staring, their white pupils and purple irises all the more disconcerting in the glow of the tomb's luminstones. Briel had the odd feeling that the slight movement was just the knife—the *freyd*, the king had called it—laughing at them.

Meanwhile, the king had recovered enough to rush to Quivalen's side near the entrance to the tomb. To Briel's relief, the prince had stopped screaming. He lay in a blistered, blackened heap. He no longer burned, but a glance at the wreckage that had once been the man's face told Briel that the prince was dead. Nevertheless, the king tried to rouse him, shaking him and calling for help.

The only one who might have saved him is the woman he just stabbed. Briel managed to force himself onto his feet, cradling his broken arm. With his good hand, he retrieved Knightswrath off the ground. He had never held such a sword before, and the feel of the dragonbone hilt almost startled him into dropping it. *Why is it so damn warm?*

He circled behind Rowen, sword ready. He considered stabbing the man in the back, but the king shouted for him to fetch the healers. Rowen turned, too, and snatched up Briel's shortsword. Though tears of grief ran from the Knight's eyes, mingling with the dried blood covering half his face, Rowen's expression bristled with an altogether different emotion. The Knight stood, white-knuckling his sword.

Briel backed off. *I have his sword, and he has mine. But I'm fighting with a broken arm. He's fighting for vengeance. He'll kill me in an instant.* Briel cursed himself for not protesting the king's order that the guards remain behind. *If Rowen kills me, he'll kill the king. And, gods, I wouldn't blame him!*

Briel backpedaled to the king's side. "Get out of here, my king. I'll hold him back."

"No, we need a healer! The prince—"

"Your son's dead. Get out, Sire. There are guards down below. Bring them."

The king stared as though he had not understood, then he faced Silwren. Briel followed his stare and saw the glass knife stir again.

The king choked, "Chorlga can save my son. But first, we have to make sure she's dead."

Though the king spoke in Sylvan, Briel could tell that Rowen had understood. The Knight barred their path. He jabbed his sword—Briel's sword—in the direction of the king's face. "Try," he spat back in Sylvan.

Briel said, "Let the king go, Knight. She's dead anyway. Lay down the sword and—"

Rowen charged, steel flashing. Briel raised Knightswrath to meet him, trying to ignore the strange heat emanating from its hilt. Briel parried one blow and dodged a third before Rowen cut a fresh groove in the outside of his thigh. Biting back a curse, Briel kept himself between Rowen and the king, Knightswrath extended before him, counting on its greater reach to save him. "Sire, go!" he called over one shoulder.

But Rowen gave no quarter. Despite his fury, the Isle Knight moved with lethal quickness. He attacked one side then the other. While Briel was unaccustomed to the long, curved blade of an Isle Knight, he could tell that Rowen had fought with all manner of swords before. All Briel could do was try to keep him at bay until the guards arrived.

King Loslandril still had not fled the tomb. Though the Sylvan monarch seemed content to use Briel as a shield, he'd drawn a small dagger from his robes and appeared to be waiting for an opening.

Not to help me, though. He just wants to make sure Silwren's dead! But even that probably had less to do with saving Sylvos than some wild hope that Chorlga would repay the deed by bringing Quivalen back to life.

Briel fought back his rage and concentrated on fighting Rowen. Since the Knight was forced to use a shorter blade, he had to get closer to inflict a wound. Briel did his best to utilize that advantage, always turning to prevent Rowen from flanking him. Luckily, the king knew enough to move with him, thus preventing himself from being caught and used as a hostage. But Briel needed two hands to wield Knightswrath properly. *Unless I can manage to—*

Rowen dashed in, parried, tried to grab Knightswrath by the unsharpened side of the blade, and very nearly took off Briel's head. Briel sidestepped and aimed a kick at Rowen's kneecap. Rowen lifted his leg and took the kick on his ankle. But the engagement gave Loslandril the distraction he needed. He dodged around the combatants with surprising speed and made for Silwren.

At the same time, Briel moved sideways to close the gap. Though he understood his opponent's rage, Sylvos needed its king. Briel could not let the Isle Knight kill him. "Me, Knight. You face *me*, not the king."

Rowen's expression changed as desperation replaced rage. With his back to Silwren and the king, Briel could not see what the king was doing. But Rowen could.

He'll gamble, Briel thought, readying himself.

Rowen charged. At the last instant, the Isle Knight slid sideways, feigned for Briel's wounded leg, then swung for his throat. Knightswrath met Rowen's blade and held it long enough for Briel to drive his knee into Rowen's side then elbow Rowen in the cheek.

Briel rammed the edge of his sword toward Rowen's temple, intending to finish him. Rowen ducked and kicked the back of Briel's knee. Rowen dove into Briel, but Briel answered with another knee. Rowen grunted. The shortsword swept down. Briel blocked it, then slammed Knightswrath's dragonbone hilt into Rowen's sternum. Rowen grabbed the hilt with his free hand, pinning it to his chest.

Another kick swept Briel's ankle out from under him. Letting go of Knightswrath, Briel landed in a roll, bit back a scream as pain lanced his broken arm, and kicked blindly. He struck something and heard his opponent grunt. With speed gained from thousands of hours of training as a Shal'tiar, Briel dove headfirst toward the sound. Somehow, he avoided being stabbed and caught Rowen in the stomach.

Rowen fell in a tangle of bloodied limbs, taking Briel with him. Their swords clattered away. Briel fought his way on top, took a knee to the groin, and elbowed Rowen's forehead. Then he stabbed his fingers toward Rowen's eyes. To his amazement, the Knight caught his fingers and bent hard. Bone snapped. Briel bit back a scream and tried a head butt. Rowen shifted and took the blow on the side of his head, though it was enough to stun him.

Fighting back pain and exhaustion, Briel pushed himself up on his broken hand and tried to angle his knee toward Rowen's throat. But Rowen blocked Briel's knee with both hands and shoved him off balance. For a moment, the two were parted, though Briel still barred Rowen's path.

Rowen picked up Knightswrath. Wincing, Briel fumbled for his shortsword. He gripped the weapon with his good fingers and got to his feet. He turned to check on the king.

Loslandril had reached the wytch, but a gigantic Isle Knight in ancient, dusty armor held the king by the arm, immobilizing him. Silwren lay on the floor, motionless, her eyes wide and staring. Loslandril tried to twist free, but the new Knight held him so firmly that the king's wrist might just as well have been encased in stone.

Briel frowned. *Where in the gods' names did he come from?* He saw by Rowen's stunned expression that he must have been wondering the same thing. Both men regarded the new Knight with confused fascination.

Crane and stag emblems covered the Knight's ornate breastplate, but the largest and most central symbol was a nine-pointed flower. Though the Knight's helmet had no visor, shadows seemed to obscure his face. An empty silver scabbard hung at his side. He held the king a moment longer then tossed him away. The Sylvan king struck the far wall like a ragdoll. He whimpered and lay still for a moment then crawled back to Quivalen's body and wept.

The ancient Knight of the Lotus turned his head, momentarily fixing his shadowy gaze on Briel. Though the ancient Knight appeared to be unarmed, Briel stepped back. The ancient Knight turned to Rowen. Though neither spoke, Briel sensed something pass between them. Rowen Locke trembled. Then he fell to one knee, laying Knightswrath on the floor before him. He said something that Briel could not understand, though he thought the words were Shao.

The huge Knight turned to Silwren and knelt. As Briel and Rowen stared, one dusty mailed fist opened over the glass knife. The ancient Knight of the Lotus seized the *freyd* and pulled it slowly from Silwren's breasts. Another hand closed on the blade. The knife shattered. Tossing away the pieces, the ancient Knight of the Lotus rose.

His shadowy visage regarded Silwren a moment longer then turned to face the sarcophagus at the far end of the room. His body began to shimmer. The luminstones flared, flooding the tomb with so much light that Briel was forced to shield his eyes. A moment later, the radiance dimmed.

The Knight of the Lotus was gone. But he had taken something with him. The dreadful pallor faded from Silwren's cheeks. She blinked. Then she wept. Slowly, she sat up, tentatively touching the ghastly tear in her gown. She turned. "Ro-Rowen?"

But Rowen was already rushing to embrace her.

Gods save us... Briel turned and caught Loslandril's eye. The king still leaned over his son's charred body. With wet, desperate eyes, the monarch indicated the shortsword in Briel's hand. But Briel shook his head, turned away from his king, and faced Rowen.

Briel raised his sword. Rowen tensed, raising Knightswrath in answer. Briel drew his own sword across his left cheek, so deep that he felt the edge scrape bone. Warm blood flowed down his cheek. He resisted the impulse to press on his wound. Instead, he bowed.

"*Os'lum hen-tar'i,* Isle Knight." He straightened. "We surrender to your justice."

CHAPTER FORTY-FOUR

KNIGHTSWRATH

A THOUSAND MAD THOUGHTS RACED THROUGH Rowen's mind. Had he really just seen Fâyu Jinn? Moreover, had the founder of the Knighthood—or his shade—appeared out of thin air to save Silwren? Had he healed her wound, or had he actually brought her back from the dead?

Like El'rash'lin did for Hráthbam...

Rowen shook his head. He did not have time to think about that. He stepped protectively in front of Silwren and fixed his gaze on Briel. He tried to think of a reason not to cut the Sylv in half—surrender or no.

By any reasonable measure, he had every right to do so. Briel had shown signs of misgivings, sure, but he had still kept fealty with the king. He had tried to kill Rowen a moment ago. And he had stood by as the mad prince murdered Silwren. *And didn't he try to kill us at Que'ahl?*

Rowen tightened his grip on Knightswrath's dragonbone hilt. Heat raced up his arm. He scrutinized his Sylvan enemy as they stood, bloody and unblinking, in the pale illumination of the luminstones. "You don't actually think I'll spare the king after what he did to Silwren, do you?"

Silwren touched his arm, but Briel said, "Actually, I do. Besides, my surrender has terms, Isle Knight. One is that you stay away from Loslandril. One dead royal is enough for today, I think."

Rowen glanced at the king, who knelt with blank, stunned eyes over the charred corpse of the prince. "She was just defending herself."

"I didn't say otherwise."

"Something she wouldn't have had to do if you'd stood up to the king."

Briel sheathed his sword. "We don't have to fight—at least, not each other. Forgetting about this Dragonkin for the moment, if the Olgrym have not breached the World Gate yet, they will soon. I'm out of men. We need magic… especially if Fadarah and his sorcerers show up. If the wytch helps us—"

"Ask her yourself."

Briel blinked then directed his gaze at Silwren. "A pact, wytch. No more knives in the dark. Help us defend the city, and I swear to you, we'll let you leave unharmed." He paused. "If you want, I'll throw in as many gold coins as you can carry. Gods, I'll even build a statue of you with my own two hands if I survive."

When Silwren still did not answer, Briel added, "And… I'll make sure things change after you're gone. No more Shel'ai infants will be killed. I don't know what we'll do with them—maybe send them to you—but they won't be killed. That's my pact, wytch."

Rowen glanced at the Sylvan king, who seemed completely oblivious to his surroundings. "Do you really think *he* will honor that agreement?"

Briel tapped his sword hilt with one of his unbroken fingers. "I'll see that he does. In fact, I'll swear it on my honor as a Shal'tiar."

Rowen smirked. "A little late to talk of honor, Sylv."

"Maybe not. We both have blood on our cheeks. Besides, we have shared enemies. Besides Fadarah's lot, this Dragonkin—"

"Your king's gone mad, Briel. There probably *is* no Dragonkin!"

"Yes, there is," Silwren said at last.

Something in her voice made Rowen turn. "Silwren—"

"He's near," Silwren said. Her voice trembled. "I couldn't feel him before… I think he was hiding… but I can feel him now. Whatever healed me… Jinn, if that's who it was… maybe he did it. But I *feel* him, Rowen!" Her violet eyes widened. "He doesn't want to face me

371

himself. He's lived too long to risk that. But I can feel how powerful he is."

She took Rowen's arm, and he fought to keep from screaming as wisps of wytchfire leapt from her fingertips. "I can't kill him. He's too strong. Don't you see? He's been draining Shel'ai infants for years, taking ones abandoned outside the forest, draining them the way his kind used to drain dragons. He's been draining others, too. And he's been doing what *we* did! Cadavash... Namundvar's Well..."

The luminstones flickered.

"His name is Chorlga. He stayed here when the other Dragonkin left. Or maybe Nekiel left him behind on purpose, to try and find a way to break down the Dragonward from the inside."

"Silwren..." Rowen tried to pull free of her scalding grasp, but her grip was like iron.

"Jinn showed me, I think. Chorlga has been *hiding* in Ruun for a thousand years! He's been here all this time, turning us against each other, and we never knew. He *wanted* us to learn about Namundvar's Well!"

Silwren's grip tightened even further. "He *wanted* Fadarah to turn us into Dragonkin! He knew we wouldn't be able to control the power. He thought we'd all end up like the Nightmare, that we'd destroy ourselves."

She released him suddenly. "Only he forgot about Knightswrath. He forgot about what Nâya did..." She lowered her eyes. Then she stretched out her hand and took Knightswrath from his grasp. "He forgot what she did for her people. For Jinn." She stared down at the blade. One hand held it by the hilt. The other wrapped around the blade so tightly that blood trickled down its steely length. "For the man she loved."

Too late, Rowen understood. He called out her name and dove for her, but she stepped just out of his reach. Her white pupils flared. And Rowen could not move.

For one long moment, Silwren stared at him, her violet eyes brimming with tears. Rowen tried to hold her gaze, tried to speak. But before he could find the words, wytchfire flared to life.

Rowen watched in horror as the flames spread up her arms and flickered down her shoulders, tracing her back and thighs, trickling down to the stone floor. Her clothes burned away. Silwren's bare flesh glowed white hot. An awful, six-winged shadow spread on the stone floor behind her.

When she spoke, her voice had grown louder, and several spoke in concert. "Nâya gave her life to undo the treachery of her father, Nekiel, foul servant of the Undergod. Other Dragonkin joined her. What they did was remembered by no one—not the Sylvs, not the Dwarrs, not even the Knights. But their sacrifice crafted a relic."

Rowen strained against whatever magic held him immobile. He had the thought that Silwren might be reading his mind, as she had done so many times before. *Don't do this*, he pleaded. *We'll find another way—*

"There is no other way." Silwren smiled sadly. *"When this is done, look to the east. Jalist needs you. So do the Knights. So does everyone—as I did. Goodbye, Knight of the Crane."*

Before Rowen could think his answer, Silwren's body blazed brighter than ever. Unable to blink or look away, Rowen wept. He lost sight of her face in the fiery glare. White wings spread behind her. Violet eyes—still familiar somehow—met his.

For one brief moment, everything froze. Then Rowen heard a scream—half pain, half triumph—followed by a sound like rushing water, as if an entire ocean were being drained. With frightful quickness, the fire imploded. Dimly, Rowen saw Knightswrath at the center of the maelstrom. He realized the sword was sucking all the fire, every last tendril, into its blade.

No, not fire. That's Silwren! I have to stop this. I have to stop her before—

As quickly as it had begun, it was over.

The luminstones dimmed then returned to normal. Rowen blinked. He realized he could move but made no effort to do so. Silwren was gone. Knightswrath hovered for a moment in midair, then clattered to the cold stone floor, rocked, and lay still.

CHAPTER FORTY-FIVE

THE OPEN GATE

FADARAH STRODE THROUGH ASH AND shattered iron—all that remained of the World Gate—and surveyed the ruined, corpse-strewn fortifications around him. All his bodyguards had been killed, down to the last Olg. Still, his heart swam in exhilaration. True, they had hardly ascended from the forest floor, but they were in Shaffrilon. They had breached the World Tree. Olgrym streamed past him, crazed and howling. The stink of their passage both sickened and elated him.

Too many to be stopped. By nightfall, all of Shaffrilon will be ours.

Of course, sooner or later, Fadarah and his remaining Shel'ai would face a different challenge: killing the last of the Olgrym and claiming Shaffrilon and the surrounding forest for themselves. *Might as well let Shaffrilon's ailing defenders do their work. After all, every Sylv and Olg killed here is one we won't have to face later.*

He spotted Doomsayer leading the Olgrym charge against the next gate. Fadarah sneered. Armored in blackened iron, the hulking Olgish chieftain might have been mistaken for Fadarah himself were it not for the Olg's long hair—braided with animal skulls—and the way he fought: mace in one hand, sword in the other. Fadarah thought of the two-handed sword he'd left behind, remembering where he'd left it. He felt a pang of guilt then chided himself.

A fresh chorus of screams caught his attention. He turned in time to see two Olgrym tormenting a young Sylvan warrior, little more than a boy. Each held him by an arm and a leg. The Sylvan warrior screamed for mercy. The Olgrym ripped him in half, laughing.

Fadarah had the urge to burn the Olgrym to ashes, but before he could make up his mind, Shade joined him. His young second-in-command still bled from an arrow that had struck his shoulder. Shade had already broken the arrow in half but had not had time to dig out the barbed point.

"You should stop to heal that."

"They're reinforcing the Moon Gate, General. Should we burn this one down, too, or let the Olgrym do it for us?" Shade spoke in Sylvan, though Fadarah doubted any of the charging Olgrym cared enough to eavesdrop.

Nevertheless, he answered in kind. "Let the Olgrym do it. The more that die here, the better it will be for us later." Fadarah drew Shade aside to let more Olgrym pass. "How many of us remain?"

Shade's face darkened. "Nine, I think. I can't find Hasiel, but I saw Tamrien go down from arrows. I ordered the rest to the rear after we breached the World Gate."

Fadarah frowned. He could not recall the faces of the two Shel'ai that Shade had just mentioned. "Good," he said. The Sorcerer-General pressed his fingers to Shade's wound.

Rather than recoil, Shade merely hissed through clenched teeth as Fadarah grasped the arrowhead and wrenched it out. Then Fadarah pressed one hand over the wound. Before Shade could protest, Fadarah sent a flood of energies into the wound—more than was necessary, so that by the time he was done, the wound had healed almost without a scar. Fadarah pulled his hand away and turned back to the Moon Gate. "Did you see what Doomsayer did to their general?"

Shade nodded. "I half considered putting him out of his misery, but his men carried him away."

"Better for us that they did. The sight will make them more afraid. And he'll bleed to death soon enough, if he hasn't already."

"I'm not sure they *can* be more afraid, General."

Fadarah saw a wild glint in Shade's eyes. He remembered the man's fondness for blood and murder and marveled that Shade seemed as calm as he did, given all the torn corpses heaped around them and the slaughter still taking place only a few hundred yards ahead. "One can *always* be more afraid."

Fadarah wondered why he'd just said that, then he eyed the Moon Gate again. The tides of battle were turning. What had seemed like a rout moments before had ended with the Sylvs flooding through the Moon Gate and sealing it behind them, just as archers and trebuchets along the parapets unleashed a fresh flood of devastation on the charging Olgrym. Gray bodies twisted and fell, shredded by arrows and burned by fire.

The remaining Olgrym, still over a thousand strong, howled in unison and hurled themselves at the new obstacle. A great many still carried ladders and ropes fixed to grappling irons. But the Olgrym carrying them made only a token effort. Fadarah immediately saw why.

Like the World Gate, the Moon Gate resembled the front wall of a fortress, crowded with defenders. But it was shorter, made of stones carved with ornate Sylvan reliefs that provided a myriad of convenient handholds. Meanwhile, the gates were too broad and thin, constructed more for appearances and ceremony than actual defense.

As the Sylvs busied themselves with frantically defending the parapets, the rest of the Olgrym simply took axes to the wooden doors. Before long, the sound of chopping wood drowned out even the screams of the dying. Fadarah wondered why the Moon Gate's defenders didn't tip cauldrons of burning water and oil on the attacking Olgrym. Then he guessed that they'd run out. A few trebuchets fired, sowing more destruction in the farther-back ranks of Olgrym, but the missiles did nothing to slow the decimation of the gates themselves.

Silwren, are you in there somewhere? If so, why aren't you helping them?

"They never expected an enemy to get this far," Shade muttered.

"They never expected a lot of things. They never expected us to survive. They never thought we'd come back. They didn't think we'd seek justice." Fadarah formed a fist, pulsing with wytchfire. "Bring up the others. We'll let the Olgrym do their work then follow them into the city."

"And... Silwren? I haven't sensed her."

"Nor have I. She could be hiding from us. Or she fled. No matter. Bring up the others. Tell them we've nearly won. Tell them Shaffrilon is ours."

Shade nodded and left.

Fadarah stared at the Moon Gate a moment longer then stooped to retrieve a curved Sylvan blade off the battlefield. The blade seemed small and puny in his half-Olg fist. He laughed. Then he turned back to the gates and let loose a mad, howling cry of challenge.

CHAPTER FORTY-SIX
NÂYA

ROWEN FELT AS THOUGH HE were wading through fire. Somehow, it did not kill him—but it singed his skin and burned him deeper than that. His mind buzzed like a hornet that had burrowed in through his ears and nested in his brain while he slept. But it was awake—and angry.

He ran. He thought he was running from the fire, but somehow, he ran to it. Dimly, he heard screams of panic and terror on the other side of the flames, but he paid them no mind. Once, he thought he heard someone call out his name, but the buzzing in his head drowned out the sound. Then he was running again.

My name... My name...

He realized he had just forgotten his own name. He began to wonder if he'd ever had one, if he'd ever been anything but a nameless, wretched thing set at the center of a firestorm. An image formed in his mind: a great, burning flower with a skull at its center. A death's head.

That's me, he thought then laughed.

Only then did he realize he was holding something. Alternately cold and hot, it frightened him. It hurt him more than the flames did. He tried to throw it away, but it seemed to have become a part of his arm. Red tendrils snaked through it, into his skin, winding up his arm, into his chest. He imagined them flowing into his brain—not tendrils but rivers. Rivers of blood. Blood on fire.

Gods, I've gone mad. What am I? Where am I?

He heard someone call his name again. He knew somehow that it was his name, though he could not hear it over the buzzing roar. He knew, too, that the voice should have been familiar. Someone he knew—the voice belonged to someone he trusted. *A woman*, he thought, but he could not reach her. Every step toward her voice only seemed to lead him in the wrong direction.

He concentrated on the flames instead of running from them. For the first time, he distinguished their color—purple—and something else: the flames were coming from his own body. They were him.

Fear turned to fascination. He stopped running and stared at his hands. He still could not drop the thing he was holding in his right hand, but whatever it was, it no longer frightened him. He studied it. It looked like a span of white-hot fire, slightly curved, a little longer than his arm. The end he held seemed to be composed of tiny twisting dragons.

The woman called to him again. Her voice came from all around him. His panic returned. Though he knew she only wanted to help him, he couldn't let her see him panicking. He had to free himself first—or at least figure out what he was, what he'd become. He ran again.

But the woman followed. The voice eased in all around him, into his mind, soothing him like water. Slowly, slowly, the buzzing faded. In its place, he saw forests, walled cities, faces he could not recognize. He thought that the visions must be memories, though not his own, and he had the odd feeling that this had happened to him before.

One image commanded his attention. It was a woman, though she was not the woman who had called to him. Her face seemed both strange and familiar. He could not wrest his gaze from her. She had long, tapered ears, violet eyes, and hair the color of a vast, starless sky. And she was naked.

Gods, she's beautiful...

She turned to face him, as though she'd heard his thoughts. Though she looked young, he had the strange feeling that she was old—far older than anyone he had ever known. She smiled sadly. Then she, too, was surrounded by fire. It surged about her thin, pale body, ferocious but absolutely silent—purple at first, then white. When she opened her mouth as though to speak—*To warn me*, he thought, though he did not know why—she stiffened in pain.

He tried to approach her, to help her. But suddenly, he could not move. She turned away from him. Wings of white-hot flame blossomed from her naked back. She leapt into the air and was gone.

Moments later, he heard her scream. Darkness flooded his senses, as though all the flames had been sucked from his universe. Pain vanished, but something fell from his grasp. Something precious. A fresh panic filled him. He turned and twisted in nothingness, trying in vain to scream.

A new image flooded his sight. It began as a cold, rocky landscape beneath a starless sky. Then stars burst to life, forming the constellations one by one. On the earth below, bare rocks blossomed into dark grass and deep-purple flowers. The landscape blurred, shimmered, and cleared. And he saw dragons.

They filled this new, alien landscape of dark plains and silver lakes. Some slept while others flew on two, four, even six wings. Some were feathered, others scaled. One with horns that curved like scimitars flew next to another dragon with antlers and broad golden eyes.

Something compelled him to turn his head. He rotated slowly, taking in the whole horizon. More of them dotted the dark, endless plains. Hundreds, thousands, even millions. Far away, a great kaleidoscope of them leapt into the air and passed over the stars like a cloud of moths. Such was their beauty that he wept.

He was still weeping when the storm began. No water fell from the heavens, but he heard great and terrible thunder in the distance. The dragons reared their heads, craning their long necks toward the sound. Many of them cried out, screeching like enormous birds—not in fear, he sensed, but with grief.

Something blinded him. At the same time, a man's scream filled his mind, the horizon, then the whole world. By the time his vision returned, he saw a great burning shape fall from the heavens, arcing toward the distant horizon. It looked for a moment like a man, flailing in pain. Then it was gone. Everything disappeared. A new horizon of green forests and ash-gray mountains appeared—the same world, but it was older. Much older.

He still saw dragons, but far fewer. Then his vision focused on one in particular. Tiny compared to the rest, covered in scales of alternating brass and silver, with two wings like wind-filled sails, it still dwarfed the creatures hunting it. The hunters, men and women in dark cloaks, carried no weapons. But flames leapt from their hands.

The little dragon screamed and fell. For some reason, it could not fight back. He could do nothing but watch as the hunters encircled it. One by one, they touched it, laughing. And the dragon screamed as the hunters' touch sucked the fire from beneath its scales and sapped the life from its bones, until its eyes darkened to the color of ash.

Then he was burning again. The old panic returned. He ran. But he had not gone far when the flames parted like a curtain. He saw himself. Small, frail, and bloody, he stooped to pick something off a wooden floor. A sword. Just a sword. But as soon as he touched it, the blade turned to white light. Light turned to fire. He screamed. He tried to throw away the sword. But he heard a woman's voice—but not the woman from earlier. It was Silwren, telling him what he must do.

At last, he saw her hovering in front of him. Naked, burning but unharmed, she embraced him. His skin tingled as though he were being prodded by alternating jolts of fire and ice. He felt a surprising surge of lust, replaced quickly by panic.

She was not melting into him. No, she was melting into the sword! He cried out for her to stop, but it was too late.

"I'm sorry," she said then said it again.

He opened his mouth to answer, but a fresh wash of violet flames flooded his sight. The awful buzzing returned. He could not tell whether he was running or being carried. But the sensation did not last long.

As though a veil had been pulled from his eyes, the madness left him. He remembered his name. He realized what he was holding. And for the first time, he saw that instead of a wooden floor, he was standing on a marble walkway, surrounded by corpses.

Shade screamed in victory and wrenched his sword from the body of a dying Sylv. Another came at him—one dressed in the black fighting garb of a Shal'tiar—but Shade burned the man's legs out from under him, stepped forward, and cleaved the head from his shoulders. Then he stepped through the shattered remnants of the Moon Gate.

The actual wooden gates had already been hacked to splinters, letting wave upon wave of Olgrym through. More Olgrym scaled the walls, scattering most of the Moon Gate's defenders.

Shaffrilon is ours. Gods, we've done it! We've finally won.

Shade wept even as the sight of so much blood quickened his pulse to a maddening rhythm. He took a deep breath to calm himself. The battle was far from over. The Sylvs would try to flee Shaffrilon via the walkways that joined the city to the surrounding trees. If they were not stopped, they would regroup and continue the fighting.

Moreover, glancing up at the sky, beyond the endless height of the World Tree, he saw the sky roiling with dark clouds. A storm was brewing. That could slow the fighting and give the surviving Sylvs a greater chance to hide.

He spotted Fadarah ahead of him. Fury had seized the Sorcerer-General, prompting him to outdistance the Shel'ai and fight side by side with the Olgrym, slaughtering the few stubborn Sylvs who stood their ground. Only a few yards separated Fadarah from Doomsayer himself. For a moment, they seemed almost identical.

Shade resisted the urge to fight his way to the Sorcerer-General's side. Fadarah could take care of himself. Better he guard the remaining Shel'ai in case Silwren came back.

He had already tried repeatedly to reach Silwren via mindspeak. She had not answered. He could not sense her nearby. Perhaps she and the Isle Knight had already fled. A surge of jealousy brightened the wytchfire smoldering from his fist. That his wife had betrayed her own kind was bad enough, but to think of her sharing company with a Human—

A fresh sound interrupted the thought, rising over even the screams of dying Sylvs. For the first time in his life, Shade heard Olgrym screaming in terror. The bottom dropped out of his stomach. He turned to the other Shel'ai and found them staring back, equal parts alarmed and horrified.

"Silwren?" one gasped, looking to him for confirmation.

"Stay back," Shade called to the other sorcerers. He started toward Fadarah. *Gods, don't let it be Silwren!* He was not sure he could really face her, and *kill* her, as Fadarah had commanded.

The panicked howls of the Olgrym grew even louder. As far as he could see, their entire charge had ground to a halt. Some Olgrym had fallen prostrate on the battlefield. Others covered their eyes. Still more threw down their weapons and fled, nearly trampling Shade in the process.

Doomsayer passed him, brushing his shoulder. The Olgish chieftain was backpedaling to keep pace with the ranks, but his expression spoke of brutal fascination. Shade remembered that look.

He directed his gaze up the Path of Crowns, but the retreating Olgrym obscured his view. Shade wished he still had his bloodmare so that he might have risen in the saddle for a better view. He spied a nearby heap of bodies and scaled it. Ignoring the dampness of warm blood and the press of cold flesh, he reached the ghastly summit.

What he saw made him wish it was Silwren after all. All the fight and bloodlust drained out of him in an instant. He stared a moment longer then fell with a choking sob. He fell hard, bashing his forehead on a dead Sylv's armored shoulder, but he hardly noticed. Shaking, he started to crawl away on his hands and knees. Then something stopped him.

A woman's voice echoed in his mind. *"Kith'el."*

Shade froze. Then he straightened. He stood, wiping the blood from his eyes. "Silwren?" he called out weakly. He turned.

By then, nearly all the Olgrym had fled beyond the shattered Moon Gate, but a few remained prostrate. They whimpered like frightened children.

The remaining Sylvs might have killed them with ease, but most had already withdrawn farther up the Path of Crowns. They formed a shield wall so that they could stare, terrified, at the bizarre scene unfolding below.

Shade stared as a familiar red-haired Human made his way down the Path of Crowns. Instead of armor, the Knight wore bloody, singed clothing. With a burning sword, he cut down Olg after Olg. Then he jerked to a stop, as though he had been struck by an arrow. The flames dimmed, still pulsing, and the sword's bearer looked down at himself as though waking from a daze.

The remaining Olgrym pulled back. Fadarah stood alone. Shade was about to cry out to him, beg him to withdraw. Fadarah charged. Wytchfire flowed from both hands in bright gouts, more furious than any spell Shade had ever seen him cast. The bruise-purple flames flowed over the Isle Knight, completely obscuring him.

The flames surged past where the Knight had stood, even causing the Sylvs massed behind him to cry out and withdraw farther up the walkway. Shade felt a surge of hope. But the flames cleared, absorbed into the sword, and the Knight stood unharmed.

If Fadarah was afraid, he did not show it. The Sorcerer-General stood as straight as a statue while the Isle Knight strode up to him, hefted his burning sword, and cut a blazing swath through breastplate, flesh, and bone. Shade thought the Knight would strike again. Instead, he stepped back, the burning sword held in the crook of his arm.

Fadarah stood a moment longer, wobbled, and fell. His body crashed to the ground and rolled down the marble walkway. Shade screamed in rage and grief then ran to where Fadarah stopped. Fadarah lay on his side. Shade could not see his face, though he saw blood and smoke seep from the great rend in the Sorcerer-General's armor.

All at once, the silence shattered as the Sylvs broke into a thunderous cheer. At the same time, those Shel'ai Shade had left at the Moon Gate howled in despair and ran to join him. Thunder rumbled, and Shade felt the first drops of rain. Shade came to his senses. He helped the others seize Fadarah by his arms and legs and haul him toward the Moon Gate. As they moved, he glanced at Fadarah's face. His eyes were blank and wide open, but Shade thought he saw a flicker of movement from one of Fadarah's tattoos: a weak pulse beneath the taut gray skin of his throat.

Shade expected what remained of the Sylvan army to bear down on them. But even amid their celebration, the Sylvs had drawn no closer, still blocked by the Isle Knight and his burning sword. For his own part, the Knight met Shade's gaze, his soot-smeared expression unreadable. Shade looked away.

EPILOGUE

BRAHASTI IGNORED THE CLAPS OF thunder, but he could not ignore the mailed fist pounding on his door. Cursing, he climbed off the Sylvan girl and made his way to the door without bothering to dress. "Stay still," he called over his shoulder. But the girl had already used one hand to wipe the blood from her nose and the other to drag a sheet over her body. He made a mental note to have Karhaati send him captive Sylvs who spoke Common Tongue.

Dagath stood in the hallway, his hollow eye socket illuminated by the lamp he was holding. His good eye blinked at Brahasti's lack of clothing. Meanwhile, Brahasti grimaced. So far, the mercenary captain had obeyed Brahasti's orders to keep the socket covered. Apparently, tonight was an exception.

Brahasti considered striking him, even though Dagath was far bigger than he was. "Since you're interrupting something I ordered not to be interrupted, I trust you have a good excuse."

"Four men just arrived outside the villa. No sigil. All on foot."

"Four?"

Dagath nodded.

Brahasti stroked the Dhargothi-style goatee he'd spent the last few months growing. The hair was braided with copper bands that jingled when he touched them. *It's too early for Karhaati to recall me to the front. Besides, he'd send men on bloodmares—and enough of them to haul me back in chains if I refused.*

A dreadful thought occurred to him. "Are they Shel'ai?"

"No, General."

"*Excellency*. I told you, I'm tired of *General*." Brahasti poured a cup of wine. As he turned, he saw that the Sylvan girl had crawled out of bed and armed herself with Brahasti's favorite weapon—an Ivairian-style shortsword he'd taken from Dagath for some infraction he couldn't remember. The girl had drawn the sword and, still nude, stepped into a fighting stance that indicated she knew how to use what she was holding.

Brahasti rolled his eyes. "Another damn Wyldkin! When is Karhaati going to send me some baby-soft city dweller to play with?"

Dagath had already drawn his replacement sword—a curved, long-handled sword supposedly taken off a dead Isle Knight. He set down his lantern. As soon as Brahasti stepped aside, Dagath growled and charged.

The Sylvan girl's eyes widened at the sight of Dagath, but she reacted quickly. Stepping aside, she flicked the shortsword, drawing a bright scratch in Dagath's thigh plate. The sellsword howled in rage, using his sword's greater reach to hold the girl at bay while he fingered the deep scratch in the metal.

"Now you've done it," Brahasti muttered. He retrieved a goblet off the floor, filled it from a pitcher of wine, and sat in a chair to watch.

The Sylvan girl was even better than he'd expected. She dodged each of Dagath's blows as though she were made of smoke. She carved a scratch in Dagath's breastplate then drew real blood when a well-aimed lunge caught him just beneath one spaulder.

Dagath swore and beat her back. Steel rang on steel. Brahasti watched with growing interest. He wondered if she hadn't just been playing meek with him, waiting for a chance to strike. The thought that he'd actually been in danger excited him.

Dagath took two more blows, neither of which drew blood, but it was clear that for all the Wyldkin's skill, she was used to fighting on the open plains. She backed into a table, and Dagath almost had her. She managed to slip past his blade, but the sellsword kept advancing. Gradually, he used his height and greater reach to drive the girl into a corner.

Brahasti took a sip of wine and savored the wild fear he saw in her eyes. He had half a mind to order Dagath to take her alive. Dagath loomed over her, so close that she could only avoid his blade by dodging. She ducked beneath one swing, then another, before Dagath split her open.

Brahasti drained his goblet. "Pity. Now, someone will have to clean my floors." He stood. "Thank you, Captain. But as I recall, you came here to tell me something."

Dagath was breathing hard. He wiped his curved blade on his sleeve, sheathed it, then stooped to retrieve the shortsword. As though just remembering his master had addressed him, he turned. "General?"

"Excellency," Brahasti corrected, with a laugh. "The four men outside. I trust they aren't beggars, or else you'd have killed them already. So who are they?" *And should I be worried?*

Dagath blinked. "Don't know, Excellency. But there's something strange about 'em. Three are big as houses. Lem and Will fired crossbows at two of them, and the bolts glanced off. Rang like armor, but there ain't no armor but kingsteel that can block a crossbow bolt at that range."

"And I trust these men aren't Isle Knights." Brahasti seized a Dhargothi-style silk fighting robe and slipped it on, followed by a sword belt. Seeing that the scabbard was empty, he held out his hand. Dagath reluctantly handed over the shortsword. Brahasti sheathed it. "Did they say anything?"

"Just to bring you before they burned the whole fort to ashes. The shorter one killed Lem just by pointing at him."

Brahasti stopped pulling on his boots. "You said they weren't Shel'ai."

"Wasn't wytchfire that killed Lem. He just kind of"—Dagath grimaced—"turned him inside out. Surprised you didn't hear him screaming."

I was busy. Brahasti finished dressing. "Captain, remind me to have you flogged. In the meantime, bring all the men to the front. Arm them with crossbows. If this goes bad, tell them all to shoot at the one who sent our valiant friend Lem to the gods. Is that clear?"

Dagath nodded. "Yes, Excellency."

Brahasti glanced back at the dead Wyldkin girl. He sighed again then hurried out into the night to greet his guests. The night air made him shiver, but he rushed across the narrow bridge over the dry moat. His men stood at attention. Brahasti passed what he guessed was Lem, covered by a stained cloak, and faced the newcomers.

One of them, a tall bald man dwarfed by the cloaked immobile figures standing around him, stepped forward and grinned as if Brahasti were an old friend. Brahasti noted his black, rotten teeth.

"Here is one worth saving. A clever one. Mortal, weak, not brave, exactly... but clever."

Brahasti frowned. "You have the advantage over me. I don't see purple eyes or pointed ears, but my captain tells me you did something rather interesting to one of my men."

"So I did." The man bowed, though there was something mocking about the gesture. "My apologies, but I needed to prove a point. Now, I will prove another." The man cast off his cloak and burst into flames.

Brahasti screamed. To his relief, he was not alone. Several sellswords even fired their crossbows. Some shot wildly, but a few managed to aim for the burning man threatening their lord. The crossbow bolts blurred past him then withered to ash before they could strike their intended target.

The flames vanished. The tall man stood unharmed, though his plain, Human features began to change. His jaw narrowed, his ears tapered, and his eyes turned to purple fire. The purple flames encircled pupils that were white, like icy moons. The man had not stopped smiling.

"I trust I have your attention. Now, I don't mean to question your knowledge of history, but at the very least, you should have guessed by now that despite some of my more prominent features, I am not a Shel'ai."

In the glow of torches, Brahasti saw a great shadow spreading behind the man. A moment later, he realized the man's shadow—just his shadow—had grown wings. "A Dragonkin..."

"So I am." The Dragonkin bowed. "My name is Chorlga. And I'm talking to you here, in front of your men, because I want everyone to hear what I have to say." He raised his voice. "I have walked among you for a thousand years. I have killed more people than any plague your mother ever told you about. And I know what you're doing here."

He stepped forward with the speed of a striking serpent. Brahasti jumped, but Chorlga only squeezed his shoulder. "Lucky for you, I'm here to help. There are fertility potions that will quicken the process. With my assistance, what might otherwise take months and only work once in a thousand cases will yield lucrative results every time." The Dragonkin raised one hand and seemed to produce a book from thin air. He handed it to Brahasti.

"By working together, my... particular hungers will be sated. And in return, you—*all* of you—will hold rank in my new empire. So long as you follow my orders, of course." Chorlga gestured, and his three companions cast off their cloaks. Brahasti's eyes widened. He heard the other mercenaries swear but resisted the impulse to draw back a step.

Chorlga said, "In the meantime, I will leave these here for your protection. In my absence, Dhargot, they will obey your commands. If you know what I am, I trust that you know what *they* are, too. When I return to check on your progress, I trust you will have the results I'm looking for." Chorlga shimmered then vanished.

For a long time, no one spoke, though Brahasti eyed the blackened grass where Chorlga had stood. The charred grass formed the shape of wings.

Dagath turned and spat on the ground. "Am I cracked, or did that really just happen?"

Another sellsword answered, "If you have to ask, lift up that cloak and take a look at what's left of Lem."

Brahasti said, "Get back inside." He glanced uncertainly at the three metallic figures looming over him. "You three... guard the prisoners." He pointed.

Brahasti half hoped that nothing would happen. But with just a faint metallic creak, the three Jolym started forward. As they shambled across the bridge, the other sellswords dove out of the way. Brahasti noted that each of the Jolym's hands ended in a weapon.

Brahasti was the last to enter the villa. He replayed the Dragonkin's words in his mind. It seemed impossible that so much could have happened so quickly. Then he remembered the book. He stood beneath a torch and opened it. To his relief, he recognized the language: an ancient form of Dhargothi, said to have been a precursor to Shao. He could not read more than a few words of it, but he knew Dhargots who could. He could bring them to translate it.

That will take time. Time, and a great deal of money. But I can afford it. Besides, what choice do I have?

Nearing the bridge that led back toward his villa, he paused beside Lem's corpse. After a moment's hesitation, he lifted the cloak but almost immediately let it fall. He covered his mouth to keep from retching and eyed the three Jolym in the distance. They loomed over the pit where the prisoners were kept. Brahasti smiled.

Sooner or later, Karhaati or Fadarah will send for me. They'll need me. Maybe they'll even come to get me themselves. He hoped they would. He glanced behind him, out into the dark and endless night. He wondered where the Dragonkin had gone. He had the feeling that whatever the man had gone to do, it would involve actions that even Brahasti would find disquieting. He shuddered. Then he hurried back inside, shouting for Dagath to bring him another prisoner to play with.

APPENDIX

THE CODEX LOTIUS (CONTINUED)

XXVI.   Those who crave revenge will never know peace.

XXVII.   Doubt is the seed of wisdom, but if ignored, it will choke all it touches.

XXVIII.   To be a Knight, be half crane and half dragon.

XXIX.   Legends are like laws: when they cease to function, change them.

XXX.   Fortune and misfortune are not opposites but the same priest in two differently colored robes. To attain wisdom, heed not the priest but learn well his religion.

XXXI.   Good fletchers are known by the straightness of their arrows. Like this, know a Knight by his enemies.

XXXII.   One should not enter a privy and expect the smell of roses.

XXXIII.   To learn a proud man's true nature, knock him off his horse.

XXXIV.   In the next life, the lamb rules the wolf.

XXXV.   Let the accused face the accuser. Let the verdict end the trial, not preface it.

XXXVI. All are bound by law, or else none are bound by law.

XXXVII. Many a fool has followed a wise man off a cliff.

XXXVIII. Slay your enemies without pause, mourn their deaths without pretense, and brood long on the contradiction. This is the path to honor.

XXXIX. Impatience leads to death. Prudence leads to death. Honor leads to a *good* death.

XL. Speak and act justly, but to shame one's enemies is to shame oneself.

XLI. Fish yearn for the sunlight, only to be lured into the fisherman's net. Like this, men yearn to be ruled.

XLII. One should not become a Knight if one desires a long life.